Also by Pamela Callow

INDEFENSIBLE
DAMAGED

TATTOOED

PAMELA CALLOW

MIRA®

MIRA®

Recycling programs for this product may not exist in your area.

ISBN-13: 978-0-7783-1302-1

TATTOOED

For questions and comments about the quality of this book please contact us at Customer_eCare@Harlequin.ca.

www.Harlequin.com

Printed in U.S.A.

For Dan,
my beloved husband.

Hell is empty,
And all the devils are here.
                    —William Shakespeare, *The Tempest* 1:2

_1_

Ten.

Roman numeral X.

X marks the spot.

In John McNally's case, prison.

On the tenth day of serving his ten-year prison term for manslaughter, John McNally had tattooed an X over his heart.

Ten years. Seven, with parole.

He knew the system. He'd been in and out of it for the past five years. Before that, he'd been in and out of the foster care system. Hell, yes, he knew the _systems_.

He got parole thirty-seven months ago. He lasted two months on the outside. If that moron at the White Elephant hadn't laughed at his prison tattoos, he would have been long gone from this hole. Even though he barely touched the guy, he was sentenced to two additional years to be served consecutively, based on his history of violent assaults.

They wouldn't give him parole again. But he didn't give a shit. Parole _sucked_. Reporting to a parole officer and being told what he could and couldn't do frustrated the hell out of him. He knew what he wanted to do, and he couldn't do it with a fucking parole officer breathing down his neck.

So, he did his time on the inside.

Until May 19. Today. His second sentence was complete. The sentence for the manslaughter conviction had expired two years ago.

He would be *free*.

No conditions, no parole officers, nothing.

McNally sat on his bunk and waited for the CX—aka the correctional officer. The air closed in on his ears. He remembered that sensation—as if he was in a wind tunnel—from his days in the band, when he stood at center stage, the amps blasting at him in surround sound, the air vibrating from the noise.

His bed was made, his locker emptied. He had disposed of his personal items last night, giving them to the guys who had done him favors over the years.

He clasped his hands together, studying the tattoos that had shaped his life: LOVE tattooed on the back of the fingers of his left hand; HATE tattooed on the knuckles of his right hand.

The classic ink of the tattooist's psyche.

The love and the hate had never stopped, never changed, never gone away.

For over half his life he had loved Kenzie Sloane.

And for over half his life he had hated her for what she had done to him.

But he had a plan.

A plan that would bring them full circle.

Back to the day they had planned to make Imogen Lange their first victim. Imogen had been the key, the catalyst, the blood tie that would have bound Kenzie to him. He and Kenzie had had it all planned out....

And then Imogen was taken away from them. By her sister, Kate Lange.

In her stupid attempt to "save her sister" from doing coke at Kenzie's party, Kate Lange had killed Imogen in a car crash on the way home.

After the night that Imogen died, Kenzie began to drift away from him. He wasn't sure if Imogen's death had scared her. Or if she was getting tired of him. She accused him of being too possessive. Desperate, he arranged for another girl— Heather Rigby was her name— to come to the bunkers on Mardi Gras night to take Imogen's place. But it wasn't the same. Too much time had passed. The opportunity had been lost.

If Kate Lange hadn't interfered, Kenzie would still be with him. And he would be running his own tattoo shop by now, Kenzie at his side.

Every plan, every dream he had harbored, had been derailed by Kate Lange the night she killed her sister.

And now, seventeen years later, he was ready to set things right.

First he had to track down Kenzie.

And then he would find Kate Lange.

He flexed his fingers, watching the skin pucker at the knuckles. He fisted them into his palm. The letters of the tattoos strained with tension.

He wondered where Kenzie was now. What she looked like. Did she still have that long red hair? Had she gotten any more tattoos?

Was she with someone?

Sweat dampened his skin. He imagined the spider's web tattooed across the back of his skull glistening with his perspiration.

It didn't matter if Kenzie had a boyfriend. Or if she was married. She belonged to him. He knew it, she knew it. She'd just have to tell the other guy to get lost. Or he'd do it for her.

He jumped to his feet and stared through the bars of the cell.

The corridor was empty.

Roberts glanced at him from his cell across the hall and shrugged.

McNally spun away.

Where the fuck was the CX?

From the top bunk, Digger crossed his arms and leaned his head back against the wall. His eyes appeared shut, but McNally knew they were opened a crack, not missing a thing. He was waiting, everyone was waiting. It was McNally's release day.

But the CX scheduled to work today was Aucoin. McNally wondered if he had requested this shift.

Everyone knew that Aucoin didn't like McNally. The feeling was mutual. Aucoin had gone out of his way to write up McNally over the years, sending him down to the hole at least eight times.

At 0720, Aucoin strolled down the corridor and unlocked McNally's cell. "Let's go."

McNally glanced at Digger. They had shared this cell for the past thirteen months. "See you on the outside."

Digger had another five years to go.

He nodded and closed his eyes.

Aucoin led McNally to Admissions and Discharge. It was a nondescript room, with posters on the wall urging him to get screened for various STIs, reminders that all phone numbers had to be on an approved list, and a list of weekly religious services if he had an epiphany that Jesus was waiting for him in this particular federal penitentiary.

Aucoin tossed a sealed bag onto a table. "Hope they don't smell too bad," he said, his face impassive.

McNally grabbed the bag. He knew that Aucoin was taunting him. Most offenders had family who would bring them fresh clothes to wear on their release date. It had not gone unnoticed that McNally's phone list included only his lawyer and his social worker. He had been estranged from his brother, Matt, since he'd killed that girl in the bar. And he had crossed his foster mother off the list, oh, about eight years ago. The only recent change to his phone list was the addition of Rick Lovett, his old band mate.

McNally tore open the bag, his heart thudding.

His fingers dug into the soft knit of his T-shirt.

"Come on, McNally. Move it. You'd think you'd be itching to get out of here." Aucoin crossed his arms.

McNally yanked the shirt out of the bag. A belt fell to his feet. He'd forgotten about the belt....

He cinched the belt around Aucoin's neck, tighter, harder. The man's bulbous eyes bulged. Aucoin gasped, his hands clutching his throat. McNally grinned. The CX looked like a fucking fish.

Aucoin snatched the belt from the concrete floor. "Give me your uni. Get your clothes on."

If they were two dogs, the fight to the death would have begun at this moment.

McNally yanked the prison-issued golf shirt over his head, feeling the flex of his muscles as he tossed the uniform onto the floor. *You can pick that up, too, Aucoin.* The shirt had changed size in direct proportion to the number of hours he had clocked in the weight room.

Aucoin's gaze flickered over the tattoos on McNally's upper arms. It was well known he was the resident tattoo artist of the unit. Usually, the prison staff turned a blind eye unless they had a particular reason to discipline an inmate. Aucoin had been one of the few who went by the book, stripping away McNally's privileges whenever he was able to establish that McNally had done the ink.

But when Aucoin wasn't around…supply and demand was the governing law of prison. Whoever had supply was in demand. And there was pent-up demand for tattoos when McNally arrived twelve years ago. It had taken less than a day for the other inmates in his unit to discover that he could sling ink for them. He just needed the tools. When it became obvious that McNally didn't have anyone on the outside to send him supplies within the thirty-day admission period, the other guys on his unit began to smuggle the necessary parts to make a tattoo gun.

Within a week of his incarceration, McNally was in possession of an empty pen tube, an E guitar string, and a pencil eraser. Electrical tape and an emery cloth were smuggled from the machine shop. But he still needed a motor. After some pressure from Hodder—a lifer who controlled the unit's contraband supply chain—the kid two cells down sacrificed the rumble pack from his video game controller. "My girlfriend won't even let me get a prison tatt," he muttered.

McNally had filed the tip of the guitar string with a piece of emery cloth, and slid it into the tube. Billy Lyman, his cell mate, had watched with a mixture of fascination and fear. "I don't want no more trouble," he'd told McNally. "I've been down in the hole three times since the summer."

McNally threaded the other end of the guitar string through the top of the pen tube, and pushed it into the eraser.

"See? That's how you do it. The eraser works as a cam," he told Kenzie.

He studied her studying the contraption. "A cam?"

The winter sun cast her face in a cool, unforgiving light. But with Kenzie's features, there had been nothing to forgive. Her skin, always pale and smooth, appeared to be composed of marble. He had a sudden appreciation for the thrill Michelangelo must have felt when confronted with such pure material on which to create his art.

"The cam connects the guitar string to the motor. It's like a spinning wheel. It makes the needle move."

He couldn't wait to create his masterpieces on her.

He had created one masterpiece on Kenzie.

Soon after, she had fled—and left him to dispose of Heather Rigby's body.

Five years after Kenzie had run away, he had killed the girl at the bar where he worked, and got a ten-year sentence. And on the tenth day of serving his sentence for manslaughter, he had made sure he would never forget Kenzie. Or what she owed him.

He had concentrated on getting the cam just right. After several adjustments, the "needle" moved up and down at the correct depth. Too short, and the needle wouldn't hold the ink. Too long, and the needle would make raw meat out of flesh.

Hodder had slipped him two disposable razors. McNally put them in the unit's microwave. Once burned, the plastic handles left a soot residue, which he mixed with soap and water.

He had sat on his bunk, drew ink into the tube, and tattooed an X on his heart. The needle hurt like hell. His blood thudded. If he had closed his eyes, he would have said that his heart was pounding enough to make his skin undulate.

For whatever reason, the lines of the tattoo had bled. Billy Lyman had laughed. "Can't be straight edge if the lines are blurry."

McNally had ripped the tattoo gun across Billy's cheek. Blood welled from the slash. "You son of a bitch." He had dropped the tattoo gun onto the bunk. "I'm not straight edge." His fingers curled into his palms. He wanted to crush that ugly Adam's apple in Lyman's throat so he could never laugh again. He pointed to the large spider's web tattoo spread across the back of his skull. In the center was a death's head. "You think this is fucking straight edge?"

Lyman backed away. "Didn't mean anything by it. Nothin' wrong with not wanting to do drugs or booze." He lowered his voice to a whisper. "I won't say nothing about the tattoo gun. Or this—" He touched the cut. "It was an accident. Shaving. Trust me, you don't wanna spend time in the hole." Eight months later, McNally learned from bitter experience how right Lyman was.

But then, just ten days on the inside, he shrugged and threw himself onto his mattress. He stared at the underside of Lyman's bunk. He hated Lyman for lying to protect him from solitary confinement. He did not want to owe any favors.

It would be so much easier if I just killed him. He could kill him the same way he had killed that girl who had taunted him at the bar. Just grab him by the throat and smash his head on the floor.

McNally hadn't inked any more tattoos on his upper torso after that first X. Partly to make it stand out; partly because it was a difficult angle to tattoo unless he used a mirror. Even when he got an additional two years for assaulting that jerk in the bar, he didn't change the tattoo. The tattoo meant more than just the number of years he spent in prison. It symbolized his heart, his commitment, his willingness to do whatever it took to get Kenzie back with him.

Aucoin whacked the loosely coiled belt against his thigh. "I don't get you, McNally. You could be walking out of here. Instead, you stand there daydreaming."

What are you, the fucking Gestapo? McNally glared at him, pulling his own T-shirt over his head. Despite being sealed in a bag for two years, it didn't smell so bad. The soft, worn knit slid across his skin. He wanted to close his eyes, savor the feel of his own clothing stretching across his body. The shirt strained at his shoulders, hung loosely at the waist. He didn't care. It felt so damned good, he didn't ever want to take it off.

The CX whacked the belt again.

As soon as McNally was dressed he was one step closer to leaving this behind him. One step closer to attaining something that had only been a fantasy. He reached into the plastic bag and removed his boxers and his pants. He stepped out of the prison jeans, then yanked down the worn underwear and kicked it away from his body. Tomorrow, someone else would wear his freshly laundered uniform.

He slid on his boxers, the neon yellow that he'd worn when he was arrested appearing brassy and cheap in the fluorescent lights. His jeans were looser at the waist, snugger across the thighs. He held out his hand for the belt.

Aucoin dropped it into his palm and watched him tighten the buckle. McNally shoved the T-shirt into his waistband. He picked up the plastic bag and scrunched the handle in his fist. His wallet was in the bag, as were his keys. The former was empty, the latter no longer relevant. He had stayed at a halfway house when he'd been out on parole. Lovett, his old band mate, had sold the house in which he had been crashing before his manslaughter conviction. He wondered if the new owners had changed the locks....

He tightened his grip on the bag and gave Aucoin a brusque nod.

The CX led him out of the security areas and buzzed open the gate to the parking lot.

McNally stepped through it.

An early-morning mist hovered over the small patches of green that "naturalized" the parking lot. He breathed in, enjoying the cool damp on his face.

Where was Lovett's Mercedes? He knew Lovett would not come into the penitentiary. Not once had he visited in the twelve years McNally had spent there. He had built a real estate empire while McNally rotted away on the inside. It would hurt his reputation, he told McNally, for an upstanding member of the business community to fraternize with someone like him. McNally knew that wasn't the real reason, but he wasn't in a position to argue. At least Lovett had—reluctantly—agreed to help McNally return home to Halifax.

McNally scanned the parking lot again, averting his face so the CX couldn't read his expression. No sign of Lovett's gleaming black SUV. Shit. Had he forgotten that McNally would be released today?

He crouched outside the school, under an overhang. The rain poured in a sheet three inches in front of his face. He had stuck his tongue in and out of the stream, making patterns, watching the shifting globules of water. His mom said she would come after school. She had scooped him into a big hug and promised him.

He had made her promise again. She had. But when he asked the third time—hoping that three promises would work better than two—she grew impatient and pulled his arms off her neck.

He shoved his hands in his pocket. They were numb from wet. He wished he had a watch so he could tell how long he'd been waiting, but he still got confused with the little-hand stuff so it wouldn't have made any difference anyway. All the teachers had left. So he knew it had been a long time since the bell went.

He watched the water running in long cascades of silver. He was an explorer, he was hiding from the bad guys behind a waterfall. He flexed his thumb and forefinger in his pocket. He would shoot them if they found him. He would. Shoot them dead. He stared through the rain. The school grounds seemed to grow darker, the rain had mysteriously changed from silver to black. He needed to pee so bad. His sneakers were soaked. His legs were soaked, too. Would it matter if he just peed a little? No one would know....

A cab pulled into the parking lot.

He exhaled. Why had he thought Lovett would personally come to pick him up? He should have known that wasn't going to happen. Anxiety tightened his chest. He did not have enough money to pay for his trip all the way back to Halifax.

Aucoin flagged the cabdriver. The cab eased over to where they stood. The cabdriver studied him through the windshield. He was having second thoughts, McNally could tell. He wished he had a ball cap to cover his death's head tatt.

"Oh, by the way, you received this mail." Aucoin held out a FedEx envelope.

McNally snatched it from him, relief overriding his

anger that Aucoin hadn't given him the envelope with his belongings in Admissions and Discharge. He tore open the envelope and shook out the contents.

Lovett had sent a chit for the cab, a train ticket and some cash to get McNally started.

He stepped forward to open the cab door—throwing a glance behind him. His cheeks flushed as his gaze met the CX's.

You'll never stop looking over your shoulder, Aucoin's eyes told him.

McNally's pulse pounded in his ears. He hated himself for the involuntary gesture, he hated himself for being so conditioned to the CX's authority. *Fuck you.*

Aucoin gave him a mock salute. "We'll keep your bunk warm for you, McNally."

McNally's jaw tightened. *Just you wait, Aucoin.*

He jumped into the cab, tossing the plastic bag onto the floor. "Take me to the train station."

He leaned his head back against the car seat. Everything appeared dull: the cracked asphalt of the road, the modest homes that multiplied along the roadway the farther they drove away from the penitentiary. A large golden dog tied to a fence post barked. He smiled.

Clouds threatened rain. But the air held its breath. Promising spring. Promising freedom.

Promising.

Kenzie.

His heart pounded so hard he felt the X undulate under his shirt.

He had lost twelve years.

It was, at long last, time. Nothing would come between them now.

He would make sure of it. Kenzie and he shared the

same soul, traveled the same darkness. And this time, he would make sure that Kenzie never strayed again.

Kate Lange would bring them full circle, back to the night when her sister, Imogen, should have been their first victim. One Lange was as good as another.

X marks the spot.

2

You would think that after surviving two near-death experiences in just over a year, you would be more prepared when death showed up at your door.

That was what the undaunted optimist in Kate Lange hoped. But the logical part of her brain knew better. Despite her semi-celebrity status as the slayer of a serial killer, she had seen how random, how inexplicable death could be. What she didn't know—didn't understand and was afraid to ask—was why it kept searching her out.

This time it appeared self-evident. Her client, Frances Sloane, was afflicted with a terminal disease: Amyotrophic Lateral Sclerosis. Made famous by Lou Gehrig, it was a disease that attacked the motor neurons. For Frances Sloane, it appeared to have attacked everything and left a crumpled cage of bones and tissues. If anyone ever wondered about the role of motor neurons, all they would have to do was look at Frances Sloane.

Though her body was clearly in a state of ruin, Frances' sky-blue eyes remained the same: sharp and penetrating. As had happened in her youth, Kate found herself mesmerized by them. She could almost—almost—forget the elaborate motorized wheelchair, the hand controls, the torso that could barely hold itself erect—when she met Frances' gaze.

She fought to keep the pity from showing on her face. Knowing Frances Sloane, it was the last thing she wanted. Or needed.

Frances Sloane's helper, a middle-aged woman named Phyllis wearing the uniform of a professional caregiver, set the brakes on the wheelchair. She gave her client a quick nod and left Kate's office.

"Mrs. Sloane, nice to see you again." It had been a complicated string of events—and emotions—that had led to this meeting.

"Kate," her client said, her once-crisp voice slurred and oddly nasal, "call me Frances."

Kate smiled. "It will be hard to break the habit. I've always thought of you as Mrs. Sloane."

Saliva pooled in one side of Frances' mouth. Her hand rose, a tissue clutched in her grip, reminding Kate of a bird struggling for liftoff against hostile winds.

That small movement, which was now a gargantuan effort, made Kate's throat constrict. Frances Sloane's independence and vitality had been her trademark. She had built her own award-winning architectural firm in a profession still dominated by men. Now, if Kate correctly understood her client's circumstances, Frances was all alone. Just she, her caregiver and her wheelchair. Facing a terrible end.

Kate thought of her elderly neighbors, Enid and Muriel Richardson. They, too, were a strong pair near the end of their lives, but the younger Richardson sister had been in a slow decline due to the effects of Alzheimer's. Unlike Kate's client, Muriel had the benefit of the caring companionship of her sister Enid. *I haven't spoken to Enid and Muriel in over a week. I need to call them tonight.*

Frances wiped her mouth, studying Kate. "You've been through a lot. I read about it in the papers."

"It appears we both have," Kate said. "I'm sorry about your illness…."

Frances' hand slowly made its descent to her lap. "I need your help, Kate."

The irony of this statement was not lost on Kate. She doubted it was lost on Frances, either.

Frances must remember the last time they had seen one another. It had been at the funeral of Imogen Lange, Kate's sister.

Imogen had died in a car crash when she was fifteen—with seventeen-year-old Kate at the wheel.

After Imogen's funeral service, Kate had barely been able to look at Frances Sloane when she stopped in the receiving line to offer her condolences. Not because of her shame. Or guilt. Or grief.

But because of her rage.

Perhaps it was unfair. Frances, after all, had been out of the country when her daughter, Kenzie, hosted the party on the night of Imogen's death.

Surely she must have known her daughter would hold a party at their house in her absence?

Surely she might have guessed that Imogen—who had begun hanging around Kenzie with puppylike eagerness—might be induced to join Kenzie's well-known drug binges on her back porch?

Frances must have read those questions in Kate's gaze. Or perhaps they were the very ones she had asked herself after Imogen's death, for she said, "Kate. I'm so sorry. I didn't know about the party. I would have stopped it if I'd known."

Kate's eyes had welled with tears. Frances' words were a form of absolution; a recognition that the blame for Imogen's death did not reside solely on Kate's seventeen-year-old shoulders. And Kate's rage melted into liquid warmth, spilling down her cheeks.

She had nodded at Frances, unable to speak.

Frances had moved onward to offer her condolences to Kate's shell-shocked mother—leaving Kate to face Kenzie Sloane as the line of mourners passed by.

Kenzie had averted her sky-blue eyes.

And then she walked past Kate to the cathedral door.

Frances Sloane had cast one last look over her shoulder and followed her daughter out of the cathedral, her bearing erect but her step slow.

Had the disease been lurking even then?

Focus, Kate.

She stared at the file folder on her desk. It contained all the legal reasons why her client could not ask someone to help her kill herself.

"Mrs.—I mean, Frances," Kate said. "You are seeking an opinion regarding the legality of assisted suicide in Canada. Correct?"

And it was as simple—and as complicated—as that. "Yes."

The hope, the determination—and worse, the desperation—in Frances Sloane's eyes made it difficult to meet her gaze. "I'm sorry to tell you this, Frances. But there are no circumstances under which it is legal. The Sue Rodriguez decision made it clear."

Sue Rodriguez had put a face to both ALS and the matter of assisted suicide in 1993, taking her battle all the way to the Supreme Court of Canada.

"That was an old decision," Frances said. "And it was close." Five to four, Kate had noted. Only one vote to change the entire course of legal precedent and redefine when and how one could legally end someone else's life.

Kate didn't envy that judge.

"Hasn't anything changed?" Frances asked.

Kate shook her head. "The decision was based on the fundamental tenets of our Charter of Rights. And those haven't changed."

"But why can't I choose how I want to die?"

"You can."

A smile twisted her client's face. "If I was able-bodied I could choose. But I'm not. It is discriminatory to say I can't kill myself because I am physically unable."

"It was a close decision when the Supreme Court of Canada voted." Seeing her client slumped in her wheelchair barely able to keep her head up, hearing her speak, watching her struggle to lift her limbs, it seemed unfair. But Kate couldn't let her sympathy obviate the legal reality: "The Supreme Court felt that it was necessary to protect the interests of the vulnerable. It also wanted to preserve the sanctity of life—" her client's lips twisted "—by ensuring that assisted suicide remain a criminal offense."

"The old slippery slope argument..." Frances grimaced. "Sue Rodriguez had the right question—Who controls my life? Me or the government? But the court gave the wrong answer."

Kate leaned forward. "Look, you aren't the only one who feels that way. I think the court of public opinion is shifting. Right now, there are two different challenges to the law underway. Those plaintiffs are arguing that other countries do allow assisted suicide. Several states in the U.S. do, as well. The question is—Are you willing to go through the long and arduous process of mounting a challenge?" *Would you even be alive by the end of it?*

"How long would it take?" Frances asked.

"We would have to start with the provincial courts and work our way up," Kate said. "We could ask the courts to expedite the process, given your condition. Even so, you are looking at six to twelve months for the first hearing."

Frances gazed at her hands. They rested on the armrest, flaccid.

The few times Kate had seen Frances in the past, she had always gripped a pencil, ready to jot down an idea or make a rough sketch of the buildings she had made a career of designing.

"I'll be dead by the time the courts are done," Frances said.

There wasn't much point in denying it. With ALS, the afflicted never lived long enough to be effective activists. "The question, in my mind, is whether you want to spend the final days of your life in court?"

Frances gave a mirthless laugh. "Of course not. I was hoping you would tell me that there was a loophole. There usually is. At least for criminals."

Kate shook her head. "I wish there was."

Frances was quiet. Finally, she said, "If I can't ask someone to help me kill myself without getting them into trouble, can I tell my doctor to top off my painkillers when the time comes?"

"Frances, that is between you and your doctor. I think most doctors are very compassionate…." *Read between the lines, Frances.*

Her client's gaze was pensive. "But Dr. Clarkson got into trouble for it a few years ago. That's why I called

Randall to advise me. But he told me he is in New York on a leave of absence...."

"Yes," Kate said, keeping her tone neutral. "He is working on a corporate merger in New York. But he has briefed me on the Clarkson case."

The Clarkson case was legendary in Halifax. A prominent heart surgeon had been accused of injecting a fatal cocktail of drugs into a patient in extreme distress—who had no chance of surviving—to prematurely end her suffering. Detective Ethan Drake, Kate's ex-fiancé, had been the primary homicide investigator on the case. The case hinged on the testimony of the victim's son, who told the police—and the court—that Dr. Clarkson had assured him that his mother would not suffer any longer.

Dr. Clarkson bankrupted himself to pursue his defense, but he was convicted. It was the desire to help out his old friend that triggered Randall Barrett's return to Halifax years before, that had yanked the raveling thread of his marriage and had led him to leave his Bay Street career and relocate to Halifax. He had masterminded (and funded) Clarkson's appeal—Old Soccer Teammate Launches Appeal was the newspaper headline—calling into question the victim's son's testimony, specifically by alleging that Detective Ethan Drake had improperly influenced the teen.

"As you might remember from the news, Frances, Dr. Clarkson was convicted on charges of murder. He was unsuccessful on appeal. The court of appeal upheld the conviction 2-1."

Neither Randall nor Ethan had forgiven one another.

"How can I prevent the same thing happening to my doctor?" Frances asked.

"Legally, the only thing you can do is to provide specific directions to your physician that you are not to be given any life-extending treatments." Kate closed the folder. "I'm sorry, Frances. I wish I could be of more assistance."

Frances laughed. Loudly.

Kate stared at her. *Did she think I was joking?*

"Sorry," Frances said, sputtering. "ALS makes me laugh when I'm upset." She swallowed. "It's frustrating," she added, as if reading Kate's thoughts. "The way I talk—people think I'm drunk or crazy." Her hand twitched.

After that outburst, Kate could understand why people might question whether Frances was mentally competent. And yet she knew it was rare for ALS to affect cognitive function. That was what made the disease so terrible. And terrifying for the afflicted. To know that one's body would slowly lose its ability to function, until even breathing had to be provided by a machine, while the mind remained alert and excruciatingly aware of everything that had been lost.

Unlike the Creutzfeldt-Jakob disease that could be lurking in her own cells. That disease robbed its victim of all cognitive function.

Stop it, Kate.

She hadn't thought about it in months, had not allowed herself to dwell on it. Although it was hard not to be confronted with your own mortality when facing a client who clearly was losing that battle. And whose very reason for seeking legal counsel was to hasten her own death.

"You probably are wondering why I just didn't kill myself while I could." Frances gazed at Kate, dwarfed by the heavily padded frame of her wheelchair. Her eyes, still watery from her laughing episode, held a defiance that made Kate's heart squeeze. Why should someone have to defend their decision to live? Or their decision to die?

"I wanted to live." Frances' words were soft.

Her client gazed down at her hands. Frances' eyelids were translucent. Embryonic. The cycle of life nearing its end and returning to where it began.

"I so very badly want to live."

Her gaze met Kate's again. She did not try to hide her despair. Or her determination. "But not like this."

"I'm sorry." A sense of failure weighed Kate's words. She wished, in a moment of cowardice, that she had not agreed to take Frances as a client. Then she wouldn't have to face her own inability to help her.

You can't overturn the Supreme Court of Canada's decision, Kate.

She could only put up a challenge to it, if her client was willing.

And Frances Sloane was not.

"I'm afraid there isn't anything more I can offer you," Kate said, rising to her feet. *How did doctors do this all the time?*

Frances took a shaky breath. "I understand. Could you get Phyllis for me?"

Kate nodded. "Of course."

She hurried to the foyer. The cool air of the corridor refreshed her. She hadn't realized how thick the atmosphere had become in her office.

Kate hovered in the hallway while Phyllis guided Frances' wheelchair down the corridor.

She raised her hand in farewell. "Take care, Frances." That sounded horribly inadequate to her ears. But what else could she say? "Hope you have a peaceful death," or "I'll come to your funeral"?

Frances slurred, "Goodbye."

Oh, no. Those were tears in Frances' eyes.

Kate watched Phyllis guide her client's wheelchair to the elevators.

This is probably going to be the last time you'll see her.

Her stomach clenched. She spun on her heel, closing the door to her office with more force than necessary. *You couldn't have done more, Kate. The law is the law. She didn't want to take on a court challenge.*

She threw herself into her chair, closed her eyes and leaned her head back.

An image of Frances Sloane, crumpled in her wheelchair, her eyes burning into Kate's, jumped into her head.

"Damn!"

She leapt to her feet, trying to rid her brain of the image, and rushed out of her office. Frances and her caregiver waited at the elevator.

"Frances!" Kate planted herself between her client's wheelchair and the elevator doors. "I just thought of something—"

"There *is* a loophole?"

"No. But there is one other way to change the law," Kate said. "You could lobby your M.P. to amend the Criminal Code. Or get the government to strike down the provision."

Frances' gaze sharpened.

Kate lowered her voice. "If you can convince them of the merits of the issue, then they will fight for it in Parliament. You won't have to engage in a lengthy battle in the courts."

The elevator bell chimed. Frances' caregiver began to push the wheelchair toward the doors but Frances reached for Kate's sleeve. Her fingers were unable to grip the fabric. Her hand sank back to her armrest.

The elevator began its descent without Kate's client.

"Can you help me?" Frances asked, reaching out her hand again. Kate didn't remember Frances Sloane ever being so touchy-feely. Perhaps it was because she was losing the ability to do so that compelled her to attempt it while she could. "Can you write a legal argument for my M.P.?"

Kate shook her head, regret twisting her mouth. "I'm not a lobbyist, Frances."

"But you know the issues. You could do this for me."

Kate shook her head. "Frances…I'm sorry," she said, her tone gentle. "You need to find a professional lobbyist. I'm sure there are ones with legal training who could help you."

"I've chosen you." Frances' gaze became pleading.

A weight formed in Kate's chest. "Why?"

"You fought the Body Butcher so you wouldn't die a horrible death."

The foyer had become very quiet. The back of Kate's neck prickled. She was certain that the receptionist listened intently. She was also certain that Melissa would be looking anywhere but at them.

You've got this all mixed up, Frances. It was pure survival instinct, not a well-thought-out plan about my means of departing this earth. Kate rubbed her arms. "I fought him because I wanted to live, Frances."

"But you didn't want to die like that, did you?"

Kate saw exactly where Frances was heading with her question. Yet she couldn't lie to her. "No." The desire to live had fuelled her fight to the death with Halifax's first serial killer. But Frances was right. Fear underlay her desperate fight with the Body Butcher. Fear of dying in the manner that had earned the killer his moniker.

"And your fame could help my cause, Kate."

God. She gave a shaky laugh. "I'm not that famous, Frances."

"You are a hero. You saved other girls from being killed. This disease is my killer, Kate. There is nothing—" Frances swallowed. "Nothing that will help me fight it. No pills, no surgery. It is incurable and omnipotent. So I will choose to die the way I want. Not the way it chooses for me." She paused. "You still can choose. I can't."

And you can choose to help me. Frances didn't need to say it—they both knew it.

Kate could not face the plea in those weary sky-blue eyes. She would be doing this woman a disservice by agreeing to her request.

And, she was afraid, she would be doing herself one, as well. After being plagued by post-traumatic stress disorder from her encounter with the Body Butcher, she didn't want to revisit her experience in any way, shape or form.

"Frances, I am not qualified to be a lobbyist." Kate eased around the wheelchair. "I will find someone who can help you. Someone who can be successful. I'll call you as soon as I find someone."

The disappointment in her client's gaze sliced into Kate. Finally, Frances said, "If that is your decision."

Kate forced a reassuring smile. "I'll call you."

Even to her ears, that promise sounded inadequate.

The elevator chimed and the doors slid open. Her client drove into the lift. "Goodbye," she said. Her voice had a finality to it.

Every goodbye was probably uttered with that intention. She had no idea when death would claim her.

Kate returned to her office, her footprints smoothing the track left by Frances' wheelchair in the plush nap of the carpet.

You can't be everyone's savior, Kate.

But it wasn't everyone who was asking.

It was just one woman.

One very sick and helpless woman.

Kate sank into her chair and closed her eyes.

3

Flushed with triumph at finding *sarracenia purpurea*—also known as the purple pitcher plant—Rebecca Chen crouched above the surprisingly clear and shallow water of the peat bog. *Bag this last plant and then I'm outta here.*

It was a pretty plant and yet, according to her notes from biology class, it was a predator, capturing its food in its petals. She plunged her hand into the muck, her fingers scrabbling down the plant's stem, searching for the root ball. But the stem curved sideways under the dense thicket of hummock. She exhaled, her forehead prickling with sweat.

Farther up the slope and beyond the cliffs, lay the outer mouth of Halifax Harbour. Fog hung over the horizon, a ghostly waterfall hovering over the deep blue of the ocean, but the cooling breeze carrying its afterdamp did not reach her.

With a grunt, she pushed her hand deep into the underside of the hummock. Her fingers hit a rock. The stem appeared to be wrapped around it.

Frig. She sat back on her heels. The peat bogs stretched around her, serene blue pools dotting scrubby hummocks of low-lying shrubs. She had never even been out to Chebucto Head until her biology teacher assigned this lab, and she cursed him when she had missed the class trip and had to find her own way to the peat bogs. After a twenty-five-minute drive, she found the road to the headland. It was flanked by a protected nature reserve, but it eventually opened to a cove dotted with houses. They huddled, higgledy-piggledy, on the granite bedrock cliffs, as if holding their collective breath.

The peat bogs were a twenty-minute hike across the headlands. "Just find the old bunkers," her teacher had told her. "There are two. The bogs are down the slope. You can't miss them."

True enough, after twenty minutes of following a scraggly, muddy path, she spotted the bunkers on a crest of the cliff. There were two: one facing the water, the other offset behind it. The bunkers had been built eighty years ago as the outer battery to defend Halifax Harbour. The lower bunker perched on a slope, its flat, sharp roof appearing crooked against the sky. Tall shrubs and a handful of stunted evergreens grew around the squat concrete boxes. Rather than softening the forbidding exterior of the wartime posts, the tangled thicket of shrubs and the dense branches of the evergreens served to emphasize their brutal purpose.

Even in the May sunshine, they were creepy. She veered around them, and headed downhill to the peat bogs. They gleamed in the sun, the area a large, open marsh with a pleasant piney scent. It hadn't taken much time to find the samples for her biology lab.

Until now.

Last lab of the school year, last lab of high school, Rebecca. That knowledge lent extra urgency to her scrabbling. She wrapped her fingers around the rock anchoring what she now viewed as "her" plant. She yanked the rock-and-plant specimen from under the hummock, falling back on her heels. She staggered to her feet, the prize clutched in her hand.

Her butt was soaked from her efforts. *Figures.*

She unraveled the roots clinging to the rock.

Her fingers froze.

Beneath the plant debris and muck, the rock appeared calcified. And smooth.

God. It felt suspiciously like a bone.

It's not a bone, Rebecca.

It *was* a bone. Her heart pounding, Rebecca tore away the roots of the plant.

The smooth curve and calcified exterior were obvious now.

It's just an animal's bone. Probably a deer.

She peered at the hummock, searching for the hole she had tunneled through the underside.

Her breath caught in her throat.

She couldn't move.

Couldn't blink.

Couldn't scream.

All she could do was stare at the two bulging colorless eyes that pinned her in their malevolent gaze. Then she saw the hooked nose, the gaping smile, the hair floating from the head. Everything tinted the same brownish color.

Horror in sepia wash.

Her brain, at first, couldn't process what she saw. Finally, her lungs forced her breath out in a gasp. And her brain interpreted the image.

The bulging eyes belonged to a mask. A rubber Halloween mask that someone had thrown into the bog. Her insides liquefied with a warm rush of relief. Then she remembered the cold, smooth length of bone in her palm.

It hadn't been just a mask she had dislodged. The mask had been on a dead body.

She was holding proof of it.

A scream built in her throat.

The dead body was under the hummock. Under *her*.

Oh, dear Lord. She was holding a dead body!

She threw the bone into the water so forcefully that water splashed onto her torso, her face. And into her mouth. An earthy, decayed taste swelled the taste buds on her tongue. Bog water.

The water had a putrefied body in it.

She wiped her mouth with the back of her hand. With the hand that was filthy with muck.

Muck that contained a dead body.

Her stomach heaved. Vomit flecked her rain boots.

She began to scream.

4

The random movements of people on the sidewalk set McNally's teeth on edge. The rows and rows of bread in the grocery store…nine grain, whole grain, vitality, soy, cracked wheat, organic this, vegan that. Everything was so…complicated.

And the girls and women… Everywhere.

His first few days on the outside had been a blur. Rick Lovett, who once had hung on his every word, was as of today his new boss. His old friend had greeted him with a warning: "Stay away from me. No drugs. No police." Lovett had unlocked the now-vacant superintendent's apartment in one of his lower-rent apartment buildings in the North end. "You are on call 24/7. You have weekends off. Rent is included. Don't scare the tenants." He had tossed the keys to McNally, doubt in his eyes, regret already twisting his lips. "And wear a baseball cap on your head until your hair grows in. You look like you belong to a gang with that tatt."

A flush prickled McNally's neck, but he slipped the keys in his pocket. He walked through the doorway of the apartment.

It was small. It was bare. It was his.

He could do whatever he fucking wanted to do in here.

His heart began to race.

"Will do, boss," he drawled and closed the door on Lovett's ugly face.

The next morning, he woke up at 5:04 a.m. He grimaced. It was early even for prison time.

He buried his face in his pillow. He had wanted to sleep in to celebrate his first day in his new life.

But neither his mind nor his body had made the leap yet.

He jumped up from his mattress, unable to stay still. He would make a cup of coffee, write a list of things he needed.

Half an hour later, the list was two pages long and frustration made his body tight. At the wage Lovett paid him, it would take at least a year to earn enough money to afford everything he needed.

And wanted. Like a professional tattooist's kit.

He put on his running shoes. He didn't have any gym clothes, so his jeans would have to do. He slipped into the hallway, locking his door—pushing down, down, down the memory of the thousands of times that he had watched a CX lock him up—and headed to the parkade.

Lovett had given him the keys to a company truck. It was navy blue, parked in a corner, easily identifiable with the large gold logo of Lovett's real estate company: Lovett Group Limited.

The vibration of the V8 engine dug pleasantly deep into his bones as he drove across the bridge and headed to Cole Harbour. Fifteen minutes later, he turned down Bissett Road—snorting at the religious exhortations on the billboard of a local fundamentalist church—and drove to the turnoff for Rainbow Haven beach. He sensed, but could not yet see, the ocean in the distance. He turned into the parking lot. His tires crunched, the truck's engine a low throb in the hush of near-dawn.

He was the sole visitor. He jumped out of the truck.

Sea air—tangy, damp, invigorating—brushed his face.

He broke into a run, savoring the air on his skin, empty space all around him.

He jogged past the canteen and change rooms. His sneakers made a hollow thud on the wooden boardwalk. It took only a minute to arrive at the beach.

He stopped. The sweeping majesty of sand, water, sky made his chest feel hollow. His heart pounded.

Quiet.

When had he last heard quiet?

As he stood, he became aware of the soft roar of the tide, the muted call of a seabird, the wind confiding in his ear.

The waves were low today. When he was a teen, he had surfed on white, foaming breakers that carried the energy of inestimable particles of water. They had been some of the best days of his life.

He let his gaze wander down the long, sandy beach.

Sea foam, a dead crab, pebbles worn by a hundred thousand waves.

Dawn imbued the sky with a luminous gold. It moved under his skin, seeping through his cells, injecting light where there had been gray for as long as he could remember. Color bloomed through his blood.

For the first time since his incarceration twelve years ago, tears tightened his throat.

He put his face to the wind and began to sprint down the beach. He eventually slowed into a steady run, only stopping when the frantic energy in his muscles had subsided to a manageable buzz.

Just over an hour later, he climbed into the truck, his body sheathed in sweat, eager for another cup of coffee. He switched on the radio and found a station that played classic rock. By the time he reached the bridge leading to Halifax, he was singing at the top of his voice.

The hope had been short-lived. As soon as he walked down Spring Garden Road, ready to throw himself into the bustle of one of Halifax's main shopping districts, his muscles tightened. Became twitchy.

There were eyes watching him, all the time. He stood at the intersection, waiting for the light to change. He glanced over at the girl who stood just behind him, in a tiny tank top and cutoff shorts. He had been all ready to smile at her, but she edged away.

He hurried into the drugstore. He needed a razor and shaving gel. He took his time, his brain adjusting to the overwhelming variety. The back of his neck prickled. The sales clerk was staring at him. He chose a five-pack of disposable razors. He tucked it under his arm while he sniffed the shaving gel. One of them had a clean, fresh scent.

"Mmm...you smell so good," Kenzie murmured into his neck. "Like citrus or something."

This one smelled citrusy. He added it to the package of razors tucked in his arm and walked to the back of the line at the cash. He skimmed the tabloid magazines until it was his turn to pay. The cashier eyeballed the pockets of his jacket.

He dropped his purchases on the counter—enjoying the cashier's flinch—and paid for the items. But as soon as he resumed window-shopping, his neck prickled again. Everyone stared at him. He shoved his hands in his jean pockets and retreated to a magazine store.

It was cool. Quiet. He drifted down an aisle. The images from the magazines jumped out at him. For years, he had only been permitted to use a black or blue pen for his drawings. The saturated color and pictures of beautiful women stirred a desire to create something in ink. Preferably in the flesh.

The tattoo magazines were tucked into the bottom shelf of the far corner. His heart rate quickened. Tattoo magazines had been contraband in prison. The few that circulated were before his time. He crouched down, his gaze jumping from cover to cover. He couldn't decide, so he grabbed a copy of each, and strode to the cash. It added up to more than he expected—more than he could afford—but he bought them anyway.

Half an hour later, he lay on his mattress, flipping through the magazines. Midway through one of the most popular tattoo magazines, his fingers paused. He stared at the page.

Kenzie Sloane, The Goddess of Japanese Tattoos. The headline slammed into him.

Kenzie gazed at him—only a foot and a half from his face—glossy and in hi-def. So now he knew how the past seventeen years had treated her.

Well.

Very well.

Black eyeliner outlined those sky-blue eyes. The years had given her face a new assuredness. A plain black tank top provided stark relief to the riot of Japanese designs swirling on the skin of her arms, her chest, her neck.

Her neck.

His eyes flitted back and forth between the words of the article and the exuberant images of the photo spread.

The more he saw, the hungrier he grew.

The more he read, the angrier he became.

Had Kenzie ever once acknowledged that *he* was the one who had introduced her to tattooing?

No.

She'd used him.

And then abandoned him. "The bitch!" He threw the magazine onto the floor, jumping to his feet, his heart racing.

He knew she had been successful with tattooing, but he had had no idea what a celebrity she had become.

Had he just been naive? Willfully blind?

Or stupid?

He snatched the magazine from the floor and studied her face again.

The chronic infection of his heart—which had not eased over seventeen years—intensified.

He needed to see her. Talk to her. Make her see how terrible her mistake had been.

Make her sorry for never once calling. Never once visiting. Never once letting him know how much she regretted running away that night.

No, instead she hooked up with some guy who made her an apprentice at his shop in Montreal. And then she moved to the States. And now—his jaw tightened—she had a Q&A column called KOI—"Kenzie On Ink."

You think you're so clever, he thought. *But I bet all that tattooing advice you dish out is the stuff I taught you when you were seventeen.*

"Kenzie welcomes questions from tattooists at all levels," the magazine gushed. It then listed her website, where "All of Kenzie's guest studio appearances are listed."

He stuck the magazine in his jacket, grabbed his set of master keys and strode down the hall to the manager's office. One of the tenants turned from the row of mailboxes that stood sentry to the office door. "You're the new super, right?" the short, tubby guy asked with an ingratiating smile.

McNally flipped through the key ring, searching for the one to unlock the office. "Yeah." He gave him a look that had ended more than one conversation in prison.

The guy stuffed his mail into a grocery bag. McNally wanted him to scurry back to his apartment, but the tenant pulled out a flyer to the discount store and began to flip through it.

McNally swallowed his irritation.

This key looked about right. He stuck it in the lock and turned the knob.

Bingo.

He walked into the office. He felt the tenant's eyes on his back, felt them tracing the lines of the spiderweb inked on his skull, sensed the man's indecision about whether to ingratiate himself further—or keep a safe distance.

He shut the door on the tenant. Then bolted it.

It was for the man's safety, he decided. Because if that guy bugged him any more, he'd punch his face in.

He turned on the computer. He had little access to computers on the inside, but he had received some job training while out on parole a few years ago. The computer was old and slow. By the time the software loaded, his teeth were gritted. He typed Kenzie's website URL, and watched the site load.

His throat tightened. Koi fish swam up the sides of

the computer screen. The background was a faint image of a waterfall. He entered the site and faced Kenzie, full screen.

His entire body flushed at the sight of her long, tattooed limbs. Her full breasts. Her mocking smile.

Had she ever tried to find him? Had she ever looked up his phone number or tried to search for *him* on the internet?

She had told him he was her soul mate. And he had believed her. He had been desperate to believe her. After years of being sent from foster home to foster home—and never once hearing from his own mother—Kenzie had been the one thing he could call his own. He had let her into the darkest parts of his soul—and she had reveled in them.

He had given her everything.

He had done everything she asked.

They would be bound by blood, sin and complicity.

And then he never heard from her again.

His heart twisted.

He scrolled through the pages of her website. He read her "tips" with a curl to his lip. Then he realized, his stomach tightening, that he didn't know many of the techniques she described.

The bitch.

He clicked on "Events and Appearances."

Hey, all you East Coast ink lovers, I'm coming to Halifax! Book an appointment at Yoshi's.

The post was dated last week.

His entire body broke out in chills.

Kenzie. Back in Halifax.

He didn't even have to go looking for her.

She was coming here.

It was a sign.

He exited the website, and cleared the browser cache. He did not want Lovett discovering that he had been on Kenzie's site.

The phone rang. He glanced at the clock. Shit. It was already after 10:00 a.m. He had better get his work done.

If he was quick, he could finish by early afternoon and head over to Yoshi's.

He answered the phone. It was Lovett, checking on him.

A vein in his temple throbbed.

It pissed him to no end that he was being bossed around by Lovett.

It won't be for long. Now that Kenzie's in town, you can move ahead with your plans.

Plans.

He liked that word.

For too long, it had seemed like a pipe dream. Fantasy. Whatever you wanted to call it, it had seemed unattainable.

The X inked on his heart had been a constant reminder to keep the faith.

And now, the universe handed him Kenzie on a platter.

Kate Lange would be next.

5

Sweat trickled behind Detective Sergeant Ethan Drake's ear. It was one of those glorious May days, a chimera of summer's arrival. He wiped his forehead, impressed with the pace set by forensic anthropologist Darcie Hughes, Ph.D., as they followed the worn footpath to Chebucto Head.

He was still trying to wrap his head around the fact that Dr. "Darcie" Hughes was a woman. Judging by her indifference to his double take when she jumped out of her four-wheel drive, he guessed she was used to it.

Dr. Hughes swatted a blackfly on the back of her neck. Her ginger-colored ponytail got in the way and she missed. He was tempted to slap it away but sensed whacking the back of her neck could be misinterpreted. She was all business, Dr. Hughes. From the top of her ball-capped head to the bottom of her rubber boots. Over her long-sleeved plaid shirt, she wore a vest in a hideous shade of green, covered in pockets. He couldn't wait to see what she pulled out from them. He guessed that the kit bags they carried contained the usual excavation equipment: bags, markers, labels, tape, rubber gloves, string, stakes, notebooks and cameras.

Usually, if unidentifiable bones were found, the medical examiner sent them to Dr. Hughes' lab. But very occasionally, the province's forensic anthropologist was called to the scene. When Dr. Hughes learned that the body had not yet been removed from the site, she told Dr. Guthro that she wanted to see the remains in their untouched state. And given the challenge of excavating a peat bog, Dr. Guthro was more than happy to have her attend the scene.

Her excitement was palpable when they set off down the track toward the crime scene. "Haven't excavated a bog before," she said, swinging her mud-encrusted spade.

Ethan tore his gaze from the blood that welled from the bug bite on Dr. Hughes' densely freckled neck and studied the terrain. The place was full of scrubby bushes and stunted trees, a living testament to the bleak ocean winds. No question that the first rule of survival for flora on this headland was to hunker low to the ground. *Trench warfare for plants.*

"So, Detective, do you have any missing-persons cases that fit this scenario?" Dr. Hughes asked, wiping the back of her neck with her sleeve and falling into step beside him. No easy task on the trail they followed.

He shifted the strap of his duffel bag. It held a bottle of water, some protein bars that he'd snagged from the station's kitchenette, a camera, notepad and two missing-persons files. "I brought the most relevant files with me. One is for a fifty-three-year-old male, last seen in October of 2003. He had refused to take his antipsychotic meds."

She gave him a thoughtful look. "You think it's him?"

Ethan shook his head. "No. I think it's someone else." A girl. Whom he had once known. "Her name was

Heather Rigby. She went missing on the night of Halifax's final Mardi Gras. In 1995."

Dr. Hughes shot him a look. "God. I went to those Mardi Gras parties."

He raised a brow. "Who didn't?"

Mardi Gras. Halifax's wildest street party. So wild, it eventually was banned from the streets. Held on the Halloween weekend, it attracted twenty to thirty thousand partiers—mainly university students—all in costume. And amongst those drunken revelers were the criminals, who took advantage of the costumed chaos to exact revenge and settle scores.

She threw a glance at his duffel bag. "So, what are the details on the missing girl's file?"

Spill the dirt, Detective, her eyes said.

He dug out the file from his bag and flipped it open, although in truth, he had long ago memorized every word on the page. "'Status—missing. Last seen—Mardi Gras, 1995.'" He stepped around a root. "'Age—eighteen.'" He glanced at Dr. Hughes. "She was a student at Hollis University." She had been a sweet, ordinary girl in his criminology class whom he had barely noticed until her disappearance became a headline story. He often wondered if it was Heather's case that had sparked his desire to become a homicide investigator.

"What were her physical attributes?" Dr. Hughes asked.

Of course, for an anthropologist it was all about the body.

Heather had a cute smile. He glanced at his notes. "Five foot four, one hundred and fifteen pounds, shoulder-length brown hair, brown eyes, birthmark on lower back."

"And the night she went missing—" Dr. Hughes

brushed a blackfly away from her face. "What was she wearing?"

He skimmed the page. "A black minidress, boots, fishnet tights and a green wig." He closed the folder, stuffing it back into his bag. "No one saw her leave the bar. The crowds were too heavy and everyone was drunk."

"And if everyone was costumed, it would be difficult to recognize anyone. Especially a witch—" Dr. Hughes slapped his arm. "Sorry. You were about to get bitten."

"Thanks." He flicked the dead fly from his sleeve. "If I recall correctly, the sexy witch costume was very popular." He caught Dr. Hughes' eye. *I bet you probably went as a skeleton.*

"And what about the other missing guy? The psychotic one?" Dr. Hughes asked. "Was he the same size as Heather?"

Ethan shook his head. "No. He was a big guy, at least six feet tall."

"Well, if the skeleton is fairly intact, we should be able to at least rule out one of them *in situ.*"

His step quickened. The case had been one of those that haunted everyone who heard of it. When he was transferred to Cold Case last year, Heather Rigby's file was the first one he had pulled up. He had pored over the witness statements, reviewed the security footage from outside the bar and contacted police forces across the country to see if there were any new leads.

Nothing.

Now the question of where she had disappeared might finally be answered. And a slew of new questions would arise.

He wanted to be the guy to help solve this case, bring closure to Heather's family—*if it is Heather lying in that bog,* he reminded himself. He wanted to get his hands dirty every way possible and do some good, solid police work. He wanted a case to rekindle his passion for the job.

Not only was he eager to get started, he was relieved that something had finally come his way that would force him to work 24/7. A case that would fill up those empty evenings and sleepless nights, when memories of Kate Lange drifted into his mind.

Inevitably, he would jump on the treadmill and run. Despite the endless miles he clocked, he couldn't chase her out of his thoughts.

He was frustrated as hell. He hated to even admit that he was lovelorn a year later. What was it about Kate that kept him wanting her?

He knew she'd had a thing for Randall Barrett—but the guy had upped and left town. He was crazy, leaving Kate all alone, after everything she'd been through.

But if Randall was stupid enough to turn his back on a woman like Kate, it was his problem.

Ethan had punished himself long enough for the mistakes he'd made with Kate.

He was ready to take a chance.

And try one more time.

Ahead, yellow crime scene tape fluttered in the breeze, the water of the bog surprisingly blue and clear within its confines. Dr. Guthro stood in water up to his knees, the rolled-up cuffs of his khakis dark with wet, studying a hummock with his usual unflappability.

"Ah, Dr. Hughes, Detective Drake," he said, as if ushering them into his study rather than a bog. "This is quite a case we have here."

Dr. Hughes grinned. "Tell me about it." The two doctors exchanged glances. Their excitement was palpable.

"Is this the site of the remains?" Dr. Hughes nodded toward a thick, spongy hummock.

"It's been rather cleverly hidden." Dr. Guthro pointed to the small hole that the high school student had dug to remove the plant.

Dr. Hughes walked into the pool of water that was the center of the bog, and crouched down until she was eye-level with the hole. "Nice," she said, when she saw the mask. "Someone had a sense of humor."

Detective Constable Lamond—Ethan's former Homicide partner until he was switched to Cold Case last year—edged toward them, pacing in small circles by the yellow tape, his gaze glued to a three-inch radius in front of him.

"Find anything, Lamond?" Ethan called over.

He didn't glance up. "Just test tubes." Then he added, "The girl who found the body was collecting water samples for a science lab. When she discovered the body, she freaked and dropped all her samples." He pointed at the flagged test tubes that were visible in the scrub. "The good news is that she says she didn't remove anything from the bog except the bone she found. So far, I can't see anything to disprove it."

Dr. Hughes opened her backpack and removed a DSLR camera with a massive lens. "Hopefully, she didn't disturb any loose bones. I'm going to take some photos *in situ*. Then we'll stake the area into a grid, and set up a datum point. And *then*," she said, giving Dr. Guthro a conspiratorial grin, "it's time to get our hands dirty."

Gridding, Ethan knew, was painstaking work. And he guessed that this particular grid would prove to be more challenging than most.

He was right. Once the general area to be gridded

was determined by Dr. Hughes, and the datum point had been established, they began the process of staking twelve-inch-by-twelve-inch sections and marking the grid with rope. The stakes had a nasty habit of either sinking into the hummock or being yanked out by a too-enthusiastic tightening of the rope.

Sweat soon ran down their backs, attracting a cloud of persistent blackflies. Several hours later, Ethan figured he had personally supplied the local blackfly population with enough blood to keep them going for a week.

As soon as the grid was complete, Dr. Hughes took more photos. Ethan rubbed the back of his neck, glancing upward. Over the time it had taken to lay out the grid, a massive bank of clouds had obliterated the blue sky. No sign of the sun now. It would be dark in about two hours. He hoped that the M.E. would be able to remove the body by tonight…but that was assuming there was an intact skeleton. It would all depend on what they found when they began the process of removing the layers of hummock covering the remains.

"Clarence," Dr. Hughes said, turning to Dr. Guthro, hands on her hips as she surveyed the gridded area. "We aren't going to be able to sift through this. It's too spongy and wet. Not to mention all the roots from the scrub." She swiped a strand of hair from her forehead, leaving a streak of mucky water in its stead.

Dr. Guthro offered her a handkerchief. "What do you propose?"

She dabbed the sweat on her forehead with the neatly pressed cotton square, which Ethan noted were monogrammed with the medical examiner's initials. "We are going to have to remove the hummock in sections. We can take the sections back to the lab and try to break the peat down. If we can't sift through it all, we will have to X-ray each piece."

Dr. Guthro's brows rose. "I can just imagine how popular we would be with the X-ray techs. Hopefully, we won't need to do that."

Dr. Hughes stuffed the handkerchief in one of her pockets. "I'll give this a wash, Clarence," she said with a grin, and picked up the spade that lay under an open kit bag. "I'm going to remove the first section. I'll start with the one over the mask."

She climbed onto the hummock, and knelt next to the flagged section. "Clarence, can you help me on the other side? I need someone to take the section when I lift it up." She groped in one of her many vest pockets and extracted a plastic bag, which she handed to Dr. Guthro.

The Forensic Identification Services team, which had been searching the area, grouped behind Ethan, a wall of white bunny suits peering over Dr. Hughes' shoulder as she sliced the edge of the spade into the hummock. Water squelched up its sides as she pushed the spade deeper. Then she slid it up, and repeated the process along the other three sides of the section. "I think I've loosened it enough," she said.

All eyes were fixed on the spade as she pushed it into the section, tipped the edge under and lifted the edge of the hummock up. It appeared about two feet deep. A mass of torn roots thatched the underside. A fresh, piney scent filled Ethan's nose, undercut with a damp, mossy smell.

Dr. Guthro held open the bag horizontally. The forensic anthropologist slid the hummock section into the bag, her movement quick and precise, avoiding the disturbance of any potential evidence caught in the tangle. Ethan studied the cross-section of the hummock. There were no obvious bones sticking out, which boded well for the prospects of finding an intact skeleton. It would make identification much easier. And if they could find some clothing or jewelry…or even a murder weapon… *If* the decedent had been murdered, he reminded himself.

He bit down his impatience.

The removal of the first section of the hummock left a perfectly square hole. Dr. Hughes gazed into it. "It's definitely a rubber mask…."

"Do you see anything else?" asked Sergeant Deb Ferguson, head of the Major Crimes Unit, craning forward with a scowl of concentration on her milkmaid features as she peered into the hole.

Dr. Hughes adjusted the camera lens. "No. I can only see a bit of the mask. It's covered in soil."

"May I look?" Ethan asked.

Dr. Hughes stepped back, handing him the flashlight. He directed the beam into the hole.

Despite the many dead faces he had seen over the years, this one caused him to gasp. He realized, with a start, that he had been visualizing Heather's face, post-mortem, possibly decayed, most likely a skull.

But not a witch's face.

It glared at him. The mask had lost its paint years ago, but it was almost creepier in monochromatic shades of brown. A few strands of hair were visible.

Dr. Hughes caught his eye. "Did your missing girl have a rubber mask as part of her costume?"

He shook his head. "No one reported it. But it doesn't mean she didn't."

"Looks like she was strangled," Dr. Hughes pointed to the lower right quadrant of the exposed square. "See the rope?"

It was covered in dirt, with roots growing around it. Good catch by the forensic anthropologist, Ethan thought. He stood. "Definitely looks like foul play."

He was itching to have a closer look at the mask, but there were still several hours of meticulous dusting and sifting of loose soil to be completed. There could be key evidence in the strata soil above and below the remains.

He glanced at his watch—6:53 p.m. The light was changing, the landscape subtly hazed by twilight's first encroachment.

The next section of the grid came out a little more easily than the first. Dr. Hughes and Dr. Guthro followed the same procedure, bagging the section and placing it in a large plastic container. The forensic anthropologist peered into the hole. She threw Dr. Guthro a look of astonishment. "There's a body."

"You mean a skeleton, right?" Ethan asked.

Dr. Hughes shook her head, the expression of wonder in her eyes quickly replaced by excitement. "No, an actual body. I can see a corpse."

"So this is recent?" Ethan frowned.

Dr. Hughes shook her head. "No. The body is mummified." She flashed a grin at Dr. Guthro. "We have found ourselves, sir, a genuine bog body."

Dr. Guthro slowly shook his head. "Are you sure, Darcie?"

"I can definitely see a mummified shoulder."

"How can you have mummified remains in water?" Ethan asked, trying to peer over Dr. Hughes' head into the hole.

Dr. Hughes still had a slightly dazed look on her face. "Bacteria cause decomposition in a body. But when there is a lack of oxygen in the environment—such as bogs, which are highly anaerobic—there is no bacteria.

So the body will mummify, instead. I knew this was a possibility when I heard about the location, but I still didn't really believe that we'd actually find a mummified corpse. I thought we'd just find skeletonized remains, since the high school student had discovered a bone."

"But what about the fact the body was exposed to water? Why isn't it rotten?" It seemed kind of bizarre.

"The tissue actually dries up from the acids in the water," Dr. Guthro said, rubbing his hands, a clear sign he was dying to embark into a pathology lecture. "And the tannins in the bog environment help preserve it."

"If we have actually found a preserved body, Clarence, this is a huge scientific find," Dr. Hughes said. "As far as I'm aware, there has never been a bog body found in Canada—"

"—until now," he interjected with a smile.

"And there are very few cases of contemporary bog bodies. Anywhere." The implications of what she was kneeling on seemed to be hitting her. "We could really do some fascinating research—"

This could be Heather. Who had never come home.

The haze of daylight had dramatically dimmed in the past few minutes. Rain appeared to be imminent. And night would soon follow. Ethan shifted impatiently, his foot squelching on the hummock. Time to break up the bog body love fest. "Doctors, it will be dark in about an hour," Ethan said. "It also looks like it is going to rain. What is your plan?"

"I think we should continue excavating. Let's bring in the floodlights," Dr. Hughes said. "And we should set up the tent over this."

Ethan could tell there was no way on earth the forensic anthropologist would leave her find. This was what academics lived for. She probably foresaw years of funding for her lab with the research she could conduct with this one body. There was just one problem: it was not hers to keep. There was a family out there. Waiting for a phone call.

Ferguson called over the team. Within minutes, they had fashioned a tentlike structure over the gridded area. "If the wind picks up, this will be down in a flash," Lamond said. "There is nothing to anchor the stakes."

"Hopefully, we'll get the body out by then."

If not, Ethan foresaw a long, wet night ahead for Dr. Hughes.

6

As it was wont to do in Halifax, the weather had turned. Gray clouds—thick and voluminous—canopied the blue sky that had been so promising earlier in the day. Kate ran through the stone gates marking the boundaries of Point Pleasant Park's upper parking lot, hugging the perimeter so she wouldn't have to stop for the traffic.

It had been a good run. A necessary run. Kate's mind had been cleared of all the emotions that Frances Sloane's visit had brought to the surface.

But despite the tangy sea air, her chest felt heavy.

She knew she had made the right decision. Assisted suicide was a huge policy issue, a public touch point. Trying to convince a member of Parliament to strike down a provision of the Criminal Code—especially this one—required the finesse of a professional lobbyist. It was clearly in her client's interests that she initiate her fight with the right team. Otherwise, the door could be slammed before her client even got her wheelchair past the threshold.

Alaska, Kate's white rescue husky, and Charlie, Randall Barrett's chocolate Labrador, trotted at her heels. Charlie's tongue lolled with the happy abandon of her breed, although her gait was not as smooth as it once had been. Her pelvis had been injured last year. But despite the limp, she kept up.

A year ago, Kate would have continued to run straight ahead, all the way down Tower Road toward the universities and back home. Instead, she turned left toward Randall Barrett's show-stopping residence. Charlie gave a little whine, her tail wagging, and began to pull on the leash.

"Whoa, girl." Kate slowed to a walk. Her thigh had never been the same after the Body Butcher's attack a year ago, and she needed to stretch it after her run. Charlie—ever obedient—*you could learn from her, Alaska*—settled back at Kate's heels.

She's a good dog. Kate had grown used to Charlie's lumbering body, her sloppy kisses, her tail-with-a-mind-of-its-own that had cleared Kate's coffee table of any breakable objects within a week of living at her house. But most of all, she had grown used to Charlie's unconditional love. Charlie was, in fact, Randall Barrett's pet. But Kate had earned Charlie's trust when she took care of the Lab during the dark period of Randall's arrest last August.

A small whine erupted from Charlie's throat. She had spotted Eddie Bent sitting on the front porch of Randall's house.

"Nice job on the garden, Eddie," Kate called as she walked toward him. "Looks like Randall won't kick you out, after all."

"Gracias," Eddie replied from the deep confines of the Adirondack chair he had dragged onto the front porch of Randall's house. Eddie was Randall's oldest, most trusted friend from law school. Randall had asked him to house-sit while he was in New York City. "I

managed to rake the leaves without killing any of the new buds, too."

"Obviously this place is rubbing off on you," Kate said, giving the porch a furtive scan for drag marks from the wooden chair legs. She grinned. Looked as if Eddie was in the clear with Randall. The porch remained unmarked.

Charlie bounded up the steps and threw herself at Eddie's legs. "Down, Charlie!" Kate called, anticipating imminent disaster. But somehow Charlie managed to avoid knocking over Eddie's makeshift ashtray. It suspiciously resembled Randall's white china sugar bowl, which he had served alongside Kate's tea eight months ago.

"It's all right." Eddie tamped out his cigarette and rose from his chair. "I have to check on supper." He opened the door. "You staying?"

"Depends what's for supper." Kate flashed him a grin.

Eddie shook his head. "All this cooking with Enid is going to your head, Miss Lange." Enid Richardson, sister of Muriel, was Kate's elderly neighbor. They had grown close over the past year, and Kate viewed them as family. "I can recall a time in the not-so-distant past when you were desperate for a home-cooked meal."

Kate laughed, bending down to remove the dogs' leashes. "Times they are a-changin', Mr. Bent. Did you know I just bought a pasta maker?"

Eddie snorted. "But you actually have to take it out of the box, Kate."

"Touché." Kate rolled the leashes into her hand. "I *have* taken it out of the box. Then I put it back in again."

Eddie wagged a finger. "Don't tell me you are going

to buy every useless cooking accessory in every high-priced kitchen store...."

"You are just jealous," Kate said, following Eddie into the kitchen. It was a study in sleek architectural efficiency, with endless white cupboards, gray granite countertops and gleaming stainless steel. Its monastic severity was relieved by a series of murals on the walls. But they were different from the ones Kate had admired the first time she had seen Randall's kitchen. Those had been of the ocean, abstract, yet with enough form that the ocean's moods could be felt twenty feet away.

Kate knew why Randall had removed the triad of ocean paintings by his mother, Penelope Barrett. The ocean had almost stolen someone he loved. It had revealed its terrible beauty—a reminder which he did not want to face every morning over his coffee.

The replacement set of paintings by his mother was equally compelling: inviting yet bleak, they depicted abandoned barns—weathered, and still standing the test of time.

"Take a look at this kitchen. How could I be jealous, Kate?" Eddie asked, waving a hand while stirring the pot of spaghetti sauce on the stove. Coordination was not one of his strengths, and a few drops of red sauce spattered the stainless steel oven door.

Blood dripping down the elevator wall.

Kate shook her head, trying to rid herself of an image that had imprinted itself on her brain a year ago.

"This kitchen already possesses every useless cooking accessory from every high-priced kitchen store in Halifax." Eddie winked. "Don't tell Randall I said that."

Kate slid onto a white-leather bar stool next to the granite island. She tore her gaze from the spattered sauce and forced a lightness into her voice. "I think he already knows." She crossed her legs, trying to appear casual. "How's he doing, anyway?"

God. You are pathetic, Kate. You just spoke to him a few days ago.

But it wasn't the same. It had been about Frances Sloane.

Not about them.

Eight months ago, after Kate had successfully defended Randall Barrett on the charge of murdering his ex-wife, they had both recognized that their feelings had deepened beyond those of lawyer and client.

"I think the merger finally got the go-ahead. He's pleased." About a month after he had been vindicated from the charge of murdering his ex-wife, Randall had been contacted by an old law school classmate from Harvard. His classmate offered his condolences for all that Randall had been through—and offered him the opportunity to work on a complicated corporate merger of an international technology company.

That, of course, wasn't what Kate wanted to know. She tried again, "How are the kids doing?"

"Good." Eddie reached down and patted Charlie, who sat by his leg. "Lucy misses the dog, though."

A Manhattan apartment was no place for a large chocolate Labrador, Randall had told Kate. She'd offered to take Charlie while the Barretts were gone, not realizing how hard it would be to have a constant reminder of Randall when there was no real commitment between them. And when he came back, who knew? Who knew what decisions he would have made about his children's needs, about his own needs?

About his feelings for Kate?

Eddie scooped some sauce onto the wooden spoon

and gave it a taste. "Mmm…just the right amount of salt."

Kate raised a brow. "When are you going to give me your meat sauce recipe?"

"It's a Bent family secret, Kate." Eddie hummed under his breath as he tossed a bag of garlic bread into the oven to warm. "My mother would roll in her grave if I gave it to you." He closed the oven door, leaning his large bulk against its warmth. "And besides, why do you need my recipe? You're going to get the real deal when you're in Italy."

"True, but that's a few months away. And I'm starving!" Kate grinned.

Eddie's gaze softened. In that instant, Kate saw Eddie the father—the father who yearned for the daughter who had moved to Montreal with her mother and who had thrown her alcoholic father out of her life for good.

"Oh, look," Kate said, "Nat's on the news." She hopped off the stool, glad for something to relieve the melancholy that had descended on her friend, and turned up the volume.

Nat Pitts, Kate's old friend from university, had landed a job on the local news show after her work on Randall Barrett's murder case eight months ago. She had made the transition from print to air more successfully than some reporters. Today, she was covering a news story somewhere on the coast, the wind ruffling her no-longer-bleached-blond-but-viewer-friendly light brown hair, a microphone clutched in her hand, a trench coat tightly belted to show her trim figure to advantage. Behind her, mist blurred the shot of a crime scene investigation. "…Police have brought in a forensic anthropologist to investigate what appears to be human remains discovered by a local high school student in a peat bog."

A shot of the taped-off peat bog filled the screen. A team of people laid out a grid of rope over scrubby plants. It appeared pretty mundane, but the police gazed at a hole in the scrub with apparent fascination.

A pang—a tiny pang—darted through Kate. A familiar dark-haired figure stood in the middle.

Ethan.

Detective Ethan Drake, former-homicide-turned-cold-case detective. Former fiancé whom Kate had believed would be with her in sickness and in health, to love and to cherish, for better or worse.

Only the last part had proven true. Ethan had been part of some of the worst moments of her life. Not in a good way.

She had tried to put him out of her mind over the past year. Mostly, she had been successful. Once in a while, usually late at night, when she had had a glass of wine and lay in bed, unable to sleep, she would wonder if he was with someone else. Would he bring that other someone a café latte in the morning, with perfectly foamed milk and fresh shavings of chocolate?

That's what Starbucks is for, Kate. A marriage is not built on espresso coffee.

Now he was just a three-inch figure on the TV screen, his head bent, his gaze absorbed. The wind ruffled his hair.

The news camera cut back to Nat. A tall, ball-capped woman stood next to her, wearing a vest with multiple bulging pockets. "Joining me is Dr. Darcie Hughes—"

"Darcie?" Kate exclaimed.

"You know her?" Eddie asked, grating a small block of parmigiano.

"Law school," Kate said. She fell silent, concentrating on Nat's interview, but her brain was still processing the fact that her old law schoolmate was now a forensic anthropologist.

"—peat bogs are known for their preservative qualities, correct, Dr. Hughes?" Nat said.

Darcie Hughes nodded, a few wisps of ginger-colored hair escaping from her ponytail. "Yes, they are. This is an exciting find. It is the first of its kind in Canada."

"How long do you think the body has been there?" Nat asked.

The camera tightened a shot on Darcie Hughes' face. Her eyes, a light gold-green, stood out amongst the blur of freckles on her skin. She gave a rueful smile. "We aren't talking about finding an Iron Age mummy, such as the Tollund Man of Denmark. The body is from modern times. Within this century, for sure."

"Why do you say that, Dr. Hughes?" Nat's eyes had narrowed in a way that meant she knew something—and was trying to lead her wary prey into revealing it. Kate held her breath. She rooted for Nat to score a coup, yet didn't want Darcie Hughes to stumble into a trap.

But Darcie Hughes had picked up a few things in law school. She gave a small laugh. "Sorry, I cannot reveal any more details at this time. The police will provide an update when information is confirmed." She yanked the rim of her ball cap farther down on her forehead. "I've got to return to the dig. Before the rain comes."

The camera closed in on Nat while Darcie Hughes made an off-camera exit. "That was Dr. Darcie Hughes, a visiting professor at Saint Mary's University, who was called in by the Halifax Police Department to excavate the remains found this afternoon by a high school student completing a biology lab." A gust of wind lifted Nat's trench coat collar. "Unconfirmed reports suggest that a rubber Halloween mask was found with the remains."

The segment finished with an interview of the unfortunate high school student Rebecca Chen, who appeared dazed that life would do this to her—and who confirmed that she had glimpsed a rubber Halloween mask. Definitely a coup for Nat, but Kate knew the police would be ticked that a major forensic detail had just been released to the public—before they even knew whether this was a homicide or not.

"Whoa," Kate said. "I wonder who that poor person is. Probably a wino—" Her hand flew to her mouth. "Oh, damn. I'm sorry, Eddie—"

He shook his head. "Don't be. It probably is some poor guy out partying who aspirated on his own vomit. It happens." He dropped the pasta into a boiling pot of water. Steam billowed upwards. A speculative look came into his eyes. "Although, I wonder…"

Kate turned down the volume of the television. "What?"

"That mask…"

"What about the mask?"

"There was a case…."

"Don't tell me…. You knew the victim?" Eddie never ceased to surprise her. Before he became a criminal defense lawyer, he had followed his father's footsteps in the family plumbing business. He had once told Kate that living in Halifax reminded him of the plumbing in an old home, with curious connections and the odd kink here and there.

He shook his head. "No. But I do remember a case that involved a girl who went missing on Halloween… It haunted me…." His voice trailed off.

"Why? She wasn't your client, was she?"

Marian MacAdam flashed through her mind. *Don't go there, Kate.*

Eddie stirred the pasta in the pot, studying its contents as if the answer lay in there. "No. This girl—Heather Rigby was her name—went missing the year my daughter was born. I remember cuddling this fragile, vulnerable baby to my chest and feeling horror-stricken that someone else's daughter could just disappear like that. Heather was the kind of girl you'd want your own kid to grow up to be." Eddie sounded as if he had known her. Kate suspected he had studied the case carefully, applying his incisive mind to the facts, parsing the details, trying to find an answer to a terrifying question.

And did your daughter grow up to be like her? Kate wanted to ask. But she didn't. She never would remind Eddie of what he had lost. Thrown away, was how he put it.

"And this girl was never found?"

Eddie shook his head. "No. There was a lot of media coverage—and even more false leads." He drained the pasta in a colander. "I wonder if this discovery will give them something solid."

"Do you think it could be her?"

Eddie shrugged. "Hard to say. On the one hand, I hope it is—her family would finally get closure. They never gave up looking for her, you know." He turned away, busying himself with the act of serving their meal. Kate took the garlic bread out of the oven, and placed it on a wooden cutting board. She now knew Randall's kitchen as well as her own, having mooched more than a few meals from Eddie.

Eddie set the plates on the granite counter. A typical bachelor, he didn't use the table. At least he sat down to eat, Kate thought. They settled down with steaming plates of Bolognese, topped with the freshly grated parmigiano.

"On the other hand, I hope it isn't this girl," Eddie said, as if he hadn't trailed off five minutes before. He twirled spaghetti on his fork. "Especially if it turns out whoever was found in that peat bog met a violent death. I know many families want to have closure, but sometimes not knowing is better than knowing."

Tell me about it.

"So," Eddie mumbled through a mouthful of spaghetti, "what is your itinerary for your trip to Europe?"

Kate took a sip of water. Eddie never served wine and Kate never offered to bring any. "Well, Nat and I decided that we'd each choose a country and surprise each other."

Eddie arched a brow. "That could either be a spectacular idea or…" He dug a spoon into the bowl of grated parmigiano and sprinkled even clumps over his meat sauce. "Let me guess, Italy was your pick?"

Kate grinned. "Uh-huh. I'm all about the food."

"And Nat?"

"England. I have a feeling I'll be tramping through a lot of old castles. She's obsessed with the history there. And the whole royalty thing. She's hoping to see Kate Middleton's wedding gown." Kate rolled her eyes. She would never admit it, but she wanted to see it, too.

"From the sounds of it—" Eddie shook the saltshaker vigorously over his pasta "—each of you choosing a country to plan the itinerary falls into the 'spectacular idea' category. You are each passionate about different things—could be very educational for both of you."

"Are you sure you don't want to come?"

Eddie snorted. "Kate, you don't need a fat old fart like me trailing you around the streets of Italy."

Kate put down her fork and stared at Eddie. "What are you talking about? You are not an old fart."

Eddie shook his head. "I am, Kate. I'm overweight. I chain-smoke. I'm fifty-three years old. Not only that, I'm a recovering alcoholic—"

Kate tried not to let her concern show on her face. Eddie rarely sought sympathy, but he seemed to be fighting the blues tonight.

"Who still has a full head of hair—" *Darn, that didn't even garner a smile.* She plowed on. "Who is also a brilliant criminal defense lawyer, and a pretty mean cook." She bit into her garlic bread and, trying to sound casual, mumbled, "Something happen today?"

He stirred his spaghetti around his plate. "No."

Kate hesitated. They were good friends, but she usually stayed away from the-inner-life-of-Eddie-Bent territory. But there was pain vibrating beneath the surface of his rumpled exterior. She sipped her water. "So what's up?"

He patted his pocket. Then dropped his hand. She wasn't sure if he hadn't pulled out his cigarettes out of courtesy to her, or if he belatedly remembered Randall's strict prohibition on smoking in his house. The silence between them reminded Kate of when she was little and would sit outside at twilight, holding her breath and wondering if the crickets would sing.

Eddie pushed his chair away from the counter. It scraped against the floor. He made to rise, but then slumped against the back of his chair. "It's my anniversary today."

Oh...

Kate's heart constricted. Eddie never talked about his wife, but it was love, not hate, that stilled his tongue.

"I'm sorry." Kate put her hand on Eddie's arm.

He gave her a bleak smile. "So am I."

"Have you spoken to her recently?" Kate asked.

He shook his head. "She told me not to call her."

"But she knows you are going to AA and everything, right, Eddie?"

I know what you are trying to suggest, but it is too late, his eyes said.

"She knows you're practicing again, right?"

He shrugged. "I'm sending her checks for Brianna's support, so I presume she has put two and two together."

"Maybe she hasn't…."

He ran a hand over his breast pocket, his fingers caressing the shape of the cigarette package. He pushed his fingers through his hair. "It doesn't matter, Kate. She doesn't love me anymore."

He said it simply. Matter-of-factly. Without an ounce of self-pity or anger.

But the pain in those shrewd, nonjudgmental eyes of his killed Kate.

"I'm sorry, Eddie." Kate didn't know what else to say.

"Don't be, Kate. It was my fault."

Anger at this unknown woman and the pain she was causing this man who was trying so hard to put his life back together shot through Kate. "What about forgiveness? Isn't the word in Elaine's vocabulary?"

"It was once," Eddie said. "But I've had to ask for it too many times, Kate. Every time you ask, it loses its elasticity. Eventually it just snaps like a worn rubber band."

He reached into his breast pocket and pulled out his cigarette pack. "If you will excuse me, I need to obscure my thoughts in a haze of smoke…."

Kate hated to see her friend kill himself on cigarettes—he'd started wheezing lately on stairs, and she had promised herself that she would wean him off them this year—but at that moment, she was grateful for anything to help him forget.

"Go ahead. I'll wash up."

There wasn't a lot to do. For a man so disheveled, Eddie was a surprisingly orderly cook. Kate loaded the dishes into the dishwasher, put away the leftovers and cleaned the counters.

It was strange to think that eight months ago, she had stood in this kitchen with a different man, a man so tortured that he had thrown a phone through the window, a man so haunted that he had taken his children to New York....

Had he called?

She had left her cell phone at home. Deliberately. So she couldn't obsessively check it for messages.

For God's sake, Kate, stop acting like you're in high school.

She hung up the dish towel and walked out to the front porch. It was strange that Eddie didn't sit in Randall's back garden to smoke, but Kate guessed that Eddie needed to look outward.

The dogs lounged by his feet. Both thumped their tails, a lazy drumming on the porch boards, as Kate lowered herself into the matching Adirondack chair.

"I never asked you how you are doing on the drunk-driving case."

Eddie knew her history. He knew the challenge for Kate to stay objective.

"It's going fine. I'm hoping they'll settle. But today I met with a new client I wanted to talk to you about."

"Oh?" He turned to look at her. "You look worried."

"Confused is more like it."

"I'm listening."

And Kate knew that, despite whatever was bothering him, Eddie *was* listening. He always did. "Randall referred a new client to me."

"Frances Sloane?"

"How did you know?"

"He called me just before supper. He was concerned about you."

"Oh, really?" Kate bent down to pat Alaska's head so Eddie couldn't see her face.

"He said you knew her. From a long time ago."

Kate glanced away. "Yes."

"It was good of you to see her, Kate."

Kate threw him a glance. So Randall had obviously told him of her history with the Sloane family.

"I like her. I feel sorry for her. She's dying. She asked to see me. How could I say no?" She gave a wry smile. "Besides, I thought it would be a one-time deal."

"It isn't?"

Kate exhaled. "No. Yes. Well, from a legal perspective, it's over. But she asked me to help lobby an M.P. to change a law." She was bound by solicitor-client privilege to not say more. But she wished she could have Eddie's insight.

Eddie blew out a cloud of smoke, away from Kate. "And did you agree?"

"No."

Eddie turned to look at her. "Why not?"

A flush heated Kate's cheeks. "I'm not a lobbyist, Eddie. I have no desire to become one. I would be terrible at it, anyway."

He said nothing.

"Besides, I'm not sure what I think about the whole thing."

"You mean about helping someone kill herself?"

Kate bit the inside of her cheek. "I killed my sister, Eddie."

He shot her an admonishing look. "Kate, it was an accident—"

"I've had enough of death and destruction."

"But the philosophy behind assisted suicide is to allow people to die with dignity. Peacefully." Light was fading fast. Eddie tapped the glowing ember on the end of his cigarette, the ashes reminding Kate of a dying star. "You've seen your share of violent deaths. Perhaps this an opportunity to change that."

"Eddie, I don't want to screw this up for Frances Sloane. This is too important. I don't know the first thing about lobbying. She told me that she thinks I'll be successful because I'm 'famous,' but I don't think that's true." She watched the mist drape itself along a branch, the water globules suspended from its underside. Eventually they would crash to the ground or evaporate.

What would it be? Crash? Or fade away?

"Why don't you think it's true?" The question drifted through the twilight.

"I don't think my fame will change people's minds. And besides, I really don't want to dredge that all up again. It was one of the worst periods of my life." Kate clipped the leashes on the dogs. They lumbered to their feet. Alaska nosed Kate's thigh. "Nietzsche sums it up pretty well—*Battle not with monsters lest ye become a monster....*"

"So you think if you become an activist for assisted suicide you will become the Angel of Death?"

"Of course not." Kate pushed a wisp of mist-curled hair off her face. "I agree in principle with assisted suicide. I just don't want to be the one fighting the fight."

Eddie pushed himself to his feet. He stood next to her,

feet planted wide as if the wooden planks of the porch were a ship's deck, gazing at the mist that shrouded Randall's front garden. "I shouldn't have pushed you. I was playing devil's advocate. I obviously touched a nerve." He gave her shoulders a squeeze. The cigarette came perilously close to her sleeve. "I don't think you should do this. You've been through too much. You need time to heal." His voice sank. "And...you need to forgive yourself."

For what? Killing two people? Not saving someone else?

"Gotta run," she said. "Thanks for dinner. It's my turn next."

He nodded. "I'm expecting you to use that new pasta maker."

"First I've got to baptize my new roasting pan," she said, tugging on the dogs' leashes.

The mist had become heavy, on the verge of drizzle. The therapeutic effects of her earlier run had disintegrated with the cigarette ash on the porch. She sprinted up the hill, desperate to reclaim some equanimity. A full stomach and two tired dogs made for a long slog home.

Her feet pounded on the wet pavement. Her mind pounded on her conscience. She did not want another stain on her soul, no matter the reason. Eddie thought it would bring peace, but she wasn't so sure. She thought it was more likely to bring nightmares of the Body Butcher variety.

She was no Angel of Death.

7

The headlights of Kenzie Sloane's rental car swooped over the curve of the long driveway to what was once her family home. The family had dispersed years ago, and had disintegrated long before that. Now, the lone occupant of the stunning architectural structure was her mother. And for how much longer, nobody knew.

Tall, spindly evergreens flashed into view, receding as the headlights found new targets. Kenzie's hands tightened on the steering wheel. Foo Dog, her black pug, was barely visible in the dark, but she was grateful for his solid presence. She hadn't been home in seventeen years. She had never wanted to return.

Still didn't.

But here she was.

Why?

Was it her brother's email? The years spent inking memorial tattoos on grieving clients?

No. It had been the sound of her mother's voice on the phone. Her voice but not her voice. Maybe that was why she had been so disarmed: she hadn't recognized it. That shocking, slurring, nasal voice. "Kenzie. Please come home." A pause. An audible swallow. Then the plea that sealed the deal: "I want to see you once before I die."

Guilt came crashing out of nowhere.

Years ago, when Kenzie had made her escape, her mother had written her. Angry and hurt, Kenzie had never opened the letters. But instead of tossing them in the trash, she'd scribbled, "Return to Sender" on them. Her mother had gotten the message.

Kenzie hadn't heard from her in seventeen years.

Although she had heard from her brother three times. Once to inform her that their parents had split. There had been no avoiding the accusation that lay behind those words. The second time was to tell her that her father had remarried. There had been no mistaking her brother's glee. And the last missive had come via email. He had contacted her through her online blog site KOI to inform her that, "Mom has ALS and will die in the next year. She doesn't know I'm contacting you. And God knows you are the last person I want my children to meet, but out of respect for her I am asking that you come home to say your goodbyes."

The email had been caught in her spam filter for three months. She had been traveling all over the U.S. doing guest stints and hadn't found it until three weeks ago. She called her mother.

And here she was.

Out of any disease to afflict her mother, the general consensus was that Amyotrophic Lateral Sclerosis, or ALS, was a terrible way to go. As Kenzie learned, it was a disease that strangled the body and left the mind to suffocate within its confines.

The irony had not escaped her. She had felt strangled within the confines of the award-winning home her mother designed. It had been both lauded as "cutting edge and forward thinking" and panned as "unrealistic and unlivable." Perched near Chebucto Head, it stuck out on the cliff as if it, too, had been carved by a glacier, its surfaces layered with glass and melded with curved steel. The ocean's turbulence reflected in its window-like walls as if it were a mood ring.

It was the "unlivable" criticism that had gotten to her mother. "What do they mean, 'unlivable'?" she'd asked, throwing the magazine on the table. She swept her arm in a fierce gesture, as if drawing to her chest the elements of her house that had both astounded her admirers and provoked her critics. "Do you find it un-livable?" she had demanded of her son, Cameron.

But she hadn't asked Kenzie. She was too afraid of what her unpredictable daughter would say. And Ken-zie knew that if her seventeen-year-old self had been asked, she would have gladly thrown the critics' words in her mother's face and stomped out of the room with the knowledge she had succeeded beautifully in wound-ing her mother.

"Be on your best behavior, Foo," Kenzie said as she parked the car in front of her mother's house. Kenzie unclipped his seat belt, enjoying the visual contrast of the sensible blue polyester harness against Foo's spiked-silver leather collar. She knew that most people might find it surprisingly against type for a tattoo artist to buckle her dog into a car seat—they probably found it surprising she had a pug instead of a Rottweiler—but she would never risk Foo.

He leapt out of the car behind her, his nose at her calf, his walk jaunty. He was unfazed by the otherworldly quality of the house. Kenzie had always thought it un-natural, the antithesis of the kind of home she wanted. She had yearned for a traditional house like those of her friends, with rugs scattered on the floor and over-stuffed sofas. Instead, her mother had created an irregular glass rectangle that was accented with steel. There was no corner in that house in which Kenzie could lose herself. Everything was too exposed. Her father, Gus, had seemed displaced, too. He built a covered porch in the back, one with traditional wood posts and patio furniture. Kenzie and her father often retreated there, she with her sketchpad, he with a crossword puzzle.

Lately, though, the house appeared to have hunkered itself down to the ground. Bracing itself for death's appearance.

The Japanese maples by the front entrance had barely begun to leaf. Their spindly branches reminded her all too vividly of decimated limbs. Kenzie scooped up Foo and held him against her chest as she rang the doorbell. A light chime echoed within the house.

A woman appeared at the door. She peered through the glass. Kenzie straightened to her full height, which was a decent five foot ten. With her hair bunched up on the back of her head and the two-inch heel on her Doc Martens white-leather boots, she topped six feet easily.

"Kenzie?" the woman said, pulling open the door. "I'm Phyllis. Your mother's caregiver."

"Hi."

Foo squirmed in her arms. She put him on the floor, keeping a tight hold on the leash while she glanced around. It was home. And yet she didn't feel at home, she didn't feel she could let her dog go or run upstairs to see her mother unless she was invited to do so.

Phyllis must have seen her glance upstairs, because she said, "Your mother does not use the rooms on the upper floor anymore. She's moved into the living room."

"Oh. Of course." It made total sense, and it gave

Kenzie her first glimpse of how radically her mother's life had changed. Seventeen years ago, her mother would never have allowed a living room to be used as a bedroom.

It was sacrilege.

Kenzie followed Phyllis to the back of the house. Their footsteps were lost in the open space. "She's in here," Phyllis said, gesturing to the living area.

Kenzie paused on the threshold, bracing herself for the bombardment of family memories, but there was no room for those as her brain took in the implications of the scene before her.

Her mother, whom she had not seen for half of her life, was unrecognizable. Kenzie would have walked right by her if she'd been on the street. She might have glanced at her—yes, she would have—for it would be hard to miss the motorized wheelchair, although it was the awkwardness of the body that would have made Kenzie give a second look. Her profession demanded the ability to create a picture on a curved canvas—the skin covering a limb—and she was intimately famil- iar with how limbs were angled. Any irregular form always caught her eye.

Her mother leaned to one side of her wheelchair, her head resting against a curved headrest, hands lying in her lap.

"Kenzie. You came." Her mother's eyes scanned her face. Kenzie had remembered her mother's eyes as bright and sharp. Always assessing, calculating, ready to find the flaw. "Lives depend on it," she had once told a five-year-old Kenzie when she had asked her mother why she was always pointing out the "mistakes" on her blueprints.

The tables had been turned most cruelly on her

mother. The structural integrity of her body now depended on others to keep it functioning.

"Hi, Frances," Kenzie said, trying to sound casual. For the past three weeks, she had flip-flopped over how to address her mother. "Mom" seemed too intimate given the distance between them; "mother" was too formal and made her sound like an ass. So she had decided to call her mother by her first name.

Her mother blinked. Kenzie inwardly squirmed. "Frances" had sounded pretentious.

"How are you?" Kenzie asked. That wasn't much better. Anyone could see her mother was a train wreck.

"I'm dying."

She swallowed. "I heard."

Her mother's eyes traveled over her face, lingering on the multiple piercings curving up Kenzie's ear, then headed downward, skimming her long-sleeved distressed leather jacket and low-slung skinny jeans. The weather had been damp—and the chill had really gotten under Kenzie's skin after being in Texas last week. It was only natural for her to cover up. And yet, if she was being honest with herself, she knew that she wasn't ready to expose her tattoos, her art—her life's journey— to this woman who was now at the end of her own.

Her mother's gaze fell to Kenzie's hands, which were unadorned with the exception of a small black tattoo in Asian script on the back of each thumb.

"This means strength. In Kanji." Kenzie held out her right hand. "And this one means tranquility," she said, holding out the other so her hands were extended symmetrically. "Strength" was just two bold strokes, fluid and curved, with forward movement. "Tranquility," on the other hand, was smaller, with many strokes working together to appear balanced.

"With strength comes tranquility," her mother said. "And with tranquility comes strength."

Had either of them achieved that? "That was the idea."

The quiet of the room was broken by a loud, uncontrolled laugh that burst from her mother's throat. Frances began to cough. Within seconds, she was choking.

Kenzie turned and sprinted to the door. "Help!"

Her mother's caregiver ran into the room. She thrust a suction tube down her mother's throat and cleared the airway. Frances leaned her head back against the headrest and closed her eyes. Tear tracks marked her cheeks, her breathing hoarse and rapid.

"God, Mom," Kenzie said, and realized she'd forgotten to call her mother by her first name. She sat in the armchair by her mother's wheelchair, her legs shaking, her pulse racing.

That choking sound...

It had taunted her in dreams for years. She had never thought she would ever hear it again.

Foo sat by her feet, leaning against her shin.

Her mother opened her eyes. They were watery from tears, washed in defeat. "I can't believe I'm seeing you again." The words were so painful, and so painfully slow, that Kenzie couldn't bear it.

"Foo. Come here, buddy." Kenzie scooped up the pug from where he sat by her feet, observing these follies of human nature with his usual *je ne sais quoi*. Her shoulders lost some of their tension at the feel of his solid, velvety body in her arms. Kenzie stepped toward her mother. "You want to hold him?"

Frances glanced down at her hands. "Please put him on my lap. Help me move my hands first."

Kenzie bent over and clasped one of her mother's hands. The coldness of her skin, the laxness of her muscles, made Kenzie's throat constrict. She averted her face from her mother's too-observant gaze. "Right here?" Kenzie asked, placing her mother's hand on the armrest.

"Yes."

Kenzie gripped her mother's other hand with the lightest, briefest of touches and placed it onto the armrest. "There," she said. She lowered Foo onto her mother's lap. Her pug met her mother's gaze with his own, and then sniffed her face. "Hello, Foo," her mother said. She looked at Kenzie. "Could you put my hand on his back?"

Kenzie guided her mother's hand onto Foo's fur. "He's soft," her mother said.

Foo curled his body and lowered his head onto Frances' lap. "He's a lug," Kenzie said. Foo gave a long, gentle sigh and closed his eyes.

"Such peace," her mother said.

Silence descended on them.

Shit.

Kenzie didn't know what to say. The distance, fuelled by hurt and lengthened by years, was not going to be breached in one visit. Or ever.

And yet she couldn't just leave.

She had only arrived.

"Are you happy, Kenzie?" her mother asked.

Kenzie tensed. She did not want to explore this territory now—at this late stage—with her mother. And yet, she could tell by the urgency in her mother's eyes, that the question was of vital importance to her.

"Yes." There was truth in that answer. She was as happy as she had ever thought she could be.

"That's all I ever wanted for you."

Kenzie exhaled. Really? *Really?* It hadn't felt that way when she was a teenager. Yet her mother now watched her with such obvious concern and love in her eyes that Kenzie almost believed it.

"I'm leaving you half of everything."

That brought Kenzie to her feet. "I don't want it." Foo lifted his head.

"Please." The laughter bubbled in her mother's throat. *Shit.* She was getting her mother upset. "It's all I have left to give."

Too little, too late.

Kenzie shook her head. She didn't want this visit to end in an argument, but she didn't want to give in, either. She didn't need her mother's money now.

She had needed it seventeen years ago.

And had been rebuffed.

Phyllis came into the room, carrying a cup of pills.

"It's time for your meds, Frances," she said. She turned to Kenzie. "It will take a bit of time. She has difficulty swallowing."

"I should go," Kenzie said. She stood, trying to hide her relief. "Come on, Foo."

The pug sprang off Frances' lap and trotted over to Kenzie. She clipped on his studded leash. "Good night, Mom."

"Will you come back?"

The question hung in the air. Her mother's eyes held hers.

Kenzie's heart tightened.

"Of course," she said. "I'll call."

"I'll be here," her mother said. It was a feeble attempt at humor.

Kenzie knew she should kiss her mother's cheek.

She raised a hand—the one marked with "strength"—
and left.

The other, she shoved in her pocket.

8

Kate's cell phone rang just as she launched—full *voce*—into the chorus of "What's Love Got to Do With It." She scrabbled for the volume dial on her kitchen radio, muting Tina Turner's throaty call to arms, and snatched her cell phone from the counter.

She knew who it was. She hated the fact her heart was pounding—and he wasn't even in the same country.

"Hello." She gazed out the window overlooking her backyard. Large drops of water streaked the glass. She had made it home just in time. The rain had begun. The dogs lay on their mats on the floor, content.

She wished she were a dog.

"Hi, Kate." Randall Barrett's voice was warm.

"Hi."

There was an awkward pause. Kate was used to it. Both of them trod the high wire of their relationship with caution. Kate supposed that was a good sign. Her relationship with Randall had taken so many twists and turns since she'd joined McGrath Woods: from rookie associate on probation versus antagonistic managing partner, to last-hope criminal defense lawyer representing desperate accused. The magnetic undercurrent in their relationship mirrored those twists and turns, vacillating from attraction to repulsion.

It changed last summer, when they joined forces in a small motorboat on a desperate mission to save Randall's children from a killer. The undercurrent deepened to an elemental pull. And although they both were caught in its force, the timing was about as bad as it could get.

In the end, they both came up for air.

Separately.

In the first few weeks after the trauma, Kate had dropped by Randall's home. She had brought Alaska, ostensibly to visit Randall's daughter, Lucy, who loved dogs.

But even armed with a husky as an ice-breaker, her visits to Randall's family had never gotten past, "How are you?" To his children, she was their dad's lawyer, former colleague and "friend," someone who had been with them during the very worst time of their lives, been privy to their secrets, their anguish, their pain—and yet didn't know them. It was an uncomfortable place to be. And neither Randall nor Kate wanted to force an intimacy that wasn't there. One that would most certainly be rejected.

That was the first barrier. The other was more difficult to scale, for it came from within.

Kate understood all the dark niches and secret hiding places of grief, guilt, loss, pain. She understood what had driven Randall to leave, to find peace.

But the part of Kate that wasn't ready to abandon the emotional intimacy she had shared with Randall was…lonely.

And the part of Kate that had only gotten over the pain of her failed engagement with Ethan Drake a year ago urged her to move on. Her heart could only take so much.

"Did your meeting go well?" Randall asked.

She pushed a wisp of hair behind her ear. "Sort of."

"Mrs. Sloane knows assisted suicide isn't in the cards?" His voice was low.

"Yes. But she changed tacks."

"In what way?"

Legal ethics dictated that she maintain her client's confidentiality. But Kate needed some advice. And she figured that since Randall had been the referring lawyer, it wasn't unethical to get his opinion. Junior lawyer to senior mentor, et cetera, et cetera.

"She wants to strike down the provision in the Criminal Code that makes assisted suicide a crime," she said.

"She's going to mount a challenge?"

"No. She doesn't feel she will live long enough to appear in court."

"So…" he said, his tone thoughtful, "she's going to attack it from the legislative end."

"Bingo."

"I suppose it could work. It will keep the fight going even if she dies. Who is her member of Parliament?"

Kate exhaled. "Harry Owen."

"Isn't he the 'tough on crime' guy?"

Kate could picture Randall, brow furrowed, as he tried to puzzle out the implications of this situation.

"Yes, indeed, he is."

"She's going to need one hell of a public relations campaign."

"I agree." Kate hesitated. "That's why I told her I wouldn't be her lobbyist."

He was obviously as surprised by Frances' request as Kate had been. "Why did she want you to do that?"

"She said that since I had survived an attack by a serial killer, then I would understand her desire to dictate the terms of her own death...."

"So she thinks you would be more personally invested in it?"

"I think so. She also said that my so-called fame would help her cause."

Darkness had fallen. The window reflected her face against a background of dark, streaked glass.

"Well, you are quite a public-relations coup, Kate. Frances' team could put a good spin on this. It would certainly help her case, at least in the court of public opinion."

"I'm not a professional lobbyist, Randall. I don't know the first thing about it. She'd be much better off with someone who knows how to work the system."

"I'm not sure I agree with you, Kate." Randall's tone was thoughtful. "I think, given you are trying to sway Harry Owen's tough-on-crime position, you are better off letting the voters do the talking. He's pandering to fear. You have more credibility than he does. He talks the talk, but you walked the walk, Kate. You are the epitome of toughness. You can show that being 'tough' on vulnerable, dying people is inhumane."

God. That kind of made sense.

"It was actually a very savvy suggestion by Frances," he added.

"But that's exactly the reason why I don't want to do this."

"Because you're famous?"

"I'm not famous," Kate said with a slight edge to her voice. "What I meant was I don't want to dig up the past again. It's taken me a long time to get over what happened to me. I'm finally moving forward." She swallowed. "I can sleep again."

She heard him exhale. "Sorry, Kate." His voice was gentle. "That was presumptuous of me. You've been through a lot."

She wanted to throw herself against him, to let him stroke the tension from her shoulders, to murmur that he was wrong to add more to her already burdened conscience.

But he had chosen to move over six hundred miles away and lick his wounds in private.

"Kate, I understand how you feel." His voice became low. "I wish I was there with you. I should never have asked you to see Frances Sloane. I'm sorry. It's just… I trust you. I knew you would do right by her."

"How would you feel if you were asked to trade your notoriety to help her cause?" she asked, trying hard not to sound defensive—but failing.

There was a pause. "I would…" She could tell he was choosing his words carefully. He cleared his throat. "Kate, I'm different than you. I guess I would do it because it would make me feel that I hadn't been made a victim in vain. That I could do something positive with it. That the person who hurt me and my family had not triumphed in the end."

Kate's fingers gripped the phone. Would the Body Butcher triumph in the end? Would she die from the same disease that had robbed him of reason?

"Oh, God." Kate could hear the blood rushing in her ears. It pulsed through her veins, sustaining her body.

And yet, it could be infected.

She herself could die a terrible death.

The inverse of Frances'. One where her mind became a sponge, full of holes, little vacuums of dementia.

She would be helpless. Unable to reason. Unable to communicate her wishes.

Unable to ask someone to take her out of her misery.

Because she wouldn't even be aware she was in it.

She had almost died alone last year. Just her and a serial killer.

If she died tomorrow, the only being whose life would truly be affected would be her dog, Alaska.

Would she be in the same situation as Frances? Asking someone to help her before it was too late—and no one would? Not even someone who could end up in the same situation? She pressed her hands to her temples. Her veins throbbed against her fingers.

"Oh, damn. I'll do it."

"I don't think you will regret it, Kate. She needs your help." Randall paused. "Do you realize," he said, his tone pensive, "that if Frances succeeds and the law against assisted suicide is struck down, then we might have an argument to get Don Clarkson out of jail?"

Kate exhaled. "No…" She hadn't even thought about Don Clarkson since her meeting with Frances. But, of course, the whole reason that Frances had come to see her was because of Randall's involvement in the Don Clarkson case. His old friend had been rotting in jail for the past five years, serving a sentence for murder after he had tried to end a patient's suffering. The law was, indeed, a slippery slope. And he had tumbled down it. "But that wasn't assisted suicide." It had been considered euthanasia.

"But if we could strike down assisted suicide, it might crack open the door for Don."

She swallowed. "Good point."

"I was only incarcerated for a few days, Kate. He's been in there for five years. It sucks the soul out of you.

You were the one who got me out of there. I will never forget how hopeless—and helpless—I felt."

The weight in her chest had returned full force. "I will do my best, Randall. But I think it's an uphill battle."

"Perhaps. But it might spur other people to agitate."

Kate sat down at the kitchen table. Alaska leaned against her leg. She stroked his head, his fur soothing under her hand. "You're right. It isn't just Frances' fight." *Or mine.* She felt lighter. "Thank you. You've given me some clarity."

"I miss you." His voice was low. She remembered last summer, after they had saved Lucy and Nick, how he had pressed her numb, wet body against his in the boat. His arm clasped her to his side as if he would never let go.

But he had.

And so had she.

So much for clarity.

The silence on the other end of the phone expanded. Randall waited for her reply. She wanted to say, "I miss you, too." Hell, she wanted to say, "Fly home." If she was really honest with herself, she wanted to add, "And spend the weekend at my place."

But those words stuck in her throat. She had no idea where Randall's head—or heart—was. He had chosen to move six hundred miles away and lick his wounds in private. Why the hell had he left her? She was hanging in limbo, getting older, watching her biological clock ramp up into overdrive. She cleared her throat. "How are things?"

"So-so. Nick is still sticking pretty close to his room, but he has had a good year at his new school." His voice dropped. "Lucy is still suffering from a lot of night-mares."

"I'm sorry." She hesitated. "I had those too, after... I was attacked. They do lessen over time."

"Sometimes I get so angry I have to punch the wall. You should see my knuckles."

She bet the wall didn't look so hot, either.

He cleared his throat. "Listen, Kate, the kids are still a long way from getting over Elise. I can't..." He exhaled.

"I understand, Randall." And she did.

Yes, indeed, she did.

The sprinkle of rain had paused. The clouds held their breath. "Look, I've got to run. I have some work to do. I don't have the first clue about being a lobbyist."

"Of course." He did an admirable job keeping his tone casual, Kate thought. Too admirable. "Let me know if you need anything."

"Will do," she lied.

9

McNally switched on the shaver, humming under his breath.

After years of shaving with cheap disposable razors, this mundane task had become one of his daily pleasures. His adrenaline surged when the vibration of the electric shaver connected with his jaw. He took his time—because he could.

He ran his hand over his cheeks. Nice and smooth. He guided the beard trimmer along the sides of his goatee. His hand was steady, the edge precise and symmetrical. He cleaned up the line running down the middle of his chin with a triple-blade razor. It had been expensive—but he would never use a cheap blade again.

Nice work, McNally. He wondered if Kenzie would recognize him with the goatee. He had filled in, too. His face was squarer, his neck thicker, his shoulders dense with muscle.

He squirted the citrus-smelling aftershave gel into his palm and smoothed it over his skin. *Mmm.*

He turned his head back and forth, examining his reflection in the mirror. A week's growth had obscured the tattoo, but his hair needed cleaning up. The uniform one-eighth inch burr cut had a few uneven patches.

And today, of all days, he wanted to look his best.

He grabbed the clippers, flicked on the switch, and ran it over his scalp. Christ. He had nicked himself.

He took a deep breath and leaned in closer to the mirror. The nick wasn't noticeable behind his ear.

Steady now. He ran the clippers over the back of his skull, imagining it skimming the threads of the spiderweb tattoo stretching from ear to ear.

His freshly cut hair bristled under his palm, yet the hair was soft. When he had been out on parole, he discovered that women loved to rub their hands over his burr cut, never failing to compare it to a cat's tongue.

Kenzie, he remembered, liked cats.

Kenzie, massaging his shoulders, licking his neck, whispering to him that he was the only one for her.

The familiar pressure tightened his chest.

Easy.

He tapped the stubble out of his grooming supplies and laid them side-by-side in a drawer in the vanity. He glanced at his watch. It was 8:40 a.m. He grabbed his jacket, put on a ball cap, despising Rick Lovett for making him wear it in the apartment building. McNally didn't have much choice. This was the best job he could get. Right now.

Who the hell do you think you are, you ugly son of a bitch? It was a familiar refrain. He could write a song about it. Lovett had never dared to tell him what to do before McNally had gone to prison.

He's got it all, now.

And you've got nothing.

But his luck was changing. He locked the door to his apartment, shoved his hands in his pocket and headed down the hallway, his step slowing as he neared number 114. A faint throb sounded through the walls— the stereo was turned up too high. He knocked on the door.

No answer.

Music was too loud.

He knocked again. "It's the superintendent," he yelled.

He heard the chain sliding out of the lock. His blood thudded in his veins. The door swung open.

"Yeah?" A cute girl in her early twenties cracked the door open a few inches. Her hair was disheveled. She wore no bra under her tank top.

He fought the urge to push the door open.

Her gaze traveled over him. A flicker of fear in her eyes gave him a corresponding shiver of satisfaction.

"Your music is too loud. Turn it down," he said.

He smiled and walked away, lifting his ball cap and rubbing his hand over his death's-head tatt. He smiled all the way down to the car park.

He had parked the truck—screw Lovett, it was *his* now—right by the stairs. He loved the gearshift. He could control the engine, make it do what he wanted. He backed out of the parking spot, then shifted up to second gear and roared out of the underground parking. Lovett would shit bricks if he saw that. He switched on the radio, the tunes feeding his adrenaline. He was going to get his work done, and then wait outside Yakusoku Tattoo until Kenzie finished her appointments.

She would be so surprised to see him.

He could just imagine her reaction.

Her mouth, painted a deep red to match her hair, curved in delight. "John," she said. She grabbed his face between her hands and kissed him on the lips. A hard, excited kiss that grew soft. And lingered.

"I've missed you so much," she murmured into his ear. "I should never have left."

Pain twisted his gut.

No. You should never have left.

His palms smoothed over her shoulders, a hard ridge beneath his palms. He collared her neck with his hands. "Why didn't you call?"

"I'm sorry. I was so stupid." *Tears glittered in those gorgeous, heartless eyes.* "I still love you, John."

His hands tightened, squeezing.

She accepted her punishment.

"How much do you love me?" *He increased the pressure.*

She gasped, "With all my heart."

10

"Everyone and their dog is here," Ethan said to Lamond, as they walked into the autopsy suite.

Any of the staff of the medical examiner's office that hadn't been required at other scenes were clustered around the autopsy cart. Ethan spotted the gingery ponytail of Dr. Hughes, and took a final gulp of his coffee, tossing the cup in the garbage. He hadn't shut down his computer until close to three last night. He wished he had time to run upstairs to Tim Hortons for another cup but it looked as if Dr. Guthro was getting ready to start. Lamond handed him a gown, and they slipped them on as they walked over to Sergeant Detective Deb Ferguson. Ethan was surprised to see the head of the Major Crimes Unit here. Usually only the primary investigator and an FIS detective showed up for autopsies.

But as they and the rest of the world knew, this was no ordinary autopsy. Although the conversation was muted, there was an undercurrent of suppressed excitement amongst the medical team.

Ferguson was already gowned, her unruly hair pinned in a bun. Freckles dotted her broad features.

In her blue gown, she resembled a Scottish milkmaid awaiting her annual checkup. "Did you see the paper this morning?"

"Yup," Lamond said, rolling his eyes.

Ethan hadn't had a chance to look at it, but he had heard the reports on the radio.

"I've had to triple patrol at the scene. And we've already caught one journalist trying to sneak in from the woods." Her jaw was tight. "I had three reporters calling me this morning to see if this was a burial ground for multiple victims."

Lamond glanced at Ethan. They had both worked Halifax's last sensational murder case. They knew how tough it was to control the media when they got the scent of blood. "It's the Body Butcher hangover," Ethan said, shrugging. Last year, Halifax had been shocked into the gruesome world of serial killers when the Body Butcher had been killed in the act of trying to commit yet another horrendous murder. Since then, every time a homicide-victim was discovered, there was always the fear that there were other victims not yet discovered. It wasn't just the media or the general public who harbored this anxiety—the murder squad did, as well.

"Have FIS or Search and Rescue found any bone scatter around the scene?"

Ferguson shook her head. "So far, it seems like just one body was buried in the peat bog. The sooner we can get a positive ident on it, the better. Not only for the family. We need to keep the media from getting the public all stirred up."

"Good morning, detectives," Dr. Guthro said, joining the trio with a broad smile on his face. He held a camera in his gloved hands. "We are ready to begin."

They followed him to the autopsy cart. Several of the

onlookers broke away, leaving room for the detectives to view the procedure. Ethan nodded to Dr. Hughes, who appeared surprisingly fresh given the arduous work of yesterday.

The morgue attendant, a young woman whose impassive expression was in stark contrast to the anticipatory gleam in the gazes of the medical examiner's staff, unzipped the bag. Even though they all knew the body wore a rubber Halloween mask, the sight still caused indrawn breaths upon first viewing. Dr. Guthro walked around the cart, taking photos of each section of the decedent, and of the dirty rope coiled into the corpse's shoulder.

The body was removed from the bag and placed on the autopsy table. While Dr. Guthro photographed it, the staff from the M.E.'s office took turns at the head of the table, examining the mummified tissue. Ethan had seen many bodies, in many stages of decomposition, but never a mummified body. He edged closer to study the remains. They were lucky that the neck and upper body weren't skeletonized. The M.E. might actually be able to determine cause of death. And from what he could tell, the body had breasts. It must be female.

It must be Heather.

"I was going to have chicken for supper tonight," Lamond whispered. "But I just changed my mind."

"Is that what chicken looks like after you cook it?" Ethan asked under his breath. "Remind me not to eat at your house." He had to admit, though, that the mummified tissue resembled an overcooked chicken breast: yellowy-brown and dry.

Ferguson gave them both a look. "Dr. Guthro, what are your initial thoughts about the gender of this body?"

The medical examiner leaned over the bog body's

pelvis. Unlike the torso, it was mainly skeletonized. "I'd say female. The sacrum is short and wide. And the body of the pubis is quadrangular."

Ethan hadn't realized he had been holding his breath until now. If the body had been male, then all his work on the Rigby case would have been futile. And they would have to start over.

"Now for the X-rays," Dr. Guthro said. "Everyone please clear the area." The X-ray technician rolled the portable X-ray machine over to the autopsy table. "We will recommence in half an hour."

"Perfect," Ethan muttered to Lamond. "Time for at least one coffee."

Lamond arched a brow. "Is Cold Case so dull that you are willing to aggravate that ulcer?"

"The ulcer is fine. Ever since I left Homicide," Ethan said, throwing a dark look at his former partner. It was part jest, part truth. He missed Homicide, but he had been on a downward spiral. There had been too much stress, too much frustration, in the past twelve months. He had given up coffee, but as soon as his ulcer had settled, he had warmed up his espresso machine and was back to his usual habits.

After they grabbed a coffee and a muffin—Ethan couldn't resist advising Lamond to eat something that wouldn't stain his clothes if he brought it all up during the autopsy—Ethan bought a newspaper at the gift store while Lamond hit the men's room. He hadn't realized how bang on he had been about the phenomenon of the Body Butcher hangover until he saw the front page. The media were all over the titillating question of whether the bog body could be victim zero of the Body Butcher. Accompanying the article was a photo of Kate taken after the Body Butcher's attack last year, her face battered, her eyes haunted. His gut clenched at the sight of it. *God.* A year later, and his heart still rushed into his throat when he thought about her lying in the parking lot, nearly dead.

She had almost died. And he had let her walk out of his life.

But he couldn't keep living like this anymore.

One of them could die at any time—he could take a bullet in the head on his job, or she could develop CJD. Either way, life was too short. He would never be able to live with himself if he didn't give things one more try.

Third time's the charm.

He folded the paper, ensuring that the front cover was tucked inward, and stuck it under his elbow.

When they arrived back at the autopsy suite, the dregs of their coffees consumed in the elevator, the X-rays had been loaded into the view box. Dr. Guthro hovered in front, his tall, gowned form hunched in concentration.

"Excellent news," Dr. Guthro said, peering at an X-ray of the chest area. "Looks like there's a bullet in there." He pointed at the glowing white firefly lodged between two lower ribs.

Ferguson grinned at Ethan and Lamond. "We are in business, Dr. Guthro."

"We certainly are."

The rest of the X-rays showed no obvious signs of trauma or injury. "No skull fractures, no major bone fractures," Dr. Guthro murmured. "Let's take the mask off and see what we have under there. Dr. Hughes, would you like to hold the skull?" His request was an act of professional courtesy, a nod to the assistance that the forensic anthropologist had provided yesterday.

Dr. Hughes stood at the head of the table and gently

held the top of the skull. Dr. Guthro gripped the bottom edges of the mask. As he peeled up the first inch, he nodded to himself. "A ligature," he said. The rope, which they knew was attached to the neck, had been tied with a slipknot. It obviously had been very tight, because even with the shrinkage of the tissue, it was still taut around the throat.

The rubber was brittle, and it took some time for Dr. Guthro and Dr. Hughes to ease it off the skull. "The epidermis has slipped," Dr. Guthro said, "hence the lack of hair and eyebrows. But there appears to be a considerable amount of hair on the interior of the mask." He placed the mask on a tray, and with a pair of tweezers, removed a hair for the standard for the homicide team, which they would use as a benchmark for comparison and analysis with any other hairs found on the scene, then bagged and labeled it. The mask would be bagged and labeled later, and sent to the FIS lab for analysis.

As one, the team studied what remained of the face of the victim. Her eyes were long gone, her lips dried and shriveled. Both ears were still intact, as was her nose. The mask had obviously protected her face from rodents. Ethan mentally overlaid an image of the smiling, fresh-faced girl from his university criminology class and decided that this shriveled, eyeless head could be her face.

Or not.

Who knew? He needed to keep reminding himself that they had no objective confirmation that this dead girl was Heather Rigby. He had jumped to conclusions before, with disastrous results.

Right now, all they knew was that the body was likely female.

It could be any female.

And that realization chilled him.

Kate could have ended up in the morgue last year, along with the Body Butcher's other victims.

She could have been the one on the autopsy table, her remains being examined to determine how she had died, how she had defended herself.

She would have been identified as "female, age twenty-five to thirty-five, shoulder length brown hair."

But what she felt, and who had occupied her last thoughts, no one would have ever known.

He wanted Kate's last moments to be with him. With love in her heart. And the knowledge that they had been happy together.

When he faced his maker, he wanted to be with Kate the same way.

And have no regrets.

He had seen enough dead bodies on these autopsy tables to know that some would have regretted their actions that led them to this final destination; others would have regrets for actions not taken before this final destination.

He did not want regrets.

This desiccated body, this leathery shell that had once housed a vibrant young woman was impetus enough.

Why was he wasting time?

Life was too short.

He'd never know until he tried.

Remember, third time's the charm, Drake.

He would call Kate. Tonight.

If nothing else, to stop the self-help clichés that kept urging him on.

"The hair inside the mask is brown," Lamond said, as if reading Ethan's mind. He shivered. Kate's hair was brown. That must be a sign from the universe.

Stop it, Drake.

Dr. Guthro began the external exam. The mummified tissue extended to just below the diaphragm. The left arm was also mummified, but the rest of her limbs were skeletonized. The skeleton was surprisingly intact— again, a sign that rodents hadn't found it—with the exception of the ulna that Rebecca Chen had unwittingly removed in her zeal to complete her biology lab.

"Some evidence of adipocere on the left anterior femur," Dr. Guthro said. Adipocere, Ethan had learned from experience, was a white waxy substance that occurred when the fatty tissues of a body had a post-mortem enzyme reaction due to cold, moist conditions, resulting in saponification of the tissue. Essentially, the chemical reaction of the fatty tissues created a soaplike substance, known as grave wax.

The morgue attendant turned the body over. At first glance, the decomposition on the posterior view was almost identical to the anterior: mummification of the tissue to a midpoint of the torso, as well as the entire left arm. The rest of the body was skeletonized with adipocere on the coccyx and upper left femur. A member of the FIS team took photos while Dr. Guthro slowly circled the body. But it was Dr. Hughes who noticed the mark first.

Dr. Hughes pointed to a spot almost at the base of the corpse's neck. "There. Do you see that mark, Dr. Guthro? It's not dirt."

Dr. Guthro picked up a magnifying glass. He frowned. "Looks like a very crude tattoo."

Ferguson threw Ethan a look. *Did Rigby have a tattoo?*

He did a mental run-through of Heather's description in the dog-eared missing-persons file, and gave a subtle shake of his head.

No, she did not.

11

Yoshi, her old friend and owner of Yakusoku Tattoo, had told her to park in the back of the building. He hadn't mentioned that finding the driveway would be so difficult. All these old buildings were connected. Kenzie slowed her car and peered through the side window.

There. Three buildings over, she spotted the narrow carriage lane that led to the parking lot. She eased her car between the brick buildings, careful of the rental vehicle's side mirrors. The lane was barely wide enough for her car. But, she discovered to her surprise, the parking lot behind the buildings was actually quite big—one of those strange lot divisions from earlier times.

She glanced at her watch. She was early. Hardly surprising, since she hadn't slept last night. God, she felt like hell. She grabbed her Americano, slung her kit bag over her shoulder, and led Foo down the carriage lane to the front entrance of Yakusoku Tattoo. The tall buildings had protected her from the weather, but as soon as she reached the sidewalk, heavy drizzle dampened her skin.

Ugh. She wasn't used to this chill damp anymore. She craved warmth and sun.

One more reason she should have just flown in and out again.

I shouldn't have let Yoshi talk me into this.

This was supposed to be a quick trip, but when Yoshi heard she was coming to Halifax, he asked her to do some guest spots.

He wasn't someone to whom she could—or would—say no.

Yoshi had been the tattoo artist to design the arm sleeves and koi design on her back. Whenever he was in her neck of the woods, she would book off a few days and have him work on her. He had finished the final section of her tattoo a year and a half ago. No, she could never say no to Yoshi.

She'd never been to his studio before. They had met eight years ago when she was in Tokyo at an international tattooing conference. He had been demonstrating the technique of *tebori,* something she had always wanted to learn. Not only had Yoshi been willing to share his vast knowledge of traditional woodblock designs and the art of *tebori,* but while she was in Japan, he had been instrumental in making an introduction to the famed Horifuyu, one of the great masters of the art of Japanese tattooing. It had been a lifetime ambition for Kenzie to meet him, and she was beyond thrilled when he tattooed a crane taking flight around her ankle.

Four years later, Yoshi had created a tattoo studio that was known across North America. His clients, who were willing to invest the time and money into the art on their bodies, booked vacation to come to Halifax to have their tattoos done.

And now, here she was—about to ink clients in a studio owned by a Japanese artist in good ol' Halifax. If someone had told her seventeen years ago that she would be doing this, she would have laughed. But her life had many strange twists. This, fortunately, was one of the more pleasant ones.

There were already a few clients hanging around the waiting area when she shouldered open the door. They all turned to stare. She gave a quick smile, and scanned the room. It was exactly what she expected Yoshi's place to be: cool, eclectic, immaculate. The room had an urban industrial vibe, the tall ceiling crisscrossed with venting and pipes, the slightly uneven floor finished with distressed concrete. It was all gray. But serene gray. Zen gray. On the walls hung Hori's designs in the most brilliant, breathtaking colors. Dragons, koi and serpents curved with sinuous grace. Above the counter were designs and flash from the other artists at the studio: skulls, hearts, pinup girls, Celtic and tribal. She eyed a Celtic cross. Nicely done but a bit mechanical.

"*Yookoso,* Kenzie." Yoshi walked around the front counter and gave a small bow. She bowed back. It was a little ritual they had, from one professional to another. Then she reached over and gave him a hug. He was shorter than she, stocky in build. A soft goatee contrasted with the thick stubble bristling his head. "How are you?" he asked, stepping back.

"Good." She flipped her hair off her shoulder and stretched.

He scrutinized her, his gaze concerned behind the tinted John Lennon–style glasses. "You look like shit."

She shrugged. "I went to my old house yesterday."

"How's your mother?"

"Dying." She took a big gulp of her espresso. "So, what's my schedule like today?"

Yoshi took the cue and sat down at the computer behind the counter. "Let me see… Your first client is in ten minutes. You've got a full day ahead of you."

"Great." She needed that. She needed to take her mind off her mother. "Where's my station?"

Yoshi led her to a far corner with an exposed brick wall, and a bonsai garden in a gray bowl on a shelf. Kenzie was pleased to see that the tattoo chair was fully adjustable and hydraulic. She placed her kit bag next to the metal-and-glass workstation, and gave it a quick check. Thermal paper, green soap, inks, ultrasonic cleaner, razors, Vaseline, surgical gloves. Good. She had her own needles, power supply, needle tubes and sketch pad in her bag. "Nice place, Yoshi." Perfect for zoning out and tuning in to inking her clients.

"Gracias." Yoshi grinned. "Glad you like it."

"What does Yakusoku mean again?"

Yoshi's eyes gleamed. "It means the promise one has between a customer and the tattooist."

"Cool." She liked that. The client trusted the tattooist in so many ways: to perform a safe procedure, to create the design they want, to not hurt them. But the biggest promise was to create something they would be satisfied with for the rest of their lives.

She had just settled Foo on his fleece blanket in the corner, and laid out her equipment when her first client arrived, a burly teddy bear of a guy who asked her to tattoo a portrait of his cat on his chest. "He's been with me through some tough times," he told her, handing her a photo of a fluffy gray cat with white socks and quartzlike eyes.

Kenzie nodded to Foo, who snored gently on his blanket. "I hear ya."

His cat was cute, and Kenzie's spirits lifted as she began the outline work of his tattoo.

An hour and a half later, she surveyed her work with satisfaction. "This is amazing!" her client declared, studying the tattoo of his cat curled on his chest.

After he left, she broke down her workstation, disposing of her single-use items, then cleaned and sterilized her equipment. She glanced at her watch. Her next client was due any minute, but hopefully he was late and she could grab a bite of the muffin she had packed in her bag. Foo watched her, knowing that his best chances of a treat were after her clients had left.

"Your next client is here," announced the receptionist, with an impressive collection of piercings.

Any frustration at not having her muffin vanished at the sight of her new client. Tall, tanned (how could he get a tan in this weather? she wondered), well-muscled with an easy grin and shaggy blond hair, he was definitely an acceptable substitute for her muffin.

"Hi, I'm Kenzie."

"Finn." He shoved his hands in his front pockets.

"Can you tell how long the victim would have had the tattoo before she was killed?" Ethan asked Dr. Guthro.

Dr. Guthro shook his head. "No. Did your missing girl have one?"

Dr. Hughes threw a glance at Ethan.

He rubbed his jaw. "There is no tattoo listed under identifying marks." And he certainly could not recall one from his university class. Back in the '90s, a neck tattoo on a Halifax university student would have been memorable. But Heather had long hair. The tattoo was on the back of her neck, so it might have been covered. "But I'll have to check with the family."

"We are lucky that the teeth are intact. You don't have

to worry so much about identifying marks if we can get a positive match with the dental records."

"May we have a look at the mark, Doctor?" Ferguson asked.

Dr. Guthro handed her the magnifying glass. Ethan and Lamond stood behind the sergeant. The mark on the victim's skin was faint, just a blurry outline. "Looks homemade," Lamond said. "It isn't even shaded."

"What do you think it is?" Ethan asked. "Some kind of triad?"

Ferguson shrugged. "Maybe." Ethan knew from past experience that when she said "Maybe," she meant "Not likely." Ferguson glanced up at Dr. Guthro. "Is there any way to get an enhancement of this?"

"We can try infrared camera. If that doesn't work, sometimes an amber filter on the lens will work. If the ink is black, it will absorb the light and darken the image."

"When will you be able to look at that?"

"I have to check when our camera technician is in." Dr. Guthro made a note of it on the whiteboard hanging by the autopsy table.

The rest of the external exam was completed without any more findings of note. With the exception of the victim's neck, there were no signs of external trauma and no more unusual markings.

The body was rolled back onto its back. "Let's remove the rope and see what we can find," Dr. Guthro said. He worked the slipknot, trying to avoid damage to the rope and any evidence that might have survived. The homicide team knew it was extremely unlikely that fingerprints would have lasted in the bog environment, but they were hoping there might be blood or fibers caught in the rope.

A deep groove encircled the victim's throat. Dr. Guthro leaned in for closer inspection. "Given the amount of force that would have been applied to create this kind of damage, some of the bones of her neck would have sustained small fractures. We'll have a look under the skin at the end of the autopsy." He gazed over the rim of his glasses at the onlookers. "Shall we break for lunch? Or keep going?"

"I'm all for retrieving that bullet, Dr. Guthro," Ferguson said, her tone brisk.

"Me, too." He gave a broad smile.

The morgue attendant set up the body, and Dr. Guthro began the Y incision. The skin was like leather, and he had a fine sheet of sweat on his forehead by the time he removed the chest plate.

The organs were surprisingly recognizable. "Don't judge a book by its cover, heh." Dr. Guthro chuckled. He studied the X-ray of the bullet, then examined the exposed lungs. "Hmmm… The entrance wound looks to be about…here." He stuck his gloved finger in a tiny hole. "See?"

He peered down into the chest cavity. "Looks like it hit some large blood vessels—" he checked the X-ray again "—and is lodged in the muscles of the vertebral column. Let's see if we can map the ballistic trajectory."

The morgue attendant handed him a bright pink rod. He eased one end into the hole, and gently probed downward into the tissue. "Easy does it…" he murmured. "Yes, my initial hypothesis was correct."

He removed the rod and dug his finger into the tissue. Everyone watched. No one dared breathe. "I can feel it…." He grunted a few times. His face shone with sweat. "Hold on…here it comes…"

He hooked the bullet upwards with his finger, and placed it on a tray.

Ethan studied the bullet. "A .38 S&W would be my guess."

"That narrows it down," Lamond said.

Ethan gave him a look. "I was just about to add that it looks like a vintage bullet. Probably from the second World War."

Dr. Guthro removed the organs, one by one. After he weighed and measured them, he placed a large hypodermic into a pool of fluid in the abdominal cavity. "We'll see if the lab can run a toxicology screen on the decomposition fluid."

Science never ceased to amaze Ethan. This corpse was in the bog for years, he guessed, and there was still a chance that they could test it for drugs.

The morgue attendant peeled back the skin on the skull, and removed the skull cap. Liquid streamed out of the skull onto a towel. Lamond wrinkled his nose. At the unspoken question in the homicide team's eyes, Dr. Guthro said, "That was the brain."

Brain drain.

Stop it, Drake.

He gave himself a shake, and threw a quick glance at Lamond. His former partner's eyes were wide, his gaze fixed tightly on the victim's face.

The pathologist examined the skull and dura. "No fractures, no sign of hemorrhage. Doesn't look like someone hit her on the head."

He finished the exam.

"One last thing." He sliced through the skin on the neck, peeling it back to examine the bone and cartilage. "I'm not seeing any obvious fractures, but I'll remove the neck and section it. We might see more under the microscope."

"Can you make a guess at cause of death?" Ferguson asked.

Dr. Guthro shook his head. "No. The bullet clearly caused hemorrhaging, but whether she was dead before she was strangled, I can't tell. The COD may be inconclusive." He made a note on the whiteboard. "The forensic odontologist said he'd have a look at her teeth today. And if you get the dental records for your missing girl ASAP, we'll see if we can at least get a match."

"I'll start tracking them down," Ethan said.

"I'll stay here while they look at the bog sections," Ferguson said. The excavating team had brought in parts of the bog that had been under the body. "Lamond, you take the bullet to ballistics. Let me know what you find out. Ethan, be as quick as you can."

Relief flashed in Lamond's eyes that he didn't have to stay to watch the sectioning of the victim's neck.

He, on the other hand, wanted to know everything he could learn about the tattoo.

If the dental records matched those of Heather Rigby, then she had gotten the tattoo just before she disappeared.

And if that was the case...

They had just gotten their first break in seventeen years.

12

Nervous.

Kenzie could pick up the vibes a mile away. Either this guy, Finn, had never had a tattoo or the last one was done by a scratcher.

"Hear you want a custom piece." She led him back to her station. "What are you thinking?"

"I want a Foo Dog." Kenzie bit back a smile. First a cat tattoo, now a dog tattoo. Haligonians loved their pets.

As if on cue, Foo jumped off his blanket and rushed over to check out her new client.

"A Foo Dog, huh?" she grinned. "Well, you can't have mine."

Finn crouched down and scratched Foo behind the ears. "Even though he seems to really like you." Foo practically melted against this guy's knee, his pink tongue peeking between his lips as he snorted his pleasure at Finn's deft ear massage.

"I work with dogs," Finn said. "I'm a dog walker."

"Seriously?"

"Yeah. What's your dog's name?"

Kenzie smiled. "Foo Dog."

He grinned. "Seriously?"

"Yeah."

"He kind of looks like a Foo Dog."

"Well, he's got the attitude down, that's for sure." Foo Dogs were actually not dogs at all, but "Lions of Buddha." They were symbols of protection and courage in both Chinese and Japanese Shinto mythology.

Finn stood, sliding a picture from his pocket. "I was thinking of something like this." It wasn't the standard tattoo design of a crawling Foo Dog. Rather, it was a picture of a stone Foo Dog statue, sitting on its haunches, a large paw on a sphere.

"Nice," Kenzie said. "Where do you want it?"

Finn pointed to the back of his shoulder. "Right on my shoulder blade. So that he guards my back."

"Right on." She studied the posture of the statue. It was static, stolid. If it wasn't positioned just right, it would look like he had a postage stamp stuck on his back. "Can you turn around and take off your shirt?"

Finn flushed. "Sure." He pulled his T-shirt over his head, and turned around, revealing a broad, smooth back tapering down to narrow hips. Perfect material.

"The Foo Dog will look awesome on your shoulder blade. Although you know what would look even better?"

"No."

"Two. Traditionally, there is a pair of Foo Dogs that guard the entrance to sacred buildings and houses. If you had the male on one side," she ran her palm over one shoulder blade, "and the female on the other, they would symbolically guard your soul—and they would be symmetrical."

She felt his shoulders tense under her hand. "Uh…I

don't know. I'm not sure I'm ready to make that commitment."

He had completely unmarked skin. She bet this was his first tattoo. "You want to be sure." She had a hunch that once he saw the design, he'd be in for both, but she would never push a client. "It will be yours for life." Too often she'd seen clients jump into a tattoo they would later regret. "I'm thinking it will cover about this much," Kenzie circled her finger on his skin.

"Maybe a bit smaller?"

He isn't ready. "You sure you want to do this?"

"Yeah." His gaze was steady. Good. Nothing worse than having a client who started sweating halfway through the tattoo because they had changed their mind. Once the ink was in, it was in. Couldn't use an eraser on it.

"You want to make sure it looks good in ten, twenty years. If you do it too small, you won't get the detail," she said. "And over time the lines will fade, so you want to make sure the tattoo isn't so small it just looks like a blob." He still looked uncertain. "Look, I'll show you." She lifted the edge of her tank top and pulled down the waistband of her cargo pants to reveal her left hip. On it was a brilliant blue-and-green Foo Dog, curving around her body, crawling toward her heart.

"Wow," Finn said. "Very cool."

"You see the detail in this? You are going to lose all that if you shrink it down."

She pulled her tank back over her hip.

"So if it's too small it will look like this?" He pointed to her chest.

What the—? She may have her insecurities, but not with her breasts.

Then she grinned. He was pointing to the silkscreen

on her tank top. It was a picture of the back of the cover from the Talking Heads *Remain in Light* album. The four members of the group were masked with red blocks painted over their faces. The overall effect was to render their feature indistinguishable. Blobs.

"Yeah. Exactly." She pulled out her sketchbook. "Give me twenty minutes to come up with something."

It took about twenty-five minutes, but she was happy with the results. "That's amazing," Finn said. She had sketched a Foo Dog with a paw pushing off a sphere, its mane curling and flowing, its snout open in a protective snarl. Instead of the dog sitting—which looked too blocklike to her—she drew the dog springing from its haunches, the sphere about to roll away.

"Trust me, it's going to rock!" Energy charged her blood. She had outdone herself with the design and she had the perfect canvas to work on. She couldn't wait to get started.

She traced the design onto transfer paper. "Okay, now we are going to put the design on your shoulder. So you need to take off your shirt."

He yanked off his shirt, so excited that the shirt whipped over his head. They both grinned. Kenzie gloved, then wiped his shoulder blade with green soap and shaved the skin with a razor. "This will make sure that the lines are really smooth," she said. She wiped the skin down again and applied a generous coating of adherent. "This will make the stencil stick." Now was the moment of truth. She had that feeling of sick excitement that comes when you know something you've created is really hot. She pressed the stencil on Finn's shoulder blade, patted it down and peeled it off.

"Nice," she breathed. "Take a look." She grabbed his arm and led him to the full-length mirror hanging on the wall. "Don't you think the size works?" she asked, handing him a mirror so he could see his reflection.

Finn stared at his stenciled shoulder blade, angling the mirror back and forth. "Yeah," he said. "I do. I think it will be great." He smiled. "Bring it on!"

While she was waiting for the stencil to dry, she selected the needles and inks. Green, blue, a touch of yellow in the eyes...

"I just want black with some shading," Finn said.

"You sure?"

"Yeah. I want it really simple. Kind of pure.

She mentally adjusted her vision of the tattoo. Yeah, she could see that. It would work. And it would fit her client's comfort level. He wasn't screaming "collector."

"Right on," she said. She disinfected the chair and laid protective plastic on the surface. "Have a seat. And make sure you are comfortable. This will take a couple of hours."

Finn straddled the chair, resting his arms on the back. She put together her tattoo gun, opening the needle in front of him and attaching it to the bar in the gun. Then she slid the needle tube over it. She adjusted it until just the tip of the needle could be seen from the edge of the tube. Then she bagged the motor, sealing it with a rubber band.

"We'll start with the outline, Finn." She patted down his shoulder blade, removing excess transfer ink, and then smoothed a coating of Vaseline over his skin. She dipped the needle into a cap of black ink, drawing up a bit of ink into the tube. With her right hand, she stretched the left side of the tattoo, and then began the outline.

"You're a lefty," Finn said.

"Uh-huh."

"So'm I."

"Cool." She wiped off excess ink, and began another line. "Your skin loves ink, by the way."

"What do you mean?"

"For some people, their bodies don't like ink. But the ink goes really smoothly in you. I'm the same way."

"When did you get your first tattoo?"

"I was sixteen."

"You serious?"

"Uh-huh. My mother almost killed me."

"What was it?"

"The usual. A skull." The lie came so naturally now that she almost forgot that the tattoo had not been a skull.

"Can I see it?"

She wiped off more ink, and turned to refill the tube. "No. I had it covered up. It was bad."

"Who did it?"

She got asked about her first tattoo all the time by new clients. Years ago, she could barely talk about it, but she soon was able to gloss over it and move on. But today, she felt her shoulders tensing. Maybe because she was back in Halifax. Glad that Finn couldn't see her face, she said, "An old boyfriend." She kept her tone cool. Even though she liked Finn, this was "no fly" territory.

The conversation moved on to Finn's work. The crazy antics of the dogs he walked. He laughed out loud at her stories about Foo. They talked about creating things with their hands—how he loved renovating and transforming houses. "A bit like tattooing, I guess," he said.

She felt a spark of excitement. This guy *got* her work, her art. Her soul. "Tattooing is about personal transformation for so many of my clients." She realized, at the end of their three-hour session, that she hadn't enjoyed talking with a guy so much in a long time. "Okay, we are done. And it rocks." She wiped away the extra ink and put down her tattoo gun. "Wanna take a look?"

Finn got off the chair and checked out the tattoo in the mirror. "Wow. You are a true artist."

A warm flush prickled Kenzie's skin.

She studied his tattoo. His shoulders were well-muscled, and the poised power of the dog, ready to spring across his back, blew her away.

"Can I take a picture?" she asked. "I want to add it to my collection of favorites."

"Sure."

Yoshi came over to admire Kenzie's work while she rooted in her bag for her camera. "Very fine work, Kenzie. Horifuyu would be pleased."

"Thanks." She grinned. "I was inspired. Great concept—" *great canvas;* she wouldn't say those words in front of Finn "—and the ink went in real smooth." She took a couple of pictures.

"Here, let me take one of you together," Yoshi said.

Kenzie stood next to Finn. He slung an arm around her shoulders—"My good arm," he joked—and Yoshi snapped the shots. "Give me your email and I'll send them to you."

"Thanks."

"Maybe I should send Foo over for a little exercise. It's too easy for him to get fat here." The words popped out, but as she spoke them, she realized it was a great idea.

Finn eyed Foo, who returned his gaze with lazy interest. "Yeah, I think he'd be good with the other dogs."

"How about tomorrow?" She applied some lotion to his tattoo and covered it up. "You can put your shirt on."

He pulled it over his head. "Sounds good. Where do you want me to pick him up?"

"I'll be here by ten tomorrow morning."

"See you then."

It felt like a date.

It's for Foo. Not you.

Maybe.

Maybe not.

13

Kate tapped her pen on the notepad that lay on her desk, the phone cradled to her ear. She had been on hold for—she glanced at her watch, her mouth twisting—oh, six minutes too long for her taste.

Well, what else did you expect from the Honorable Harry Owen, Kate?

She knew she shouldn't feel irritated, given that Harry Owen had agreed to a phone call with her on short notice, but her extended wait allowed her to repent the fact she had consented to this dirty job. For she knew it could not be anything but. Harry Owen was a flagrant fearmonger. She had enough terrors, thank you very much, to not be reminded of them by her elected official.

His noted dalliances did not improve Kate's opinion of him. He was probably a closet sexist, enjoying the lovely young interns on Parliament Hill while hiring all his hotshot cronies who had no real skills except the ability to spell their surnames.

Ooh, that was rather cynical.

Remember, you have a job to do, Kate. You have to

*win him over, so stop sneering. Frances Sloane—and
God help you, Don Clarkson—are depending on you....*

"Hello. Ms. Lange, this Harry Owen." The voice of
Canada's youngest member of Parliament was energetic, smooth. It fit in nicely with the findings from
her late-night Google search: a thirtysomething confirmed bachelor, former corporate lawyer, of multiple
immigrant extraction tramping unimpeded on the road
to ministerial glory.

She straightened. "Thank you for agreeing to speak
with me, Mr. Owen."

"Sorry for keeping you waiting. I was on a mind-
blowingly dull conference call. It is truly a pleasure to
meet you." His tone held genuine admiration. "I'm a
big fan of yours."

Oh?

"But I'm afraid I have another call scheduled in less
than ten minutes, so before we begin, let's make sure
that we can even have this conversation."

"Of course," Kate murmured. She knew exactly what
he was going to ask. And she knew exactly what she
was going to say.

Maybe this lobbying gig could be fun, after all.

"Are you on the registry for lobbyists?" he asked.
"My assistant checked this morning and didn't see your
name."

The first shot had been fired across the bow.

Kate studied the fax on her desk from the Office of
the Commission of Lobbying. "I sent in my report to
the registry last night. I received confirmation a few
hours ago. It was faxed to your office just after lunch."
Fortunately, the registrar had been sympathetic to her
circumstances and recognized the need for urgency.
Her bona fides were straightforward to confirm, and

within two hours she was officially a federally registered Consultant Lobbyist.

"I see. Just hold a moment, please."

Kate leaned back in her chair, a smile curving her lips. She was enjoying herself. Perhaps a little too much.

A minute later, he said, "Yes, we just received it." He cleared his throat. "Now, what can I do for you, Ms. Lange?"

"As I explained to your assistant, I am representing a client who is stricken with an incurable and horrific disease that afflicts her motor neurons."

"Amyotrophic Lateral Sclerosis," he said. "So sad."

Very impressive, Harry. You have done your homework.

"As you may remember," Kate continued, "a woman named Sue Rodriguez mounted a legal challenge against the criminalization of assisted suicide almost twenty years ago."

"And the court upheld the Criminal Code. Assisted suicide is a crime in Canada."

He was sending her a message with his subtle emphasis of "crime." "Yes. But my client is desperate, Mr. Owen. She wants to take control of her life. Die on her own terms."

There was a pause.

"Ms. Lange, the Criminal Code provision is in place for a reason. It protects the vulnerable from being euthanized."

A sweeping, emotionally powerful sound bite that would work well on TV.

"That was the concern of the Supreme Court," Kate said. "But subsequent research has shown that the slippery slope the court feared did not materialize."

"Ms. Lange, as you yourself have experienced—"

You'd better lose that patronizing tone, Mr. Owen.

"—we are facing increasingly violent criminals, as well as a severe increase in cyber fraud, child pornography, drug and financial crimes." He must have read her mind, because his voice was no longer patronizing, but instead sounded resolute. "I am one of the members working on a committee to toughen our criminal laws. Our goal is to send a message to anyone who is thinking of committing a crime, not to open a door for opportunists to commit murders. I am a firm believer in deterrence. And if that doesn't work, punishment. Someone shouldn't get away with murder." He ended on a final, passionate note.

The power of his charisma, the strength of his convictions, resonated over the phone line.

Her job would be that much more difficult with a political adversary such as Mr. Owen.

Kate knew why the member of Parliament held such passionate conviction. The *world* knew why. In fact, Harry Owen had often said that the bullet his father took in his spine during a late-night holdup when Harry Owen was eight was one of the reasons Harry chose to go into law, and then politics.

"Mr. Owen, I beg to differ. Assisted suicide is not murder. It is assisting someone to take their own life. And suicide is not a criminal offense." Before he could respond, Kate added, "I've studied your political platform. I know that you are bullish on deterrence and, if that doesn't work, punishment."

It was the third arm of the corrections model that Harry Owen had eliminated from his platform: rehabilitation. "But I also know that you are very much in favor of autonomy. That is why you didn't support the gun registry." Several years ago, the government at the time put in place a long-gun registry. Anyone who owned a gun had to register it. It was recently disbanded.

Harry Owen had been outspoken about his disdain for the registry in the past, even going so far as to suggest that the gun control legislation in Canada should be modified to allow citizens to carry handguns.

"If my father had had a gun the night he was held up, he wouldn't be in a wheelchair now. And that bastard—pardon my language—wouldn't be living off social assistance and getting his cable TV paid for by the taxpayers, of which my father is one."

Ouch.

"I don't understand why you are lobbying this issue," he said. "The Criminal Code is the only thing that keeps innocent people from getting hurt. It protects people, Ms. Lange." His voice lowered. "Pardon me for saying this, but I would have thought that after your experiences, you would be in favor of making the Code even stronger. You barely survived being murdered."

"I may have survived being attacked—" Kate said, her mind racing as she struggled to find a way to break through his indomitable wall of righteousness. *Screw it. I'll tell him the real reason I'm doing this.* "—but I may not survive the consequences of it. Did you know I might be infected with an incurable disease that would completely rob me of cognitive function?"

There was a shocked silence. Then he said, "My God. No. I had no idea. I'm so sorry."

"Me, too." Kate swallowed. "That was, by the way, confidential information."

"Yes, of course."

Was anything confidential in politics when someone was trying to come out on top?

She closed her eyes. She no longer enjoyed this conversation. She wanted to end it as soon as possible. "So, to answer your question, that is why I am helping my client. She deserves—just like any of us—to die with dignity."

"What exactly do you want from me?"

Kate tried to swallow her frustration. He was not making this easy for her. *Welcome to politics, Kate.*

"My client doesn't have the months or years it will take to mount another legal challenge of the Criminal Code. The public climate has changed since the Rodriguez case, Mr. Owen. We want the government to strike down the provision in the Criminal Code making assisted suicide a crime. This could be an opportunity for the government to show its compassionate side." Kate waited.

He exhaled. "Kate, I'm sorry. But there is a reason the Supreme Court ruled against Rodriguez, and there is a reason that assisted suicide is in the Criminal Code. People could claim that they were asked to help kill their loved ones—and then cash in on their insurance policies. It is not an issue that the government is prepared to explore. Just a moment—" He paused. "My assistant says that my next call is about to begin." His tone became formal. "Thank you for sharing your client's concerns, Ms. Lange."

"Mr. Owen, please reconsider," Kate said, her voice urgent. She was losing him. "This could be a savvy move by the government. And it would make a huge difference to my client—"

"I'm afraid you are knocking on the wrong door." His voice now had an edge to it. "Assisted suicide is a crime."

"And forcing someone to suffer terribly is not?" She let that sink in. "Call me if you change your mind."

He hung up on her.

She stared at the phone. "Jerk."

She had revealed one of her deepest secrets—and he'd told her to get lost.

She dialed Frances Sloane's number.

"Phyllis, it's Kate Lange. Is Frances able to take my call?"

"Oh, yes, Ms. Lange. She's doing better this afternoon." There was a note of excitement in Phyllis's voice. They knew about her scheduled phone call with the M.P. "I'll just take off her mask so she can speak to you."

While Kate waited for her client to have her respiratory mask removed, she thought of a few choice curses for the M.P.

"Kate?" Her client's voice held the same note of anticipation as her caregiver's.

Kate's stomach became a hard knot. "Hi, Frances. I just spoke with Harry Owen today. I won't drag this out—he was a no-go. I'm sorry."

I knew I shouldn't have let myself get talked into this. A professional lobbyist could have finessed this.

There was a pause. Kate envisioned Frances' eyes, such a vibrant blue in such a wasted body. A life force in a dead zone. "I wish I could have done more, Frances. I tried everything."

"I understand. You did your best." Frances' voice held forgiveness and acceptance.

Unexpectedly, tears tightened Kate's throat. "I'm sorry."

"I haven't given up yet, Kate." She began to cough.

Phyllis got on the line. "We have to go." She spoke hurriedly. "She will call you later. I need to suction her."

Frances' life had been stripped down to meeting basic needs. Breathing trumped talking.

Kate hung up the phone and stared out the window. Cars crawled in a steady stream below. What she did up in this office tower sometimes felt so disconnected. And yet she knew it mattered.

She should have felt relieved that her lobbying efforts were dead in the water. She had not wanted to do it; she had not wanted to put herself on the line for this cause, this client.

But now she wanted to give Harry Owen a wakeup call. As Randall had said, the M.P. talked the talk but he obviously had never walked the walk.

He was the voice of his constituents. He had a duty to listen to them.

Harry, I can make you a man of the people if you let me.

Or I can make you the target of public controversy. Your choice.

She fished her phone out of her purse. She speed-dialed *N*.

Nat picked up on the second ring.

Her takedown of Harry Owen was about to begin.

14

Kenzie hummed under her breath while she broke down her station. She had a little breather before her next client. Time to take Foo out for a pee. She clipped on his leash and headed to the entrance of the studio. It was buzzing with clients— looked like a bunch of university students celebrating their admissions with new tattoos.

"Will be back in fifteen," she told the pierced receptionist.

"Did you hear about that body they found?" a girl said to a friend, right behind her.

"Yeah. It was really freaky. Right out of *CSI*."

The receptionist appeared transfixed by the kids' gossip. She jumped right in. "They said it was perfectly preserved. Right down to the toenails."

"What time is my next appointment?" Kenzie interrupted, trying to get the receptionist's attention.

"It's probably a hoax," another guy with a brow piercing said.

The receptionist glanced at the screen. "At four," she replied without even looking at her. Kenzie bit her tongue. The receptionist was oblivious to the pissed-off vibes Kenzie sent her, staring right past her to the skeptic. "It's no hoax." She held up a newspaper. On the front page was a large photo of an area Kenzie had hoped never to see again, surrounded in crime scene tape.

Kenzie's insides liquefied.

"The body was found in a peat bog," the girl read from the paper. She looked up at the guy. "They have preservatives and shit in them."

Kenzie thrust Foo's leash at the receptionist. "Take him for a minute, please." She rushed back through the studio and into the ladies' room. Ten minutes later, she emerged, shaking and sick to her stomach.

"You okay?" Yoshi called from his workstation.

"Yeah. Fine." She exhaled slowly through her mouth and gave Yoshi a wobbly smile. "Must have eaten some bad food on the plane."

"Your client is here."

"Right." She straightened.

"You up for it?"

"Yes. No problem." Her hand was steady. She could do it.

Her next client wanted a skull tattooed on his calf. She couldn't help but wonder if it was a message from the universe.

Or, more to the point, from Heather Rigby. Whom, she guessed, McNally had left to rot in the peat bog.

Probably only minutes after Kenzie had put a bullet in her heart.

15

McNally awoke in full arousal, his heart hammering, his fingers clenched. His sheets were sticky. The dream about Kenzie had come back.

The neon clock dial on his bedside table showed it was morning. He jumped out of bed and stumbled into the bathroom. His eyes were still glued with sleep as he groped for the shower dial. The water was cold. He let it run down his body, angling his head until it hit the death's-head on the back of his bristle-covered skull.

Ten minutes later, he turned off the water and stood, naked, in front of the mirror.

His skin was ruddy. His flesh numb.

But that was as far as the dousing had gone.

He dressed quickly, having augmented his prison discharge garb with several new pairs of khakis, three T-shirts and a hoodie for the cool May weather. There was a small convenience store in the basement of the building, and he put on the coffee and a pot of oatmeal, hurried down to the store and bought every newspaper that made mention of the "bog body," including yesterday's leftovers. When he returned to his apartment, the smell of brewed coffee hit his nose. His stomach rumbled.

He threw the papers on the table and poured himself a large mug of coffee. It was a dark roast, the tribal design of coffees: bold and edgy and dynamic, with an intense aftertaste that left deep strokes on his tongue. Man, he loved the tribal energy. It kicked into his bloodstream almost immediately—reminding him that he was starving. He gave his oatmeal one final stir, scraping the bottom of the pot. Steel-cut, with fresh milk. Thick and heavy. He needed something that would hold his hunger at bay. He could be waiting for Kenzie outside the tattoo studio for hours. He set a bowl of blueberries and strawberries on the place mat by his juice glass. It was strange how all those old habits had come back to him after he was released. They were strangely comforting.

He poured the entire contents of the pot into a deep bowl, loaded it with brown sugar, and added cream. Then he sat down, dug his spoon into the steaming porridge, and picked up the first newspaper. He wasn't disappointed. The reports provided vivid detail about the crime scene, with an in-depth interview of Rebecca Chen, who had found the body. He studied her picture. She was about the same age as Heather Rigby had been. But with black hair, dark eyes…

Disappointment stabbed him. Cute. But not his type.

She clearly relished the media attention. Every other paragraph provided an extensive quote about her traumatic experience of finding a dead body while trying to get an A in her biology lab.

But it was her description of tearing her fingernails ragged to dig out the "rock" that transfixed him.

There had been a plank thrown behind the bunker, and he made Lovett drag it down to the peat bogs while he dug under the hummock. The must of decaying earth filled his nose, blocking the sharper metallic tang of Heather's blood. He breathed deeply. Anger and adrenaline, combined with cocaine, had ramped up his heart rate and his chest could barely contain the raging muscle.

His fingers ripped out a handful of roots and dirt.

It was Kenzie's hair.

Another handful.

Kenzie's skin.

He scrubbled deeper and pulled out a mass of peat. It was moist.

Kenzie's heart.

His hands dug farther and deeper under the hummock, creating a tunnel into which he would bury the gullibility that had led him to this moment.

She had betrayed him.

She had betrayed his trust. His love. His hope for their future.

Mist crawled under his clothes.

The longer it took for them to get rid of Heather's body, the farther Kenzie could get.

His muscles trembled.

She had ruined everything.

He still couldn't absorb the extent of her betrayal. He wanted to destroy something, hurt something, something more than the dead girl who lay next to him.

Something like Kenzie.

His eyes refocused on the newspaper's interview of the girl who had discovered Heather's body.

The body, according to our sources, is still intact.

"Shit."

The bog had played a cruel trick on him and Lovett. He wondered if the police had found the tattoo gun....

The oatmeal became leaden in his gut.

There is nothing to connect you to that. Nothing. The water would have destroyed any fingerprints or blood.

He shoved the newspaper aside, and grabbed the next one on the stack. It was the local paper—the *Halifax Post*.

The *Post* speculated that the bog body could be "missing university student Heather Rigby who had mysteriously disappeared on the night of Halifax's final Mardi Gras."

Yup. You got it. It's Heather.

He grinned. All those police officers and doctors and journalists—they thought they were so smart—and yet none of them knew what had happened to poor little Heather.

McNally hummed under his breath.

And they wouldn't find out.

He was sure that the bog would have erased all traces of blood and semen from Heather.

How could they ever connect her to him? Or anyone else who had been there that night?

They'd gotten away with murder.

He picked up his coffee mug, savoring the strong brew as he scanned the other headline on the front page.

The Body Butcher Killings: Are They Connected?

He had heard about this case. All the guys on his unit had talked about a serial killer operating in Halifax. He could imagine how well that went down with the old establishment of the South End. Especially when the bodies were dumped in their own backyard.

Make that *dismembered* bodies. He'd forgotten that part. Cool.

One of them was a judge's daughter? *Holy shit.*

It made his own kill seem tame in comparison. Heather Rigby had been a nobody.

Had that Body Butcher guy killed all those women by himself?

He wondered if the Body Butcher had tatts. He pictured the ones he would ink on him: a series of pinups, each one more broken than the last—

Then he read the next paragraph: "The killer had been killed by one of his intended victims."

The would-be victim stared at him from the front page, her face bruised, her eyes haunted. Brown hair, brown eyes.

Jesus. Christ.

He read the caption underneath the photo: Halifax lawyer Kate Lange kills the infamous Body Butcher in self-defense during his final, crazed killing spree.

The universe had just sent him another sign.

Kate Lange had killed a serial killer.

And he was going to kill her.

He imagined the headlines: Killer of Serial Killer Found Murdered.

You bet that would make news all over the world. Not just in the *Halifax Post*.

And if her death was a replicate of Heather Rigby's...

What would that make him?

The best.

This, more than anything else, would convince Kenzie that he meant business.

Kenzie would know he was all-powerful.

And that she could never leave him again.

Or, more precisely, he would never let her leave him again.

16

The team had assembled in the war room at the station. Ferguson stood by the whiteboard, which was covered in black, red and blue scrawls, diagrams and arrows. A large map of Chebucto Head had been tacked next to it.

"We've had a positive identification," Ferguson announced, smiling broadly, holding an extra-large cup of Tim Hortons coffee. Ethan could sense her relief. Cold cases usually stirred up considerable media interest, but this case went viral because of the "bog body" angle. Reporters from all over North America and Europe had descended on Halifax—and thus, on the crime scene—to report the finding.

As the sergeant overseeing the investigation, Ferguson had her hands full maintaining security of the site, and ensuring that none of the remaining holdback evidence about the crime—namely, the bullet and the tattoo—had been leaked. The stress was wearing on her, on all of them.

"Ethan, can you debrief the team on the dental records?"

"We were lucky that the teeth were intact on the body. We had a positive match with the dental records.

The victim, as we all suspected, was Heather Rigby, last seen at the Mardi Gras in 1995."

It was always a strange mix of feelings to get a positive ID on a cold-case victim. There was triumph and satisfaction in succeeding to piece together the evidence to make an identification; there was a sense of closure in resolving an unanswered question that never let you rest; there was sorrow that the hope for the family was now gone.

In Heather Rigby's case, the feelings ran stronger, deeper. The case had haunted the police and the city for years. To know the manner of her death made it even more terrible. "We've notified the family, and I'm going to interview them after this meeting," Ethan added.

"I've asked Detective Liscomb to brief us on the FIS results as soon as we get them," Ferguson said. "I need some volunteers to canvass the houses in the area to see if they can remember anything about that night." Ferguson looked around at the team.

"Volunteers?" Lamond asked. "What happened to patrol?"

"Thanks to the media attention," Ferguson said, "I've had to use my quota to secure the crime scene. We are going to have to do the footwork."

Lamond exhaled. "I'll go."

"When I finish talking to Rigby's family, I'll join you," Ethan said. "I've got a list of old contacts you can start with."

"And don't forget to find out whether they know who hangs out at that bunker—" Ferguson was interrupted by a knock at the door. A woman stepped inside, carrying a box with several folders piled on top. "Detective Liscomb, I see you've brought some goodies."

Detective "Lizzy" Liscomb grinned, revealing an

endearing dimple that Ethan knew had fooled many. "You guys are gonna love me," she said. "First of all, remember that strange blob on the back of the victim's neck?" She opened a folder and rummaged around in it. "It was definitely a tattoo." She pulled out three 8 x 10 photos, which she pinned to the corkboard next to a map of the crime scene. "We used an infrared camera, which helped with some of the fainter lines." Yet the outline of the tattoo was still incomplete. The lines faded and then grew bold. "This isn't the fault of the technology," Liscomb said. "The actual tattoo was crudely done, with an inconsistent depth of penetration by the needle."

Ethan glanced at Lamond. As usual, his eyes reflected what he was thinking. In this case, it was exactly what Ethan was thinking: *How the hell do you know that?* And then he remembered what was in the box….

Liscomb lifted the lid of the box and, with a gloved hand, removed the homemade tool that Dr. Hughes had uncovered at the bog. "This, my friends, is a scratcher's tattoo gun. And the one we hypothesize was used to tattoo the victim's neck."

Liscomb held out the gun so the team could see it. "Usually the homemade guns use motors from electrical cars or VCRs, and then they are hooked up to a power supply, but this one is quite clever. Whoever made it used a rechargeable electric shaver, so it was completely portable."

"And could be used in the bunker," Ethan said.

"That's right." She pointed to the tip. "Instead of a needle, they used a guitar string, which we presume was attached to the button that Dr. Hughes found."

"How exactly does that work?" Lamond asked.

"The button sits on top of the motor. The guitar string is threaded through a tube—in this case, the outer tube of a pen. The end that protrudes out of the tube is the needle. The other end is hooked into the button. When the motor is switched on, it rotates the button, which causes the string to move up and down in the tube." She smiled. "*Et voila,* a crude but effective tattoo gun. Unfortunately, it is doubtful any DNA survived on the button or the guitar string, but we've removed the duct tape wrapped around the tube, just in case something was preserved in the layers." She put the gun back in the box.

"So you believe this tattoo was made by that gun, correct?" Ferguson asked.

Liscomb turned to the photos of the actual tattoo. "Yes—the unevenness of the penetration into the skin suggests it was done by a homemade gun. What's interesting is that the tattoo itself is quite well drawn."

"How can you tell?" Ethan asked.

"We took it to one of the local tattoo parlors last night. A tattoo artist created a rendering of it, and filled in the details. When you see the finished product, it's pretty good." She pulled a sketch from the file folder and pinned it on the board.

"The tattooist thought it was a bird?" Ethan asked, studying the image. So much for his triad theory.

Liscomb nodded. "He was positive. And in fact, he said it was a raven." She flipped open a notepad. "I did some preliminary research on its meaning. In Native American cultures, the raven is considered a symbol of transformation and light."

Lamond raised his brows at Ethan. "Did Heather Rigby have Native American beliefs?"

Lizzy held up a hand. "Not so fast, guys. I haven't finished. It also has meanings for other groups. Historically, it was considered a keeper of secrets and symbol of death in Europe, a bad omen in the Middle East and a creature of evil in the Bible."

"So there could be a variety of angles on the tattoo," Ferguson said.

"Yeah. Like Heather had a thing for birds," Lamond said.

"Did the tattoo artist recognize the style of tattoo as belonging to someone?"

The FIS detective shook her head. "He couldn't associate it with anyone. But there are many more tattoo artists in the Halifax area. Someone might recognize this as a signature."

"As far as I know, Heather Rigby did not have any tattoos prior to the night she was killed," Ethan said. "So presuming she got this the night she went missing—and she was tattooed with the tattoo gun that was found with her—then we can guess that it was done locally. And we know that tattoos weren't as mainstream back then as they are now. There probably weren't as many tattoo artists around...."

"But there were probably more scratchers, working out of their basements, which means it might be harder for someone to identify this signature," Ferguson said.

Ethan nodded. "True. I think we need to release this sketch to the public. See if anyone was in a tattoo shop on the night of Mardi Gras and remembers Heather Rigby getting inked."

"Go for it," Ferguson said. "It's the best lead we've got."

Ethan grabbed his notebook and headed out the door. His meeting with Heather Rigby's family was at the top of his to-do list. He would verify their previous report that, other than a birthmark, Heather did not have any identifying markings, such as a tattoo, when she went missing. Then he would release the tattoo to the public and hope that they got some leads.

Adrenaline pumped through him. This case had haunted Halifax—and him—for over seventeen years. Heather had died a brutal death.

He wanted to be able to look Heather's parents in the eye and tell them that her killer had been brought to justice.

He wanted to be able to look himself in the eye again. And, if he was honest, he wanted to be able to tell Kate about this case. He wanted to redeem himself in her eyes.

Have her respect him again.

17

"Kate, it's me," Nat said. "Are you already at work?" She had called Kate's cell phone.

"Yes, I've been here for a while. Why? Were you able to set up the interview?" She felt a tremor of excitement. Nat had come through with her request to do a televised interview of Frances Sloane. But alongside the excitement lurked unease. Frances had been right about the appeal of Kate's so-called fame. Nat had told her that the news show would be interested in doing an interview of Frances only if Kate would agree to appear with her on TV.

"Yes, it's on." Nat sounded pleased. "But we need to do it this morning at 11:00 a.m."

"This morning?" Kate glanced at the clock. It was just after nine.

"Sorry for the short notice—but it was the only time I could make this work."

"No problem. In fact, that's fine for me." Kate was happy to get it over with. "But I'll have to make sure Frances can get there in time. She lives outside the city and her mobility issues slow her down."

"We'd like to do it at your client's house, Kate. Then viewers can really appreciate what her life is like."

"Of course." Nat was right—she should showcase Frances at home, amidst all the tubes, machines and paraphernalia that were required to keep her body functioning.

But a sense of dread hit Kate. She knew where it came from. *You are just going to have to suck it up.* "I'll check with Frances and get back to you."

Half an hour later, the interview confirmed with her client, Kate closed her office door and prepared a set of stock answers to the Body Butcher questions.

They needed all the ammunition they could get to take on Harry Owen. The final stroke of brilliance—masterminded by Nat—was that the news show would air the segment on the anniversary of the Body Butcher's death.

But that meant that she would have to dredge up that terrifying day where she'd had to kill—or be killed.

Stop thinking about it, Kate. You agreed to do it.

Armed with an Americano, she hurried to her car and tried to relax while she drove along Purcell's Cove Road to Frances' home at Chebucto Head. The Northwest Arm, a long dark blue finger of the Atlantic Ocean, gleamed.

Twenty minutes later, Kate turned onto the private road to her client's house. She thought that her memory had exaggerated its length, but no, it was a good hike from the main highway. Every pebble that crunched under her tires, every tree that she passed by, every single thing about this road set her heart jumping.

She was not on neutral territory. That was another reason she dreaded the interview. It was bad enough reliving the Body Butcher attack in front of thousands of viewers, but to do it at the place where, seventeen years ago, Kate had made the biggest mistake of her life…

Strange how time blurs so many memories, and then driving down a driveway in the early morning May sunshine brought back, in vivid detail, the dark May night when Kate was seventeen.

Her sister, Imogen, had fussed with her eye makeup in the passenger seat. She had been excited, full of nervous energy. Kate, however, was uneasy. Her sister had been acting strangely and Kate knew Kenzie Sloane was behind it. She was sure the only reason she had been invited to this party was to provide chauffeur service to her fifteen-year-old sister. But Kate had wanted to go, anyway. Everyone at her school—especially the in-crowd—was going, and she wasn't immune to the lure of hanging out with them.

The road had been lined with the poorly parked cars of her peers, most of them encroaching on the immaculate lawn. The dashboard of her car vibrated from the music pounding through the glass walls of the house. Imogen had been impatient, urging her to hurry while Kate trolled for a safe place to park their mother's car. As soon as she had backed the car into a spot, Imogen threw open the door and hurried to the house.

Three hours later, she was dead.

How many times had Kate wished she hadn't taken her sister to Kenzie's party?

Let me count the ways.

The final curve of the road crunched under the wheels of Kate's car. Frances Sloane's house came into view. She forced herself to exhale. *It's the past, Kate. You can't change it.*

Advocating for Frances to achieve a peaceful death

was perhaps her form of forgiveness. Of allowing that darkened recess of her heart to have light.

Yet she couldn't shake the feeling that something dark hovered over her head. No matter where she tried to hide, the dark bird of Death always found her.

It didn't help that Frances Sloane had left a trail of breadcrumbs for it.

Hopefully, that damned bird wouldn't assume they were meant for her.

Kate strode up the walkway, her heart hammering, studying her client's house. It had been designed to elicit intellectual awe rather than emotional attachment. And today, in the cool, clear May light, it appeared stark and unwelcoming.

She rang the doorbell. Phyllis answered the door with a warm smile. "Ms. Lange, please come in. I've been tidying the room for the interview."

"I'm sure it will be fine," Kate said. "We want to show what Frances' life is really like."

"Good. I think it's ready, then," Phyllis said. She left Kate at the entrance to the living room. "I'll go make some tea."

The living room was exactly as Kate remembered, and yet entirely unfamiliar. When she had last been here, the room had been crammed with excited, drunk, hot bodies dancing to The Cranberries' Celtic-flavored rock. Kate had vaguely recognized the song: "Salvation." That song had played over and over in Kate's head after Imogen's death, the lyrics frustratingly blurred in her memory. Four months after her sister's funeral—following an afternoon of binge-crying and self-recrimination—Kate bought the CD and read the lyrics on the insert.

She had been incredulous.

"Salvation" was an anti-drug anthem.

She had wondered if Kenzie played that song as a middle-finger salute to her parents.

And now, as Kate stepped into Frances Sloane's living room, the memory of that song bouncing off the full-length windows, the frenetic beat whipping the partygoers into a manic energy, barged into her consciousness.

Salvation.

Frances Sloane sat in her wheelchair by the massive windows that had deflected "Salvation" so long ago. Her gaze locked onto Kate's face—as if the sheer force of her stare would bring Kate to her.

Kate approached her client, briefcase in hand. The late morning light, streaming in through the glass, did little to warm the steel accents and angular structure of the room.

It did little to soften the ravages of the disease on Frances Sloane's face.

"Hello, Frances," Kate said, her voice unnaturally loud.

"Hello."

Her client's bravado from earlier in the week was not in evidence. Kate couldn't put her finger on it, but something had changed. Was she regretting her decision to fight this battle in the public forum?

Or had she sensed Kate's uneasiness at being in her home?

As Kate neared her, she realized that Frances' eyes appeared suspiciously wet. "I saw Kenzie yesterday. First time in seventeen years."

Whoa. Kate lowered herself into a chair.

She thought of her half-empty coffee cup in her car. She wished she had finished it.

She kept her voice neutral. "How is she?"

"She seems happy. She is a tattoo artist now."

"Really."

Kate was surprised—and yet she wasn't.

Kenzie had grown up with all the trappings and privileges of her parents' success. And had consistently thrown it in their faces. Becoming a tattoo artist was entirely consistent with Kenzie's behavior.

She had been the figurative Painted Lady of their school.

Was this another carnivalesque choice?

Or a true career?

"She's very successful," Frances added.

"Good." The faintest hint of nausea uncoiled in Kate's stomach. With the exception of the orange she had been slicing when Nat called, she had skipped breakfast in her rush to get ready, and now regretted it. She opened her briefcase and pulled out a notepad. "I wanted to run a few points by you. Key messages for the audience."

"I know what I want to say."

"Just in case—"

"I know what I want to say."

Kate smiled. "Good. Then I'll just have one more look at my own notes before Nat arrives."

She kept her head bowed, flipping through her speaking points, staring hard at the lines she had scrawled after her shower this morning. The words were weighty. She knew they could change lives.

But it was no use.

Her gaze kept drifting to the back porch.

Damn it.

The memories that had been crowding at the gates of Kate's subconscious now surged through the barrier.

Kate was getting bored. All around her, kids were obnoxiously drunk. And Tim Roth, one of the more popular guys on the school hockey team, would not leave her alone. At first, she had enjoyed his attention. Until she discovered that he was not interested in having a conversation.

She edged away, looking for her sister. She wanted to go. Now.

Behind her, a group of kids huddled together on the back porch. She knew what they were doing.

Then she saw her sister in the center of the group.

Imogen's brown hair fell in a gleaming wing across her face. Another girl leaned toward her, her hair molten copper. The way the girls huddled over the table reminded Kate of how she and her sister would crouch on the sidewalk to peer at a ladybug so many years ago. But they weren't young children anymore. They were in high school. And this wasn't one of nature's wonders at which Kenzie Sloane and Imogen gazed so hungrily.

Her sister's hair lifted in the breeze as she bent over and cut a line of coke.

The drunken antics of the partygoers around Kate took on an obscene quality.

So that was why her sister had been so irritable.

So remote.

So unlike the Imogen she'd taken care of for so long.

Imogen's shoulders rose as she inhaled sharply through the rolled five-dollar bill.

She was only fifteen.

And yet, this wasn't the first time. It was obvious from the ease with which Imogen cut the line, the intensity of her gaze. She wasn't scared or nervous.

She was hungry.

Desperate.

Her sister's shoulders relaxed as soon as she got her fix. Kenzie leaned close to her and murmured something in her ear. Imogen flung back her head and laughed. It was shrill, manic. Kenzie doubled over, tears streaming down her face. Then another girl joined in.

The laughter grew raucous. Her sister lifted the rolled bill in the air in a victory salute. She bent over the table.

No. Not more.

Kate pushed Tim aside and shouldered her way onto the porch.

"Imogen!" She grabbed her sister's shoulder. "What are you doing?"

Imogen shook herself out of Kate's grasp, giving Kate a defiant look. "Go away, Kate."

"You're coming with me," Kate said. She glared at Kenzie. "I can't believe you let my sister have this stuff!"

"It was easy. She wanted it." Kenzie's gaze was cool. "Time for you to leave, big sis." She flipped her hair over her shoulder.

"Gennie, it's time to go home." Imogen's eyes had a terrifyingly manic expression.

Don't let Gennie see your fear. Make her come.

Gennie's face flushed bright red. "I'm not leaving."

Kenzie patted the empty space next to her. "Come here, Immy."

Immy. Kate hated that nickname.

Imogen grinned and edged toward Kenzie.

Kate grabbed her sister's wrist. "You are coming with me. Now."

Anger beat the blood in Kate's head so hard, so fast, that she couldn't hear what was being said, couldn't see the faces of the kids around her. All she could focus on was the fact that Gennie, her best friend, confidante and little sister, was deserting her for something so seductive, so destructive that it terrified Kate more than anything had terrified her before.

She had to get her away from it.

And from the girl who supplied it to her.

Kate snatched the phone from a side table, waving it in front of the group. "If you don't come with me right now, Gennie, I'm calling the police!" She shook the receiver at her sister. "Now, Gennie!"

That threat—unlike all the others—got under Kenzie's skin. She flushed. "You wouldn't dare."

Kate shook her head. "Just watch."

"Don't, Kate. Please." Imogen shot a terrified look at Kenzie.

Kenzie's lips curled. "Tell me, Kate. Why do you think the police would believe the spawn of a con?"

Spawn of a con. *The words hung in the air. Crystal Burton snickered.*

Imogen's eyes widened.

But she didn't leave Kenzie's side.

Pain grabbed Kate's heart, squeezing and twisting it.

She put the receiver to her ear, her index finger hovering over the number nine. "Tell my sister to leave, Kenzie."

Imogen's gaze was expectant, but uncertainty lurked beneath the bravado.

Kenzie's gaze flickered past Kate's shoulder to a group of guys huddled outside. Her jaw tightened. "No. We have plans for tonight, right, Immy? And they don't include your sister."

Kate punched the numbers 9-1-1.

Kenzie shot her a look of such hate and anger that it took all of Kate's will not to shrivel.

She pressed the receiver against her cheek.

"Wait!" Kenzie half rose from the bench.

"911. What is your emergency?" the emergency response operator asked.

Kate's gaze locked with Kenzie's. Finally—thank God—Kate saw fear in her terrible sky-blue gaze.

Kenzie pushed Imogen's shoulder. She winced. "Go home. Tell your sister to stop." Then she lowered her voice and whispered something in Imogen's ear, but Kate couldn't hear because at that moment the emergency service operator repeated her question, her voice urgent: "911. What is your emergency?"

Kate cleared her voice. "I'm sorry. Wrong number." She hung up the phone. "Bet the police will come out to check, anyway."

Imogen threw her an anguished look. "I can't believe you did that!"

"We're going now. And we are never coming back."

"I am, Kenzie," Imogen said. "I'll see you tomorrow."

"No, you won't," Kate said, her voice grim.

The shocked silence in the room spoke volumes. She had crossed a line that sent her straight to pariah-ville. "Mom is going to ground you 'til the cows come home. And besides, Kenzie's going to be sitting in jail unless she gets smart and flushes all that coke down the toilet."

Kenzie's face had drained of color. "You bitch," she hissed. "You are going to rot in hell for this."

"See you there," Kate said. "Come on, Gennie."

Kate pasted a smile on her face, shaken by Kenzie's vituperation, the crowd parting before her as news of the phone call spread.

Someone spat on her sneaker.

She held her head high, cheeks flaming, ignoring the sobs of frustration coming from her sister. The night air cooled her flushed cheeks and she hurried across the lawn to her car. People had begun to trickle out behind her, spooked that the police might come.

As soon as Imogen flung herself in the front seat, Kate swung the car around and hit the gas.

Spawn of a con.

She clenched the wheel, her jaw tight.

"You are going to be in big trouble, Gennie," she said, her voice hoarse with anger. "Mom's going to ground you for weeks."

The tires squealed as she made the turn onto the highway. It was dark.

Black.

She peered into the night. She couldn't see a thing.

She'd forgotten to turn on the headlights.

She switched them on.

"I can't believe you humiliated me like that in front of my friends!" Gennie shouted, her face contorted with rage.

"Friends! What kind of friends are those?"

"Better friends than you are."

"Because they give you free coke?"

Imogen flushed. "So what?"

"You are fifteen years old, Gennie! Fifteen! You are throwing your life away!"

"But it makes me happy."

Happy.

When had they been happy?

Maybe before the summer she turned twelve. Before her father was charged with fraud and sentenced to prison.

Yes, they had been happy then.

"Lying makes you happy?" Kate said, her voice bitter. Yes, she could see now, with the painful, gut-

wrenching clarity of hindsight, that her sister had lied to her, over and over these past few months. And Kate, not ready to read the writing on the wall, had believed her.

"Lay off me, Kate. I wouldn't have lied if you weren't breathing down my neck all the time."

"Ha! That's a joke."

"No. The joke is you. Who do you think you are? You act like you're in charge of me, but you aren't. You're not Mom!"

"I was trying to help you—"

"Help me? You are going to be a laughingstock on Monday at school. And so will I. Because of you!"

Imogen's eyes were wild. Her face had contorted. Kate had never seen her like that. Rage leapt the few feet separating them as if it were a wildfire, gobbling the oxygen of their hurt.

Her sister's eyes filled with tears. "I hate you, Kate—"

The headlights caught the reflectors on the guardrail.

Kate gasped, jerking the steering wheel.

The tires hit the curve too fast, too wide, too everything.

Kate slammed on the brakes.

But it was too late.

Kate shook her head to rid her mind of the image of Gennie's expression just before life left it.

God. Stop.

Tears were perilously close. She lowered her head, aware of Frances' sharp gaze on her face.

Phyllis brought in a tray of tea holding a pot, and one cup. Frances could no longer safely swallow, but Phyllis poured a little into her feeding tube. "Ahh," Frances said. "Caffeine." Phyllis adjusted Frances' headrest and wiped the saliva that had pooled onto the collar of her blouse.

The doorbell rang.

It was Nat.

Get a grip, Kate. It's over, it's in the past, you've had your moment to wallow in it. Time to move on.

She exhaled and rose to her feet. Her silk blouse clung to her back. She was cold and hot at the same time. "I'll go let them in."

She exited the cavernous room, her heels clicking on the wooden floors, and opened the front door. Nat took one look at Kate and said, "Jeez, didn't you get any sleep last night?"

"Obviously not enough." She closed the door behind Nat and the cameraman.

Nat rooted around in her purse, and handed her a compact. "Here, put this on. All over your face. Otherwise, the audience will think you are the one with the incurable disease."

Then she threw Kate a stricken look. "Shit."

"Que sera, sera." Kate took the compact and flipped it open. Nat was right. She looked awful. The powder was dark, but when Nat saw Kate's skeptical look, she said, "Trust me. The light will wash you out."

It took Nat only a few minutes to hook them up to mics, and then they began the interview.

It had been a year since Kate had done a television interview—she had refused all requests after Randall Barrett's acquittal as she "wasn't authorized to speak on behalf of her client"—and she was initially tense.

Nat sensed Kate's anxiety and whispered, "I promise the audience will respect you in the morning." Then the camcorder light focused on them, and the interview began. Nat was relaxed, warm, empathetic. Kate was impressed with her questions about the disease, Frances' desire to die with dignity, and Kate's role in Frances' cause.

She gave the final word to Frances. Kate felt a surge of emotion tighten her throat as her client stared straight into the camera and asked: "How can wanting to die peacefully and with dignity be a crime? Isn't forcing someone to die a terrible death a crime? Where has our humanity gone?"

Nat let the question hang in the air. Then she said, "What is your next step, Mrs. Sloane?"

"I want to start a discussion in the public forum about this issue. Please contact my lawyer, Kate Lange, or my member of Parliament, Harry Owen, with your views. Death happens to everyone. But we should be able to choose how we end our lives."

After a second, the cameraman turned off the light on his camcorder.

Nat unclipped the mics, packed them in the bag, and within minutes, she and her cameraman were heading out the door. "I'll call you later and let you know how the footage turned out."

Kate nodded. "Thank you, Nat."

Nat squeezed her shoulder. "You did good." Kate closed the door, and exhaled. Her skin was clammy with sweat. She pasted a smile on her face and returned to the living room. Frances' eyes were closed, but she opened them when she heard Kate approach.

"That went well."

"Nat was pleased." Kate slid her notepad into her briefcase. She hadn't actually needed it. She had been so caught up in the interview—and Nat's questions had been so skillful—that everything she had wanted the public to hear had been said. "This is going to be aired tonight. I expect we'll get a lot of people responding to it. I will present the responses to Harry Owen. And we'll go from there."

"Thank you, Kate," Frances said. Her eyes were damp.

"It's what you hired me to do."

Hurt flashed so quickly through her client's eyes that Kate wasn't sure if she saw it. But it needed to be said.

"I'll call you after the interview airs," Kate said, picking up her briefcase. She turned to leave, relief already flooding through her, when Frances' voice slurred through the vast room.

"One last favor."

Damn. Kate had learned that those were never good words to hear, especially when they were uttered as she made her exit.

"Yes?"

"Look under the newspaper."

On a side table, out of sight of the television camera, sat the newspaper. Kate approached it as if it were a snake, lifting a corner with considerable reluctance.

Two envelopes lay under it. Kate's stomach sank even farther when she saw the names on them.

"The first one is for Kenzie." Frances struggled to enunciate her words.

"Why don't you give it to her?" Kate asked. She did not want to be in the middle of this estranged mother-daughter relationship.

"When I die. Please give it to her."

Kate started to shake her head but Frances said, "Please." Her eyes pleaded with Kate.

"What's in the envelope?" She could feel paper, but also something hard.

"It's a key. To a storage locker. Has Kenzie's things from her bedroom."

"The executor of your will should do this."

"It's my son." She swallowed. "They don't get along. He might not give it to her. You're my lawyer, Kate."

Kate exhaled. It was a slippery slope onto which she had stepped when she agreed to that first meeting with Frances. She really wanted to suggest she appoint a new executor—but had a strong suspicion that Frances would want her to do the job.

In for a penny, in for a pound. This was small change compared to the lobbying effort. She could simply mail the envelope to Kenzie after Frances' death and fulfill her obligation—without ever having to speak to her. "Okay."

She gave a questioning glance at the other envelope. It had her name written on it. "This is a small gift for you," Frances said. "Please don't open until I'm dead." She gave a weak smile. "You won't have to wait long."

"I hope it's not money beyond my fees. I couldn't accept it, Frances," Kate said.

"No. It's something more precious than that." Her gaze searched Kate's.

They must be photos. And if they were photos, they must be of Imogen—with Kenzie. Kate had a good collection of photos of her sister already, many of the two of them together. She wasn't sure if she wanted to see one of her sister with Kenzie.

"Thank you, Frances," Kate said.

Frances nodded, so exhausted her head barely moved. Kate slid the envelopes into her briefcase and hurried out of the house, as if by moving quickly all those terrible memories the house held would remain trapped within. The door closed with a hollow thud.

Kate drove down the long driveway, blocking images of the last time she had left this house, and instead noted that the leaf buds on the trees overhead were about to unfurl.

She turned onto the highway. She definitely deserved another cup of coffee.

As she passed the spot where she had crashed her car so many years ago, she glanced at the water.

It was a shining expanse of blue.

The sun glowed behind the fog, incandescent and mysterious.

Soon it would break through.

18

It was moments like these that made Ethan both love and hate his job. He stood on the front porch of the house belonging to the victim's parents, Allan and Cathy Rigby. Next to the entrance, the orange-pink petals of an azalea bush glistened in the softness of the morning light.

He yanked up the collar of his jacket and gave the property a once-over. It was a modest home, with pale yellow vinyl, a small yard and a little poodle that barked from the moment he rang the doorbell.

Heather had grown up in this house, according to his notes, and had still been living at home the night she went missing. She had possessed that cared-for look about her, he recalled. Hers was a safe neighborhood, a well-kept street, the kind of place that people bought to raise their kids with the confidence that all was right with the world. Their world, at least.

A man in his late fifties answered the door. He wore an open-necked blue and taupe checked shirt and tan trousers. Once upon a time, he was a suspect. Now, he was simply another grieving parent.

"Mr. Rigby?" Ethan said, holding up his badge. "I am Detective Ethan Drake, with HPD Cold Case."

"Detective, please come in."

Mr. Rigby led him to a living room decorated with pale blue curtains, beige fabric sofas and dark blue carpets. A woman whom he presumed was Heather's mother perched on the sofa. A tray of tea and small sugar cookies sat on the glass coffee table in front of her. "Detective, this is my wife," Allan Rigby said.

Distress had supplanted any welcome in Cathy Rigby's face. "You are sure it is Heather?" She clutched a large framed photo of her dead daughter, who smiled prettily into the camera.

An image of Heather's body lying in the peat bog superimposed itself in Ethan's mind. The memory of his shock of seeing her head, encased in a rubber witch's mask, kept popping into his head at unexpected moments, throwing him off stride.

He gave himself a mental shake, lowering himself into the chair facing the victim's parents. "The dental records are a match."

Cathy Rigby looked at her husband. He frowned at her. "My wife is worried that the police will stop looking for Heather because this body was found."

"Mr. and Mrs. Rigby," Ethan said. "Your daughter *has* been found. I'm sorry." He hesitated. Now was the moment to reveal his past association with her, as scant as it was. But he couldn't bring himself to breach that professional barrier. There was a reason it was in place. "Now we turn our efforts from searching for her to searching for her killer."

A sob broke out of Mrs. Rigby's throat, a harsh, cawing sound. "I hoped she was alive somewhere."

Her husband put his arm around her. "I know, Cathy,

I know." He gazed at Ethan. "We never gave up hope. Ever. Heather was a fighter. She would have found her way home if she could."

He had heard those words before. He knew, if he were in their shoes, he would believe them, hold on to them, keep them close to his heart. But the reality was Heather had probably been killed within hours of disappearing from the bar, had probably no chance of survival, no chance of escape, no inkling of what she had been up against. Killers had their own rules. Victims rarely understood how to react—until it was too late.

"I'm sorry," Ethan said. "We have evidence to suggest she was a victim of homicide."

"The night she went missing?" Hope and pain warred in Allan Rigby's face. Hope, that his daughter had been killed quickly and thus did not suffer unduly. Pain, that if she hadn't been killed that night, there had been a window of time to find her—and they had failed.

Ethan kept his gaze level. "We can't say for sure. The medical examiner is not able to give an exact time of death, it's been so long…" He deliberately trailed off.

"We read the papers," Mrs. Rigby said fiercely. "They are calling her the bog body. As if she was a specimen." Her lip quivered. She stared at the photo of her daughter. "No one is talking about *her*. About the fact that the 'bog body' was a real girl. Whose life was taken when she was much too young—" The sobs that had been building in her voice now erupted. "She was only eighteen! Eighteen! She was a good girl. She was in university. She was so full of life…." She buried her face. Her husband leaned over her, his eyes resigned, mute in the face of grief that was as stark and raw as when Ethan had seen them first interviewed on television seventeen years ago.

Sweat began to prickle his neck, his underarms.

Cathy Rigby wiped her eyes with the back of her hand. "We've had to live without her for seventeen years. Seventeen years of wondering where she was, what had happened the night she went missing, was she alive or dead, had someone hurt her…"

Mr. Rigby closed his eyes, his face working, his arm tight around his wife's shoulders.

"And now all they want to talk about is how a bog body has never been discovered in Canada before!"

"I understand how insensitive that is," Ethan said, treading carefully through the land mines of their grief. "The media are making a big deal about this. However, we have not released your daughter's name, so they can't really speak about the victim besides what they have found out for themselves. We plan to release your daughter's name to the press. But we are not going to share any more details beyond that due to the nature of our investigation."

"How was she murdered?" Mr. Rigby asked, his eyes reflecting an agony that Ethan had seen too many times. And still had not inured himself to.

"I can't give you more details than that while the in vestigation is under way. I am very sorry."

"Was she dismembered, like those other girls?" Mrs. Rigby asked, darting a terrified glance at her husband.

Ethan swore silently at the media. Heather Rigby's family had read the speculation about whether the bog body could have been "victim zero" of the Body Butcher.

"No. She was not. We do not believe, at this point in time, that her death was connected at all to the Body Butcher."

A tear rolled down Allan Rigby's cheek. "Thank God."

"I know that you've been asked these questions many times before, but I'd like to go through Heather's movements leading up to the night she went missing."

The tea and cookies went untouched—as Ethan knew they would—while he led Heather's parents through his questions. He was about halfway through, when he asked, "Did Heather have any piercings, tattoos or cosmetic surgery?"

"Like breast implants?" Mrs. Rigby asked. "No, she never had anything like that done. Did the body have it?"

Still hoping it's not your daughter.

"How about piercings or tattoos?"

"Well, she had her ears pierced, if that's what you mean. She was wearing earrings with skeletons dangling from them."

"I think she had her belly button pierced, too," her father murmured. Mrs. Rigby shot him a startled look.

Oh, so the father was in on his daughter's little rebellions.

"No, she didn't," Cathy Rigby said.

Allan Rigby gazed at Ethan with regret in his eyes. He didn't want to cause his wife more pain—he didn't want to remind her that her beloved daughter had concealed things from her.

"And tattoos? Any of those? Girls her age often got them on the lower back, the ankle, sometimes on the shoulder…."

"Absolutely not," Cathy Rigby said. "She knew our opinion about those."

Ethan looked at Allan Rigby. He shook his head. "None that I am aware of," he said.

"Did she have a fascination with birds? You know, did she collect pictures or have a pet bird, or anything like that?" Ethan asked. Cathy Rigby was already mouthing no before Ethan had finished.

"No, I don't think so," Allan Rigby said.

"Any other animals or mystical creatures?" The tattoo artist could have been wrong. Never hurts to check.

"She loved rabbits. We had one when she was a little girl. She called it Fou Fou. You know, after the song 'Little Rabbit Fou Fou'?" Cathy Rigby stared at the photo in her lap. "She really loved that bunny."

Ethan wrote down "rabbit." Could the raven actually be a rabbit? Seemed unlikely that a rabbit could be mistaken for a bird, but nonetheless...

The rest of the questions yielded nothing new. Ethan stood, relieved to have this duty completed. He had tried to be as compassionate and respectful as possible.

When he walked outside, he heard the dog run after him. "Come here, Fou," Cathy Rigby called. He glanced over his shoulder.

She picked up the poodle, and buried her face in his fur.

19

Kate drove into the parking garage, mulling over the interview she and Frances had just given. Had they said enough to motivate the public to call Harry Owen's office and force him to change his mind?

Her phone rang. "Kate Lange."

"It's Enid." Her elderly neighbor's voice sounded weak, breathless. Not like Enid at all.

Enid Richardson lived two houses down from Kate. Fifteen months ago, when Kate bought a house in her old neighborhood, Enid and her sister Muriel befriended her. No matter the Richardson sisters weren't related by blood to Kate, they had shown in so many ways that they considered her a cherished member of their singular lives. Honorary niece, goddaughter, whatever.

"Are you all right, Enid?" She most definitely did not sound all right.

"It's my heart. I can't get up."

Can't get up? Enid was the most energetic, unstoppable woman Kate knew. "Okay. Just stay there. I'll be right over." Kate did a 180 in the parking garage. As soon as the parking exit barrier lifted, she hit the gas.

Ten minutes later, Kate unlocked the door to the old

Victorian home of the Richardson sisters and rushed inside.

"Enid?" she called, running into the kitchen. It was empty.

She sprinted upstairs. Although she knew the Richardson sisters quite well by now, she rarely went to the upper level of their home. "Enid?"

No answer.

The first door on the left was Enid's bedroom.

"Enid!" Kate cried.

Enid lay on the bed, her breathing short and rapid. "It's my heart. I took the nitro…but it hasn't helped." She paused for breath.

"I'm calling an ambulance."

Enid's lack of protest was indicative of how badly she felt, Kate realized as she dialed 911.

The dispatcher answered on the first ring.

"My neighbor is in heart failure," she said, trying to keep her voice calm. "We need an ambulance."

"What are her symptoms?"

"She's short of breath. Sweating. She can't walk. She says her medication isn't helping."

"We'll be there in less than ten minutes. Stay with her."

As if she would leave her.

"Please go to Muriel," Enid whispered. "I told her to have a nap. But she'll be scared when the ambulance arrives."

Kate hurried from the room. Muriel's door was shut. She paused outside, listening. She heard a tell-tale snore. She wouldn't disturb the elderly lady until the ambulance arrived.

She rushed back to Enid's bedroom, checking her

color carefully. Had her lips become more purple? Had her breathing worsened?

"I'm sorry," Enid whispered. "This is such a bother for you, Kate."

I'm the one who is sorry. This is my fault.

Neither Enid nor her sister Muriel had been the same since they had been trapped by Elise Vanderzell's killer last summer. Both had grown noticeably frail. Kate had watched their decline, trying to keep her anxiety and guilt at bay. But seeing the once-vibrant Enid unable to lift her head off the pillow terrified her.

"Can you stay with Muriel while I'm in hospital?" Enid asked. "She knows you."

"Absolutely—"

The strident wail of the ambulance announced the arrival of the paramedics. Kate sprang to her feet and ran downstairs to the front door to admit the Emergency Medical Technicians. She followed them as they ran up the stairs with a stretcher.

It was only then that Kate saw Muriel. She stood by Enid's door, wearing her big black coat. Her hair hung in limp strands around her face. "Enid?" she asked. "Enie? What's wrong?"

Kate took Muriel's arm and drew her away from the doorway. "She'll be okay."

Muriel pulled her arm out of Kate's grasp. She returned to the doorway. "What's wrong with Enid? What's the matter?" Tears gleamed in her eyes. "What did they put on her face?"

"It's an oxygen mask," Kate said. "She's not feeling well, Muriel. They are helping her."

The EMTs strapped Enid into the stretcher. Kate's heart constricted. The elderly lady appeared shrunken as she was carried down the stairs. Enid gave her sister a thumbs-up, unable to speak with the mask on her face, and then let her eyes droop closed. Her eyelids were tiny mollusk shells, bruised and blue against her bloodless face. Kate put an arm around Muriel's shoulders.

"Muriel and I will come as soon as we can," Kate called, not sure if Enid could hear her.

Please don't die.

"Where are they taking her?" Muriel asked, trying to shake off Kate's arm. "I want to go with them."

"She's going to the hospital. We'll go very soon."

"The hospital?" Terror flashed through Muriel's eyes. "Enid has to go to the hospital?" She began to cry. "No, not the hospital!"

Kate didn't know why Muriel was so upset about the hospital, and wished she could take back the words. It took her fifteen minutes to calm her down, although she suspected it was the presence of Muriel's cat, Brulée, that soothed the Alzheimer's-stricken woman.

Now Muriel sat at the kitchen table, threading Brulée's tail through her fingers. Kate put on the kettle. "Would you like some tea?"

"When is Enid coming back home?" Muriel asked.

"Soon, Muriel."

Muriel started to rock. "Where did she go?"

"She's at the doctor's." Kate said the words tentatively, hoping that Muriel's experiences at her doctor's office were better than the hospital. Muriel nodded, fingering the cat's tail. Kate exhaled. Another land mine avoided.

The kettle boiled. "Let's have some tea," Kate said, relieved she could offer this comforting routine to Muriel.

While Muriel drank her tea, Kate called Finn, the shaggy blond dog walker-cum-Guy Friday who had proven his friendship time and time again. His voice mail answered. *Damn.* "Finn, it's Kate. Please pick up."

He didn't. She called again. Voice mail.

This time she left him a message. "Please call me at Enid's house. It's urgent." She couldn't take Muriel to the hospital with her; it was too confusing and upsetting for her. But she desperately wanted to go the hospital and stay with Enid.

She found the ancient address book that Enid kept in a kitchen drawer. The Richardson sisters had several close friends, and searching through the book filled with crossed-off names underscored Kate's worry about Enid. Would she become a scratched-out entry in some other friend's worn address book?

Stop being morbid, Kate. She tried to funnel her worry into more productive channels, so she called the homes of Enid's friends. Her relief was almost palpable when one of them answered. Kate knew Mary was one of the Richardsons' closest, oldest friends, but even so, when she offered to spend the night with Muriel, Kate hesitated. "I told Enid I would stay with Muriel."

"Listen, Kate. I can only do tonight," Mary said. "My granddaughter is coming on a visit tomorrow. Don't worry, Muriel still knows who I am. Give yourself the night off, because you could be in for a long week."

"Thank you," she said. It would give her a chance to check on Enid in the hospital, do her laundry and catch up on the Sloane file.

"I'll be over in an hour."

"Thank you," she said again. She hung up the phone and turned to Muriel. "Do you want to watch some TV, Muriel? I can put on *Fawlty Towers* for you."

"That would be nice," Muriel said. They went into

the sitting room. While Muriel watched the show, Kate called the hospital to get an update on Enid's status.

The doorbell rang just as she got off the phone.

Kate hurried to the front door. It was Finn. She almost melted with relief.

He stepped inside and followed her to the kitchen, a concerned expression on his face. "I just got your messages. What's wrong?"

Kate leaned against the kitchen counter. "It's Enid. She's in the hospital. Her heart is acting up."

"Oh, no. That's terrible."

"I know. I'm really worried about her." She felt the tension ease from her shoulders. It was good to be able to share her worry with someone who knew and cared about Enid.

"How's she doing?"

"She's stable. She's in the E.R., still waiting for a hospital bed."

"Sorry I didn't get your call right away."

"It's okay." Finn's personal life was still a mystery to her. He spent a lot of time at her house, but she knew very little about him, except that his family lived on the West Coast, where he had attended university before dropping out and heading east. *They wanted me to be a dentist,* he'd once said, rolling his eyes. "How long do you think Enid will be in the hospital?"

"They thought a few days."

"What are we going to do about Muriel?"

"I'm going to call some home-care agencies as soon as they open. I thought we could get someone to help during the day, and then you and I could take turns at night starting tomorrow." She held her breath. Finn had no obligation at all to help the elderly sisters, but she knew he had a soft spot for them. *Who wouldn't?*

"Sounds good."

Kate exhaled in relief.

"I'll check in on you after I take the dogs for their walk," he added. "I'll do that right now." He headed to the door. There was a stain—looked like pus—on the back of his T-shirt, by the shoulder.

"Finn, did you cut yourself?" Kate pointed to the spot.

He shook his head. He had a strangely bashful expression on his face. "I was…um…gonna surprise you."

That didn't sound good.

"Oh?"

"I got a tattoo." He grinned, pride and excitement all over his face. It was hard to resist Finn when he smiled like that, but Kate felt a little twist in her heart nonetheless. *He's your friend, Kate. Nothing else. He doesn't have to share every detail of his life with you.*

He pulled his T-shirt over his head, wincing a little when the fabric stuck to the fluid dried on his skin.

"Let me help you." Kate eased the stiff patch off his skin. His shoulder, once so smooth and tanned—she'd seen it many times last summer while he worked on her home—had a large bandage taped to it.

Pus stained the gauze, crusting the skin below it. "It looks infected," Kate said.

"Where?"

"I can't tell with the bandage on it."

"Lift up one side. Then you can see it."

She had the feeling he was more interested in showing off his tattoo than investigating his infection. As a precaution, Kate washed her hands before lifting one edge of the bandage.

"It's not too infected," she said. "Just on the edges."

"But do you like it?" Finn asked. "It's a Foo Dog, the symbolic protector of the home."

Kate studied the tattoo. The Foo Dog crouched on his shoulder. It had been so artfully created that it appeared to be breathing, its muscles tightening, ready to spring against any foe.

"Yeah. I love it." She forced enthusiasm into her voice. "It's really striking." It *was* really striking.

It just wasn't Finn.

Or at least the Finn she thought she knew. When had he changed? Why hadn't she noticed? Even though the redecorating of her main floor had been completed in the fall, she still saw him almost every Sunday, when he, the Richardson sisters and Kate would meet for Sunday-night dinner.

His voice slightly defensive, Finn added. "When Yoshi—" *Yoshi? Who was Yoshi?* She really didn't know any of his friends, she realized "—told me that Kenzie Sloane was going to be a guest artist at his shop, I decided to get this piece done. She's considered one of the best artists of the Japanese style on this continent."

Oh, God. You can't be serious. "Kenzie?"

"Kenzie Sloane. She's from here but lives in New York now." Finn pulled his arm back through his sleeve and winced. "Still a bit tender."

Most people are after an encounter with Kenzie. She exhaled. So, Frances had been correct when she said her daughter was a successful tattoo artist.

"Are you planning to get more?" Kate asked.

Finn shook his head. "I don't think so. Although she thought I should get a matching one on the other side."

I'll bet she did.

Kenzie was putting her mark on him.

And he'd never be the same.

Don't say anything you'll regret, Kate.

"You need to keep an eye on the infection. So it doesn't get worse."

"I'll get Kenzie to check it," he said. "I'm walking her dog for her. Alaska likes pugs." He kept his tone light, but a faint blush tinged his cheeks.

Oh, God. Not you, too, Finn.

Kenzie Sloane had stolen Imogen from her in the worst possible way: through addiction. And now she was about to poach one of the good guys.

"You'd better get home and put some antibiotic cream on your tattoo," Kate said. "I'll wait until Enid's friend arrives."

He nodded. "You sure you don't need anything else?"

"No. But I bet Enid would love it if you called her."

"I'll take a detour down to the E.R. before I walk the dogs. Just to say hi."

Bless you, Finn.

He left, hands shoved in his pockets. The stain was barely visible on his shoulder.

She hoped that Foo Dog would guard his back.

20

You can prepare yourself for days, months, *years*, but still not be prepared. It was like deciding to get a tattoo, savoring the design, imagining the art on your flesh—*in* your flesh—and then wincing from the first sting of pain when the needle penetrates the skin.

McNally had just taken a bite of pizza when the door to Yakusoku Tattoo opened. He slid down in his seat and peered out from under his ball cap.

Konzie Sloane hurried out, her kit bag on her shoulder, holding the leash of a little black dog.

McNally spat his mouthful of pizza onto his plate. He wiped the back of his mouth with his sleeve. And stared.

It had been seventeen years.

Seventeen years of wanting. Waiting.

Hating.

Her hair was longer than the photo he'd seen of her in *ExtINKshun!* magazine. It curled in the damp, tentacles of dark red whipping around her face. Medusa in hi-def. The tentacles reached toward him, sensing his presence, and then whipped away from her face. The light caressed her neck, and the purity of her porcelain skin through the design of her tattoo made his throat ache.

Oh, God.

He thought he could handle seeing her. That the long-ing he felt could be tamped down.

But it spilled through him, boiling and raging, the magma of betrayal and unrequited love.

When they had been together, everyone had always talked about Kenzie's eyes—the remarkable sky-blue shade, the tilted shape, the way she could slay you with a glance from under her delicate lids.

But for him, it had always been her neck that had driven him crazy. He'd stroked that neck, kissed that neck, bitten that neck. But it wasn't enough. It had never been enough.

His gut clenched. Her neck was covered in tatts. She had made sure that he would never be able to tattoo her neck now.

But what about the raven?

Was it still there on the back of her neck?

She yanked the collar of her jacket higher as if sens-ing his searching gaze and glanced over her shoulder. He averted his eyes, suddenly nervous. She disappeared down the driveway to the back of the building. He took a deep breath. *Take it easy, McNally. She won't like it if you are all freaked out on her.*

He jumped out of his car and smoothed his hair, an automatic gesture from the years before he had shaved his head. Nervous sweat pricked his T-shirt.

What would she say?

Would she be happy to see him?

Would she kiss him hello?

He still remembered how her lips felt, how they clung to him, how they teased him, taunted him, made him scream in the agony of pain-drenched pleasure that was a Kenzie specialty. *Redheads don't feel pain,* she had told him.

He hurried down the driveway to the rear parking lot, searching for the whirlpool of red hair. At first, he didn't see her. She was bent over the passenger side of her car, strapping her dog into the seat.

He could pinpoint the moment she saw him. *Really* saw him.

The shock of recognition.

The disbelief.

He smiled at her. Fear was good.

He could do a lot with fear.

She rushed around the hood of her car, trying to reach the driver's side.

Her hand was on the door when he blocked her escape.

"Kenzie."

Up close, she was older than the Kenzie in his dreams. Her face was more defined, her makeup more skilled.

"Stay away," she said, her voice tense.

He flinched. "I need to talk to you."

"You are the last person I want to talk to."

"Kenzie. Please." He hated the pleading note that had crept into his voice. He cleared his throat. "I just want to talk."

His hand trembled with the effort of keeping it by his side. He longed—*ached*—to touch her hair.

It gleamed in the sunlight. Shades of red, each highlight more glittering and complex than the last.

"Haven't you seen the news?" she hissed. "We should not be seen together."

"We can meet at my place—"

She was already shaking her head. "I don't want to talk to you. Ever."

She opened the car door. Before he could grab her arm, she dove into the driver's seat, slamming the door shut.

She just missed his fingers.

"Hey!" he shouted, pounding on the window.

She turned on the engine, slammed the gear into Drive and hit the gas.

Her eyes flashed at him.

Those merciless eyes.

He jumped backward. His heart pounded as he watched her car disappear down the driveway.

She had left him.

Again.

How the fuck had he let that happen?

He'd been too nice to her, that's what had happened. His head had been so messed up imagining her lips that he had been totally unprepared for the real Kenzie.

The heartless Kenzie.

The bitch Kenzie.

Who the fuck did she think she was?

Seventeen years ago, she had run away, leaving him with a dead body to dispose of.

She thought because she had managed to escape that night that she could do it again.

He stalked back to his truck.

She had no idea who she was messing with.

He had been young, naive, when he met Kenzie. She had wrapped him around her little finger. She was willing to try things, do things—things that no other girl would ever do.

And in return, she had goaded him to prove his love.

He had proven his love beyond what any ordinary man would do. He had demonstrated the lengths he would go for her. He had given up his whole future to please her.

And what had she done?

She had left him holding the bag and disappeared without a word.

It had turned out perfectly for her: she had gotten away with murder and followed her dreams.

He needed to make her realize that she could try to cover her true nature in symbolic Japanese art, but the tattoos couldn't conceal her soul.

Kenzie was as cold-blooded as he was.

In fact, more so.

Then he grinned. She didn't realize it, but when she chose to ink a koi on her chest—her symbol of "transformation"—her subconscious had kicked in.

Fish were cold-blooded, right?

21

The key card shook in Kenzie's hand as she slid it into the lock on the door to room 549. She had kept her nerves under tight control after her run-in with McNally and the two hours previous to that while she inked her last client. Her fingers would no longer hold steady. It was a good thing her clients couldn't see her now. They would never let her go near them with a needle.

After three attempts, the green light on the lock blinked and she pushed the door open.

Foo rushed in, knowing that this signaled his mealtime. Kenzie dropped her kit bag to the floor, locked the door behind her, and hurried into the tiny white kitchenette of her generic hotel suite. Within a minute, Foo had been served his dinner and it had been consumed. He now licked his bowl, either hoping for magical food to appear, or savoring the micro dust left by his kibble.

A message blinked on the desk phone. She ignored it.

Her brain still processed her encounter with McNally in the parking lot.

One minute she'd been strapping Foo into his seat, the next minute she was confronted with the person who had forced her to flee Halifax a lifetime ago.

It *was* a lifetime ago and it had shov n on John McNally. She knew he had been in prison, but even if the thicker build and jailbird tatts hadn't given that away, it was evident in the harsh lines etched in his face. Gone was the smooth-cheeked passionate wanna-be rocker of her youth, whose handsome features were made edgy not by years spent in an eight-by-eight cell, but by his punk haircut. In its stead was a physically threatening man, with a buzz cut, goatee and a look of desperation in his eyes.

That look, more than anything else, convinced her that the body in the peat bog was indeed Heather Rigby's.

It could be no one else.

She had fled before Heather's body had been disposed of. She had guessed that Lovett and McNally tipped her over the edge of the cliff. Not buried her in a peat bog. What the hell were they thinking?

But they hadn't been thinking that night.

She closed her eyes. She wished she had never come to Halifax, she wished she had never left her apartment in Manhattan.

She wished, as she had wished a thousand times before—until she knew it was a barren trench into which she had dug herself—that she had never met McNally.

Her fingers scrabbled for the remote. She turned on the TV, standing in front of the small flat screen, flipping channels until the supper-time news came on. She waited, impatient to learn more about the discovery of Heather's corpse. Halfway through the local news segment, the anchor provided an update on the "bog body."

She sank down onto the sofa.

Everything came rushing back to her: the rubber Halloween mask, the naked girl, the rope…

The rope.

The tantalizing, pleasure-inducing, terrifying rope.

But it hadn't started with a rope.

It had started with a gun.

Months before they picked up Heather Rigby at the Mardi Gras.

The first time they played was at two o'clock in the morning, after a gig. McNally had pulled his grandfather's service revolver out from under his bed.

"Holy shit, you've got a gun?" Lovett chortled.

Kenzie had stared at it. It looked like an adult version of her brother's toy guns that he had flourished with great machismo when they played cowboys and Indians as little kids.

She couldn't tear her eyes away from it. She had never seen a real one before.

McNally held the revolver up to the light. "It was my grandfather's. It's an Enfield No.2 Mk I."

"Lucky you," Lovett said, his gaze avid. "I'd die to have one of those."

McNally pointed the gun at Lovett's head. "You can have a bullet, instead." He grinned.

"Hey!" Lovett flinched.

"Hey, what?" McNally mocked. "It's not loaded."
His finger caressed the trigger.

"You idiot! If it was loaded, you could have shot someone! The hammer has no spur."

Kenzie had no idea what Lovett was talking about, but he seemed pissed.

"So what?" McNally's voice was casual, but his gaze sharpened.

"The spur on the hammer was removed from the Enfield during World War Two because it kept getting caught on things inside the tanks."

McNally had lost his smirk. "So?"

"It makes it a double-action revolver."

At Kenzie's blank stare, Lovett added, "You don't have to keep cocking the hammer. Once it's cocked, you just have to pull the trigger to empty the cylinder."

Clearly wanting to demonstrate that he was the real expert in the room, McNally released the lock on the cylinder and pushed down on the front of the barrel. The action pushed the cylinder upward, exposing six empty bullet chambers. "See? There's a hinge at the bottom. Makes it easy to load." He grabbed a box of bullets. The box looked like a cigarette package, but made of heavy brown paper. There was some kind of serial number, with the words: 12 Cartridges Revolver—380-inch, with the date stamped on it 24 JUL 1942. "These are military issue."

Envy twisted Lovett's mouth. "You are so lucky. Those are hard to come by."

McNally loaded bullets in five of the chambers. "You need to leave one empty, otherwise it could discharge accidentally if you drop it." He snapped the barrel up, locked the cylinder, cocked the hammer, and pointed the barrel at a flower vase sitting on his bureau, all in one smooth motion.

Kenzie didn't even see him pull the trigger. She heard the gun fire, saw the vase explode into smithereens, smelled the gun smoke. "Sorry, Grandma." McNally grinned.

Lovett snickered.

McNally fired again. The bullet grazed the lamp. He blew gun smoke from the barrel and smiled. "Bingo."

"You can blow your brains out doing that, McNally," Lovett said. "There's still a bullet left."

"Oh, yeah?" McNally flipped off the lock on the

cylinder. But instead of breaking open the revolver, he spun the cylinder and locked it. He held the gun to his head. "Bang, bang, I'm dead."

"John, don't—!" Kenzie screamed.

Lovett stared at him, fear mingling with excitement in his eyes.

McNally pulled the trigger.

He fell backward, moaning.

"John!"

Then Kenzie realized she had not heard gunfire.

She shook him. "You faker."

He grinned. "Your turn." He thrust the gun at her.

"Me?" Her heart lurched at the look in McNally's eyes. "No way."

He grabbed her hand, uncurled her palm and placed the gun in it.

Kenzie stared at the revolver. A sculpture of extinction. Or rebirth. Depending on your beliefs.

Her fingers curled around the grip. It felt so natural, that she relaxed. She hefted the weight of the cold metal in her palm. It felt good.

She held in her hand the power to end a life.

Her blood surged.

McNally grabbed her wrist and forced the gun up to her temple.

"Stop it, John." She tried to shake him off but he wouldn't let go.

He pressed the gun to her temple.

"Shoot it."

"No!"

"You scared, Kenz?" he asked, his voice soft, teasing. "You want to be a tattoo artist and you're scared of one little bullet? You need balls to be a tattooist, Kenzie. Balls."

Lovett gave a slow smile.

The air was thick from her sweat, the booze exuding from McNally's pores, the animal excitement that both McNally and Lovett gave off. Kenzie could hardly breathe.

"Do it, Kenz," McNally breathed in her ear. She shivered. His breath was moist, warm, erotic. "Do it for me, baby."

Her nerves screamed with an exhilarating rush of fear and adrenaline.

Do it.

Her finger tightened on the trigger.

Do it.

She pulled the trigger.

The sex they had that night was the best sex they'd ever had.

Kenzie had packed her memories of that night with Heather Rigby—and the months leading up to it—into a tidy little box, along with her passion for the fiddle and any goodness that she'd once possessed, and buried the box in a tiny corner of her memory.

And she'd done everything she could to preserve the entombment of those memories—she left her home, deserted her friends, abandoned her family and struck out on her own. She had slept her way into a tattoo apprenticeship and used every skill at her disposal to create the KOI brand.

She wasn't going to let those memories be exhumed now. She wasn't going to let all those years of damned hard work go down the drain.

She wasn't going to let herself get caught now.

Why had McNally come to see her today? What was so important that he was willing to risk being seen in public with her—one day after Heather Rigby's body was discovered?

He was no fool.

Her cell phone rang. It better not be her mother. No, the call screen flashed the number for Yakusoku Tattoo.

"Kenzie?"

"Hey." She exhaled. "What's up, Yoshi?"

"Listen, we are getting many, many phone calls from customers wanting to book with you. Would you consider staying a few days extra?"

She almost laughed. "Sorry, can't do that. I've got some stuff to attend to back in New York."

"Of course, I understand, Kenzie." There was silence. She sensed his hesitation. "I'm wondering if you could do one extra client tomorrow. She's a special client. It would be a great favor." Knowing Yoshi and the über-politeness that had been ingrained in him, Kenzie recognized how important this must be to him.

She closed her eyes. Every cell of her body urged her to leave Halifax before it was too late. But she knew that would be a big mistake. If she was connected to Heather Rigby's murder, high-tailing it the day after the body was discovered was a sure sign she was running away from something.

No. She should stay and act as if nothing had changed. And take her scheduled flight back to New York on Monday.

"Yes, of course. Just add your client to my schedule."

"Arigato," he said, his voice soft. "See you tomorrow."

"See you tomorrow." Kenzie exhaled.

Speaking with Yoshi had its usual calming effect. She had panicked when she saw McNally, maybe because she was used to being in control.

She stripped off her clothes and ran the bath.

The warmth of the water relaxed her. As did her ritual of gently washing her tattoos. Each one on her leg was a token that had been earned, a reminder of what she had lost or gained.

When she decided to train in *tebori* and learn the secrets of Japanese *horimono* from the masters, she devoted her upper body to Japanese designs. The image of the koi had spoken to her the moment she saw it. A symbol of transformation in Japanese and Chinese mythology, the koi represented wisdom, knowledge and loyalty. In the traditional fable, a koi traveling up a waterfall symbolized courage and an aspiration to overcome life's obstacles. If it reached the Dragon's Gate, it would transform into a dragon—a most powerful symbol.

Kenzie had no desire to become a dragon. For her, life was about change and fluidity. Horifuyu, one of the great masters, tattooed the koi on her upper body. It began under her left breast, traveled diagonally across her chest, until the head of the fish curled around the right side of her neck.

Every time she looked at it, she felt a sense of accomplishment. She had grunted away for years as an apprentice, honing her craft, deflecting the occasional sexist attitude of her coworkers or clients, and clawed her way to artistic prominence. She had picked up the pieces of her shattered life and made something of herself.

She worked hard to remove any reminder of the girl she had been in Halifax. Including the tattoo McNally had inked just below the back of her neck.

Yoshi had created a most exquisite peony over it.

Calmer now, she stepped out of the bath.

Just four days of scaling this waterfall.
She had been through worse.
You are a wily old carp, Kenzie.

22

McNally had parked behind a large SUV, farther down the street. His camera sat on the seat beside him.

Tall, slim, her brown hair pulled into a ponytail, Kate Lange was so much *more* than he remembered. Perhaps because Imogen had been the one that people had gravitated toward. Imogen, with her laughing brown eyes, her impish smile. She had captured the light; Kate had moved with the shadows.

That had been seventeen years ago. Somewhere along the way, Kate Lange had torn through the tightly woven chrysalis of her younger insecurities. She had emerged strong. Feisty. A monarch of monarchs.

For her, a butterfly tattoo would be appropriate. In bold orange and black.

Although he could imagine a tiger in the same colors, crawling along her back, ready to pounce on any man who was not her match. Yes, a tiger tattoo would be most fitting for Ms. Lange.

It was funny—he had thought the same thing about Kenzie when he first met her. With her deep red hair and glittering eyes, she had immediately reminded him of a predatory cat.

Kate's coloring was more subdued, although her eyes had an amber glint to them that was most definitely feline.

But it was more than outward appearances. Or even the way she moved.

There was something in her—a tightly suppressed energy, a suggestion that those lithe legs could uncoil at any moment—that was feral.

Powerful.

Exciting.

She was way too confident, way too proud.

She probably thought she was hot stuff, killing a serial killer.

It was time to give her a taste of what was to come.

He slipped a rope over her head, flipping her brown locks tenderly out of the way. He slid the knot until it was snug against her throat. She gazed at him, eyes defiant, lips curled in a snarl, her body twitching. He held up the other end of the rope until her eyes shone with anger. With fear.

"*Nice kitty,*" *he said.*

John McNally was back.

Ethan rubbed his hair dry with a towel and threw it on his bed. He had done a quick workout on the treadmill after supper, and then had taken a shower, just in case….

He had watched Kate on the supper-time news with her client Frances Sloane. Most people wouldn't have caught it, but he had seen the distress lurking behind her steady gaze as she discussed why surviving the Body Butcher attack had made her an advocate for assisted suicide.

He turned away from his reflection in the bathroom mirror.

He needed to talk to her. He couldn't stand it any longer. The frustration. The longing. The pain.

Especially when he was so sure it didn't have to be that way.

He picked up the phone.

Just do it, Drake.

His fingers had never forgotten Kate's number. He dialed it quickly, not letting himself think about what would happen if she hung up on him.

She answered on the third ring. "Hello?"

"Kate?"

He felt her shock of recognition bounce through the cellular waves. "It's Ethan."

Kate dropped the newspaper she had been reading when she heard Ethan's voice.

"Hi."

"How are you?" Ethan asked, concern in his voice. "I saw your interview on TV earlier. I wanted to make sure you were okay. The media are all over the Body Butcher anniversary."

Kate glanced down at the papers that straggled by her feet. As if the media hadn't had their cup overflowing with the bog body investigation, this week heralded the anniversary of the Body Butcher's death—by her hand. The front page was devoted to the bog body murder and the Body Butcher anniversary, of course seeking to tie them to one another. She had skimmed those sections. But she had faltered when she read the victims' families' recollections. Especially those of her grief-stricken former client Marion MacAdam, whose granddaughter had been the Body Butcher's first obvious victim. A photo of Lisa, whom Kate had never met but would never forget, had been tucked into the body of the article. "Lisa's death has left a large hole in my life. She didn't deserve to die like that," Marion had told the paper.

No. She did not.

"I'm okay." She gave a shaky laugh. "I knew the papers would mark the occasion, but I hadn't realized they'd put it on the front page."

"Listen," Ethan said. "Do you want to go grab a coffee tonight and catch up?"

Whoa. She hadn't expected that.

She shifted, the newspapers collapsing around her feet.

What the hell. It sure beat thinking about how she had failed Marion MacAdam a year ago. Or worrying that she was failing Frances Sloane. And it would take her mind off Enid. "Sure."

"Great." He sounded a bit surprised. She was surprised, too, at the alacrity with which she accepted his invitation. "How about Starbucks in half an hour?"

"See you then."

Kate hung up the phone and ran upstairs, the newspapers still lying haphazardly on the floor.

She knew if she stopped to think about it, she'd wish she had said no.

So she didn't stop.

23

A knock on the door jolted Kenzie.

"Room service!" a man's voice called.

Foo began to bark.

Room service?

She hadn't ordered room service.

She forced herself not to panic. McNally wouldn't be that stupid.

Would he?

Foo's barking intensified.

"Hey, Foo, calm down," the voice on the other side of the door said. "Kenzie, it's me, Finn. I was just joking."

She pulled the belt of her robe tighter, and hurried to the door. A peek through the peephole confirmed it was, indeed, her client of today. He smiled, aware of her scrutiny.

Damn.

She was not in the mood for casual conversation.

On the other hand, after McNally's surprise visit today, maybe having a guy around would keep McNally at a distance. She had seen the look of fury in his eyes when she drove away.

She unlocked the door. "Finn, hi."

"Hi. I left you a message…." He shrugged. "I know you are only in town for a few days, so I was hoping I could take you out for dinner."

"Oh." She drew the robe closer around her throat. "I suppose so."

"Hey, if this is a bad time…"

"No! No, not at all." She stepped away from the door. "Come on in. I'll throw some clothes on."

Foo jumped on the bed while she dressed. He watched her, his brow furrowed. Her unease worsened. What if McNally found her room and broke in? What if he found Foo?

She knew it wasn't very probable—but then, neither was the discovery of Heather Rigby's remains, or of McNally seeking her out on her second full day in Halifax.

She scooped up Foo and strode into the living area of her suite. Finn sat on the edge of the sofa, his hands casually clasped between his knees. He wore jeans and a fresh T-shirt. When he saw her, he smiled. "You look great."

She felt a bit of the day's tension ease in the glow of his appreciation. "Look, I was wondering…could we order room service? I'm beat. I just arrived yesterday and had a crazy busy day today…."

"Sure, no problem." He picked up the hotel menus from the coffee table. "I'm always a sucker for room service."

"Me, too." She grinned and sat down next to him.

His warm, solid presence eased the cold lump in her chest.

Inevitably, the conversation turned to tattoos. The power of the medium. The reasons for people getting them. Some of Kenzie's more bizarre requests. Their food arrived and they dug in.

Then Finn said, "Did you know that tattoos can last beyond the grave?"

A chill skittered down her arms. "What do you mean?"

"I heard on the news today that the dead girl they found in the bog had a tattoo. The police were actually able to re-create it."

Kenzie bent over to sip her water, letting her hair fall over her face.

Shock ran in icy waves through her body.

No.

God, no.

"What did it look like?" she managed to ask.

"It was a bird. A crow or something." He shook his head. "It was creepy looking."

"I'll bet. Nothing looks good on you when you're dead."

Or in jail. She could not believe that the police had identified Heather's tattoo. Could they link it back to her?

Anxiety dispelled Kenzie's enjoyment. She desperately wanted to search the news reports online about the tattoo discovery on Heather's body. She glanced at her watch. "Oh, Finn, I'm beat. I've got an early start tomorrow…."

He took the hint with good grace. "Me, too."

He left, giving her a warm kiss on the mouth.

Under different circumstances, she would have taken it further.

But instead, she locked the door behind him and spent the next hour searching the internet. It didn't offer more than Finn had told her. She crawled into bed.

Thank God the tattoo that McNally gave her was covered up.

They can't connect me to Heather Rigby.
I can stay away from McNally until Monday.
Everything will be fine.
Just four days of surviving the waterfall, Kenzie.

But then the thought wormed into her head: Had Imogen Lange's sister—her mother's lawyer and the girl who had once hated her guts—recognized the tattoo as the same one her dead sister had gotten before she died?

Kate turned the corner and approached her neighborhood Starbucks. She had decided to walk, needing the cool air to clear her head. But the fog had crept in. It was more than cool, it was downright chilly. She pulled up the collar of her fleece jacket and wished she hadn't agreed to come.

Why had Ethan called her?

And, more important, why had she accepted?

She hurried up the stairs into the coffee shop. It was warm. It was dry. And Ethan was already there.

He sat at a table by the window. She walked over, aware of his gaze on her.

Every step felt awkward.

He rose when she approached the table. "Kate."

His blue eyes searched hers.

A light flush warmed her neck. *God.* This was awkward.

Why had she come?

"Hi." She stood by the table.

He pulled out a chair for her. She lowered herself into it, aware of his hand behind her back. "I can't stay too long," she said. "Enid is in the hospital."

The dismay on his face warmed her. "What's wrong?"

"It's her heart. They think they can stabilize it. But it will take a few days."

"That's a relief." He gestured to the large drink menu above the counter. "What can I get you?" He smiled.

She hadn't seen Ethan smile at her in, oh, about a year and a half. It was a strange sensation. As if they were on a first date. Instead of…whatever this was.

She returned the smile. "A decaf café latte would be lovely."

"A classic." He knew she loved those.

He stood in line. She slid off her coat, studying his back. His hair was shorter. A crisp, clean cut. It suited him. She recognized his jacket. She knew how it felt under her fingers….

He returned with two lattes. "They're both decaf, although a little caffeine wouldn't be bad right now."

She sipped the foam on her drink. "Are you burning the midnight oil on the bog body case?"

He nodded. "Yes. We've had a big break." His eyes gleamed with excitement. "After seventeen years, we might actually get justice for Heather's killer."

Heather's killer. The way he said it, it sounded as if he knew her. "That's great news." She was happy for him. He needed success at his job. There had been too many disappointments.

"How about you? How's the assisted suicide campaign going?"

Kate's eyes searched his face, trying to gauge his feelings. This could be a land mine. Ethan had fought a very public battle with Randall Barrett over Don Clarkson's euthanasia case. "So far, so good." She hoped.

"Good for you, Kate." The warmth in his voice was unmistakable.

She sipped her latte. "Why do you say that? I didn't think you were in favor of it."

He cradled his cup in his hands and gazed at the foam. "I'd like some control over how I ended my life. I guess it's an occupational hazard. I see so many people who are killed." He glanced up at her. "My grandmother had terrible dementia at the end. Running down the street with no clothes on, forgetting to put in her false teeth. This was a woman who was very religious—had almost become a nun in her youth—and extremely modest. If she had had a choice, I think she would have chosen to end her life sooner."

"It's more difficult when cognitive function is impaired. It's hard to know what they would choose." Kate's lips curved into a wry smile. "Do you realize we are taking the opposing views to what we've said in our professional capacity?"

Ethan grinned. "I guess that's why it's a slippery slope. It isn't clear where the boundaries should be drawn. There are always extenuating circumstances."

"That's why Harry Owen doesn't want to touch it with a ten-foot pole. But he might feel differently if he knew he would die a terrible death." Her tone was bitter.

She gazed down into her latte. Frances Sloane's case had stirred her fears about CJD. But people died from terrible diseases every day. Why should she be spared?

"It's not a done deal that you'll get CJD, Kate," Ethan said, his tone gentle.

Kate stared at him. How did he know that she was thinking about it?

She forced a nonchalance she did not feel. "You're right. I can't let that worry me. Who knows what will happen."

"That's why I called you." Ethan's gaze caught hers.

Kate had almost forgotten how blue his eyes were. Dark blue with black eyelashes.

"What do you mean?"

"We don't know what could happen. Life is so unpredictable." He paused. "I almost lost you twice, Kate." His voice was soft.

I would have had to be yours to lose. The thought jumped into her head.

And with it, Randall's face, after they had survived chasing down Elise's killer. His expression was of terror that he had almost lost her, thankfulness that he hadn't. And Kate had glimpsed love in his eyes.

But then he moved out of the country....

This is wrong, Kate.

Wasn't it?

Talk about a slippery slope. She pushed back her chair. "Ethan, I'm not sure what we're doing. I think I'd better go."

He placed his hand over hers. His palm was warm, dry, capable. She remembered how he used those hands to knead pasta or grate chocolate—and sometimes used them to make her forget about everything but his hands. "I know what we're doing." His thumb brushed over hers. "We are trying to make up for lost time."

She eased her hand from his and slipped on her jacket. "A lot has happened since last year, Ethan." She struggled for words, because she really didn't know what to say. "I enjoyed seeing you, but..."

"But?" His eyes searched hers.

"But I don't know if I am ready for this." Her smile was crooked. "Whatever *this* is. I thought you wanted to be friends."

"I do. Best friends. Confidants." His voice sank. "I want us to be like we were when we first met."

She had been tying her shoelace in the park. He ran by. Their gazes met. The charge of attraction was so strong, so exhilarating, that she had to look away. Or he would see the hunger in her eyes.

God.

"I'll wait for you," he said, his voice soft. "I'll always wait for you."

Her skin shivered. She glanced around. This was a busy coffee shop. She did not want to provide entertainment for any bored coffee drinkers. But no one was nearby. "Thanks for the coffee."

"I meant it, Kate."

"I know. But I don't think you should."

His jaw tensed. "Why not?"

"Because I don't want to hurt you again."

"That's for me to decide." *Don't bail on me,* his eyes said. *Don't put up barriers before we even begin.* "I'm ready to take a risk." He reached over and tucked a strand of hair behind her ear. "Are you?"

She wasn't ready for this.

It was too unexpected.

And so was her reaction. Part of her wanted to say, "Yes."

And that scared the hell out of her.

She had promised to spend her life with Ethan. And then had written him out of it a year ago. She had made an uneasy peace with it.

Did she really want to strip all that away and reawaken feelings that had both exhilarated her—and brought her so much pain?

Did she really even have those feelings for Ethan anymore?

"I don't know. I wasn't expecting this." She stood.

"Look, I have to go. I need to call the hospital and check on Enid."

"I'll call you."

His words echoed in her ears as she left the coffee shop.

She knew he would call her.

The question was: Would she answer?

24

"Jesus," he breathed, turning the final page of his sketch pad. McNally sat on the synthetic wall-to-wall carpet of his bedroom, still dressed in his overalls—he had repaired a leaky window for a tenant—and leaned his head back against the door frame to his closet.

Ever since he had opened the box of old sketchbooks, he hadn't been able to stay away from them. He was good. He was brilliant. He had forgotten how good he was until he had flipped through the sketch pads he had accumulated through his teen years, each of them marked with the date. Believing that at some point he would use them as a retrospective, as a chronicle of his development as a tattooist.

Now, he realized, they were also the chronicle of his bond with Kenzie.

And hers with him.

He leapt to his feet, shoving the box into the closet with his foot. Snatching his jacket from where he had thrown it on the bed, he strode out of his apartment. Within minutes he was on the road, heading downtown.

It was past eight o'clock on a work night, and the traffic was light in the business core—which also was home to some of the city's most popular bars and pubs. He turned down one of the side streets, cursing when he discovered that it was now a one-way street.

He sped along it, ignoring the startled honks from two cars that had turned onto the street in the opposite—and correct—direction, and swung a left onto Hollis Street.

Every muscle urged him to push his foot on the gas and race down the long, empty stretch, but he was trying to remember on which corner resided the Last Man Standing bar.

There. He recognized the building but not the sign. The bar had undergone a re-do at some point, and called itself Due South. He slowed down in front of the entrance. Stylish university students and twentysomethings drifted in and out of the bar.

In his mind's eye, he could see the stage.

Despite the threats by city council to shut down the Mardi Gras, a huge crowd turned out at the bar. Dressed in costumes ranging from Star Wars to vampires, the crowd was pumped and drunk.

A perfect audience, McNally thought. He was jazzed, wired, ready to let fly. He grabbed the mic, jumped up and down yelling, "Let's go!"

His brother Matt sat behind the drum kit. He raised his arms and hit his sticks together to the count of four. Lovett, on bass, started his first chord a half-beat early, which threw Kenzie off. McNally saw her flash Lovett a look, but she fudged a riff, her bow flying across her electric fiddle, and got back on track. Man, she was good. And hot. She wore a tiny miniskirt, barely covering her rear end, fishnet stockings on those long, deadly legs, and a black leather-wannabe corset that pushed up her already full breasts.

Tonight was gonna be amazing.

Kenzie had no idea just how amazing it would be. He had planned a special surprise for her. Something that would show her just how much he loved her. Something that would make her realize that they would be together for the rest of their lives.

A guy dressed as a police officer threw himself backward onto a table while three friends poured booze down his throat. This wasn't the usual Saturday-night dance crowd. No, Mardi Gras had brought out a different vibe. Disguised in costume, the crowd was letting loose. Everything was frenzied: their movements, their expressions, their laughter. It was nuts.

A trio dressed in bird costumes danced on the table, the occasional feather drifting into the crowd. Directly in front of the stage, girls gyrated and bounced, their sense of rhythm deadened four drinks ago.

Sweat dripped down McNally's back. The crowd was super-wound up, and their little band was giving it all they had. Lovett, his short stumpy body planted on the stage, frowned in concentration. Matt pounded it out behind them on his drum kit. And in center stage, McNally let loose. He noticed a bunch of girls dancing in front, their movements suggestive. He ran his hand through his hair—freshly cut in an edgy punk style— and checked them out.

Although they didn't know it, one of them would be joining him and Kenzie tonight.

He smiled at them.

It was then that he saw her. His heart jolted.

Her eyes...large, brown.

Like Imogen's.

Even the expression was the same: sweet, adoring.

He moved to the edge of the stage and stared straight into those eyes.

She was the one.

He knew it.

And, from the expression of surprised delight in her gaze, she knew it, too.

He ended the set on a rousing yell. The crowd erupted.

Kenzie strode over to him—eyes glittering within her ghoulish witch makeup—and slid her arm around his waist. "I've got a bottle of vodka in my bag," she said.

Electricity sparked through his veins at her touch, at the thought of what would come later tonight. He glanced at the girl. She watched him, a drunken invitation in those large velvety eyes, but her expression was unsure. She had seen Kenzie's possessive body language.

He murmured in Kenzie's ear, "Let's get drunk and then play our favorite game." He threw an inviting smile at the girl. "We'll bring her with us."

Kenzie stiffened. He liked that she was jealous. She'd been distant for the past month or so, accusing him of being too possessive, too angry, and it was making him crazy. "Why?"

"Because."

He gave her a look.

Something shifted in her gaze.

She understood what he meant.

Her gaze flicked to the girl, eyeing her witch's getup with contempt—McNally knew Kenzie was thinking that her own was so much better—and the wig that sat slightly askew. Her gaze lingered on the girl's eyes.

Kenzie's body pressed against him. He tightened his arm around her waist.

"I've got a plan," he said. He grabbed the Darth Vader mask he had left by a speaker, and wrapped his

cloak around his jacket. "Meet me by the side entrance in fifteen minutes."

Kenzie grinned.

McNally clenched his teeth. He had planned it all out for her.

And she had left him.

Not this time.

Not. This. Fucking. Time.

He slammed the truck into Drive. A shaggy guy smoking outside the bar entrance shot McNally a look.

McNally gunned the truck, shooting into the narrow one-way street, just avoiding shearing off the side mirror of a parked car.

Well, of course. Kate stared at the number displayed on her phone screen.

Of course Randall would call her the same night that she had gone for coffee with Ethan.

The phone rang again.

"Kate."

The sound of his voice both warmed and angered her. The latter emotion wasn't rational. But anger rarely was. It was the situation that frustrated her. If he hadn't left… "Hi, Randall."

"How are you?" His tone was low, intimate. "I've been thinking about you all day. Are you okay?"

"I'm fine." She pushed her coffee with Ethan out of her head. It was just one coffee. And she had told him that she wasn't ready for anything. But that didn't stop the guilt from nibbling away at her.

"Did you get any media coverage?"

"Uh…yes."

"Kate, is everything okay?"

"Sorry. It's been a long day." She filled him in on

the interview she'd given with Frances Sloane on television, and the newspaper features on the Body Butcher anniversary. She couldn't bring herself to tell him about her former client Marian MacAdam's quote in the paper about the murder of her granddaughter.

"You've been busy. I'm sorry I'm missing so much. My mother asked you to pass on her regards to the Richardson ladies."

"Randall, Enid was admitted to hospital today with heart failure. I should have remembered that your mother would want to know."

"Oh, no. Will she be okay?"

Kate thought of Enid's birdlike body. The normally bright eyes dulled with pain, sunken in her face. "I don't know." There was the faintest tremor in her voice.

"Can I help at all?"

Not when you are six hundred miles away. "It's all under control here. Finn and I worked out an arrangement to look after Muriel in the evenings."

"Well, the good news is that I should be home soon," Randall said. "The negotiations went well last night, and I think we are on our final round. We could be home by early July."

Kate stared out the window. She could see nothing but her face, pale and indistinct. "That's wonderful! It will be so great to see you all."

"It will be so great to see you, Kate."

"You, too." She turned away from her reflection. "It's not that far away. And I'm happy to report that your garden is holding up."

"Good."

There was an awkward silence. Then they both spoke at once.

"I should be going—" Kate said.

"I miss you—" Randall murmured.

"Thanks for calling. I really appreciate it."

"You know you are always in my thoughts."

"You, too," she said, her voice so soft she wasn't sure he heard her. "Bye."

"Bye."

Do it, Kate. Tell him about your coffee with Ethan. "By the way—" Kate said quickly. But Randall had already disconnected.

Kate jumped to her feet, giving herself a shake.

For nine months she had waited in limbo while Randall reassembled the broken landscape of his life. Part of her understood his need to leave, having been through trauma herself. Part of her resented his absence. And another part was scared that she was letting her life tick away waiting for a man who might decide that she was not part of his newly drawn landscape.

What she hadn't realized, until this moment, was that she had slowly been erasing him from her own.

The streetlights shone through the still-bare trees. Kate Lange's house was older. Unless she had put in new windows and doors, it would be easy to break into.

But not tonight.

The lights were off. Given it was after midnight on a week night, McNally guessed she was in bed.

He thought of her, hair spread out on the sheets, her neck exposed....

He grinned to himself and hurried over to her car.

It took only a second to slip the envelope under the windshield wipers.

A minute later, he was cruising home.

His entire body hummed with excitement. He wished

he could see Kate Lange's face when she opened the envelope.

He drove around for another half hour, restless, excited.

Then he went home, threw his jacket on the sofa and grabbed his sketch pad.

His body exploded with creative energy.

He was back.

The old McNally was finally back.

25

Kate rolled over and fumbled for the button on her alarm. Damn. Was it 6:00 a.m. already?

She threw back the covers. Alaska nosed her bare leg. Charlie gave her a sloppy kiss. "Good morning, lady and gentleman," she mumbled. "I hope you are ready for a good, long run." She patted their heads. "'Cause I sure ain't."

Nine minutes later, she unlocked her front door and stepped outside with Alaska and Charlie at her heels. Fog brushed her skin. It was cool and damp—but also refreshing. It chased away the exhaustion induced by a night of insomnia. "Come on, guys." She tugged the dogs' leashes and jogged down the porch steps.

Her body shifted into automatic, her stride lengthening as her brain began to sort through her to-do list for the day: *check comments on news site for reaction to Frances' interview, follow up with Harry Ow—*

She stopped, the dogs jostling into her legs. An envelope gleamed damply under the windshield wiper on her car.

She tugged it free.

KATE LANG.

Her name was hand-printed in blue ink, the surname misspelled. The ink had blurred from the wet. It must have been on her windshield for a while. The heavy mist had dried up overnight.

Which meant...

Someone had come to her house at night, while she slept—because it hadn't been there when she walked home from coffee with Ethan, and the dogs would have barked at anyone who had approached the driveway unless they were asleep....

She tore open the flap and removed a sheet of folded paper.

Charlie whined. She wanted her walk. "Just a sec, girl," Kate said, unfolding the sheet of paper. A newspaper clipping drifted to her feet. She bent and retrieved it, instinctively knowing before she looked at it what it was: the photo of her post–Body Butcher attack from yesterday's front page news item.

Don't think the worst. It could be a letter of support.

She held up the letter.

Oh, God.

THE BODY BUTCHER LEFT YOU FOR ME.

Her fingers began to tremble. She wanted to tear the paper into tiny pieces, throw it to the wind and kill the bastard who would try to scare her like this.

Her heart pounding, she ran up the porch and unlocked the door, both dogs dragging on the leash because they didn't want to return to the house without their walk. "Don't worry, we're still going."

She dropped the letter onto the console in her foyer. Then she set the house alarm, closed the door, testing it to make sure it was locked.

Alaska and Charlie bounded down the porch stairs,

pulling Kate in the direction of the park. Kate didn't try to slow them down.

She needed to run, to pound down the fear that pushed against her chest, tightened her throat and threatened to empty the contents of her stomach.

The streets were quiet, the fog enrobing the familiar route in drab gray.

Kate had run this route hundreds of times, had run through the park thousands of times, and had rarely felt unsafe. She was fast. She had two large dogs. Not too many people would try anything on her if they saw Alaska's teeth.

But today was different.

Her eyes searched the foggy depths behind the trees as she ran down the paths of Point Pleasant Park. The unexpected crunch of a runner behind her made her heart lurch, despite her excellent conditioning.

THE BODY BUTCHER LEFT YOU FOR ME.

Are you kidding me?

Don't you know what happened?

I killed the bastard.

I. Killed. The. Body Butcher.

But it still didn't stop her from glancing over her shoulder every few minutes until she got home.

She took a shower and did all the usual preparations for work, trying to ignore the letter sitting on the console in her foyer.

Why had someone left it for her?

Was it a prank?

Or a threat?

God knew there were enough sick people out there.

But was it merely someone envious of her so-called "heroism"?

Or someone who wanted to harm her?

You should call the police.

No. She was sick of calling the police.

Then call Ethan.

He would know what to do.

Yeah, but he will also get all protective on you. And think that you've opened the door to what he had been hinting at last night.

The note was a prank. Nothing more.

She glanced at her watch. She had just enough time to check on Muriel before going to work. She locked the door, setting the alarm, and hurried two doors down to the Richardsons' house.

Enid's friend answered the door. "Hello?" Her softly permed hair floated above her head as if it were a cumulus cloud.

"Hi, Mary. I'm Kate Lange. I just wanted to find out how Muriel is doing."

Mary held open the door. "Come on in. Do you have time for a cup of coffee?"

"Just a quick one." Kate followed her into the kitchen. Muriel stood at the counter, holding a knife with butter.

"Want some help with your toast, dear?" Mary gently guided Muriel's knife onto the bread.

"Hi, Muriel," Kate said.

"I thought it was Enie," Muriel said. "Where's Enie?"

"She's at the…doctor's, Muriel," Kate said. "She'll be home soon."

Muriel's eyes were watery. "Tell her to come home soon. I miss her."

Kate's throat tightened. "I will." Her phone vibrated in her jacket pocket. The Sloane file, she bet. "I'm sorry, I don't have time for coffee. Work is calling." She glanced at Mary. "But I'll be here at six o'clock to spend the night with Muriel."

Mary waited until they were at the door, then said, "The lady from the home-care agency is due to arrive in fifteen minutes. I'll give her a tour and make sure Muriel is comfortable with her before I leave."

"Thank you so much, Mary. I'm going to check in with Enid. If she has any news, I'll let you know."

She hurried back to her driveway, her dread rising as she unlocked her car and checked the interior. But there was no sign anyone had been in the car. She climbed into the driver's seat and started the engine, staring at the spot where the envelope had been.

There was no sign it had ever been there. It didn't matter. She couldn't erase the memory, but she sprayed windshield fluid on the glass anyway. She switched the wipers onto high speed.

"I saw your interview last night on television," Liz, her executive assistant, said. "And from the looks of it, so did a lot of other people." She handed Kate a stack of printed emails and phone messages.

Kate took them, her heart pounding. Could there be another message from the person who had left her the note?

"Three hundred and fifty-two emails so far. Seventy-six phone messages," Liz announced. She glanced at the clock. "And it's only 9:00 a.m."

"Sorry, Liz," Kate said, turning toward her office. "I think it will die down after a few days."

Liz arched one of her perfectly shaped brows. "No pun intended, I presume."

Beneath Liz's frosty and immaculate exterior lurked a rather macabre sense of humor. They were a good match, given Kate's recent cases.

The stack of messages burned in her hand. "None

intended at all. Thanks for all your help, Liz. I know it's above and beyond your usual duties."

"In this instance, I'm happy to help."

Kate hurried into her office and closed the door, spreading out the stack of messages on her desk. Her first glance was reassuring. None of the emails were written in all-caps. And any references to the Body Butcher were in the context of her "heroism."

Less nervous, she sipped her coffee. The interview had been successful for her client. She calculated that roughly seventy percent of the messages were in support of assisted suicide.

Time to give Mr. Owen a call.

She bit back a smile. *A wake-up call.*

He did not keep her on hold this time.

"Mr. Owen, it's Kate Lange calling." She tried to keep her voice neutral, not wanting to give a hint of gloating at the obvious success of her campaign.

"Ms. Lange, lovely to hear from you." He sounded disconcertingly unperturbed.

"I take it you saw my client's interview last night?"

"Yes."

"And...what did you think?"

"I think she is a very compelling figure."

Kate detected a "but" in his tone of voice. "And?"

"And I think that she is the unfortunate victim of a deadly disease that is the exception, rather than the norm."

"The norm should be a standard of compassion for the vulnerable rather than washing one's hands of the situation." Before he could respond, Kate added, "I received hundreds, if not thousands, of messages from the public supporting my client's cause, Mr. Owen." That was a teeny exaggeration, but one Kate was sure most lobbyists would make.

"That's not surprising, Kate." His tone was that of a pro explaining the rules of the game to the rookie. "You are her advocate. I have received an equally large number of messages from my constituents who are vehemently opposed to it."

"I see. Well, I'd like to propose that you meet with my client, Mr. Owen. You owe it to your constituents to hear both sides of the argument."

"Your client presented her case on television last night, Ms. Lange. A further meeting is not necessary." He paused. "And I wouldn't want to get her hopes up. It wouldn't be fair."

"What isn't fair is the assumption that you are on the moral high ground, Mr. Owen."

"Perhaps not. But there I stand, with the entire Government of Canada behind me. Good day, Ms. Lange."

He hung up before she had the satisfaction of doing it herself.

Damn him.

26

The neighborhood canvass had paid off for Lamond.

"One of the residents remembered that some teen-agers used the bunker for doing drugs," Lamond told Ethan while they drove out to Chebucto Head.

"In 1995?" Ethan bit into his sandwich, one hand on the wheel. The wrapper lay scrunched on his lap.

"That's what she said. She could date it because she knew one of the kids who went there." Lamond checked his notepad. "The girl's name was Kenzie Sloane."

At the mention of her name, Ethan gulped down his mouthful of sandwich. "Any relation to Frances Sloane—you know, the woman who is on a crusade to change assisted suicide?"

"Yup. Frances Sloane is Kenzie Sloane's mother." Lamond flashed him a look. He knew that the assisted suicide campaign struck a little too close to home for Ethan. The Clarkson case had been ugly, and even though the court had ruled in favor of the prosecution, Ethan had not come out of it smelling like roses.

Ethan took a large sip of his Zen green tea. "That's an interesting connection." So was the fact that Kate represented Frances Sloane —

The turnoff to Frances Sloane's private road suddenly appeared. "Damn." He jerked the wheel hard to the left. Lamond threw him a look. They headed down the driveway to Frances Sloane's house. *Stop thinking about Kate's reaction.*

Kate's a professional. She knows this case is a totally different matter than her client's campaign. But she also would be aware of the effect of negative publicity on Mrs. Sloane.

The assisted suicide campaign was a battle for people's hearts. The mother of a murder suspect wielded a blighted sword.

Around the bend, Frances Sloane's residence appeared.

"That is one whacked-out house," Lamond said, peering through the windshield.

Ethan parked the car to the side of the main entrance, next to a budding Japanese maple.

"It's called modern architecture."

"Looks more like a glass box. I could have designed that."

Ethan raised a brow. "If you could actually draw a straight line…"

"Not bad, Drake." Lamond grinned. "You are also looking surprisingly chipper today. Finally getting out of the house?"

Lamond had uncanny intuition sometimes. Ethan bit into his sandwich. "Just had a good night's sleep." That wasn't true. It had been hard to fall asleep after his coffee date with Kate.

You see? You don't know until you try, Drake.

Enough with the self-help crap.

But Kate *had* looked incredible. He'd had to fight the urge to pull her to him and bury his fingers in her hair.

He remembered how it slid like strands of silk through his fingers—

"Tell me her name," Lamond said, an amused expression in his eyes.

Ethan refused to meet his gaze, making a point of studying the glass-and-steel house. "Anyone else corroborate the fact that Mrs. Sloane's daughter hung out at those bunkers in '95?"

Lamond shook his head. "I knocked on eight doors. Four of them answered. Two of them hadn't lived in the area at that time. One couldn't remember a thing. The fourth one remembered the kids at the bunker."

"Could she ID Heather Rigby?" They had a photo of Heather taken shortly before she went missing.

Lamond shook his head. "She said she'd never seen her before."

"But she recognized Frances' kid, Kennedy Sloane?"

"Kenzie Sloane," Lamond corrected, biting into an apple. "She said she had long red hair. Hard to miss."

"Does she know if Kenzie Sloane still lives around here?"

"She says she moved away. But obviously her mother is here." They climbed out of the car and walked up the front walkway. Ethan could detect no movement inside.

They rang the doorbell. It echoed for a long time. They were just about to leave when the door opened.

"Yes?" A woman in a personal-care-attendant uniform gazed at them.

"We are Detectives Drake and Lamond," Ethan said. They held out their badges. "We are investigating the death of Heather Rigby, whose remains were found about three miles from here. We would like to speak to the owner of the house."

The caregiver's gaze flicked from the badges to their faces. "Mrs. Sloane is not well."

"It is important," Ethan said, his voice firm. "We won't take a lot of her time."

The caregiver glanced at the badges again and held open the door. They stepped into the cavernous foyer. "Please wait here. I'll get her ready." She closed the door behind them. "It will take a few minutes. You have to understand that she is very unwell. She can't speak clearly, and she gets tired easily, so please choose your questions with care."

Ethan felt as if he had just been reprimanded by a schoolteacher. But he respected the caregiver. She was doing her job.

The woman left them in the hall. Ethan examined the view from the windows. "I bet you could follow the coastline and get to the bunkers without ever taking the highway."

He made a note to take a hike this weekend.

They waited, studying the house, the exits, the view of the property through the windows. Finally, Lamond said, "She wasn't kidding when she said it would take a few minutes. It's been at least ten."

Three minutes later, the caregiver ushered them to the back of the house.

It was as if they had stepped right onto the ocean. The view from the back windows was spectacular. There was a sense of unfettered space—sky and ocean as far as one could see. The owner of this pièce de résistance studied him, her gaze wary.

Ethan wondered, as he noted the straps to keep Frances Sloane upright in her wheelchair, whether the vast openness she saw through the window gave her peace—or merely reminded her of her own loss of freedom.

They sat down on the sofa. Judging by the closed expression on Mrs. Sloane's face, he was sure she knew something. "Mrs. Sloane, as you may be aware, the body of Heather Rigby was discovered in a peat bog by the old bunkers, approximately three miles from here." He studied her face for a reaction.

"Yes," she responded. Her voice was slurred, nasal. He hoped she wasn't under the influence of medication. "I heard."

"We believe Heather was killed on the night of the Mardi Gras in 1995."

"I read in the paper she wore a mask."

Lamond leaned forward; it was difficult to understand her.

"Yes. The last time she had been seen was at a Mardi Gras party in downtown Halifax." He held out Heather's photo. "Did you see her that night?"

Frances Sloane studied the photo. "No."

"Did you know her?"

"No."

"Had you ever seen her in your neighborhood? Babysitting, hiking…?"

"No."

It was difficult to read her body language or the inflection of her voice. Only her eyes had remained untouched by disease. They were a startling sky-blue, sharp and incisive. But he sensed, rather than saw, fear in their depths.

"Do you have any children, Mrs. Sloane?"

If she could have stiffened, she would have.

"Yes. Two."

"And how old were they in 1995?"

"My son was fourteen, my daughter seventeen."

Lamond wrote that down. Frances Sloane's gaze darted from Ethan to Lamond and back to Ethan again.

"I understand that your daughter liked to hang out at the bunkers?"

She swallowed, working her throat to speak. "Who told you that?"

"Someone who lives close to them. She told us that a group of teenagers used to hang out there. And one of them was your daughter."

She blinked. "Yes."

"What is her name?"

"Kenzie."

"Did Kenzie ever mention Heather Rigby to you?"

"No."

Ethan had the impression that Kenzie hadn't mentioned much to her mother. "Who did Kenzie go to the bunkers with?"

"Friends."

Frances Sloane wasn't trying to be deliberately brusque, Ethan guessed. Communication—both verbal and nonverbal—was difficult for her. "Any kids that you knew?"

She exhaled. "Some girls. Crystal Burton. Imogen Lange—"

"Did you say Imogen Lange?" It was difficult to tell with her speech, but that was an unusual name.

"Yes. Why?" Her eyes scanned his face.

Ethan struggled to keep his expression impassive. Kate's younger sister had hung out at the bunker with Frances Sloane's daughter?

Was that why Kate was putting herself on the line as a lobbyist for Frances Sloane?

And yet, hadn't she told him that in her final days Imogen had been hanging out with a bad group of kids?

Was Kenzie one of them?

He made a note to call Kate.

Then crossed that off as fast. She couldn't talk about her client.

"I know Imogen's family," he said.

"Her death was so tragic." Frances' gaze searched his.

"After Imogen Lange died, who did Kenzie hang out with?"

Frances Sloane closed her eyes. A spasm crossed her face. Ethan wasn't sure if it was from a bad memory or was a symptom of her disease. She opened her eyes and said, "No one. After Imogen died, she stopped going."

"Kenzie was in grade twelve in 1995, correct?"

"Yes."

"Did Kenzie use drugs at the time?"

Frances Sloane's eyelids flickered. "I don't know."

Or you didn't want to know.

"Did her friends do drugs?"

"I don't know." She swallowed. "What does this have to do with Heather Rigby?"

"Were you at home on the night of the Mardi Gras in 1995?"

"That was a long time ago. But I believe so."

"Where was Kenzie?"

She exhaled. "She went downtown. To the bars. But then she came home."

"At what time?"

"Before midnight."

Lamond, who had been taking notes, paused. Heather Rigby had been spotted on the bar security cameras at 1:09 a.m.

"Are you sure?"

"Yes."

"How can you be certain?"

"Because her curfew was midnight. And I would remember if she had broken it."

Lamond made of note of this flimsy rationale.

Frances Sloane's head drooped sideways. Her caregiver jumped to her feet. "Mrs. Sloane is getting tired, Detectives."

"One more question, if I may, Mrs. Sloane," Ethan said.

She gazed at him. She hadn't moved a muscle but he had the sense she was bracing herself.

"Did Kenzie have any tattoos?"

The caregiver's eyes grew round. Her gaze flew to Frances Sloane.

A rather strong reaction.

"She had several." Mrs. Sloane's face was calm.

"What were they?"

"I don't remember."

She was lying, Ethan was sure of it. She had likely seen the police sketch of Heather Rigby's tattoo. But why would she lie unless…her daughter had the same one?

"Do you have a number where we can reach your daughter?"

"She's visiting from New York. She's at a hotel downtown."

Kenzie Sloane was in Halifax? Ethan managed to keep his face impassive and caught Lamond's eye.

But they both knew where they were headed next.

"She's here for only a few days," Frances added.

"Do you have her number where she is staying?"

Phyllis flipped open a binder. "She gave me her work number."

"She's working in Halifax?"

"Only while she is visiting. The name of the place is—" the caregiver squinted at the words "—Yaku... Yaku... Yakusoku Tattoo shop."

You have got to be kidding me. Ethan struggled to keep his excitement from showing. "She's a tattoo artist?"

Phyllis threw a panicked glance at her employer.

"Yes," Frances said, her voice steady. "She is."

He stood. Lamond flipped his notepad shut. "Thank you for your time, Mrs. Sloane."

"Goodbye." Her tone had an air of finality. Her eyes drooped closed. They had exhausted her.

They were ushered out quickly by Phyllis. But instead of returning to the car, Ethan detoured around to the back of the house. The property extended all the way to the cliff overlooking the ocean.

Could someone walk along the headland to the bunkers from here?

They returned to the car and drove down the long driveway to the highway.

"So..." Ethan threw Lamond a sideways glance. "What do you think? Have we found our first suspect?"

Lamond grinned. "Let me see—her daughter is close to the same age as Heather, lived near the dump site and hung out at the bunker. And, to top it all off, she works in a tattoo shop." He sipped the nearly empty can of soda left over from his lunch. "Yes, I think Kenzie Sloane is definitely a person of interest."

"Let's head straight over to Yakusoku. Her mother might not be able to warn her if she's with a client. Also, Frances Sloane looks like she is on her last legs. The sooner we narrow down the Kenzie Sloane connection, the better." Ethan took a sip of his now-cold green tea. "Have you ever been to Yakusoku Tattoo?"

"No. But I think that's the place Liscomb consulted for the tattoo drawing," Lamond said.

Ethan shot him a look. "Are you serious?"

"Yup."

27

Kenzie stretched her shoulders. "How are you holding up?" she asked Mikey, who lay on his stomach.

He sucked in his breath when the needle hit his skin. "I'm starting to lose it."

"Almost done."

One could never tell who was going to last and who wasn't. She had had skinny girls with no meat on their ribs who were able to tolerate sitting for elaborate back pieces. And then she had clients like Mikey, three hundred pounds of beef in a biker jacket, who began to wince an hour into the appointment.

She added the final red highlights to the flames bursting from the skull's eyes. "Done."

He practically leapt off the table.

"Came out pretty good, don't you think?" she asked as he admired his tattooed calf in the mirror.

"It rocks. You are the best, Kenzie."

He gave her a hug. Over his shoulder she spotted two guys standing out front. From the way they held themselves—and the closed expression on their faces—she knew right away who they were.

Police.

Her client let go of her and shot a sideways glance at Kenzie. "Is Yoshi in trouble?"

She managed a smile. "Don't think so."

He patted her on the shoulder. "Be good."

She began to break down her workstation. Her skin prickled.

Yoshi walked over to her. "Kenzie, there are two police officers who wish to speak to you. You can use my office." His voice was calm, but she read concern in his eyes.

She nodded. "Thanks." She took her time cleaning up. Then she walked to the front of the tattoo shop, feeling the cops' scrutiny as she approached.

"Kenzie Sloane?" the taller one asked. "I'm Detective Drake, and this is Detective Lamond." They flashed their badges. The receptionist watched, her eyes jumping back and forth between Kenzie and the two men.

Why don't you just take notes? Kenzie thought, trying to ignore the woman's salacious interest.

"I understand you wish to speak to me?"

"Yes, we have a few questions."

She did not want them dropping Heather Rigby's name in front of the receptionist and the all-too-interested clients, so she said, "Follow me. We can use the office."

She sat behind Yoshi's desk, a simple drafting table that disconcertingly resembled her mother's. The detectives sat down opposite her. It felt wrong. Farcical. As if she was their boss, and they were reporting to her. She sensed their eyes tracking her tattoos, skimming each limb methodically. Were they looking for a tattoo of an admission of guilt: "I, Kenzie Sloane, put a bullet in Heather Rigby" scrolling in Old English font down her arm?

Do not cross your arms. Do not cross your arms. It would look as if she was trying to hide something. She *was* trying to hide something, but it wasn't her tattoos.

"Ms. Sloane," Detective Drake said, "we are investigating the death of Heather Rigby, whose remains were found not too far from your family home."

The first mention of Heather's name made her heart thud. She raised her brows politely. "I'm very sorry to hear that. I had no idea. I don't live there anymore." A thought struck her. "How did you know I grew up there? Have you already spoken to my mother?" God knows what her mother would have told them.

"What brought you back to Halifax, Ms. Sloane?" Detective Drake avoided her question. But she wouldn't say any more until she knew whether her mother had already spoken to the police.

"My mother is ill. I came to see her. Did you speak to her already?" She directed her question to the taller one, Detective Drake.

"Yes. We saw her this afternoon. She's very sick, isn't she?"

Don't pretend you care, Detective. "Yes. She's dying."

"And you are also doing a little work?" Detective Lamond asked.

"Pay some bills?" The younger detective had impossibly large brown eyes. *Must be hard to be taken seriously as a cop when you have eyes like that,* Kenzie thought.

"My friend Yoshi asked if I would do a guest spot while I was in town." They clearly had no idea who she was.

Yet.

Detective Drake held out a picture. Kenzie's stomach tightened.

Oh, God, he wants me to look at her face.

Sweat slid down her sides. She could smell it. It was so rank, it had broken through her deodorant.

"Have you ever seen this girl before?"

She gave the picture a cursory glance. Pretending to look, but not focusing. She couldn't bear to do that. "She's the dead girl, right?"

"Right."

"And when did she go missing?"

"1995."

"So I would have been…seventeen, I guess. I was in grade twelve then."

"And which school did you attend?"

"Queen Elizabeth. I don't believe she went to my school. Did she?" She held Detective Drake's gaze.

"No. She was in university."

"So why would I know her?"

"That's what we are asking you. Did you know her?"

She shrugged. "Not from school. And I've tattooed so many people over the years. I can't say."

"Do you think you tattooed her?"

She cursed her stupidity. She had walked right into that one.

She shook her head. "No. And anyway, I was only seventeen. I didn't start tattooing until after I finished high school."

"Not even for fun?"

"No."

"So, if I understand you correctly, you never tattooed anyone, not even yourself, until you finished high school?"

"Geez, you guys." She lightened her tone. "I'm not on the stand, am I?"

"We are just trying to make sure we understand what you are telling us." Detective Drake smiled. It didn't reach his eyes.

Under normal circumstances, he would have merited a second look. He was ruggedly handsome—but clearly uptight.

She exhaled. "No. I did not tattoo anyone until I graduated from high school."

"And you graduated in June of 1995, right?"

"Right."

"Heather Rigby went missing in October of 1995. So it's possible you could have tattooed her, right?"

"No!" She shook her head. In a calmer voice she added, "No. I never tattooed her. I never even met her. I don't know who she is." She stood. "I need to go now."

"Where were you on the night of the Mardi Gras?" Detective Drake asked. His gaze locked with hers. His eyes were hard, inscrutable.

"I'm sorry, I've really got to run." She strode to the door.

"Where are you staying, Ms. Sloane? In case we have more questions."

"You can find me here."

She hurried out of the room and headed back to her station. She busied herself packing her equipment while they left. God, she stank. She grabbed her kit bag and hurried out of the studio.

Way to go, Kenzie. You just made yourself their number one suspect.

But what else could she do? Until she knew what her mother had said, she wasn't going to answer anything.

* * *

McNally parked Lovett's truck in front of a rental property midway down Kate Lange's street. A For Rent sign swung in the breeze. If anyone noticed his truck, they would assume that the Lovett Property Group had legitimate business on the street.

He took a clipboard from the backseat of the truck and studied it, sending an occasional, casual glance down Kate's street. She should be home soon. It was supper time.

He wondered what her reaction had been to the envelope he'd left on the windshield.

Was she scared?

Angry?

He wished he could have seen her face.

Twenty-five minutes later, he was rewarded for his patience. Kate pulled into the driveway. She hurried into the house before he could fully savor the sight of her.

Damn.

Would she come out?

He pulled the brim of his cap lower on his forehead and pretended to write a long note on his clipboard, throwing thoughtful looks at the rental unit.

Kate opened her front door. She carried a duffel bag. Her two large dogs followed her down the porch steps.

Was she going to the gym?

No. Not with the dogs.

He expected her to put her duffel bag in her trunk and drive away in her car, but instead she strode down the sidewalk.

Toward him.

He held his breath.

She would walk by him, her amber eyes lost in thought, the breeze lifting her hair. She had no idea

what he could do to her. That he was sitting there. Just
for her.

The dogs stopped to sniff a fire hydrant. The delay
made it that much more tantalizing. In another minute
and a half, she would walk right by him.

But she turned up the walkway of another old home,
this one with a riotous garden of tulips. She unlocked
the door and went inside.

He threw the clipboard onto the seat.

Why the hell did she have a key to someone else's
house?

The smell of pan-fried pork chops hit Kate's nose as
she opened the door to Muriel's house. Alaska lunged
through the door, licking his lips. Charlie was right
behind him. Kate's stomach grumbled. The aroma
of a home-cooked dinner was, quite frankly, the best
panacea for her lousy day. Kate followed her nose into
the kitchen. A woman in her mid-fifties stood by the
stove, flipping pork chops. She had dark wavy hair,
pulled into a chignon. A large apron dwarfed her pe-
tite frame.

Kate walked over to the home-care worker. "Hi. You
must be Corazon. I'm Kate Lange. I'm the one who contacted your agency."

She deftly switched off the burner and turned to
Kate. "Nice to meet you, Ms. Lange." Her smile was
gentle, her voice soothing.

"Please call me Kate." She turned to Muriel, who
stood at the counter stirring mayonnaise into the potato
salad. "That looks delicious, Muriel."

Muriel smiled. "Thank you. It's my mother's recipe."

"Dinner is ready," Corazon said. "It's one of my family's favorites."

"You will have to make it for Enid when she comes home," Muriel said. She looked at Kate, suddenly confused. "When will she be home?"

"Soon, Muriel." Kate braced herself for Muriel's reaction, but she nodded and placed the bowl of potato salad on the table.

"We used the chives from the garden in the salad," Muriel said, smiling, her eyes shining.

"No one can beat your potato salad recipe, Muriel."

After they ate—Kate savouring every delicious bite—Corazon pulled her car keys from her pocket and gave Muriel a brief hug. "I'll see you tomorrow. Don't forget, you promised to show me how to prune roses."

Muriel nodded. "Make sure you wear long pants. You don't want to get pricked."

Kate walked Corazon to the door. "Thank you."

Corazon smiled. "She's a nice lady. Have a good evening."

Kate closed the door, securing the dead bolt.

"Enid! Enid! Come quickly," Muriel called. "*Fawlty Towers* is on."

Kate walked into the sitting room.

Brulée had curled up on Muriel's lap. "Here's a little treat for you," Muriel said, holding a piece of cookie to the cat's muzzle. He took it from her fingers delicately and ate it, directing a look of superiority at the two dogs who sat at attention at Muriel's feet.

"Don't worry, doggies, I saved some for you." Muriel bit into the cookie and broke off two pieces. "There you go, Charlie. And here's yours—" she paused, searching her memory for the husky's name "—handsome."

She glanced up when Kate walked in. "I thought you were Enid. Where is she?" Her gaze was anxious.

"She's at the doctor's."

Muriel glanced out the window. "But it's late."

"She'll be home soon," Kate said. "I promise."

"But when?"

"When the doctor tells her she's better."

The canned laughter from the television show caught Muriel's attention.

While she watched the show, Kate watched her. Every few minutes, she would reach down and stroke the dogs' ears, being careful to take turns so they each got equal attention.

What if Muriel didn't have a sister who loved her so much? What if she had a sister or a nephew or a grandchild who wanted this big old house and whatever inheritance she might have tucked away?

What if the law did permit assisted suicide—and she ended up being pushed down that uncertain slope?

Too many what-ifs.

Kate rose to her feet. "Come on, Muriel," she said. "It's time for bed."

28

"Nice evening, isn't it, Kenzie?" McNally drawled, satisfaction slicing through him when he saw Kenzie jump. He stood by one of the few trees in the small park next to the hotel where Kenzie stayed. Having watched several dogs relieve themselves against it, he figured Kenzie's dog would head this way when it was time for his nighttime pee.

He braced himself for some kind of cutting Kenzie-putdown, but instead she glared at him and spun on her heel.

"Hey!" He grabbed her elbow. "I'm talking to you."

She shook her arm. But his fingers dug into her flesh. His heart pounded.

It felt so good.

Her rat of a dog sensed something. He pressed himself against Kenzie's legs and growled.

McNally stifled the urge to kick it. His time would come. But not now.

"Let go of me, McNally," she said, her voice low. "Or I'll call the police."

He let his gaze travel over her. "Yeah, right. The

same police who are investigating the murder of the girl you killed?"

Her eyes widened. She glanced frantically around the green area, but there were no passersby in hearing range. "For God's sake, shut up."

"Don't speak to me like that, Kenzie." He pulled her closer and let his fingers soften around her arm. "I just want to talk."

"We have nothing to say to each other."

Despite his resolve that she would not get the upper hand, her coolness chipped away at his confidence. Surely she had some feeling left for him. After all they had been through…

"That's not true." He tried to soften his approach by smiling.

She yanked her elbow out of his grasp. "We shouldn't be seen together." She glanced furtively over her shoulder.

"We had some good times, didn't we, Kenz?" His tone became intimate. "I gave you everything you asked for. I did everything you wanted." He held his finger against her temple. "Bang, bang, you're dead."

"For God's sake, that was a long time ago."

"Not for me, it wasn't."

"Listen," she hissed. "You have to stop bothering me. If the police see us together, we are screwed. It's bad enough that they found the tattoo on Heather's body."

He gave a disbelieving laugh. "They found the tattoo? How the fuck could they do that?"

"Because you buried her in a goddamned peat bog. It preserves bodies."

He felt as if she had just punched him in the stomach. Not just from the information she had revealed, but from the look of contempt in her eyes.

No matter what he did, she still thought she was better than him.

"So what that they found the tattoo? What difference does it make?" His eyes narrowed. "Unless you still have yours."

"No. I got rid of it a long time ago." The way she said that pissed him off. "But I wasn't the only one with the raven."

"Imogen's dead, so what are you worried about?"

"Yeah, but her sister is alive and well. She was on the front page of the newspaper. And she's representing my mother in her assisted suicide campaign."

A shiver ran along his spine. "So we kill her." He grinned. "She's the perfect victim, Kenz. She can take Imogen's place."

Kenzie flashed him a look of scorn. But there was a flicker of fear in her eyes. Good. She needed to see that *he* was the one in control. Not her.

"God, McNally, and while we're at it, why don't we just shine a spotlight on ourselves for the police. We have to be more subtle than that. Let me think about it." She pulled on her dog's leash. "And leave me alone. What happened in the past is in the past. I'm done with it."

"No, it's not. It's just the beginning for us, Kenzie."

She spun toward the hotel, but he grabbed her arm. *You ain't leaving me again, baby.*

"You think you can cover yourself in tatts, but it doesn't change who you are. What you want." His finger trailed down her cheek. "What you need to make you happy."

She jerked her head back. "Leave me alone."

His lips twisted into a smile. Or a snarl. He couldn't tell. She had the power to thrill him and infuriate him at the same time. "I can't. That's the problem. You fucked with my head so bad that there's no one else now. Just you, Kenzie."

"You can't have me."

Her words were so cold, so absolute.

Desperation ripped into his chest. "We never finished what we started, Kenzie."

"And we never will."

She pushed by him and hurried toward the hotel, that stupid dog throwing him a final, warning look.

"Yes, we will!" he yelled. "Remember Heather!"

He saw her entire body startle when he yelled their murder victim's name through the park.

But no one was there to hear him.

And now Kenzie had gone.

Rain began to fall. His tongue reached out to catch a raindrop.

She thought she could just walk away.

She thought he was stupid, that she was smarter than he was. *Let me think about it,* she'd said in that superior voice.

She didn't know that he already had a plan in motion.

One that would prove to her, once and for all, that he was way smarter than she was.

And that she would never, ever be able to walk away from him again.

He stalked back to his car.

He snatched his phone from the seat and loaded his web browser. The service was slow and it took a few minutes to locate Kenzie's website.

But it was worth the wait.

Kenzie had listed a cell phone business number in her contact information, because she traveled so frequently to tattoo gigs.

He entered the number in his address book.

And then he texted her: You'll never be able to leave me again.

He stared at his phone screen. His fingers gripped the phone so hard that his knuckles were white.

Nothing.

He glanced up at the hotel. Maybe reception was slow.

You have always been mine, he typed.

He waited. Staring at the hotel as if it would force Kenzie to answer. Well, screw her. He would wait until she came out again. Even if it took all night. But it took only half an hour before he saw the main door open to reveal Kenzie and her dog.

He leaned forward.

She's coming back to see me. His heart began to pound.

But then he saw Kenzie walked with a guy. A blond, good-looking guy. He carried her suitcases.

She had checked out of the hotel. Panic seized him. She better not be flying back to New York.

They climbed into the truck, and the blond guy drove them away.

McNally started his engine and pulled into traffic after them.

He would not let Kenzie leave town.

Not again.

Two minutes later, he relaxed. The blond guy drove in the opposite direction of the airport. Several minutes after that, it was obvious that he was taking Kenzie and her dog to his place.

McNally slipped his truck into a parking spot by the condo building Dumpster. He would not let Kenzie out of his sight again.

29

Kenzie shifted on Finn's sofa. His apartment was bright and airy, with an old brick wall and large windows. The entire place had a Scandinavian flavor. She dug the unfinished pine floors, the furnishings in gray, white, with the odd touch of bold blue.

Finn, she realized, studied her over his beer. "You okay?"

She rubbed her arms. "Yeah. Thanks for letting me come over."

"It's my pleasure." He slung his arm around her shoulders and gave her a squeeze. "I'm sorry that creep was bothering you."

She shrugged. "Comes with the territory."

After McNally had approached her in the little park outside the hotel, she had locked herself in her room. But the fact that he knew where to find her freaked her out. She didn't feel safe.

There was only one person whom she could call.

Finn answered on the first ring. "I was just thinking about you."

She forced a laugh. "I have a favor to ask…" She told

him some crazy fan had approached her at the hotel. He promptly offered to let her stay at his place.

Relieved, she checked out of her hotel. *It's only for a few days.* She felt at home immediately. So did Foo. After sniffing for a copious amount of time—Finn had a lot of dogs going through his place—he settled down with a long shudder of contentment on the sofa.

Kenzie placed her wineglass on the roughly hewn coffee table. "Want me to take a peek at your tattoo?" she asked.

"Sure." As fluid as the Foo Dog she had inked into his skin, Finn sprang to his feet and pulled off his T-shirt. She stood behind him, just inches from his back. She leaned a little closer, aware of the sudden stillness in his body.

She peeled off the bandage and eyed the tattoo. The dog's body seemed in tune with the muscle and bone for which it stood guard. It really was one of her better efforts, except— She frowned. The lower edge appeared inflamed. "You need some antibiotic cream on this part, Finn," she said. "Do you have any?"

"It's in my bedroom. I'll get some." He headed up the stairwell to his loft bedroom.

Halfway up the stairs, he threw a look at Kenzie.

When she arrived at the head of the stairs, he took her hand and raised it to his mouth, pressing his lips against the nautilus tattooed at the base of her wrist. His mouth skimmed the waves traveling up her arm. Every nerve in her body quivered. He gripped her hips. She felt as if she were a piece of wood that he was about to bring to life.

She cupped his jaw, tracing his lips. "Where did you say that antibiotic cream was?"

"It's under my pillow." He grinned, and pulled her to his bed.

The sheets were cool, as was the night.

She only became aware of that much, much later.

Who the hell was this guy? Kenzie seemed too friendly—way too friendly—with him.

McNally had been sitting outside the blond guy's place for at least thirty minutes, and he had not yet drawn the blinds on his windows. He was arrogant. Or stupid. McNally could not decide which. Did he think no one could see them?

The guy rose from his chair and took off his shirt. Kenzie stood behind him, inspecting a tattoo. But she was too close.

The guy walked upstairs.

A minute later she followed him.

McNally knew that look on her face.

He knew that sway in her walk.

She had walked into the basement of Lovett's grandmother's house, fiddle case in hand, dressed in a short pleated skirt with a tight white T-shirt and over-the-knee stockings. She glanced around. "I hear you need a fiddle player."

Matt walked over and put his arm around her shoulder. "Thanks for coming, Kenzie. I think you'll add a really cool vibe."

"I'm psyched," she said, and flipped a mass of glorious red hair back over her shoulder. She crouched to unpack her instrument. Her skirt barely skimmed the tops of her thighs.

She wore a red thong.

When she stood, bow in one hand, fiddle in the other, she flashed McNally a look.

The following weekend, she took him out to the bunker. It was late, about two in the morning. She turned to face him, mouth parted, eyes heavy-lidded.

He had drawn her face with that look a thousand times since. But it had never been for a customer. It had always been for him.

The light in the guy's apartment went out.

McNally smashed his fist on the dashboard.

No wonder she didn't want him following her.

I'll contact you, she had told him just hours before in the park.

Bull. She would never call him. He knew that now. She was having an affair with another guy.

God. Damn. Her.

He could not wait a moment longer. If he didn't act soon, he could lose her.

He turned on his engine. It was time to put his plan into high gear.

Nothing like being complicit in a sensational murder to keep a girl loyal.

Finn now slept. He faced her, his hand curved over the Foo Dog on Kenzie's hip. She felt safe. Protected. As if his arm connected her Foo Dog to the one she'd inked on his shoulder, creating a pair of guardians.

But could they really guard her?

She studied Finn's features in the darkness. The finger that had pulled a trigger seventeen years ago smoothed an errant wave of his hair. Tears tightened her throat.

Mr. Right.

He was one of the good guys.

And, thus, not right for her.

* * *

McNally crept around to the backyard of Kate Lange's house. This was his preliminary scouting mission. He was searching for the best point of entry.

He stepped on a few branches to see if the dogs would bark.

And waited.

But they were silent. The house was completely dark.

He paused in the shadow of a bush.

Maybe she wasn't home. Maybe she had taken the duffel bag and her dogs to her neighbor's because she planned to spend the night.

He studied the back of the house. By his estimation, Kate's bedroom was the second window on the right. These old Victorian homes, with their fussy detail and trims, were perfect for footholds. The bonus was the roof-covered back porch. He could climb on the roof....

He climbed an old maple tree that grew by the porch and jumped to the narrow porch roof, landing on the balls of his feet. He crawled to the edge of the roof. The blinds to the window on the right were only half-drawn.

The strap of her silky nightgown slipped down her arm. Her face was turned to the side, her hair fanned out on her pillow, revealing her long neck.

She didn't know he was there. He could watch her limbs move under the sheets, her breathing slow and deep while he imagined his fingers trailing over her.

He crouched down and peered into the window.

The large bed was neatly made. Kate was not in it. But he had been right—this was her room. Her clothes were folded on the chair. Two dog beds—empty—lay at the side of her bed.

He thought of Kate leaving her house with her duffel bag. And the woman from the home-care agency who had left her neighbor's house as soon as Kate had arrived. His gut told him that Kate was spending the night at her neighbor's.

He swallowed his disappointment. *You've got Plan B, McNally.*

And, fortunately, he had come prepared. He slipped the center punch window breaker from his pocket and smashed the window.

The security alarm blared through the air.

Shards of glass fell on him as he swung himself over the windowsill into Kate Lange's bedroom. He ran straight for the bureau and yanked open the drawer.

His efforts were rewarded.

He scooped up several pairs of panties, shoving them into the pocket of his hoodie, the alarm blaring in his ear.

He calculated it would take the police at least five minutes to respond.

And that was all he needed.

He dropped a folded piece of paper on her bed, threw himself out the window, leaping from the porch over-hang onto the deck. All that gym training had paid off.

He sprinted over the fence and through the yard of the house behind hers.

Fifteen minutes later, he sat on a bus and gazed out the window, taking the long way home.

Kate Lange's panties burned a hole in his pocket.

30

The shrill blaring of a siren from somewhere outside woke Kate from a deep sleep.

She sat up in bed. Her heart began to pound.

It was her house alarm.

Alaska raised his head. Charlie opened her eyes.

She threw back the covers just as her cell phone rang. She grabbed it. "Kate Lange speaking."

"It's Secure For Life Alarm Systems," a woman's voice said. "Our system indicates a forced entry at your residence."

"I can hear the alarm. Have you called the police?"

"I needed to ensure that this was an unauthorized entry. Do you want me to call 911?"

"Yes, please."

Kate threw on her clothes. She hurried over to Muriel's room, gesturing for the dogs to wait in the hallway. But the elderly lady had not woken up.

She ran to the front door. Through the window she saw the flashing blue lights of two patrol cars.

First the note on her car windshield. Now a break-in.

This wasn't random, she was sure of it.

Once Ethan heard of the break-in, he would call her. So she would call him first.

On the second ring, he answered. "Drake." His voice was surprisingly alert, given it was after three in the morning.

"It's Kate."

"What's wrong?"

"Someone just broke in to my house."

"Where are you?" Panic sharpened his voice.

"Don't worry. I'm not at home. I'm at Muriel's."

"Thank God. Have you called patrol?"

"My alarm service just did."

"Kate, promise me you will stay put. Don't go over there. Patrol can handle it."

She wanted to see what had happened to her house. But she said, "Okay. But are you coming?" There was a note of pleading in her voice that she didn't try to disguise.

"I'm on my way."

She felt bereft when she disconnected the phone. She hugged her arms.

Did her intruder know she wasn't home? Had he planned to attack her?

A patrol officer approached the Richardsons' house. "Ms. Lange? Detective Drake told me to find you here."

She nodded.

"Do you have a key so we can search inside your house?"

She rummaged in her purse and found one. He left and she stood by Muriel's front door, watching the police search her property.

The two dogs lay on the mat by her feet.

He arrived six minutes later, his hair still mussed by sleep, his T-shirt on inside out.

"They are searching the property right now," he said. She nodded.

"God, Kate." He pulled her into his arms.

She sagged against him. "Thank you for coming."

"Tell me what happened." He smoothed her hair.

She stepped back. "I don't know. I was sleeping, but the alarm system woke me up." She shivered. "Did patrol tell you anything?"

His mouth tensed.

Uh-oh.

"Someone broke the window of your bedroom—"

"But that's on the second floor."

"He climbed onto the porch roof and used a window puncher. It's kind of strange, Kate, unless…"

"Unless he was looking for me."

"Or for something in your bedroom. Do you have anything of value in there?"

She laughed, a mirthless sound. "No. The only things of value were sleeping with me over here." She felt sick. What if the dogs had been there? And someone had attacked them?

She swayed. Ethan put his arm around her. "Let's sit down," Ethan said. "I'll make some tea."

He led her into the kitchen. She was numb with fatigue—and fear. She sank into a kitchen chair and watched him fill the kettle.

"I have something to tell you." Her voice was low. "Someone left a note on my car this morning."

He spun to face her. "What kind of note?"

"It said 'The Body Butcher left you for me.'" There was the slightest tremor to her voice.

"Jesus Christ, Kate! Why didn't you call me?"

"At the time, it didn't seem important." She heard his exclamation of frustration. "I thought it was a prank.

You know, someone who saw the news coverage and wanted to upset me. They had stuck a photo of me from the newspaper in the envelope."

Ethan stared at her. "And you didn't report it?"

"No."

God. She was an idiot. She saw it in his eyes. But she knew it, anyway. She could have been attacked. "I'm sorry, Ethan. I didn't want to make a big deal of it."

"You are just lucky—"

Someone knocked on the door. Kate hurried to answer it. A patrol officer nodded to Ethan and said, "Ms. Lange, we've looked through the entire property and adjacent lots. We found a footprint in your garden bed, but that was it. We've brought in a sniffer dog."

"What was stolen?"

The patrol officer shook her head. "We were hoping you could tell us. None of the usual high-ticket items are missing."

"Of course. I'll be right over."

She glanced up the stairs. What if Muriel woke up?

Ethan saw her concerned look. He turned to patrol. "Do you have a spare constable? Someone who could wait here in case Ms. Richardson wakes up? She is easily disoriented."

A patrol officer was found, and five minutes later Kate hurried down the sidewalk to her house. The scene felt surreal: lights flashing, uniformed officers striding around her property with flashlights.

A patrol officer accompanied her to the front door and Ethan pushed it open for her.

"Let's do this systematically," he said.

"After I see my bedroom first." Kate marched up the stairs. She paused in the doorway to her bedroom. Ethan stood behind her.

"Damn," she said softly.

Jagged glass glittered in the frame of the tall window that overlooked her backyard. The blind hung crookedly at the top, the louvers bent. The bureau sat in the corner as if it were drunk, with drawers half-opened and clothes spilling out. She stepped toward it.

"Why don't you look in the top drawer," Ethan said. "That's the one patrol said had been touched."

"How do they know that?"

"Because the contents had been dumped on the ground."

He stood at the window, ostensibly inspecting the roof outside, while Kate opened the drawer. The contents were in disarray, her bras jumbled on one side, her panties crumpled on the other.

Everyone, it appeared, had gone through the contents of her underwear drawer.

She separated the items, doing a mental inventory. All her bras were there.

Where were the black-lace panties?

And the pink ones?

"Everything okay?" Ethan asked.

"No. Some of my underwear is missing." She shook her head. "What a pervert."

She stared at the drawer, tears choking her throat.

She felt so...violated.

She closed the drawer and rummaged through the rest of her bureau, hoping the missing underwear had been accidentally placed in a different drawer by the police when they searched her room.

No. The underwear was gone.

She couldn't believe it.

She spun away from the bureau and opened her closet.

Nothing had been disturbed. It looked just the same as it had looked yesterday.

"Kate." Ethan's voice was gentle in her ear, but she started nevertheless. "Patrol found something else. On your bed."

Her skin crawled. "What do you mean?" She rushed over to her bed. "I don't see anything."

Ethan handed her a bag. It held a piece of paper. "They found this on the bed."

Kate held it up to the light.

It was a sketch.

"My God." The sketch was of her. As a pinup girl. Naked, seductive Kate. The object of someone's fantasy.

She thought she might throw up.

"Who would do something this sick?" she whispered.

She pressed it against her chest, ashamed by the wanton nakedness in the picture. "Don't show it to anyone."

"Kate, I'm sorry." Ethan touched her arm. "It's evidence."

"It's humiliating. Everyone is going to see me like that."

He took the bag from her hand and cupped her face. "I'm so sorry, Kate."

"Everyone will look at me and see this naked pinup girl." Tears threatened to spill.

Ethan pulled her to him. "I'm sorry. We will find the bastard who did this. I promise. But in the meantime, you can't stay here. Or at Muriel's house."

"I have to. Muriel needs me."

"Then I'll sleep on the couch." With his service revolver, no doubt.

The thought was extremely comforting.

31

Kenzie slid from the bed, dropping the sheet behind her. They had forgotten to close the blinds in Finn's bedroom last night, and the morning sun stalked the pale oak floors. Finn dozed lightly, his face buried into his pillow. Kenzie resisted the urge to run her fingers along the smooth ridges of muscle exposed by the sheet.

Foo, who had spent the night on the rattan chair under the window, lifted his head. She pressed a finger to her lips. He whined, not willing to forgo his breakfast for Finn's sleep.

"Hey." Finn opened an eye. "Come back here. I'm cold."

Kenzie blew him a kiss. "Can't. Sorry. I've got a client booked in an hour."

He pushed himself to an upright position. "Lucky client."

She grinned. "You know all about it."

His gaze traveled over her nude body, caressing the obvious works of art and lingering on those bestowed by Mother Nature.

"Where's your shower?" she asked, stretching.

His eyes gleamed. "Let me show you."

Forty minutes later, Kenzie sat at a red light on Robie Street, her hair still damp, her skin still glowing and her heart still racing. She flipped open her smart phone and checked for messages.

She had received a text.

Damn him. Even though she had ignored all the text messages he sent last night, he hadn't gotten the hint.

She threw the phone onto the passenger seat. She wouldn't give him the satisfaction of opening the message.

Foo gazed at her.

She glanced at the phone again. "Shit!"

McNally was too dangerous to ignore. She grabbed the phone and opened the text, bracing herself for an obscenity-laced rant.

But it was a picture.

A picture that spoke a thousand words. And one that sent an unmistakable message.

It was a sketch of Kate Lange, in McNally's favorite pinup style.

A car blared its horn and she jumped, dropping her phone into the well of the steering wheel. "Damn!" The light was green. She stomped on the gas, the car lurching forward, Foo slipping forward on the seat.

"Sorry, baby." With a shaking hand, she stroked his head.

She drove the remainder of the trip to Yakusoku Tattoo with one thought in her head: McNally was going crazy.

He will never leave you alone, Kenzie.

And now that you are a tattoo artist, you can't hide from him anymore.

Her mind whirled. She was trapped. If the police didn't get her, McNally would.

A choice of life sentences.

No. She wouldn't let McNally ruin her life.

And what about Kate Lange? If McNally didn't lead the police to her doorstep with his stupid appearances at her hotel, then she still had to contend with Kate. What if she made the connection between Heather Rigby's tattoo and her dead sister's?

Her fingers found their way to her neck. She caressed the skin, imagining the koi swimming up, up.

As always, it calmed her.

I can make it up this waterfall.

She couldn't let McNally or Kate Lange drag her down.

Both of them were threats.

But how to stop them without being discovered by the police? They were hot on her scent. She was already a suspect.

Think, Kenzie.

You got away with murder once.

You can do it again.

The morning came with brutal honesty, light forcing its way through the heavy velvet curtains of the Richardsons' house. Kate lay in bed, allowing her eyes to gradually adjust to the light. A pot banged.

Alaska trotted over to her and nosed her arm. "Hello, boy," she murmured. Charlie, not to be outdone, rushed over to lick her hand. "Hey, Charlie."

Another pot banged.

Was Muriel making breakfast?

Then everything came back to her: the house alarm waking her up, the break-in, the missing panties.

The sketch.

The noise in the kitchen was most likely Ethan. She

threw on a pair of jeans and a loose sweater and pulled her hair back into a ponytail, trying to avoid her reflection on three hours' sleep.

Ugh. She really needed a shower.

She dabbed concealer under her eyes and hurried into the kitchen.

"Good morning," Ethan said. "Breakfast is ready."

She had heard those words many times during their engagement. "Wow. Thanks."

Ethan scooped scrambled eggs onto the plates, which already boasted freshly sliced oranges. "The toast should be ready in a minute."

The French press gave off a delicious aroma of coffee. She poured the hot brew while Ethan buttered the toast. They sat down at the table.

Ethan took a long gulp of the coffee. "I needed that."

He probably hadn't slept at all last night. She knew what he was like when he was on a case. And he was no doubt worried about the implications of what had happened to her.... "Thank you for coming last night," Kate said. "I really appreciate it."

"Kate, I want to be there for you. But I want you to understand something. Even if we aren't together, I would still come. I care for you. I always will."

Heat rushed to her face. "Thank you."

She forced herself to eat a mouthful of the eggs, although she had no appetite. "Why do you think someone did that last night?"

Ethan exhaled. "It's the work of a stalker, Kate. He leaves a note for you in the morning on your car. Then he takes it a step further, breaking in to your house, and leaves a drawing of you. There's no question he's escalating his behavior."

"So...do you think it's just a crazy person who saw

me in the paper? Or someone who is targeting me because of the assisted suicide campaign?" Kate sipped her coffee.

Ethan shrugged. "It's hard to know. You haven't received any notes, texts, pictures or phone calls before that note yesterday morning?"

Kate shook her head. "I read through every message that was sent to my office after Frances Sloane's television appearance, and none of them were threatening."

"We need to look at those. As well as the online news forums that reported Mrs. Sloane's story. We'll contact the moderators to see if anyone has posted threatening content about you." Ethan's phone vibrated. He glanced at the number. "I've got to go."

Kate followed him to the door. "Thank you, Ethan."

He gave her a stern look. "You can thank me by calling me if you receive any more messages."

"I will. I promise."

"Kate, don't fool around with this. I know you've been through a lot, and you are obviously a very tough woman, but stalkers are unpredictable. They live in a fantasy world. You can't assume you know what they will do next. Don't answer the door to anyone who isn't a close personal friend."

"I understand." His warning, in a strange way, warmed her. She wasn't in this alone.

"I'll be here tonight. As soon as I finish work. Unless we bring in a suspect on the Rigby case…" He paused. "Do you have anyone you can call if I can't get away?"

"I'll call Finn. It was his turn to come over, anyway. We'll all spend the night here."

"Good." He reached over and brushed his lips across her cheek. "I'll call you later."

"Thanks." There was a comforting familiarity in his words.

"And lock the door after you."

Kate smiled. "I will."

He strode out the door, yanking his phone from his back pocket. She watched him stop outside his car and scan Kate's house, the property and the houses adjoining it. She knew he was wondering the same thing: Who was the guy who broke in?

And what would he do next?

Ethan jumped into his car and gave her a final wave before heading down the street.

Kate closed the front door, securing the dead bolt. It seemed foolish in the bright light of morning. But she had made a promise.

Muriel, she discovered, liked to sleep in late. Kate tiptoed to the bathroom.

A long, hot shower refreshed her, and she dressed for work. Corazon was due in ten minutes. While she was dabbing more concealer under her eyes, her phone rang.

She checked the caller. It was Nat. "Are you calling about what happened last night?" Kate asked. The media would be all over this.

"No. What's up?"

Kate told her about the break-in. She wanted to tell her about the note and the sketch, but she knew that Nat walked a fine line between their friendship and her job. And she didn't want her friend to be in a position of having to conceal an obviously hot news story.

So she kept silent.

"Was it a random break-in?" Nat asked. "Did they take anything?"

"Not much." In fact, nothing was taken. Except two

pairs of lace panties. She wished she could tell Nat. "The alarm system went off and he ran away."

"Well, you are certainly keeping the police busy, between the break-in and your client."

Kate straightened. "What do you mean?"

"That's why I was calling. The police were at your client's house yesterday morning. In fact, Ethan was there."

The Sloane house was, of course, within walking distance of the Rigby murder site. It would make sense that they would canvass it. "Was this just the usual neighborhood canvass?"

"I don't know. But I think not. The police seem unusually tight-lipped."

As Ethan had been with her.

And as it should be, Kate. You are Frances' lawyer. Ethan is the investigating officer on the Rigby case. They each had a duty to their respective professions.

"Do you know who they interviewed?"

"Frances Sloane." Nat sounded surprised. "She's the only one who lives there, right?"

"Yes, but her daughter is visiting from out of town...."

And out of all the members of that family, Kate could guess which Sloane the police would take an interest in.

Kenzie Sloane.

Who would have been the same age as the murder victim.

Who, from Kate's own personal experience, was capable of leading a young girl down a path of destruction.

Had she done the same to Heather Rigby?

"Is this going on tonight's news?" Kate asked.

"You bet. There was practically a lineup to get a shot of the driveway to Frances Sloane's house."

Damn.

Kate had not given up hope that Harry Owen would change his mind if she could convince him to meet with her client.

But if Frances' daughter was a suspect in this notorious case, he would not want anything to do with her.

God. What a mess. "Thanks, Nat. I've got to run."

"No problem. But remember, when your client gets arrested for Heather Rigby's murder, I get dibs on the exclusive. You know, quid pro quo."

Kate laughed. "She didn't kill anyone, Nat. She's not capable of it."

"So, if it wasn't her, why were the police at her house?"

"I don't know." Kate couldn't implicate Kenzie. That could interfere with the police investigation, and she had learned from bitter experience with the Lisa MacAdam case how important it was to stay out of their business.

But she could defend her own client.

And if that meant that the media turned their focus to a different Sloane, then so be it.

32

Kenzie stretched her shoulders and reloaded the needle with ink. She found herself glancing at her purse in the corner. Even though she had erased the text message from McNally, her cell phone now seemed like a ticking bomb.

Her client lay on his back, eyes closed. Conversation had become sparse in direct proportion to the stages of completion of the tattoo. The ribs were a sensitive area, and Kenzie worked as quickly as she could. Her client had tolerated the outline of the hannya mask well. It was the shading that was killing him. After three hours, the mask was almost done. And Kenzie's nerves were almost shot.

Kenzie had tattooed many hannya masks over the years. A traditional Japanese theatre mask that originated in the fourteenth century, the hannya mask was a popular symbol for good luck, even though it depicted the demonic rage of a woman who had been betrayed. The horns, the bulging eyes, the glowering expression—it had never bothered her.

Until today.

"The police have revealed that murder victim Heather

Rigby had been wearing a rubber Halloween mask of a witch when her body was hidden in the bogs at Chebucto Head." The killer's final, gruesome act was constantly replayed in the newspaper, the radio, the TV.

Heather had not been wearing a mask when Kenzie pulled the trigger.

Kenzie wished she had. Then she would never have seen the shock in her eyes, the rictus of pain twisting her mouth, the blood that eventually erupted from her lips and ran in a rivulet down her neck.

Kenzie's hand shook. The red ink that she used to shade the demon's mask trickled down the side of her client's rib cage.

Blood gushed from the wound in Heather's chest, running in separate streams across her ribs.

Kenzie's nose stung from an acrid, burning smell. Only then did she realize that a bullet had been fired.

"Shit," Lovett cried.

A moan broke from Heather's throat. Her eyes, so brown, so afraid, locked with Kenzie's. Help me, they begged.

Help me.

McNally threw Kenzie a triumphant look. "Guess you got lucky," he said.

Heather gasped. Tried to cough through the blood. She was dying.

She knew it, Kenzie knew it, Lovett and McNally knew it.

Stumbling sideways, Kenzie propelled herself through the small door.

"Where are you going, Kenz?" McNally panted. "You're gonna miss the grand finale!"

She heard him yell after her, "I'm doing this for you, Kenzie! Come back here!"

Warm, damp air enclosed her as she stumbled down the slope. The peat bogs lay below. Silent, watchful.

Shrouded with mist that both invited and repelled.

In the distance, she heard McNally shout, "Get her, Lovett!"

She ran onto the hummocks, her feet sinking into the spongy mass. The mist crawled over her skin, under what was left of her clothes. The damp chilled her, and she began to shiver, her teeth chattering.

The cocaine-fuelled adrenaline that had pounded in her veins, rampaged through her cells—that had given life to the wings of the raven inked on the back of her neck until they beat in time with her heart was gone. The mist enveloped her and whisked the adrenaline from her muscles, leaving a chill damp that radiated from her very marrow.

She would never be warm again.

A sob threatened to break from her throat. She was moving too slowly. The bog had tricked her, promising to obscure her path but instead it grabbed her boots and wouldn't let go.

Lovett. Where was Lovett?

She glanced over her shoulder.

He wasn't behind her.

Relief bubbled through the tightness of her chest. He had taken the path that ran along the cliff.

She stumbled across the bogs toward the woods, the mist absorbing the sound of her feet splashing through the water, the thud of her body as she fell and righted herself, the panicked breathing as she gasped for air.

When she reached the woods, she heard the first splash.

Lovett had realized his mistake. He had turned around.

He had come to the bog.

And just as the mist had protected her, it now shielded him.

She couldn't stop, couldn't catch her breath.

The branches of the bushes whipped her face, snatched at her hair.

One almost took out her eye.

But she cleared the woods and found the road.

Only then did she realize that she still carried the gun.

Kenzie could barely breathe. She bent over her workstation to compose herself. After a few deep breaths, she wiped the ink from her client's skin.

The hannya mask was almost completed. *Just finish the damn thing, Kenzie. And never do a hannya mask again.*

The only area of the tattoo left to complete were the eyes. She dipped the needle in black ink and pressed on the pedal of her tattoo machine. She would outline the irises first. Her hand moved quickly, steadily. She focused on the smallest of details, not allowing herself to glance at the mask in its entirety. Then it would have no power over her.

All she needed to add were the yellow highlights. A slight sheen of sweat dotted her upper lip. She dipped the needle into the ink and drew it into the tube.

She stretched the tattoo, lowering the tattoo needle to the irises of the mask. Its bulging gaze was accusing, angry. Vengeful.

They were McNally's eyes.

They were Heather's eyes.

They were Imogen's eyes.

They were Detective Ethan Drake's eyes.

Oh, God. I'm going crazy.

Her hand shook so much that she put down the tattoo gun.

"Just need a sip of water," she told her client, and rushed to the washroom. She locked the door.

She pressed a wet paper towel to her cheeks and studied her face in the mirror. The koi, curling protectively around her neck, was exactly the same.

And yet she knew that her life had changed. The police were investigating. The media was riding this story full tilt.

The tattoo had been discovered.

But that wasn't what caused the terror twisting her intestines.

It was the drawing that John McNally had sent this morning.

He was telling her it was time to strike again.

Her breath stopped in her throat, her heart jumping into overdrive as a thought hit her.

McNally wanted to kill Kate Lange.

She could kill two birds with one stone.

She would pretend to go along with him in this ridiculous fantasy to re-create Imogen Lange's death.

She would let him kill Kate Lange.

And then she would kill him.

A murder-suicide. The police would think that McNally had killed Kate, and then killed himself.

God.

That would be perfect.

This koi would always survive the waterfall.

33

When Ethan arrived at the war room, Ferguson, Liscomb and Lamond were clustered together, sifting through photos. Ferguson glanced up. Her eyes gleamed. "Ethan, FIS struck gold."

Liscomb grinned. "We found a hair."

"Where?"

"Inside the rubber Halloween mask. If you recall, since the victim's skin had slipped—" it always seemed a strange term, to Ethan, although a very blunt description of the epidermal layer literally slipping off the dermal layer of skin "—her hair was no longer attached to the scalp. A fair amount of it still remained inside the mask. Rigby's hair was shoulder-length and medium-brown. But we found a hair that was three inches longer, and under microscope, revealed pigments of pheomelanin, which produces *red* hair color."

Ethan's pulse leapt. "Can you get any DNA?" That would be the evidentiary clincher.

Liscomb shook her head. "Unfortunately not. The hair follicle appeared to be in the *telogen* phase." That meant the hair had been in the phase of hair growth, where the hair fell out naturally from the scalp. "You only get a DNA sample when there is some tissue still attached to the follicle, and in this case, even if the hair had been pulled out, it is doubtful any DNA could have been recovered."

Without DNA evidence, hair samples could be used to differentiate or place individuals at the scene of a crime, but they could not stand on their own to convict a person. The ability of the hair examiner, the age of the evidence, and the environmental factors created too many variables for a case to rest on one single microscopically examined hair.

"Still, we now have a hair that could place Kenzie Sloane at the scene of the crime."

Ferguson nodded. "She checked out of her hotel last night. She is, at present, working at Yakusoku Tattoo."

"Where's she staying?"

Ferguson gave him a look. "With a dog walker named Finn Scott."

Are you kidding me? "What's the connection?"

"She tattooed him. And he walks her dog."

"And now she's moved in with him? Man, that's some service he provides," Lamond murmured.

Ethan wondered what Kate thought of that turn of events. He knew that Finn, Kate's dog walker, spent a lot of time at her house. She couldn't be happy that the woman who had lured her sister into drugs was now his houseguest, even temporarily.

"I say we bring her in," Lamond said.

Ethan caught Ferguson's eye. They could arrest her without a warrant and detain her for twenty-four hours for questioning. After that, they would have to lay charges in front of a judge—or let her go. If they arrested her prematurely, they might not have enough evidence to get her charged.

But she knew something, Ethan's gut was sure of it. And if she left Halifax, they might never find Heather's killer.

Especially if the killer was Kenzie.

"I agree with Lamond," Ferguson said. "Let's bring her in before she flies the coop."

Ethan nodded. "Send Redding to Finn Scott's and arrest her."

Redding was not part of the investigating team, and thus would protect them if Kenzie Sloane's defense lawyer claimed that the accused had been questioned at the scene, which created the risk that further statements would be declared inadmissible. Plus, given Finn's relationship with Kate, Ethan did not want to be the arresting officer.

"We should have Ms. Sloane back at the station by supper time," Ethan said. "I'll do the interview. Lamond, you can be the monitor." The monitor was the person who watched the interview on a video stream and would give the interviewer feedback to help direct the course of the questioning.

He pushed back his chair. "Everyone eat. This is gonna be a long night." He hurried outside. He needed to call Kate and tell her he wouldn't be over tonight.

Kenzie broke down her workstation, her movements precise and methodical. She had erased McNally's text, but she knew he would find her tonight.

And then...

She shivered.

You can do it.

You've done it before.

She rolled Foo's blanket and stuffed it into her bag. Foo pawed at her leg. She picked him up.

"By tomorrow, we'll never see this hellhole again," she murmured into her pug's ear. He gave a long exhale of contentment. His warmth, his solid little body, his heart beating against hers—it never failed to soothe her.

She knocked on Yoshi's office door.

He looked up from his drafting board. "Hey."

"Hey." She closed the door behind her. "I have to leave tonight."

"What's up?" His gaze was concerned, but not surprised.

He'd been expecting her.

"I'm heading home. I'm sorry to bag on your clients." She gave him an apologetic smile. "But this has been the visit from hell."

He put down his pencil. "What's going on, Kenzie?"

She couldn't confide in him, as much as she wanted to unburden herself. "Sorry, it's personal."

"Listen, I heard the police question you yesterday. And they were in a few days ago with a drawing."

Her body went still. "A drawing?" She cleared her throat. "What was it?" But she knew. She knew what it was.

She had seen it, raw and bleeding at the base of Heather's neck.

She had felt every line, had known every angle, had exulted in the knowledge that the waiting was now over.

Heather had been marked.

Let the games begin.

"It was a raven," he said, his voice soft.

His eyes held hers. He remembered the raven tattoo on the base of her neck—over which she had asked him to tattoo a peony years ago. He would have realized that Heather's was an identical design.

"Did you tell them it was a raven?"

He ran his hand over the bristle on his head. "I'm sorry, Kenzie. At the time, I didn't know the connection...."

She jumped to her feet. "There is no connection. None. Lots of people have similar tattoos."

"And that is what I will tell the police if they ask me," he said, his voice calm. "I didn't tell them I'd seen that design before." He let his words sink in. "Are you in trouble, Kenzie? Can I help you at all?"

She shook her head. "No. I just need to go home. Everything will be fine."

"Safe journey." Yoshi hurried around his desk and gave her a hug.

"Thank you, Yoshi," Kenzie whispered. "You've always been a true friend."

She scooped Foo into her arms and strode out of his office.

It took a minute for her brain to comprehend what her subconscious had already registered: that one by one, the tattoo machines had stopped buzzing. The room fell silent. Except for the sounds of two men walking toward her. One was a uniformed police officer. The other man, who was extremely tall, wore a suit.

Foo wriggled in her arms. He began to bark.

She put him down. "Quiet, Foo."

The tall man stood in front of her, effectively blocking her path. The uniformed cop walked to her side. Foo angled his body between the men and Kenzie's foot and glared upwards, his brow furrowed. If it had been any other moment but this, Kenzie would have smiled.

"Kenzie Sloane?"

She swallowed. "Yes."

"I am Detective Constable Redding of the Halifax

Police Department." He held out his badge. "You are under arrest for the murder of Heather Catherine Rigby."

There was a gasp from a customer in the front of the shop.

Oh, fuck off.

The rest of what the detective said was so clichéd—Kenzie had heard something similar on all those *CSI* shows—that it didn't truly register that the words were meant for her until the detective asked her to repeat it.

"Me?" she asked. Why would he want her to repeat it?

She couldn't.

He repeated himself, and asked her to tell him what he said. It was only then that she could paraphrase the caution that he had read to her.

The patrol officer snapped handcuffs on her wrists. And that snapped her out of her disbelief.

"Foo! What about my dog?" she asked the detective.

He glanced around the shop. "Can someone look after Ms. Sloane's dog for twenty-four hours?"

Kenzie searched the onlookers for Yoshi. He stood to one side, his eyes round with dismay behind his John Lennon glasses. Her face flushed with shame.

"Yoshi, can you call Finn and ask him to take Foo?" There was the slightest tremble in her voice. She held out Foo's leash.

Her old, trusty friend hurried over. His expression was so sad, a little piece of her heart broke.

But it couldn't compare to how she felt when she saw the panic in Foo's eyes as the police led her away.

He pulled so hard on his leash that he began to choke. She threw a worried glance over her shoulder. "It's okay, baby," she called.

His eyes beseeched her.
Come back.
Her heart broke.

34

Kate bent over her thigh, clasping her hamstring. Her quad had begun to act up again. She had made it through her run, all the way back to Enid and Muriel's house, but now paid the price. A sharp burning pain ran through her upper leg, radiating from the scalpel wound she suffered last year.

Finn's truck pulled into the driveway. He jumped out, and sprinted up the driveway. "Kate! Kate!"

Kate straightened as he stopped in front of her.

His face was flushed, his hair mussed, his usual laid-back manner replaced with panic.

Kate's heart began to pound. She had never seen Finn so agitated.

"Is everything okay?"

"No. No, it's not." He ran his hand through his hair. "It's Kenzie."

"What about her?"

"She was arrested at supper time."

Kate was surprised. Not because she was arrested, but because it had happened so quickly.

Kenzie, she was sure, had been on the police's radar from the beginning. "On what grounds?"

He took a deep breath. "They arrested her for the murder of that girl they found in the bog. Heather Rigby." He gazed at her, incredulous. "I can't believe it."

Kate had no response to that.

"Where did they arrest her?"

"At the tattoo studio where she worked." That was said with the slightest hint of defiance.

Kate processed the implications of that. "So she's at the police station now?"

"Yes. You've got to help her, Kate."

"Whoa." Kate shook her head. "I can't do that, Finn."

"Why not?"

"I'm representing her mother."

Finn thrust his fingers into his hair and stared at her. "Why can't you represent Kenzie, too?"

Despite Finn's naive belief that Kenzie would want Kate's help, she doubted that Kenzie would want to entrust her future to Kate's hands. But even if she did, Kate wouldn't take her on as a client, despite the fact that there weren't any obvious conflicts with Frances' legal matter and Kenzie's. "Because things could get messy," she said.

"What do you mean?" His obvious skepticism hurt her. He thought she was refusing for personal reasons. And although those were many, they weren't the reason why.

She kept her tone neutral. "What if both Kenzie and Frances are suspects, Finn?" she asked. "They could have conflicting interests. Or what if her mother is a witness?"

That didn't seem out of the realm of possibility.

Finn exhaled and ran his hands through his hair again. "Oh, shit."

"There are hundreds of lawyers in Halifax." Kate

cleared her throat. "And they would be much more experienced at criminal law than I am."

"She didn't do it, Kate." There was a desperation in Finn's eyes that stabbed Kate. "I know she's innocent. I don't want her to go through the same thing Randall Barrett did!"

This is not *the same.* "Has she called a lawyer yet?"

"No. She said she didn't want one."

"If she doesn't want one you can't force one on her."

"I can try," her loyal friend said. "Please, Kate." She had never heard Finn beg before. *Damn him.* Finn was her friend. He had helped her in ways that she could never repay. And he had never asked for anything in return.

Until now.

"Look, I can't represent her. Please believe me, I would help you if I could." And she meant it. "But I can recommend the best criminal lawyer in town."

"Eddie?"

"Yes, Eddie." She pulled out her cell phone. She didn't normally carry it with her, but since the break-in last night, she wouldn't go anywhere without it. "I'll call him right now."

Hope lit Finn's blue eyes. Kate dialed Eddie's number and studied her front garden, absently noting that the tulips were beginning to bud.

"Bent here," Eddie's growly voice answered on the third ring.

"It's Kate." She glanced at Finn. Still those anxious, hopeful eyes. She stared at the tulips. "Look, Finn is here. He told me that Frances Sloane's daughter Kenzie has just been arrested for the murder of Heather Rigby."

"And?"

That was a typical Eddie response. He would be

silently parsing the information in his head, while giving nothing away.

"He wants you to represent her."

"Where is she?"

"Down at the station."

"Tell Finn I'll be there in half an hour," Eddie said. "And ask him to give my phone number to Ms. Sloane."

"Thanks, Eddie," Kate said. "After you meet with her, do you want to come over for dinner? I'm staying at Muriel and Enid's house."

"I might be a while."

"I just need to update you on a few things." She hadn't yet let him know about the break-in or the stalker. She glanced at Finn. She hadn't told him yet, either. But this clearly wasn't the time.

"Okay, I'll come over after I brief Kenzie Sloane."

"See you then." She hung up and turned to Finn.

"Eddie's onboard." Finn's face sagged with relief. "Meet him down at the station. He wants you to give his phone number to Kenzie. Do you have a pen?"

He pulled one out of the back pocket of his jeans. "I'll write it on my hand."

Kate gave him the number.

He smiled. "Thank you, Kate. I appreciate it."

His gratitude saddened her. *He has no idea what is going down.*

She forced a smile in return. "You've got the best." She walked him to his truck. "Keep me posted. If you need me to take care of anything, just shout."

"Thanks, Kate." He gave her a quick hug.

She returned it. "By the way," she said. "Was Kenzie at your place last night?"

"Yes."

"All night?"

He flushed. "Yeah. Why?"

She smiled. "Just curious. And don't worry. Kenzie is in excellent hands."

She gave him a quick hug, her fingers brushing his bandaged shoulder. She had hoped this would be the only scar that Kenzie inflicted on her friend.

But she knew this was nothing compared to what was coming.

35

Finn sat on a varnished wooden bench in the foyer of the police station, his head against the wall, fingers drumming his knee. Eddie hadn't spent much time with Finn, but he had never seen the dog walker so tense. He jumped to his feet as soon as Eddie pulled open the heavy wooden entrance doors.

"Kenzie just called me—"

Eddie noted Kenzie Sloane called Finn rather than her dying mother.

"I told her you were coming to the station."

"And?" He brushed a stray fleck of ash from his shirt.

"She said she'd talk to you."

"Okay, I'll let the police know I'm here to see her."

The relief in Finn's eyes was palpable. "She didn't do anything. You have to tell the police they've arrested the wrong person."

"Look, Finn, there isn't that much either of us can do for Kenzie at this moment. I can tell her not to say anything, but until she is formally charged, that's about it."

He walked over to the reception desk. A police constable watched them, making no effort to hide the fact he'd listened to Eddie's conversation with Finn. They were in a public space. All was fair in love and war. Everyone wanted Heather Rigby's killer to be caught and punished. Even more reason for Kenzie Sloane to get a good lawyer. Eddie gave the constable a friendly smile. "I am Eddie Bent. I need to speak to my client, Kenzie Sloane."

The constable dialed a number and relayed Eddie's message. He hung up the phone, nodding to Eddie. "Someone will be down to let you in."

Eddie hiked up the legs on his jeans and settled down on the bench next to Finn. "So tell me what Kenzie told you," he said. "When did the police arrest her?"

"About an hour ago. At the tattoo studio."

Eddie shot Finn another look. "But she's not living in Halifax, correct?"

Finn shook his head. "No, lives in Manhattan. She came home to see her mother. And to work some tattoo gigs."

The security door opened.

"Mr. Bent," Detective Ethan Drake said, his expression closed. As Eddie expected it to be. This was a high-profile case with a sensational arrest. Kenzie Sloane was a celebrity, and her profession had a colorful enough history to make every element of the case subject to intense scrutiny. The police would make every effort to follow the process to a *T.* "Please come with me."

Eddie had not seen Ethan Drake since that day last summer at Randall Barrett's bail hearing. He wondered if Drake had felt remorse for what he put Randall through. For what he put Randall's kids through.

Eddie guessed he did. Drake seemed like a decent enough cop. He didn't know all the details about what happened between the detective and Kate, but it didn't seem like the detective had been fully to blame.

And as Eddie had learned over the ups and extreme downs of his life, no one was perfect.

Certainly not him.

They walked into a corridor, as bland as Ethan Drake's demeanor. He held open a door. "Your client is in here."

"The room isn't miked or set up with a camera?" Eddie was sure it wasn't—the police were too smart to foil their chances at a conviction—but the question needed to be asked.

Ethan flashed him a look, but his tone was neutral. "You will have complete privacy as per your client's rights."

Eddie strolled into the room and closed the door.

His client sat behind a table, her finger tracing the lines of a tattoo that covered her entire arm. She wore cargo pants and a tank top. A distressed leather moto jacket hung over the back of her chair. It looked expensive. In fact, all of her urban-style attire appeared expensive. Whatever Kenzie Sloane did for a living, she was successful.

That meant she had a certain level of discipline.

She glanced up. Her eyes were startling. Sky-blue in a porcelain face, they were artfully enhanced with makeup. They could be a great asset on the stand.

Or, as in now, they could be her worst enemy. Her gaze flicked with unmistakable contempt over his rumpled plaid shirt and baggy jeans that still bore mud on the knees from Randall's garden bed. "Are you my lawyer?"

He sat down in the chair facing her. "I'm Eddie Bent. I am a criminal defense lawyer. Your friend Finn told me that you had requested my services to represent you as legal counsel."

Her gaze traveled over his face. Her fingers, he noticed, still traced the lines of her tattoo with unerring accuracy, rising and falling on the Japanese waves as if only they knew their true destination. "I suppose so."

"First things first. These are my fees." He outlined his fee structure. Her gaze was expressionless. "Is this a problem for you?"

"No."

"Second, everything you tell me—except in a very narrow set of circumstances—is protected by solicitor-client confidentiality. I will not reveal it to anyone. So the more frank you are, the better I can mount a defense."

There was a flicker in her gaze.

She cared more than she let on. Those tough-on-the-outside girls usually did.

Unless they were psychopaths.

Was she one?

He studied her as closely as she studied him.

Her fingers ceased their meandering. She straightened in her chair. "What do you want to know?"

"Everything." He smiled. "But let's start with the actual arrest. There are certain procedures the police need to follow to ensure your constitutional rights are protected. Tell me what happened."

"I was at a tattoo studio. I had just finished work. I'm a tattoo artist," she added, glancing with defiant pride at the full sleeves of tattoos on her arms. He knew that, he had seen the item on the news when the police had gone to Frances Sloane's house. The media were all over the fact that her daughter was a celebrity tattooist. "I had just finished packing up my kit bag."

"Were you going somewhere?"

She flashed him a defiant look. "I had finished my gig. I was going back home to Manhattan."

"Were you scheduled to go home tonight?" This definitely had a get-the-hell-out-of-town desperation to it.

"Sort of."

"What does that mean?"

She glanced away, her eyes glittering. Finally, she spoke. "I changed my flight. I was supposed to go home three days from now." Her tone was flat.

"Why did you change your mind?"

"The police questioned me."

"And?"

"It made me uncomfortable. I did what I had come to do. I didn't see a need to stay longer."

Eddie decided not to push it. There was time for that later. "And what happened?"

"I had finished packing, like I said. I was saying goodbye to the guy who owns the shop. And the police arrived."

"What did they do? Did they knock, or did they make a forced entry...?" Eddie asked the question in an idle tone.

"They just walked in." That was said with the slightest edge to her voice. She took a sip of water from a foam cup. "They asked if I was Kenzie Sloane. I said yes. They read me my rights, and one of the cops put cuffs on me and took me down here."

"Did they tell you that you had a right to remain silent?"

"Yes."

"And were you silent?"

"Yes. Except when I asked them to call Finn, my boy—my friend—to take care of Foo. My dog." She blinked. "And then they drove me here."

"Did you say anything other than that?"

"No."

"And did you come straight here?"

"Yes."

"Where did they take you?"

"To a room. They said they were video recording my statement. And then they told me I had a right to counsel."

He had many clients who had been in that room. Concrete block walls painted a dingy off-white color. Hard furniture. Fluorescent lights.

"I told them I wanted to call Finn, because he knew some lawyers he could call."

"And after that, did they ask you any questions?"

"No."

That told him more than anything else that Drake and his team were proceeding extremely carefully. They either had enough evidence that they didn't want to risk contaminating their case, or they had very little evidence and didn't want to risk having her statements thrown out. Either way, they meant business with Kenzie Sloane.

"Okay, tell me everything they said to you."

It wasn't much. The police kept a tight lid on their evidence.

Eddie jotted notes. "At this stage, Kenzie, say nothing. You have a right to remain silent, do you understand?"

"Yes, I do."

"They will keep questioning you." He gave her a warning look over the top of his glasses. "They can stick their faces into yours, they can lie to you, they might try to tell you that you were seen at the crime scene that night—" Was that an imperceptible stiff-

ening of her shoulders? "—they can tell you that your
mother told them everything and they have proof you
killed Heather." He kept his eyes locked on hers. "But
whatever they say, don't respond. Be polite, but don't
answer any questions."

"Don't worry, I won't."

"It's easy to say right now, but when you are seventeen hours in and feeling exhausted, you might be
tempted to say something—especially if they seem
really sympathetic." He leaned toward her. "Look away
and keep your mouth shut. Every time they ask a question, say nothing. If you feel the need to say anything,
just tell them 'I am exercising my right to remain silent.
Please stop questioning me.' It won't stop them, but it
will be on videotape for the judge to see."

She nodded and flexed her fingers.

She had, Eddie realized, beautiful hands with long,
elegant fingers. He noted the tattoos. "That's kanji,
right? What do the letters spell?"

She gave a wry smile and lifted her left hand. "Tranquility." She raised her right hand. "Strength." The right
hand covered the tattoo on her left thumb. Then her
finger began its odyssey up her arm. "Haven't seen too
much of good ol' tranquility since I came to Halifax."

"Tonight you see won't any of it," Eddie said. "But if
you can hold on for twenty-four hours without saying a
word, you'll have a much better chance of regaining it
later." He stood. "Call me anytime. If you can't reach
me, tell the police that I am your counsel of choice and
you do not wish to see duty counsel." He dropped his
card on the table and gave her a sympathetic smile. "Just
hold tight for tonight."

"Did you see Finn?" Her remarkable eyes searched
his. For the first time, he saw some emotion in them.

"Yes. He has been pacing the foyer of the police station."

"Does he have Foo?"

"He told me he did. Finn is excellent with dogs. Foo is in good hands."

Her eyes glistened with tears.

Uh-oh. Not a good sign. If the police hammered away at her concern for her dog, she could crumble.

He patted her hand. "Foo will be fine. Remember, don't say anything. Then you'll see him tomorrow. Otherwise…"

She exhaled. Then she nodded to herself. "Got it."

His last glimpse of Kenzie was of his client staring at the wall, her fingers tracing her tattoo, navigating the waves of a hostile sea.

36

The police had removed the table, leaving two chairs in the concrete room. One for Kenzie and one for the uptight guy, Detective Drake. He positioned his chair next to her. He was so close, she could feel the warmth from his arm. She shifted away. *Nice try, Detective.*

"Kenzie, we spoke to your mother."

She stared at the wall.

"She says she forgives you."

Kenzie knew they would try to unbalance her emotionally. She had steeled herself. And yet, despite her resolve to remain untouched, the detective's pronouncement stung her. She stared at the table. "I am exercising my right to remain silent."

The detective lowered his voice. "Listen, Kenzie, you were only seventeen when you killed Heather. We know that. You were young. It was Mardi Gras. You'd been drinking. You got angry." She glanced up. And regretted it.

Detective Drake's eyes locked onto hers, his expression sympathetic. But she had had many, many clients under her hands over the years. She could judge as well as he when someone was being sincere. Or not. "You didn't know how to control yourself," he continued. "You killed her, and then panicked. But you've had to live with it for seventeen years. Seventeen years while her family wondered where their beloved daughter had gone—"

Unlike her own mother.

"—seventeen years of worrying and waiting."

I've kept quiet for seventeen years. You don't think I can handle another twenty—she glanced at her watch—*twenty hours and thirty-nine minutes?*

"I am exercising my right to remain silent, Detective," she said.

She closed her eyes.

37

"Come on in." Kate held the door open for Eddie. "I'm putting the salmon in the oven. We just came back from visiting Enid at the hospital."

"How's she doing?" Eddie asked as they walked into the kitchen.

"Better." Kate smiled at Muriel, who trimmed green beans. "Right, Muriel?"

The elderly lady nodded. "Yes, she's coming home soon."

"That's wonderful news, Muriel." Eddie settled into a chair and let out a sigh of pleasure. "I don't know how you do all that gardening. It's killing my knees."

Eddie, Kate noted with a smile, still wore his gardening clothes. She wondered what the police made of that.

"Wear knee pads," Muriel said. "I have some you can borrow."

"Good idea," Eddie said. "My knees thank you."

Muriel put down her paring knife and slipped on a pair of large green rain boots. "I'll go find them. They are in the shed outside." She hurried out the door, her cat not far behind.

"She seems to be holding up," Eddie said, watching the elderly lady stride to the potting shed.

Kate measured rice into the steamer. "Barely. Corazon has really been a godsend. But thank goodness Enid will be sent home shortly." She placed the lid on the pot. "How did it go at the police station?"

Eddie leaned back in the chair, seemingly relaxed. But his eyes missed nothing. "Business as usual, Kate."

"Do you think she did it?" Kate pulled a can of coconut milk out of the cupboard.

Eddie gave her a recriminating look. "You know I'm not supposed to talk about my clients."

"I know." Kate opened the fridge and examined a piece of gingerroot. It wasn't too wrinkly. She began to peel it. "But after what you told me about how Heather Rigby's disappearance affected you, I wondered what you thought."

Eddie's gaze met hers. "I can't think about that, Kate."

"Why not?" Kate dug around in a drawer and produced an ancient knife. She began to dice the ginger.

"Because it doesn't help."

"It doesn't help who? The family of the murder victim?"

"Kate, I'm not representing them. I'm representing Kenzie." His tone was patient, but she sensed a hint of agitation beneath his manner.

Perhaps this case was getting under the rumpled unflappability of her mentor. It certainly got under *her* skin. She put down her knife. "Did you know Kenzie was staying with Finn?" That discovery still hurt.

His gaze met hers. "Yes."

"Did she tell you why?"

"I presume it's the age-old reason—boy meets girl."

"Finn is way too trusting. She will ruin his life."

Eddie threw her a look. Kate resumed chopping. "You haven't seen Kenzie for seventeen years. She was just a teenager when your sister died. She may have changed. You have to give her the benefit of the doubt," he said.

Kate shook her head. The ginger was stringy, resistant to the knife. She should have used a sharper one. But she had developed a mild phobia of sharp knives since last year.... "I don't have to give her the benefit of anything."

"Well, I do, Kate. I'm her lawyer. And I'd like to remind you that even if you personally cannot give her the benefit of the doubt, the law presumes she is innocent. As do I." Alaska tore himself away from the possibility of food falling from the kitchen counter and meandered over to Eddie's feet. He leaned down to pat the husky. "I'm surprised at you, Kate. I thought you believed in those principles."

"I did."

"But you don't now?"

She shook her head. "Not when it comes to Kenzie."

"I think you are blinded by your anger, Kate." Eddie's tone was gentle.

"Eddie, you yourself told me how much Heather Rigby's case affected you. She was found in a bog with a Halloween mask on her head. She was murdered. She never had a chance to say goodbye. She could have had an argument with her parents, or been mean to her friend, and she never had a chance, Eddie. Kenzie stole that from her."

"Kate—" Eddie exhaled. "I know you have reason to believe the worst of Kenzie. But she was still a teen when you knew her. How do you know she hasn't felt remorse about what happened to your sister?"

"You didn't see the look in her eyes at Gennie's funeral."

"Kate, seventeen years is a long time. She might feel very differently now."

"Or she might simply be evil, Eddie. An evil teen who grew into an evil woman."

"That is for the courts to decide. But you know, Kate, just because she had a problem with addiction doesn't mean she's a killer."

Kate flushed. Eddie had struggled with alcoholism for years.

"I know. But you don't know her, Eddie. She is just… bad. And besides, there is a lot of evidence to suggest she killed Heather—the tattoo, the proximity of the crime scene to her house, the fact she left Halifax the day after Heather was killed…"

"There was overwhelming evidence that Randall had killed Elise." Kate's mouth tightened. She'd known Eddie would bring up Randall's case. *But this was different.*

Eddie's shrewd gaze was a bit too penetrating for Kate's comfort. "You know better than anyone else how easy it is to slap a biased interpretation onto the facts. How do you know Kenzie wasn't a witness?"

She raised a brow. "How do you know she wasn't the killer?"

Eddie shook his head. "I don't know. But I can't assume she's guilty of murder because she gave your sister some coke seventeen years ago."

Kate forced the knife through a particularly stubborn piece of ginger, narrowly avoiding nicking her finger.

"She's dangerous. She's a Dorian Gray pinup girl." Her voice had an embarrassing tremor to it.

Eddie's gaze softened. "Listen to yourself, Kate. Why are you so angry? Do you have feelings for Finn? Is that it?"

Kate scooped the ginger into a bowl. "Yes. I do. He's like a brother to me. I'm scared for him, Eddie."

"He's a grown man, Kate."

There was nothing to say to that. She knew she was being illogical. But she didn't care. Kenzie Sloane was a totally different beast than the usual criminals that Eddie dealt with.

She just hoped the prosecution had a damned good case.

Ethan pushed his chair back and strode out of the interviewing room, his movements deliberately abrupt. Kenzie didn't move.

He shut the door behind him and entered the monitoring room. Ferguson sat behind the microphone that connected to his earpiece. She had been murmuring suggestions to him off and on for the past three hours, but Kenzie hadn't bitten. Ferguson removed her headphones. She pointed at the monitor. "Check this out. Sleeping Beauty has finally awoken." Kenzie had hopped off the chair in the interview room and had begun to do a series of yoga poses.

He turned away from the monitor in disgust.

"She's got to be hiding something. She hasn't said a word since her lawyer left."

Ethan nodded. "I know. But nothing's working on her." The sympathy angle didn't work. He and Lamond had tag-teamed and that had no effect, either. He rubbed his jaw. "I want to show her the sketch that was left in Kate Lange's house last night."

Ferguson shot him a skeptical look. "We don't know those incidents are connected."

"I know. But the sketch was really good. Professional quality. And pinup girls are popular tattoos."

"So you think whoever did the tattoo on Heather was the guy who left the sketch for Kate?"

God. I hope not.

He shrugged. "I don't know what the connection is. But I think there is one. Maybe Kenzie broke into Kate's house and left the picture. Maybe she doesn't like the fact that her mother is trying to kill herself." That seemed a stretch, but who knew. "Or maybe Kenzie would recognize the work of the person who did it and be willing to do some negotiating."

Ferguson put the headphones back on. "Do it."

Ten minutes later, Ethan had retrieved the sketch from the incident report. Merely holding the drawing made him remember the mortification in Kate's eyes when she had seen herself depicted in that pose. Knowing she was the object of some pervert's fantasies had killed him. Heat flushed his neck.

Easy, Drake.

But he slammed the door behind him anyway when he entered the interview room. Kenzie started. Then she stretched her arms over her head, giving him a contemptuous glance, and threw herself back in her chair.

She closed her eyes.

"Nice work, Kenzie." Ethan sat down opposite her. She ignored him.

Ethan crinkled the evidence bag. "I'm surprised you would stoop this low, though."

Her eyes remained closed. But he sensed her interest. "I mean, you'd have to be pretty desperate to draw a picture like this. And I never thought you were the desperate type."

The muscles around her eyes tightened. She wanted to open them—and was forcing herself to keep them closed. "But we thank you for leaving this for Kate Lange. It gives us another piece of evidence to present to the judge tomorrow."

Kenzie's eyes slowly opened. "Why would I leave anything for Kate Lange? I haven't seen her in seventeen years."

This was the longest Kenzie had spoken since the detention began. Ethan forced his excitement not to show on his face. "You tell me." He held up the sketch. "This is a pretty cheap shot. Not worthy of you, Kenzie."

Kenzie gave it a dismissive glance. "You guys had better up your game if you want to solve any of these cases. I don't do pinups."

Ethan leaned forward. "Then who does?"

"Detective, if I wanted to be a cop I would have joined the force. I'm not doing your job for you." Kenzie closed her eyes.

Anger pounded in Ethan's veins. He wanted to shake Kenzie Sloane, force her to open her eyes and tell him who the hell had done this to Kate.

"Time out, Drake." Ferguson's voice was soft in his ear. "Let her think about it."

You need to cool down was the message. His anger must have shown on his face.

And that would only lead to disaster.

He strode to the door, forcing himself to appear relaxed. As soon as he left the room, he checked his watch. He needed to call Kate and check in with her. Make sure that Finn was with her.

A thought snaked through his head. What if Kenzie had drawn the sketch—and sent her new boyfriend to deliver it?

No. Finn wasn't capable of that.

Was he?

No. He would not harm Kate. Ethan was sure of it.

Kenzie kept her eyes closed. Her muscles buzzed with suppressed excitement. She was dying to leap off her chair and dance around the room.

She couldn't believe McNally had been stupid enough to taunt Kate Lange with that sketch of her as a pinup girl.

McNally had put the final nail in his coffin.

After his body and Kate's were found, the police would undoubtedly search his apartment. She was sure it was full of pinup sketches. And it would reinforce their theory that McNally was Kate's murderous stalker.

Well, she had to admit it. They were right.

Just not one hundred percent.

They had missed one killer.

38

It had happened too fast.

McNally's fingers trembled as he read the newspaper headline again: Celebrity Tattoo Artist Arrested for Murder of Heather Rigby.

Kenzie was being held by the police. Since sometime last night.

Would they let her go after twenty-four hours—or charge her?

He ran his hand over the bristle on his scalp, pacing the small living room. He turned on the television. But the droning of the news anchor's voice about events somewhere on the other side of the goddamned world irritated the hell out of him.

He strode into the bathroom and stood in front of the sink. Stubble dotted his cheeks, blurring the clean edges of his goatee. Everything had been going so perfectly. And now the police had Kenzie.

You are so stupid.

Every time you saw Kenzie, you let her knock you down.

You let her call the shots.

And now look what happened.

He laid out his grooming supplies. Razor. Shaver. Beard trimmer.

He switched on his shaver and ran it down his cheek. Over and over again, until his skin stung, his mind racing with questions.

Had Kate Lange told the police about Imogen's tattoo?

Had Kenzie ratted on him?

Did she turn over the gun to the police?

But his brain kept coming back to the question that scared him the most: *Would the police let her go?*

She'd been snatched from under his gaze. Taken to the police station and held in detention. What if they didn't release her? What if she never got out of prison?

What if she'd panicked after the text I sent her and called the police?

He had waited seventeen years to finish something they'd started together on a misty, warm Halloween night.

Kenzie was his.

Always had been.

No matter what she did.

And he'd just executed the perfect plan at Kate Lange's house.

He raised the shaver to his temple. He ran it across the back of his skull to the other ear. The web tattooed across the back of his head tingled.

Then he shaved his skull, his scalp gleaming.

He was ready.

The phone rang. Kate jolted up in bed.

Her thoughts were jangled, fear tinged: Was it her alarm company? Had her house been broken into again?

Kate blinked at the clock—6:55 a.m. She fumbled for the phone.

"Kate?" asked Frances in her unmistakable voice.

Kate flung back the covers. This could not be good. She cleared her throat. "Good morning, Frances. How are you?"

"Have you seen this morning's newspaper?"

"No."

"The police have arrested Kenzie. For the murder of that girl."

Kate exhaled. "I see."

"She didn't do it, Kate."

Kate closed her eyes. "The criminal justice system will give her the benefit of the doubt, Mrs. Sloane."

"Like they did Randall Barrett?"

Touché.

"Eddie Bent is representing her. Trust me, he'll make sure that the presumption of innocence is alive and well in her case."

"Well, he can save his breath."

Kate blinked. "Pardon me?"

"My daughter did not kill that young woman."

She spoke with absolute certainty. And not, Kate sensed, because she believed her daughter was not capable of such a crime.

"Why do you say that?"

There was a pause.

"Because I killed her."

And then Frances Sloane began to laugh.

39

"I have an idea," Ethan said. He drained his coffee, his taste buds so inured to the bitterness of the reheated brew that he barely tasted it.

"We could use one about now," Ferguson said. She looked as rumpled as he felt.

They had left Kenzie in the interview room to "think." It had been a long, frustrating night.

She hadn't said another word.

Of the many suspects Ethan had interviewed over the years, he could count on one hand the number who hadn't cracked at some point.

Kenzie had added herself to that number.

Those tattoos were a force field, he thought. She deflected every tactic to get her to talk. Either Eddie Bent had counseled her extremely well, or she was too scared to talk for fear of incurring the wrath of whomever had killed Rigby.

Or…she had done the deed and was too smart to say anything.

He would bet that the answer lay behind door number three—but he had also learned the hard way with Barrett's case to not jump to conclusions.

It was looking more and more as though they wouldn't get a statement from her during her detention. But as Ethan sat in the interview room with her, studying her tattoos, he remembered that Frances Sloane had said Kenzie had had several tattoos. Had one of them been a raven?

It certainly wasn't in evidence now.

Either it was under her clothes or...it had been covered up by another tattoo.

He left the room and tracked down Liscomb. "I want you to use the infrared camera and photograph Sloane's tattoos. Just stand behind the one-way glass and see what you can get."

If the tattoo had been covered up by another tattoo, the infrared camera should be able to detect it. And if it was identical to Heather Rigby's, it was one more piece of evidence to use to break Kenzie Sloane's silence.

"Mrs. Sloane, let's start at the beginning." Kate sat in an armchair that she had positioned to face her client. The May sun, a notoriously unreliable witness, decided to make an appearance.

"I killed Heather Rigby." Frances Sloane's eyes were calm, resolute.

Uh-huh. "Tell me what happened." Kate opened a notepad.

"I was out walking by the bunkers. It was late on Halloween night—"

"How late?"

"I don't remember."

Of course you don't. "Why were you walking out at Chebucto Head? Especially on Halloween?"

She swallowed. "I often walked there. It helped me think."

That could be true. "So what happened?"

"A girl ran out of the bunker. She was crying."

"This girl was...?"

"Heather Rigby. She asked me to help her. Said her friend had hurt herself and was lying inside the bunker."

Frances' disease prevented the muscles in her face from giving away any involuntary cues of mendacity. But there was nothing wrong with Frances Sloane's eyes. Right now, they gazed at Kate with determination. Not unease.

Kate couldn't tell if she spoke the truth. Or not. "What did you do?"

"I followed the girl into the bunker. But she had lied to me. There was no friend. Instead—" Frances began to cough. After a minute, she had cleared her airway. "Instead, she jumped me."

"Why?"

"She wanted money. But I didn't have any. It made her angry. She had a gun...."

Kate lowered her pen. Given Canada's strict gun laws, it was unusual for a teenage girl to have a gun. Unless it was a hunting rifle. "You mean a shotgun?"

"No, a handgun. She aimed it at me. But I hit her in the shoulder and she dropped the gun."

"And?"

"I grabbed the gun off the ground. She rushed toward me. And I...I shot her."

Had the police recovered the murder weapon?

"She wasn't very big, Frances. Why did you need to shoot her?"

Frances blinked. Swallowed. "She was strong. She was also very angry. I feared for my life." The irony of her client's current situation did not escape Kate.

"What happened after you shot her?"

"She collapsed. I realized I had killed her."

The next question was critical. If Frances could answer it correctly, she either had an inside line on the forensic holdback evidence, or had been a witness when Heather Rigby was killed—or had shot her as she said she did. "Where did the bullet hit her?"

Was that the slightest hesitation? Hard to tell with Frances. "In the heart."

"The heart?"

"The chest," she said. "Somewhere in her upper body. I couldn't tell. It was dark."

Nicely fudged, Frances. "So then what happened?"

"She died." She glanced away. "There was a rubber witch mask in the bunker—"

"Someone left it there?"

"I think it was Heather's." She paused. Fatigue already pulled at the flaccid muscles of her face. "...Wearing a witch costume."

"Heather wore a witch costume," Kate repeated to ensure she understood her client. Frances' speech had worsened over the past week.

"Yes. I put the mask on her."

"Why?"

"I was angry." She studied her barely functioning hands as if remembering their past strength. "I dragged her to the bog."

"How did you bury her?"

"I dug under it. Rolled her body in." She blinked several times.

"Mrs. Sloane, do you understand the consequences of what you've just told me?"

"Yes. I will go to jail for the rest of my life. I deserve to be punished."

"Your bid to change the assisted suicide law is now

dead in the water." Kate's voice was flat in her effort to not sound accusatory.

Despite the details provided by Frances in her confession, it rang false to Kate. The evidence against Kenzie was compelling. And Frances' sudden decision to confess when she learned Kenzie was under suspicion reeked of desperation.

The classic mother-protecting-offspring act.

But in this case, Frances was throwing away a chance to do something really good with the end of her life. And she was making that sacrifice to protect someone who had probably killed Heather Rigby—and who deserved to be punished.

Kate gazed at her notes, her mind whirling. But no matter which avenue she explored, she came back to the inevitable conclusion: she had a legal duty to proceed with her client's instructions. She had no evidence that her client had lied, or that someone else had committed the crime. Ethically, her path was clear. She raised her head and said, "What are your instructions, Mrs. Sloane?"

"I want you to tell the police they have the wrong suspect. Just like Barrett's case."

It was nothing like Randall Barrett's case, Kate thought wearily. "Okay, we'll do this by affidavit. I'll draw one up, and then you need to sign it. After that, I'll contact the investigating officer—" her stomach tightened at the knowledge that it was Ethan "—and inform him that you are confessing to the murder of Heather Rigby."

"Too bad they don't have the death penalty anymore," Frances slurred.

The death penalty, in this case, would have killed two birds with one stone for Frances Sloane.

If Frances had been the killer.

"One more thing," Frances said.

Kate glanced up. This couldn't be good.

"As soon as you give my affidavit to the police, I want you to issue a public statement that I have confessed to the murder of Heather Rigby."

And thereby make the police's job that much more difficult. Kate flipped her notepad closed.

Nicely done, Frances.

It was not surprising, Frances supposed, that she thought of her disease in terms of right angles. ALS destroyed her body in discrete stages. One day she could still swallow, the next day it was an act of gargantuan effort. It was as if she had taken a step on an escalator. And the previous step of functionality was swallowed by the machine, never to return.

She knew from the early days of her diagnosis, when she had participated in ALS support groups, that some patients viewed their illness as the final stage on a journey to a better place, an "up" escalator to paradise.

She, however, had stepped onto a down escalator. Every time her disease progressed to a worse stage, she became more isolated, more trapped. Her son, Cameron, who had bought out her partnership in her architectural firm three years ago, made an effort to see her. But he and his wife, Karen, had their hands full with twin three-year-old boys and a nine-month-old daughter named Lily Frances. The children were too young to have patience with her slow speech, her inability to move—and, in fact, were frightened of the wheelchair, the tubes that connected her to oxygen, the coughing fits that gurgled and choked her breath. "Grandma is scary," she heard young Joshua protest one afternoon when Karen and Cameron arrived, loaded with diaper bags, Cheerios for snacks, and toys to keep their children busy.

The visits dwindled to the obligatory one-hour Sunday afternoon cup of tea.

The remaining 167 hours of her week were consumed with the many hours it took to get bathed, dressed and fed. She had, once upon a time, taken those simple tasks for granted—in fact, had dealt with them impatiently— as she juggled raising two children and succeeded as a lone woman running a large architectural firm, with an academic husband who retreated to the comfortably undemanding and arcane world of seventeenth-century Asian history.

Gus left her for a Ph.D. student ten years ago. But he had, in truth, left her seventeen years ago, when Kenzie had contacted them after she ran away, begging for money. They had a bitter fight. Frances wanted to send Kenzie an airplane ticket home; he wanted to send her money.

"You always let her walk all over you," she had said, her voice bitter. Kenzie was a true Daddy's girl, who basked in his attention. It was easy for him—he just gave in to her demands. Discipline was not a technique at which he excelled.

And look where it got them. Their daughter abused drugs, ignored her curfew and threw wild parties. Frances was convinced that Kenzie had some blame for what had happened to Imogen Lange.

And when Kenzie disappeared from home—the same night a girl went missing at Mardi Gras—Frances had a terrible feeling Kenzie was involved. But Gus became enraged when Frances broached the subject, accusing her of believing the worst of their beautiful, talented daughter.

Kenzie called a week after she left home. Frances told her that she would send her an airplane ticket. Kenzie begged for cash.

Frances refused. "You should have plenty of cash from my silver teapot that you stole."

"It wasn't worth much," Kenzie said. Frances hung up on her, furious and bitter. What had she done to deserve a child like that?

"She'll come home if she has no options," she told Gus.

"She said it herself—she has no place to sleep. She's on the streets, Frances! She could be abused, or killed, even."

He sent her money.

And she never came home.

Her husband was heartbroken. Frances, however, was angry. Then she became scared. But not about Kenzie's safety. As the search went on for Heather Rigby, and the grieving parents pled for the girl's return, her certainty that Kenzie was involved in her disappearance intensified.

Especially when the Japanese wisteria, which had been thriving, died. And Frances removed it. What she found, buried under the wisteria, horrified her. And convinced her that her daughter had committed a terrible crime.

But Kenzie stayed away. Heather Rigby remained missing. And neither Gus nor Frances was forced to confront the terrible truth.

They only had to face each other.

They stayed together for Cameron's sake. When he

started university, Gus seized his opportunity and married his student.

How pathetic, Frances had told herself.

And then, one morning, she woke up on an escalator. Her left leg was weak. She could not lift it over the edge of the bathtub. Her supporting leg twitched violently.

Four months later, after she was tested for many terrible diseases, she was diagnosed with ALS. The worst of them.

After the initial shock, she slipped into depression. She toyed with the idea of suicide—never fully appreciating that the choice would eventually be taken from her without any warning—but Cameron's wife had just given birth to twins.

And, for a brief period of time, before her body stumbled farther down the escalator, she had something to live for. When Lily Frances was born—with the red hair of her grandmother and her never-discussed aunt—Frances realized that she deeply wished to see Kenzie again.

She had followed Kenzie's career, amazed at the success of her daughter. She lurked on Kenzie's blog regularly, studying the designs her daughter created. She had never appreciated the art of tattooing until then. She had never appreciated the passion that drove her daughter to strike out on her own. She admired her daughter's success and was relieved that she had made something of her life. Those terrible events of Kenzie's seventeenth year were relegated to the secret crypt of family sins.

Cameron caught her lurking on Kenzie's KOI blog one day. Her son had never gotten over Kenzie's abandonment of her family. As far as he was concerned, the older sister who had embarrassed him for so many years with her insolent and wild behavior was dead. Good riddance, he had told Frances.

But he had seen the tears in his mother's eyes.

And Kenzie, summoned by her brother, had returned.

It had been a moment that Frances would hold tight when her body no longer could hold anything at all.

But then Heather Rigby's body had been discovered. All the doubts, all the fears were excavated with her remains.

Buried for so long in Frances' psyche was the fear that it had been her inadequacy as a mother that had ultimately led to Kenzie's involvement in Heather's death. Had the tensions in their home life led Kenzie to act out, spiraling downward into drug abuse—and murder?

Or had Kenzie's delinquent behavior been a facet of a gene, preordained from when egg met sperm?

Frances would never know if it was nature or nurture that led Kenzie to be involved in the crime against Heather Rigby—and she would never know the extent of Kenzie's involvement, either—but she was in a position to offer closure to Heather's parents. She wanted to offer penance before she died.

And by so doing, she would also demonstrate to her estranged daughter, with the only means she had left at her disposal, that she loved her as deeply as a mother could love a child.

She would protect her daughter until the day she died.

But there weren't too many steps left on the escalator. The machine ate them with progressive rapidity.

She just hoped she had enough days left to get the job done.

40

Kate flipped through the completed affidavit, still warm from the laser printer. She had been at her office for the past eighty minutes, typing up the document. All the while, her brain rejected each and every word.

The whole confession stank. Frances Sloane was taking the fall for her daughter. And if Kate had had even one smidgeon of doubt about Kenzie's culpability, the fact her mother was willing to prolong the suffering of her final days of life was the most compelling evidence of all.

The sun beat on her back. The air-conditioning had been turned off for the weekend and the stale, warm air in her office felt suffocating. Sweat trickled under her arms. She needed some guidance about this mess. Eddie was off-limits, since he now represented Kenzie.

Kate dialed Randall's cell phone number.

Answer the phone, Randall. Please.

On the fourth ring, he answered.

She sagged against the chair. "Randall, it's Kate."

"How are you? Is everything okay?" His concern was a balm to her horrible day. But guilt wormed its way through. She hadn't told him about the break-in or the stalker. Nor had she told him about her coffee with Ethan—or that he had spent the night on Muriel's sofa after the break-in.

She pushed a wisp of hair from her now-sweaty forehead.

"I need some advice. Do you have a minute?"

"Give me a sec." She heard a door close. He came back on the line. "The kids are in the other room. I will have to go shortly—we have an outing planned this afternoon. A new exhibit at MOMA."

"That's nice." It did sound nice. And very far away from where she was in her life right now.

She shouldn't have called him.

"So what's up?" Randall asked. "Is it Frances?"

Kate exhaled. "Yes. And Finn. And Kenzie. Her daughter. Oh, and Eddie."

"I see. This sounds complicated. Start at the beginning."

She told him about Harry Owen refusing to help Frances, about the police questioning Frances and Kenzie, about Kenzie being arrested, how Finn revealed he was dating Kenzie and asked Eddie to represent her, and then, the final bombshell: Frances confessing to Heather's murder.

"This is crazy," Randall murmured. "I can't believe this all started with a simple legal opinion. I'm sorry I got you involved with Frances Sloane, Kate."

"It's not your fault. I could have said no. But I wanted to help." She stared at her law degree mounted on the wall. "What should I do?"

"About what?"

"Frances' confession! She didn't do it, Randall!"

"You believe that she's protecting her daughter."

"Yes!"

"And you think Kenzie did it?"

"I have no doubt."

"And are you a judge or a lawyer, Kate?"

He let his words sink in.

What he said was true.

But was he biased in favor of Kenzie based on his own experiences?

"Kate, I know how destructive speculation can be." His tone softened. "You have to give her the benefit of the doubt."

Kate stared at the file folder holding Frances' affidavit. *Don't do this to me, Randall.* "I don't have to give her the benefit of anything. I'm not her lawyer."

"I'm surprised at you, Kate. I thought you believed in the principle of innocent until proven guilty. If you hadn't, I would still be in prison."

He didn't say the words, but they hung in the air between them: *You are being hypocritical.*

Kate exhaled. "I did believe in it. I do believe in it."

"But you don't now?"

She shook her head. "Not when it comes to Kenzie."

"I think you are blinded by your anger, Kate."

"Maybe you are, too, Randall."

"What do you mean by that?"

"Maybe you don't want to consider the fact that she is guilty of murdering an innocent girl—and that her mother created a false confession to protect her—because you are still angry at how the police targeted you. Maybe they didn't make a mistake this time."

Silence.

"Jesus," he said. "Things really are still a mess, aren't they?"

He wasn't referring to the Frances Sloane case.

"I don't know," Kate said. "I don't know what to think."

Tell him, Kate. Tell him everything.

"I just don't want you to make a mistake you'll regret, Kate," he said softly. "It took a long time for you to get over what happened to your sister."

"I know. And the person who caused all of it is now going to get away with murder."

"Not necessarily, Kate. The police might suspect Frances is lying. And they can test her with the holdback evidence."

"True." The tension in her chest eased a little.

"But, Kate…" He paused. "Has it occurred to you that Frances may, in fact, be guilty of the crime? You have some baggage—quite rightly—about Kenzie. But it does not mean she is a murderer."

"Frances is even less likely to be a murderer than Kenzie."

"How do you know, Kate? Not too many people walk around with 'killer' tattooed on their foreheads."

"So what you are telling me is that I have to give the police this confession, even though I believe my client is lying."

"You don't have any proof that she is lying, do you?"

"No."

The file folder looked so bland, so innocuous, lying on her desk.

"Then your duty is to follow her instructions."

Kate exhaled. "Okay."

"You knew that anyway. You didn't need me to tell you that."

"I suppose not. It's just…you haven't met them, Randall. It really kills me to turn in this confession. It seems so unfair."

"It was Frances' choice," Randall said. "She will now have to face the consequences."

Kate took a deep breath. She had to tell him. She couldn't avoid this any longer. Like Frances, she had to face the consequences. "Something else has been going on."

"I can tell by the tone of your voice that it isn't good news."

"No." She swallowed. "Someone is stalking me."

"Jesus Christ, Kate! When did this happen?"

"The day before yesterday," she whispered.

"Why didn't you call me?" His voice was strained.

He knew. He sensed the distance, too.

"Because it happened so fast."

He exhaled a long, slow breath. "Start at the beginning."

She told him about the note and the break-in.

"Did you call the police?"

"My security firm called. They responded right away."

"And what are they doing to find the stalker?"

"There is a detective who is following up leads on the sketch." She fought to keep her voice steady, but the memory of the drawing made her stomach churn.

"You aren't staying in your house, are you?"

"No, I'm at Muriel's."

"Just you and her?"

Kate closed her eyes. "Ethan slept on the couch."

"How did he get involved in this? He's in Cold Case," Randall asked, his voice terse.

"I called him, Randall." Kate closed her eyes. "He came right away."

There was silence.

"I see." She felt his hurt, his anger, pulsing over the

phone connection. "What, exactly, are you trying to tell me?"

"All I'm telling you is what happened. It was a factual recounting of the incident, Randall."

Oh, for God's sake, she couldn't believe she had lapsed into her lawyer persona.

It was self-defense.

"I see. Well, thank you for the factual recounting. Are you sure you did not miss any salient details?"

"No," Kate said. "That covers it all. I just thought you should know."

"I don't know if I'm angrier that you didn't tell me about the stalker or that Ethan slept on the sofa." He cleared his throat. "Are you seeing him?"

"No." She paused. "I don't think so."

"What the hell does that mean? You either are or you aren't."

Her temper flared. "The same could be said about us, Randall. I have no idea what your feelings are or when your children will ever be ready to accept me into their lives! How long do you expect me to wait for you? I don't want to spend my life waiting for something I may never have."

Silence.

Kate counted the beats of her heart.

"God." Randall exhaled. "I'm sorry, Kate. This isn't fair to you. I promise we'll sort this out when I return in July."

July seemed a long time away.

"Bye," she said.

41

"I want you to give this to Lily for her seventeenth birthday."

This clearly was not what Cameron had expected when Frances called him at lunchtime and asked him to come right away—and without his family. She was sure he would have read about Kenzie's arrest in the papers.

Cameron waited patiently for her to finish her sentence. Speaking had become so laborious. Frustratingly, the harder it became, the more Frances had to say.

Phyllis, at her request, had placed the small jewelry box on her wheelchair tray. Frances could no longer lift her hand more than an inch or two, so she said, "Take it, Cameron."

Her son opened the box. A sapphire ring encircled with diamonds glinted in the morning sun. "This is your grandmother's ring, isn't it?"

She forced the muscles of her face to smile. "From one redhead to another."

His mouth tightened. Obviously thinking of the redhead who had been in police custody yesterday. "Thank you. Lily will treasure this."

Her heart squeezed with the knowledge that she

would never see Lily at the age of seventeen years. Not even the age of seventeen months, she was sure of that. The escalator moved too quickly.

Her granddaughter would never know her. The worst thing was that she would believe that Frances was a coward and a murderer.

It was a steep price for her daughter's love.

No regrets, Frances.

Even if Kenzie still distrusted Frances' motives, she would recognize eventually that Frances had acted out of love.

And for the exquisite baby Lily, who had a loving mother at her beck and call, Frances would simply be a family ghost, spoken about in hushed whispers, who bequeathed an expensive piece of jewelry to her.

Her son shifted. "You seem to have considerable public support for your assisted suicide lobby."

"Yes."

"So what's going to happen next? Is Harry Owen going to take this to Parliament?"

She held his gaze, although pain constricted her throat. Turning her back on the people who had responded to her campaign had been one of the toughest things she had ever done.

Blood is thicker than water. Remember that, Frances.

"No. He's not. It's over."

He clasped the box in his hands loosely between his knees. "I need to talk to you about Kenz—"

"One more thing—" she said at the same time. And then she began to cough.

Oh, God. She threw a panicked look at Cameron. She could not clear her throat of the mucus. *Get Phyllis,* her eyes said. She gagged, choking.

"Phyllis!" Cameron roared.

Phyllis ran into the room. She flicked on the suction machine, swishing the tube in the back of Frances' mouth.

She couldn't breathe, she couldn't breathe.

Her lungs screamed for air.

Pressure built inside her head, her eyes bulging with the effort to clear her throat. She imagined her hands clawing at her neck, her lungs forcing the dreaded mucus from her airway.

But only a tube could save her.

Eventually, it did.

She gasped, a thin stream of air shooting into her oxygen-desperate lungs. She gasped again. And again.

She became conscious of Cameron's stricken face, of the panicked look he threw at Phyllis: *Mom's getting worse, isn't she?*

Why did he think she'd asked him to come?

She only hoped that the escalator would deposit her gently, smoothly, at her final destination. Wherever that was. It could be simple oblivion. And she welcomed it.

Because she would be free.

Instead of this useless, dilapidated structure that housed her soul, she would be weightless. Surrounded not by machines that beeped, metal that supported and tubes that transported fluids in and out of her body. Instead, she would be encased in...nothing.

A few minutes later, her heart had stopped racing enough that she could attempt speech again. "I confessed to the murder of Heather Rigby."

Cameron sprang to his feet. The box tumbled to the floor. "What are you talking about?"

"I did it."

"Mom, that's crazy." Suspicion narrowed his eyes. "Kenzie asked you to do this, didn't she?"

"No."

She met his gaze. His eyes, the same mosaic of hazel as his father's, gazed at her with disbelief. "Why are you protecting her?" he asked, his voice low.

"I'm not."

"You are. She doesn't deserve it, Mom."

I owe it to her.

He must have read her mind, because he spat, "She is evil. She always has been. You are taking the fall. And now everything that you worked for will be tarnished by this. People will look at your buildings, and not see what a visionary you were—instead, they will see the mark of a murderer."

Her heart spasmed. *God, take me now.* Her skin grew clammy. He was right, she knew he was right, but what other choice did she have?

Should Kenzie be forced to lose everything because of one terrible mistake?

Don't cry, Frances. Don't.

If she cried, her sinuses would drain down the back of her throat and cause another coughing jag.

"I'm sorry," she said.

Cameron stared at the ring box that had tumbled by his feet. "Your grandchildren will think you are a killer," he said. "Lily will want to change her middle name."

Are you trying to hurt me deliberately? Do you think I love you any less for what I am doing for Kenzie?

"I'm sorry," she said again.

"It's not too late, Mom. You can tell the police the truth."

But I don't know what the truth is anymore.

All I know is my truth. That I cannot die without my daughter knowing that I loved her enough to do this for her.

"It's done."

"Mom, please, she doesn't deserve it. She never loved you. She never loved any of us."

Tears ran down her son's cheeks. The only time she had seen him cry as a grown man was at the birth of his children.

"I'm sorry."

"How could you do this to us? You are dragging us all down into her muck."

That hurt. It was true. Cameron and his family would be affected by this. But they had each other. He had a career. They would weather this storm.

"I love you."

His eyes pleaded with her. She remembered him as a small boy, those big hazel eyes begging her to help him fix his electric car. She had helped him.

She had always helped him.

Because he was the easy one. It was easy to help him, easy to love him.

Kenzie had been the difficult one.

It was easy to get frustrated, easy to wash her hands of her.

It would be easy to wash her hands of Kenzie before her death, too.

But she would not, could not, take the easy way.

Not this time.

"Always remember I love you."

Her son leaned down and kissed her goodbye. A tear dropped onto her cheek.

She sat in the afternoon sun, her eyes closed, her son's tear absorbing into her skin until there was no evidence it had ever been shed at all.

And waited for her lawyer to call.

42

"I need to speak to Detective Ethan Drake," Kate told the police officer at the front desk of the police station. "Please tell him Kate Lange is here to see him." She sat on the wooden bench and placed the legal-sized envelope containing the affidavit next to her. It would not have surprised her to hear it ticking.

The security door opened. Ethan strode toward her. He looked exhausted. She knew he had been involved in questioning Kenzie Sloane through the night.

"Kate! Are you okay?" His eyes scanned her face, concern softening them, pleasure warming them.

"I'm fine." She forced a smile. "I'm here on official business."

He glanced at the envelope on the bench. "Come on upstairs."

Kate followed him through the security door and up the stairs, unable to stop her eyes from staring at his long frame.

What was the state of the Ethan nation?

"We'll talk in my office. One of the perks of being in Cold Case." Ethan used to be in the bullpen, Kate remembered. He led her to a room with the standard office furnishings: file cabinet, desk, computer, chairs. Kate sat down opposite his desk. She placed the envelope on her knee.

He sank into his chair, and leaned back. She knew he only revealed his fatigue because he felt comfortable with her.

She shifted on the chair. This was going to be a difficult conversation.

She slid the affidavit from the envelope and placed it on the desk in front of him. "My client asked me to draft this today, Ethan."

A muscle in his eyelid twitched as he scanned the first paragraph.

I, Frances Sloane, do hereby confess to the murder of Heather Catherine Rigby—

He flipped through the statement. Then he glanced up. His mouth was tight.

She sensed his anger.

He believes Kenzie did it.

She wanted to tell him he was right, that Kenzie was capable of the crime that her mother had confessed to committing, but ethics forced her to keep her mouth shut.

"Are you kidding me?" he finally said.

"No." Her gaze was level.

"Goddamn it."

"Precisely." She couldn't meet his gaze. This was eating her up. It really was. But she couldn't let Ethan see it. "I'm sorry."

He ran his hand through his hair. "Your client needs to come in. Now."

"I know. I'll call her." Kate stood. "You know she's dying, right?"

"Yes."

She left Ethan's office.

When she reached the sidewalk outside the station, she pulled out her phone and dialed her client's number.

She fought to keep the anger out of her voice. Frances had jeopardized Ethan's opportunity to find Heather's true killer. And she had to hold his feet to the fire with her client's confession.

"See you ASAP," her client said with an unbecoming eagerness. "And don't forget to call the media."

Kenzie Sloane slumped in a chair. A half-empty water bottle rolled by her feet. Despite her obvious physical exhaustion, her eyes remained watchful as Ethan entered the room.

He held open the door. "Ms. Sloane, you are free to go."

She stood. "You aren't keeping me for the full twenty-four hours?"

What the—?

He shook his head. "You are free to go."

Triumph raced through her exhausted body. She had beaten the cops at their own game. And very soon she would beat McNally.

She should thank Detective Drake for having her arrested. If he hadn't done so, she would never have known that McNally had left the sketch for Kate. She now could set in motion the perfect plan.

Detective Drake led her down the stairs to the main entrance.

"Can you call a taxi for me, please?"

The officer at the main desk called a cab. It was then she noticed the woman sitting on the bench.

She stiffened.

Kate Lange.

Why was she here?

Those eyes were the same. Sky-blue and laser-sharp. The hair was longer, the teenage bangs grown out. Still that shade of deep coppery red, Kenzie's trademark mane fell in sweeping layers past her shoulders.

Her clothes underneath the leather bike jacket were rumpled. She walked toward Kate. Up close, Kate could see the circles under Kenzie's eyes, the smudged makeup, the fatigue pulling at her face.

A tattoo of a koi leapt from her cleavage and curled around her neck.

Kate tried to not stare.

Kenzie stopped several feet away. It was as if they both sensed an invisible line separating them. One that neither of them was yet ready to cross. It would be a fencing match, rather than hand-to-hand combat.

But Kate sensed—no, she knew—that Kenzie wouldn't hesitate to cross the line if she felt the need.

"Kate." There was no animosity in Kenzie's voice— nor was there any warmth. She trod cautiously, aware that she was under surveillance by both Ethan and the constable at the main security desk.

"How are you, Kenzie?"

"Just great." She brushed a lock of hair over her shoulder. The sleeve of her jacket rode up, exposing her wrist. Elaborately layered scales in shades of white, green, blue and black unfurled at the base of each wrist, and appeared to travel up her arm.

Did she tattoo armor on herself?

No, the design began with a nautilus at the base of each wrist. The scales of armor were actually ocean waves, presumably traveling up her arm. The tattoo was so vivid, so detailed, so full of movement and light and shadow that Kate had a hard time pulling her gaze back to Kenzie's face.

The ghost from Kate's past had become a masterpiece of inked flesh.

"I understand you've been acting as my mother's lawyer," Kenzie said, with the slightest edge to her voice. The first feint had been thrust.

"Yes. I'm sorry about her illness." Kate's tone was bland.

Kenzie threw a quick glance over at Ethan, but he remained several feet away. "So, why are you here?" She kept her voice low.

Wouldn't you like to know?

"I'm sorry, Kenzie, but I can't say. Why don't you call your mother?"

Kenzie's mouth tightened. "I will."

A cab pulled up to the curb and honked. Kenzie headed for the door.

"By the way," she called over her shoulder, "Finn is a great guy." Her gaze met Kate's across the foyer of the police station. "We've been spending a lot of time together."

Kate's heart hammered. She knew what that look meant.

Don't hurt him, Kenzie.

Kenzie strode out of the station without another glance.

Kate knew that Kenzie didn't know the reason she had been released, but she would soon enough.

Kate tasted bile in her throat.

The whole thing made her sick.

Frances protecting Kenzie. Finn protecting Kenzie.

They needed protection *from* Kenzie.

Especially Finn. He knew nothing about her.

Why had he allowed himself to be drawn into the persona of Kenzie Sloane, celebrity tattoo artist?

All those tattoos emblazoned on Kenzie's body were a decoy.

A *trompe l'oeil* to deceive the eye.

43

Kenzie wouldn't let her see how much the look of contempt in Kate's eyes rankled. She acted so superior to her.

And maybe she thought she had good reason to.

Well, she would see soon enough how wrong she was.

She strode outside.

Fresh air.

She'd only been inside for less than twenty-four hours, yet it seemed much longer. The breeze warned of fog, but she slipped off her jacket. The air stirred the tiny hairs on her arms.

She was alive.

She was free.

For now.

The cabbie honked again.

She flashed him a look and climbed into the backseat. She gave him the address to Yakusoku Tattoo. His gaze flickered over her tattooed sleeves. "Got room for any more?" he chuckled.

Kenzie stared out the window.

A van pulled into the handicapped zone, in front

of the cab, forcing the cab to reverse out of the parking spot.

The cabbie swore. He backed up and swung around the larger vehicle. Kenzie glanced at the driver as they drove by.

The face was familiar.

The cab drove past Citadel Hill, a saturated green from all the rain. It was so vibrant. Kenzie had a favorite ink in that exact same shade—

Phyllis. The driver of the van was her mother's caregiver.

The passenger must have been her mother.

Kate Lange—her mother's lawyer—was already at the station.

Waiting for Kenzie's mother.

The dots finally connected. "Jesus Christ."

Was her mother going to implicate Kenzie further in Heather's murder?

But if that were the case, would the police have let Kenzie leave before the twenty-four-hour period—especially with no conditions?

She fumbled in her purse for the business card that Eddie Bent had given her.

He answered on the second ring.

"Eddie? It's Kenzie Sloane."

"How did things go?"

"I did as you said. I didn't say a word."

"That's good." Pause. "So the police didn't keep you for the full twenty-four hours."

"No."

"You sure you didn't answer any questions?"

The implication was obvious: Eddie thought she had leaked some information that had given the police what they were looking for.

"No. I honestly didn't say a word. You should have seen me."

"Okay. I believe you, Kenzie." His voice was a soothing growl in her ear. She had been skeptical of him when she first saw him: rumpled shirt, dirt-stained jeans, nicotine and garden soil on his fingernails. The only reason she hadn't sent him on his merry gardening-gnome way was because of his eyes. They were incredibly astute. They saw past all the tattoos and gazed straight inside her. Now he said, "But it's a bit unusual for the police to let you go before they need to."

"Just as I was leaving the station, I saw Kate Lange."

"I see." His voice was neutral.

"And then my mother arrived."

"I didn't know she was able to travel."

"Only in emergencies." She nibbled a nail, a habit she had broken when she was eight. "So why do you think she's at the station?" Kenzie knew the answer. But she wanted her lawyer to tell her she was mistaken.

"They obviously want to videotape her statement." Eddie Bent let that sink in. "Why do *you* think your mother is at the station?" She had the distinct feeling she was in a therapy session.

Mom, what are you doing? "I don't know."

"Are you sure?" *Don't bullshit me,* his tone warned.

"Yes. I have no idea why my mother wants to talk to the police." She bit off the end of her nail. She had forgotten how satisfying it felt. "So what's the next step?"

"We wait. I'll call you when I hear something. If the police call you, you do not need to return the phone call. If they bring you in again, make sure that you say nothing except that you wish to call me, and that I am your counsel of choice."

"Okay," she said. As an afterthought, she added, "Thank you, Eddie."

"Remember, I'm on your side, Kenzie. If there is anything else you need to tell me, call me. The more I know, the better I can defend you."

"Thanks. I've got to go now." They had arrived at Yakusoku.

She paid the driver and hurried to the parking lot behind the tattoo studio. Thank God. Her car was still there. The police hadn't seized it.

She unlocked her car and slid behind the wheel. Fatigue crashed into her. She had had no sleep last night. She leaned back against the headrest and dialed Finn's cell phone.

He answered on the first ring. "Kenzie! Are you okay?"

"Yes, I'm fine."

"Did the police let you go?"

"Yes." Her voice was amazingly calm. "They have no evidence to hold me, Finn."

"Of course not. That's because you are innocent."

Bless your trusting heart, Finn.

"Well, you never know what they'll try to twist to fit their theories," she said. "How's Foo?"

"He's great. But he misses you."

Her heart squeezed. She could not wait to hold her dog again.

But she had one last *t* to cross before she was home free. "Will you be at your place in an hour? I need to collect my stuff."

"You're leaving tonight?" No mistaking the hurt in his voice.

"Look, Finn, I need to go back to New York. With the

exception of you, this has been a spectacularly crappy visit." He would see the truth in that.

"I'll be home."

"Thanks." She said it softly. It would hurt to leave him. Maybe he could visit....

Enough with the fantasies.

"See you soon. I just have a quick errand to run."

She turned off the phone's ringer. It was time to pay a final visit to her mother's house.

44

Ethan chugged his entire mug of coffee in one gulp, swallowing several ibuprofen with it. He had hit the wall about an hour ago. His head pounded. He couldn't believe the twist this case had taken.

They were screwed.

And by none other than Kate's client.

Don't shoot the messenger.

Kate hadn't appeared too happy about her client's confession. The assisted suicide campaign had officially committed its own act of suicide. And now this case, which had appeared so promising, appeared to be crumbling in front of his eyes. They couldn't hold Kenzie once Frances had presented her confession—which meant there was no time for the infrared photos. Just one more possible lead that was now out of reach.

He could not let another case go down the tubes.

Enough was enough.

Lamond walked next to Frances Sloane as her finger single-handedly drove her wheelchair into the interview room. She wore some kind of breathing tube in her nostrils.

Her caregiver, Phyllis, checked the portable oxygen

tank and fussed with the tube. She plucked at the blanket on Frances' legs, her face drawn in lines of disapproval.

"I'm fine, Phyllis. You can go now," Frances said.

Ethan placed the affidavit on the table, flanking it with a thick file folder and a blank notepad. "Mrs. Sloane, this interview will be videotaped. You have the right to remain silent—" he read her the caution "—you have the right to speak to a lawyer—"

"I have already spoken to her." Her eyes were uncannily like her daughter's. She swallowed. "I confess to the murder of Heather Rigby." She spoke slowly, taking great care to enunciate her words as much as she was capable.

"Tell us what happened that night, Mrs. Sloane." Ethan leaned back in his chair.

She told the exact same story as Kate had written in the affidavit.

He listened, his face impassive. Then he picked up a sheet of paper in the folder and read it with a frown, aware of her eyes on his face.

He wanted her to worry. He wanted to make her unsure.

He wanted her to wonder what she didn't know, what she was inadvertently revealing to the police.

He placed the sheet of paper in the folder, closed the folder with great deliberation and looked up. His gaze locked onto Frances Sloane's.

She was doing an admirable job of keeping her composure. But he had seen the flicker of unease in her eyes.

"Mrs. Sloane, your daughter has red hair, correct?"

"Yes."

"Had she dyed it for the Mardi Gras?"

His question posed a dilemma for Frances Sloane: *Had the police found a dyed hair? Or a red hair?*

After a few seconds, she said, "No." She watched him closely for his reaction.

He sipped a freshly topped mug of coffee, smothering a wince when his stomach reacted to it with an immediate protest. "A rubber Halloween mask was found on Heather Rigby's skull."

"Yes. I put it on her."

"Why?"

"Because I was angry."

"Was it Kenzie's?" He asked the question quickly, trying to catch her off balance.

But when a woman has very little control of her muscles, everything appeared to throw her off balance.

"No. It was on the floor of the bunker."

He opened the file folder and wrote a note. Then closed the folder again.

"Had you ever seen the mask before?"

"No."

"How do you think it got there?"

"Could be Heather's."

"Did you try it on before you put it on Heather Rigby's head?"

She hesitated.

Why would he ask that question? she would wonder.

Of course: a hair had been found in the mask. But what color? And whose?

"No."

He eyed her short, silvery hair.

"What color was your hair seventeen years ago, Mrs. Sloane?"

"Mainly gray. But I still had some natural color." At his questioning look, she said, "It was red."

Red.

Now, that was interesting.

"Did you have the same hairstyle back then?"

"No. It was long." She swallowed. "I cut my hair when I became too ill to manage it."

"How long was your hair?"

Triumph gleamed in her watery eyes. "Past my shoulders. Just like Kenzie's."

Damn. He sipped his coffee to hide his frustration. Acid blossomed in his gut.

He contemplated her for a moment, trying to increase her anxiety, smothering his discomfort at trying to agitate an obviously dying woman. She had chosen this path. Finally, he said, "What happened after you shot her?"

"I dragged her body to the bogs."

"How?" He asked the question in his most casual tone. The rope was a key piece of holdback evidence. They couldn't hammer Frances with the tattoo—Heather could have gotten it before she showed up at the bunker.

"Under her arms." Mrs. Sloane's speech had slurred drastically. She was tiring.

"So you dumped her body in the bog?"

"No. I buried it."

"How?"

"I dug under the bushes."

That would have been extremely difficult.

But not impossible.

"What happened to the gun, Mrs. Sloane?"

"I threw it into the ocean." Her chin sank to her chest. She slurred, "Are we done?"

He pushed back his chair and picked up the file folder.

Her eyes studied the folder. *What did it hold?* he

knew she wondered. *What evidence was there to incriminate her daughter?*

Plenty.

He held open the door. "You can go home, Mrs. Sloane."

"You aren't charging me?"

"We need to assess all the evidence, Mrs. Sloane."

"But I said I did it!" Saliva pooled by the corner of her mouth.

"I know."

"So arrest me! Handcuff me, detective."

"That's not necessary."

He waited until Phyllis returned to the room. With a look of gratitude, she unlocked the brakes of her employer's wheelchair. "Time to go home, Frances."

Frances stared into Ethan's eyes. "My daughter is innocent. Do not make another terrible mistake like you did with Randall Barrett."

She was baiting him.

Not a great way to get the cops on your side, Frances.

He led them to the elevator, pressing the down button. It opened immediately. Frances maneuvered her wheelchair with the toggle button. Ethan and Phyllis entered behind her. The doors closed.

Not another word was said on the ride down.

But Frances had made her point.

Did he have blinders on?

Or was he being manipulated into believing Frances' implausible story?

Heather Rigby's self-confessed murderer pushed the toggle button with her finger and drove her wheelchair out of the station.

* * *

No one should be at home—Kenzie had seen both Phyllis and her mother arrive at the police station—but she approached her mother's house with caution nonetheless. Several lights had been left on. They gave the fog-wreathed building the iridescence of an opal.

She skirted around to the side of the house. In the deepening twilight, the row of evergreens that edged the path appeared impenetrable.

When she had run down this path seventeen years ago, the evergreens had been newly planted. Now they towered over her, guarding the family home, it seemed, *from* her.

She rounded the corner to the back of the house. And gasped. The old porch her father had built in defiance of his wife's aesthetic had been replaced with a Japanese-style garden. Kenzie would have appreciated its simple perfection if she had not been so alarmed by the unexpected change.

If the porch was gone, did that mean…?

She broke into a run, her sleep-deprived body resisting the urgency that made her heart race. Her panic dropped a notch when she saw that the small, shingled shed her father had built at the far end of the property still stood. Her mother had not had it removed.

Instinctively, she glanced at the woods behind the shed. Her skin broke out in goose bumps. The small break in the trees leading to the oceanfront path was still there, albeit overgrown. She had spent many hours walking the path as a child, and many hours sneaking back and forth to the bunker on that path as a teen.

The last time she had used that path was in the very early morning hours after the Mardi Gras.

When she finally arrived at the end of the path, she wanted to throw herself on the ground and weep. She was home. She was alive.

McNally and Lovett had not yet found her.

She crouched in the wild underbrush and stared across the lawn at her house. The shrine to her mother's daring, her mother's ambition, her mother's ego.

She tucked the gun into her waistband and sprinted to the back door. As she expected, her mother had left the door unlocked for her. She slipped inside, grateful for the new, silent hinges.

She paused in the kitchen, listening.

No sound of anyone still awake. But she could not risk going up to her room. She might wake someone.

She tiptoed through the living room. Then she crept down the basement stairs and paused at the bottom.

Still silent.

Thank God.

She hurried to the laundry room.

The phone hung on the wall right next to the doorway. She snatched the receiver, her hands shaking.

In her mind's eye, she pictured Heather Rigby lying on the ground. Blood gushing from the wound in her chest.

She could not speak from the blood entering her airway.

But her eyes begged Kenzie.

Why? she asked.

Help me.

Help me!

Kenzie had turned and run.

Did Heather think Kenzie was going for help?

Was she hanging on by sheer force of will, believing that Kenzie would send someone, anyone, to save her?

But if she called 911, they would trace the call.

They would figure out she killed Heather.

Kenzie slammed the receiver back onto the handset. Her body broke into a rank sweat.

It's too late, Heather.

It was too late when you flirted with my boyfriend.

The gun was heavy and awkward against her hip bone. She put the gun in the sink and stripped off her torn, dirty punk witch costume, fingering the fabric stiff with dried blood. Heather's blood.

She stuffed the shredded clothing into a small plastic grocery bag and tied it so tightly that the only way to open it again would be to cut it.

She soaped off the worst of the dirt and blood from her body. Then she washed the gun. She rinsed the sink thoroughly, praying that the sound of the water running through the pipes would not wake anyone. For once, she was grateful for her mother's design work. The house's internal functions were incredibly quiet.

She changed into a pair of jeans and a large flannel shirt that lay in the laundry basket, and grabbed some more clothes, which she shoved into another shopping bag. She slipped the gun back into her waistband. The barrel dripped cold water down her stomach.

Money.

She needed money.

She ran back upstairs, clutching both grocery bags, and unlatched the curio cabinet in the kitchen.

The solid silver teapot set that had belonged to her maternal great-grandmother should give her a bit of cash. Her mother had always hated it, anyway. She wrapped it in her fresh clothes, hoping the weight of the silver wouldn't tear the plastic bag.

Then she slipped back outside. She glanced at the sky.

Dawn lit the edges of the horizon in a fiery glow.

She had very little time.

She ran through the mist-soaked grass to the shed in the back. Three months ago, her mother had planted a Japanese wisteria at the corner of the small outbuilding.

Kenzie knelt on the ground behind the bush and out of sight of the house, oblivious to the wet soaking the knees of her jeans. She dug with both hands until she hit the substratum. It was only three or four inches below the topsoil. Not very deep.

It would have to do. She didn't have time to run back out to the cliff. And she didn't dare run the risk of encountering McNally.

Besides, the bush would grow over it. No one would find it.

She dropped the gun into the hole, glancing over her shoulder at the sky. Dawn was in full throttle, sending the night scurrying for cover. She scooped the earth over the gun until the hole was filled. Then she smoothed the soil until the hole was indistinguishable.

She grabbed her two shopping bags and hiked into town, trusting her secret to the Japanese wisteria.

It had not proven a faithful confidante.

In fact, it had disappeared.

Kenzie checked behind the shed, wondering if she had mistaken the location of the shrub.

But there were no plants there, nothing. Just overgrown grass that her mother would never have permitted in her younger, healthier years.

Kenzie eased open the shed door. The interior was dark, barely any light showing through the dusty window. And musty. Her nose wrinkled at the smell. Something had died in there recently.

She stepped inside. And walked straight into gossamer strands of an elaborate spider's web.

Wiping the web away with the back of her hand, she groped along the wall for the shelf where her father had kept his gardening tools. Something rustled in the shed's nether regions.

She hurried out the door, shutting it behind her, and threw herself on the ground where she remembered burying the gun. The soil lifted relatively easily, a sign that it had once been tilled for a garden.

Ten minutes later, she had dug a small trench down to the substratum.

No gun.

Who had found it?

And what did they do with it?

Would they know its significance?

She scooped back the earth into the trench, smoothing the loosened turf over the excavated patches.

Then another thought hit her. Actually, it slammed into her. Leaving her breathless.

Was that why her mother went to the police station today? To turn in the gun?

A pain that she'd banished seventeen years ago snaked around her heart, choking her breath. She lumbered to her feet.

Why should she be surprised?

She returned the trowel in the shed and closed the door.

Save for the ruined spider's web, no one would ever know she had been here.

But what if her mother had taken the gun to the station? And was placing it in the hands of Detective Drake?

They could be on their way here.

She broke into a run, cursing the time she'd lost searching for the gun that most likely was encased in an evidence bag on Detective Drake's desk. She rounded the corner of the house.

And stopped dead in her tracks.

Her mother waited by Kenzie's rental car, her wheelchair effectively blocking the driver's door.

Kenzie could take her down. Easily. Move the wheelchair and get the hell out of here.

She approached her mother, slowly, warily, searching her mother's face for signs of betrayal.

But the disease that trapped Frances in the crumbling structure of her body also provided her with a poker face.

When Kenzie was a child, she could never hide from her mother's all-seeing gaze. Those sky-blue eyes had an intensity that was not deflected by mere skin and bone. They could see into Kenzie's very core.

In that moment, as twilight surrendered to night, Kenzie acknowledged why she had been fascinated with full body tattooing from such an early age.

It had been a means of protection. Of allowing one element of herself to be revealed with abandon and passion, while protecting the most tender parts of her psyche.

Those parts that her mother had prodded with unerring precision when Kenzie was a child.

Kenzie now realized she could never hide from the woman who had created those parts. There would always be a lifeline between them, one that each of them had cast aside at different stages of their lives, but now pulsed in the dusk.

"Why are you here, Kenzie?" her mother asked.

Her mother's gaze flickered over Kenzie's mud-stained knees, the panicked expression in her eyes.

Kenzie could revert to her seventeen-year-old self's lying ways and proffer a host of different explanations, but she knew her mother had given her a chance to explain herself. *Why did the police suspect her and why was she digging in the back garden?* That's what her mother wanted to know.

Kenzie glanced down at her hands. Dirt ringed the edges of her nails.

It was damned obvious why she was here—if her mother knew that the gun had been buried under the bush.

"I was looking for something I had left behind," Kenzie said.

"Did you find it?"

"No." *Did you, Mom?*

And, more to the point, what did you do with it?

Had she turned it in to the police, one final act of clearing her conscience before she left this mortal coil?

They gazed into one another's eyes. So identical in color, shape and acuity. So different in the things they had seen. Kenzie wondered, somewhat hysterically, what her mother would do if she possessed Kenzie's eyes and could replay all that they had witnessed.

"The winter that you left home was hard on the Japanese wisteria," her mother said, her speech painstakingly slow. Kenzie bit down her impatience. She needed to know what her mother had done with the gun.

An engine throbbed in the distance.

Were the police already on the way?

No, the noise grew softer, not louder.

"The roots did not have enough time to establish

themselves," her mother said. "It didn't survive. I took it out the following spring."

"That's too bad," Kenzie said. *Just say it, Mom. Just put me out of my agony.*

"I was sad to see it die."

Her mother knew. She *knew.*

She had found the gun.

Kenzie's pulse pounded in her veins. "Wher—" She cleared her throat. "What did you do with it?"

"I took care of it. You don't need to worry. It's gone."

It took a moment for Kenzie to comprehend what her mother had just told her.

She had gotten rid of the gun for her.

"Thank you," Kenzie said. Her heart lightened.

If the gun was gone, the police had nothing to connect her to the murder. She could go back to New York. And never set foot in this godforsaken place again.

But what about Kate Lange? She still had to deal with her.

And she needed the gun to do it.

Her heart began to race. What had her mother done with it?

"Kenzie, I confessed—"

Confesssssed. Her mother spoke so laboriously, the shock hit Kenzie in slow motion.

"—to the murder of Heather Rigby."

"Why?" Kenzie stared at her mother. *Why would she do that?*

"I don't know why I killed her," her mother said, deliberately misunderstanding her. "But I've regretted it ever since." Her mother paused. "I wanted to spend my final days getting to know you again. I'm sorry."

Tears sprang to Kenzie's eyes with such force that

her face twisted from the stinging pain. "You shouldn't have done that," she whispered.

"It is the right thing to do. Her family will have closure."

"You'll die in prison."

"ALS has already taken my freedom, Kenzie," Frances said. "This is a short detour to the end."

"Oh, God." Kenzie closed her eyes.

Guilt constricted her heart. Yet she reveled in the knowledge that she had escaped a terrible fate.

Her mother was dying.

How many days would she actually spend in prison? A few months? Weeks?

Versus the years Kenzie would spend in jail. Everything she had worked for would be gone.

But she couldn't leave her mother without closure. She needed to know the answer to one question. Otherwise, she would never be able to rest. "What did you do with the gun?"

Her mother's gaze held hers.

Oh, God. She didn't throw it in the ocean.

Panic gripped her. "Where is it, Mom?"

"I packed it up with your things and put it in a storage locker."

Kenzie could not believe her ears.

Her mother had packed a murder weapon with her bedroom furniture?

"Where's the key?" she asked, her voice urgent.

Tears welled in Frances' eyes. "I gave it to someone I trust. To deliver it to you after I die."

"Who is it, Mom?"

Her mother's eyes beseeched her. "Wait until I die, Kenzie. Then you will be safe."

"Mom, please, just tell me who you gave it to."

"Kate Lange."

The blood froze in Kenzie's veins.

Are you kidding me?

Kate Lange—who was the one person who could link her to Heather Rigby's tattoo—now had the key to the location of the murder weapon?

Kenzie's stomach churned from the effect of no sleep, no food—and no murder weapon.

"I'm sorry, Kenzie," her mother said. "I gave it to her before…before the girl was found."

Kenzie stared into the face that was her mother's face and yet not her face. At the short, sparse gray hair that had once been as long and gloriously red as her own. At the cool determination in her gaze that had been the one constant in Kenzie's life.

This would probably be the last time she saw her mother. "It's okay, Mom."

"I'm sorry, Kenzie," her mother said again, her speech slurring. "I'm sorry I wasn't there for you."

Was her mother sorry that she hadn't sent Kenzie money when she needed it—or she was sorry for Kenzie's entire childhood, when Frances was more interested in things she could design in steel and glass than in something she had created from her own flesh and blood.

"Goodbye, Mom." Kenzie leaned down and kissed her mother on the cheek.

Her mother moved her wheelchair, unblocking Kenzie's access to her car. "I hope you find peace, Kenzie."

Her eyes added, *For the terrible crime you committed.*

Judgment had been passed.

Kenzie's heart thudded.

Was her mother making the ultimate sacrifice—
or simply reinforcing, yet again, that she was morally
superior to her daughter in every way?

Rock, paper, scissors.

It didn't seem to matter which of the three she chose
in her life's match against her mother. Her mother
always won.

Kenzie unlocked her car door, her fingers shaking.
She reversed the car, careful to leave a wide radius from
where her mother watched from the wheelchair.

The wheelchair had become a small black speck in
Kenzie's rearview mirror by the time she reached the
road. Her mother, encased within its padded confines,
was no longer distinguishable.

Her phone buzzed. She glanced at the call screen. It
was her brother.

God. She couldn't face him right now.

But the phone kept buzzing.

He would give her no peace, she realized, until he
vented his spleen.

"Yes?"

"It's Cameron."

"I know."

"Do you know what Mom just did?"

Her jaw clenched. "I heard."

"You heard? You heard?" She could imagine his face,
apoplectic and red.

"She told me."

"She's protecting you."

He must know that she would never admit to that.

"She confessed, Cameron."

"Yeah. To your crime. You filthy murderer."

"Don't call me again."

"She's prolonging her suffering because of you—" he shouted.

She hung up on him.

But his final words rang in her ears.

She's prolonging her suffering because of you.

45

"I'm home, Kate," her client said.

Pain zigzagged in Kate's temple at the sound of her client's voice. She had been expecting this phone call. But it didn't mean she was prepared for it. "Hello, Frances."

"Why didn't they arrest me?" Frances asked.

Kate pressed her index finger into her temple. Sometimes pressure helped the throbbing.

But, as she expected, one finger was not going to make a difference in this case. "I suspect you didn't convince them of your guilt."

Silence.

"But I am guilty."

"Tell me again what the police asked you."

Frances recounted the interview again.

Ethan's questions had been little traps, designed to catch the unwary in their teeth. He had focused on several key elements: her client's hair color, the costume worn by Heather Rigby, how many times Frances had shot her, and what Frances had done with the gun.

The hair was a dead end, Kate thought—managing the briefest of smiles at her unintentional pun—because

Kenzie had inherited her mother's hair color. Frances, when her hair was longer, favored wearing her mane of silver-streaked red in a chignon. If a red hair had been found, it would be difficult to prove its owner unless they had DNA.

Which seemed impossible in this case.

On the other hand, there appeared to be a surprising amount of forensic evidence from the pathology results. "How many bullets did you fire, Frances?"

"I'm not sure," she said, her speech even slower than it had been a day ago. Was it fatigue? Or was she declining again? "One, maybe more. I panicked. I don't remember."

Nicely done, Frances. A perfectly plausible hedge.

"And where did you put the gun?"

"I told the police I threw it into the ocean."

"And is that the truth?"

Calculation weighted the silence on the phone. Kate knew her client debated whether she should answer Kate honestly—or stick with her story.

Kate's finger pressed harder into her throbbing temple. *Too bad it's not a gun,* she thought, because she sensed things were about to get very complicated with Mrs. Sloane.

"If I could prove that I fired the gun," Frances said after a long pause, "would the police believe me?"

How could they not?

"How could you prove that, Frances? You told the police that the gun is in the ocean."

"Answer my question, please."

"I don't know what holdback evidence the police have. But if you produced the weapon that killed Heather, and it had fingerprints or blood spatter that matched Heather's—and it could be proven that the bullet was fired from that gun—then I think the police would be hard pressed to discount that evidence." She paused. Would Frances admit that she had the gun in her possession?

"Thank you, Kate," Frances said.

And then she hung up.

Why? Why are you protecting her?

If she really killed this girl—and you must believe she did or you wouldn't have confessed to this crime— she does not deserve to go unpunished.

Frances knew where the gun was—Kate was sure of it.

But the gun was a double-edged sword. If it was still in Frances' possession, she would put her fingerprints on it—and convince the police that she had fired the gun.

But if Frances didn't have it in her possession—and it wasn't hidden somewhere—there could be forensic evidence that could connect someone else to the crime...

Someone like Kenzie.

46

"Nat, I've got a scoop for you," Kate said. She stared out the window of Muriel's kitchen, watching the elderly lady sprinkle fertilizer on her garden. Alaska and Charlie lay on the back porch.

"Does it have to do with the assisted suicide campaign?"

Kate exhaled. "Frances Sloane just confessed to the murder of Heather Rigby."

Nat inhaled. "Are you kidding me?"

"No."

"Can I use this?" The excitement had left Nat's voice, and now she was every inch the professional.

"Yes. My client instructed me to issue a public statement as soon as her confession was given to the police."

"So they have it?"

"Yes."

"Give me all the details, Kate. When, how, what was the murder weapon—" Kate visualized her with a notepad, pen poised to capture all the damning elements.

"I'm sorry, Nat, I'm not permitted to disclose that. All I can say is that Frances Sloane has confessed to the killing of Heather Rigby. Got that?"

"Yes. Okay, I gotta run, Kate. I want this to make the six o'clock news!"

Nat hung up.

Kate closed her eyes.

Alaska whined at the door. She let in the dogs, and gave them each a treat before supper.

What the hell.

"McN—John. It's Kenzie."

She heard the quick intake of breath. She had never called him before. "Where are you?" he demanded.

"The police let me go."

"I need to see you." She could hear the need in his voice.

She shivered.

She was running on fumes right now.

She took a deep breath. Time to roll the dice. "I need to see you, too." She let him absorb the implications of that. "Meet me at the tattoo studio in half an hour. I need to talk to you." She forced her voice to sound seductive. "It's about Kate Lange. You are going to like this, I promise."

47

Kate's phone rang just as she had begun tackling her billables at the Richardsons' kitchen table. She had fallen woefully behind on office work. The minutia of this task was ordinarily something she loathed, but right now she welcomed it. "Kate Lange," she answered, while jotting a note on a file.

"This is Cameron Sloane."

She stuck the pencil behind her ear. "Yes?"

"My mother just passed away."

No.

She hadn't said goodbye.

Tears pricked her eyes.

"I'm sorry." *I'm sorry, Frances. I'm sorry that things ended this way.*

"It was a blessing."

She watched Muriel push a wheelbarrow across the backyard. Would they say that about her eventually? *Not yet. I'm not ready for that yet.* "Yes. It was."

"Phyllis found her. She had gone to bed early—the stress of the day was too much for her. When Phyllis came to check on her, she was gone."

"Thank you for letting me know."

She hung up the phone and rested her head in her hands.

A complex, talented and haunted woman was dead. Her suffering was now over.

The assisted suicide campaign had lost its most vocal champion.

And the police had just lost an integral person in the Heather Rigby case.

Kate picked up the phone and dialed a number that her fingers had never forgotten.

"Ethan, it's Kate."

"Hi." *At least he doesn't sound like he's angry about Frances' confession.* She couldn't have coped with that.

"I'm calling as counsel. Frances Sloane died this evening."

"Where? How?" He sounded exhausted.

"At home. In bed. Her caregiver found her."

"She had excellent timing," he said. "I'll send the medical examiner over. Just in case."

I know. I understand your frustration. "I just wanted to let you know, in case it affects your investigation at all."

She couldn't hint more broadly than that.

"Thanks, Kate. I mean that." He assumed a more neutral tone. "We have just finished drafting a search warrant for her house."

"I see." Good. Ethan had seen through Frances' confession. "I believe the executor of her will is her son, Cameron Sloane. He would be overseeing her real property."

He paused. "Will I see you later?"

She hesitated. She thought of her conversation with Randall. She had hurt him, she knew that. And he had hurt her.

But she didn't want to play that game.

She just wanted to live her life. No more waiting. No more regrets. "Call me."

"As soon as I'm free."

Kate rubbed her arms.

Frances was dead.

The police were going to search her house. Probably hoping to find the gun.

What a mess for her son to deal with.

She stared at the numbers she had jotted on her billables. Her life, in six-minute increments. Had they been well spent?

She put away her billables and went outside to help Muriel.

Fatigue crashed into Kenzie in waves. She had been running on adrenaline—and nothing else—for the past twenty-four hours, and she could barely think. She narrowed her eyes until all she could see was the asphalt winding in front of her. She clenched the steering wheel of her car.

You can't stop yet, Kenzie.

Just a few more hours, and you'll be home free.

Literally.

The fog had come in from the water. Mist shrouded the roads, the trees.

It reminded her of the night she'd escaped over the peat bogs.

She couldn't wait to leave this place.

But first she needed to call Kate Lange and get the envelope that her mother had left for her.

Why had her mother put the gun in storage?

Was it another lesson about "consequences"? *I pro-*

tected you from the police, but you are going to have to do the dirty work and dispose of the murder weapon.

Well, she had certainly learned the lesson.

In spades.

And now she would have to use that lesson to ensure that her mother's confession had not been wasted, and she could get back to Manhattan without being incriminated in murder.

She was so tired.

A sign for a coffee shop caught her eye. She pulled into the parking lot and hurried inside the store. She ordered an extra-large coffee and a Danish. Sugar and caffeine should get her through.

She returned to the car, sipping her coffee, savoring the strong brew on her tongue. It was so good.

She tore a piece of Danish and ate it, thinking of Foo, how his little pink tongue would peek out when she ate something. She desperately wanted to see him. But she needed to get this out of the way. Finn would take care of him.

She licked her fingers of the last bit of Danish and dialed Kate Lange's number.

God, she hated her. She was so sanctimonious, so sure of herself. Out of all the lawyers in Halifax, why had her mother chosen Kate to represent her?

Hadn't she realized how much Kate Lange hated her guts?

It was another message: *Kate is worthy of my trust— and you aren't.*

Kate picked up the phone on the third ring.

"Is this Kate Lange?" Kenzie tried to infuse some warmth in her voice. "It's Kenzie Sloane."

"Yes." Kate Lange cleared her throat. "I'm sorry about your mother."

"She wanted to go." Her voice was tight but she raised her coffee cup to her lips. It was empty.

"What can I do for you, Kenzie?" Kate's tone was professional. Lawyer to family member. There was no hint that she had ever known her. No hint that she knew about her sister's tattoo.

"My mother told me you had a key for me."

"She did? She didn't tell me what was in the envelope," Kate said.

Damn. She was so tired, she had told Kate more than she needed to.

"I'd like to collect it now, please. I'm leaving."

"Before the funeral?" No missing the edge to her mother's lawyer's voice.

"I'm coming back." It was a blatant lie, and she hated the defensive quality in her voice.

Kate got under skin like that. Made her feel inadequate. As if she could never measure up to her sterling character.

"I'll drop the envelope over at Finn's place. I can be there in an hour."

"An hour? I have a flight to catch."

"Sorry. I can't make it sooner than that." She didn't sound sorry at all. "If you want, I can put it in the mail."

Bitch.

Kenzie's teeth clenched, but she managed to keep her tone even. "Okay, but can you meet me at the tattoo studio? I have to pick some stuff up from there."

Kate agreed. Kenzie disconnected and strode into the coffee shop. She ordered another extra-large coffee and returned to her car.

She would need as much caffeine as possible to get her through this night.

* * *

Frances was dead.

And now Kate had one final duty to her client that Kenzie Sloane would not let her forget—even when she had forgotten it herself.

The envelopes.

Frances had given her two envelopes, one for Kenzie, the other for Kate.

She spun on her heel, bumping into Charlie, who had ambled over in hope of a treat, and hurried to the kitchen. Her briefcase sat next to the kitchen table. She fished around the bottom and found the two envelopes.

It was hard to believe Frances had given them to her mere days ago.

A pang squeezed her heart when she saw the names printed on the envelopes. Clearly not written by her client—she had lost the ability to write.

She held Kenzie's envelope up to the light. The paper stock was too opaque to see what it concealed. She ran her finger along the outline of the hard object. It was thin, flat, with a triangular shape.

Not a key to a safety deposit box.

But a key to a storage room.

What had Frances locked in a storage room that could only be given to Kenzie after her client's death?

Was it a simple "Grandma's locket is in the box on the right?"

Or "I hid the murder weapon all these years and it's on the lower shelf."

Her gut screamed it was the latter.

But her client had clearly told her that she threw the gun in the ocean. She'd given a sworn statement.

Kate had no evidence to suggest that the storage room held anything but Kenzie's belongings.

In fact, when Frances gave Kate the key, Kenzie was not a suspect and Frances had not confessed.

There was no hint from her client that this key led to a murder weapon.

Could she, as Frances' counsel, call Ethan and tell him what she suspected?

No.

She would have to give it to Kenzie.

But she would do anything to be a fly on the wall in that storage locker.

She dropped Kenzie's envelope onto the bed and picked up the envelope with her name printed on it, her heart thudding.

A quick tear of the flap, and the contents slid out into her hand.

A pair of old 4 X 6 photos.

The images were blurry and dark.

But Kate could clearly see her sister, smiling.

Her throat tightened. Gennie had been so full of life. The vibrant one. The one who laughed easily—and cried just as easily.

In the first photo, her sister stood with her head leaning against Kenzie's shoulder, a broad smile on her face. Kate's heart twisted. Her sister used to put her head on Kate's shoulder, just like that.

She studied the second photo.

In this shot, her sister and Kenzie stood with their backs to the camera, pulling the collars of their shirts to reveal the backs of their necks, glancing over their shoulders with grins on their faces.

Kate stared at the picture. Her mind whirled.

Her sister had a tattoo. Kate held the snapshot up to the light and squinted. But she couldn't tell what it was. The quality of the image was too poor.

Kate had walked into Imogen's room to see if she could borrow a T-shirt. Imogen had whirled around, a sweater clutched to her chest, a snarl on her face.

"Get out!" she yelled.

Kate froze.

"You didn't even knock!" Imogen smoothed her hand down the back of her hair, momentary panic in her eyes.

The strangeness of her gesture had been lost on Kate. She blinked back tears of hurt and anger. They had always roamed into each other's bedrooms, flopping themselves down on the bed next to the other, sharing their day, their hopes, their dreams, their secret crushes.

Everything.

But it had been slipping away. Kate knew that. Her sister had ebbed out of her life, as inexorable as the tide and beyond Kate's control. There were other forces, stronger forces, eddying her sister into a world where neither of them belonged.

She had hoped that tonight she might gain some ground, pull her sister back from enemy territory. They were both going to the same party, to the house of a girl Kate despised: Kenzie Sloane. At the very least, she could scope out why Imogen was so enthralled with Kenzie.

She studied her sister's face.

The drug use had been shocking enough.

She supposed she shouldn't be shocked by the tattoo.

What else had her sister been hiding?

She grabbed her jacket and stuffed the envelope that Frances had left for Kenzie in her purse.

Then she headed to Yakusoku Studio.

48

McNally was, as usual, waiting.

He sat in his truck at the tattoo-studio parking lot, gripping the steering wheel.

His nerves jumped in little sparks under his skin. He unscrewed the vodka bottle and took a long pull.

It burned down his throat, a fuse to his adrenaline.

When Kenzie's car eased into the parking lot, he threw open the truck door with such force it swung on its hinges. He strode over to her car and jumped into the passenger seat.

"Hi."

The strain of the past twenty-four hours showed on her face. She gave him a cool smile.

He cupped his hand around her jaw and kissed her. *Sweet Jesus.*

He had waited for seventeen years for this kiss. Every nerve exploded. He leaned closer. Her lips were full. Just as he remembered.

He could never share her with another man again.

She was his. For eternity.

Even if that meant a different type of eternity.

She was not going to leave him ever again.

Not for jail.

Not for her life in Manhattan.

Not for another man.

She broke the kiss. But she stroked his cheek. "I need to talk to you."

He was like a leopard, ready to pounce on his prey.

Ready to bite into the tender, moist flesh and carry it away to his den.

"I want you to take a drive with me," he said.

Her hand traced the tendons of his neck. His skin grew hot. "Where to?"

"Where do you think?" He gave her a lazy grin. He had left the duffel bag in a safe place by the bunkers. It was stocked, and ready to rock 'n' roll.

She tensed. "We can't go to the bunker."

"Why not?" he asked. "We can bring Kate Lange out there. It will be just like old times."

"The police have been crawling all over it. So have the media. We'll be seen for sure."

He threaded his hands through her hair. The tangles wound around his fingers. He yanked it. "You need to listen to *me*. I'm in charge now. This is my plan."

Something shifted in her eyes. "You're right," she said, her voice throaty.

His fingers relaxed their grip, but he left his hand lightly wrapped in a tendril by her ear. It was a sensitive spot. It didn't take much pressure to bring tears to her eyes. And besides, her hair felt so damn good. He wouldn't let go.

He would never, ever let go.

Not now.

Not ever.

The pistol he'd stolen from Lovett's safe guaranteed he would succeed.

* * *

Adrenaline coursed through Kenzie, giving her one last, desperate burst of energy.

She shifted closer to McNally, leaning over the narrow console between the car seats. "Look, McNa— I mean John, I've been thinking." She forced a placating smile. "You've been right all along."

"What do you mean?" His eyes narrowed.

"I shouldn't have run away that night. I should have stayed."

There was a flicker in his eyes—was it pain?—but he said nothing.

"I was too young. I freaked." She lowered her voice, made it seductive. "But I made a big mistake. No one has satisfied me the way you did."

His neck reddened under the collar of his jacket.

She felt a surge of excitement. This was working.

Take it slowly, Kenzie.

"And when I heard about Heather's body being found, it was like a sign, you know? It brought back all the old urges. All the old desires." She licked her lips. "Remember how we used to play Russian roulette?"

"Yeah, I remember." His voice was rough.

"Well, remember that gun we used?"

His eyes sharpened. "Yeah."

How could I forget? his eyes said. It was the murder weapon.

She smiled. "I know where it is."

"Yeah? So where is it?" Kenzie could tell he was trying to sound casual, but he couldn't disguise his interest. If he got hold of the murder weapon—with her fingerprints on it—he would never let her go. She knew that.

"It's in a self-storage locker. And Kate Lange is bringing me the key."

His hand tightened in her hair. Tears pricked her eyes. "Why would she do that?" He didn't believe her.

"It's true." She told him about her mother giving Kate the envelope. "We could play Russian roulette again. Like we used to." She gave him a sideways glance. "It was the best sex I ever had."

His lips curled. Was it a smile or a grimace? She couldn't tell.

"It would be a perfect circle," he murmured. "Imogen was killed by her sister before we could kill her, and now we get to kill the sister." He grinned.

Kenzie smiled at him, her heart pounding.

It was going perfectly.

Now all she needed was to find the gun.

And hope it was still loaded.

Headlights flashed in her rearview mirror.

Kate Lange had arrived.

49

Kate jumped out of her car, envelope in hand. She strode to the entrance of the tattoo shop and stood under the light.

Kenzie walked out of a lane by the tattoo studio.

The past few days had taken a toll on her. Her long hair was tangled, pulled back in a messy knot on the back of her neck. Tension tightened her face.

Kate thought of the photos of the younger, more beautiful, defiant Kenzie. Did she regret any of what she had done to Kate's sister?

Or, if Kate was correct in her suspicions, what she had done to Heather Rigby?

And, she couldn't help wondering, had she had a role in her mother's death?

But these suspicions had to remain unvoiced. Her client had confessed. Kate had no proof her client had lied. She had no proof that Kenzie had committed a crime. Even the photo at the bunker meant very little. They were taken months before Heather's death. The police already knew Kenzie hung out there. She had been on their radar from the beginning.

"Hi, Kate. Thanks for coming," Kenzie said. She had a friendly smile pasted on her face.

Kate did not, could not, reciprocate. She held out the envelope. "Here it is."

Take it.

I never want to lay eyes on you again.

"Thanks." Kenzie tore open the envelope, glancing at Kate. "My mom told me that this was a key for a storage locker at Bluenose Self-Storage. She said she put my old things from my bedroom in there to prepare the house for sale."

Why are you telling me this?

"And she says that there were some belongings of Imogen's that she found in my room that she wanted me to give you."

Really? When did you ever do what your mother wanted you to do?

Yet she found herself asking, "What kind of belongings?"

Kenzie frowned. "I'm not sure. I didn't realize that I had any of her stuff. But I was kind of self-absorbed back then." She gave Kate an apologetic smile, an acknowledgment of the bitch she had once been. "Kate… I've been wanting to say this for a long time—"

The hair on Kate's neck quivered. She'd been waiting to hear this for a long time.

Kenzie took a deep breath. "I'm sorry about what happened to your sister."

Was her apology for real?

"Do you want to come with me?" Kenzie's gaze was open. "I'm not sure I'd recognize Imogen's stuff if I came across it." She glanced at her watch. "I don't have a lot of time, Kate. My flight leaves later tonight." She stuffed the key into her pocket.

Kate's mind raced through the labyrinthine possibilities of Kenzie's offer.

Before she had died, Frances had alluded to the fact that she still might have the gun that killed Heather Rigby. Could it be in the storage locker?

But Kenzie wasn't stupid.

If she thought the gun was there, why would she ask Kate to come?

She wouldn't want Kate to be a witness.

Unless… The hair on the back of Kate's arms rose. Unless she was she planning to kill Kate.

That didn't make sense, either. Her mother already confessed to the murder of Frances Sloane. Kenzie was off scot-free.

She had no reason to kill her mother's defense lawyer. After all, it was Kate who had delivered Frances' final instructions.

And Kate knew Kenzie wasn't the stalker. She had a foolproof alibi with Finn.

Kenzie's best strategy was to lie low and go back to Manhattan.

And Kenzie was no fool.

So why had she asked Kate to come to the storage locker? Was it an act of kindness?

Perhaps, in her own way, she was trying to return Kate's sister to her through Imogen's belongings. Perhaps that was too generous an interpretation, Kate thought. But whatever the motive, collecting her sister's belongings was a means of taking stock of her life, and Kate was not going to give Kenzie that final authority. Frances, in disposing of her own life's work, had recognized that moral obligation.

Kenzie jiggled her car keys. "I've gotta leave now."

"I'll follow you in my car," Kate said, not knowing

what to believe anymore—but knowing she would regret it if she didn't go with Kenzie.

Kenzie roared out of the parking lot. Kate hit the gas to keep up. Fortunately, she knew that Bluenose Self-Storage was uptown from Yakusoku Studio, dead center in the city. It was a commercial area, with apartment buildings, automotive businesses and various industrial complexes surrounding it.

She dialed Ethan's number, quashing the pang that came with the knowledge that Randall would be hurt by this choice. But he wasn't here. If something did happen with Kenzie at the locker, Ethan would be able to find her quickly.

Ethan answered the phone on the first ring.

"It's Kate," she said, keeping an eye on Kenzie's tail-lights. "Look—Frances instructed me to give Kenzie an envelope after her death. It turns out the envelope held a key to storage locker. Kenzie says that some of Imogen's things are there."

"Kate, this is a bad idea," Ethan said, his voice tense. "Don't do this."

"I know what you are thinking, but I don't think Kenzie is stupid enough to hurt me. She has no reason to. My client confessed to the murder. Why would she want to hurt me?"

"She could be the stalker, Kate."

"Finn told me she spent the night at his house when my own place was broken into. It wasn't her."

"But we think the stalker might be a tattoo artist. What if it is someone she's working with?"

Kate processed that information. "But do you have any evidence that she is working with someone?"

"No." Ethan's frustration was obvious. "Do you have

to go tonight? I could come with you tomorrow. We are executing the search warrant tonight on Frances' house."

"Kenzie's leaving on a red-eye tonight."

"What if there is evidence connected to the Rigby case in Frances' locker?" Ethan lowered his voice. "You don't want to be involved in that, Kate."

"Professionally, no." She was about to head into no-fly territory from a professional perspective. She knew, on the surface, that her decision to go with Kenzie seemed foolhardy. "Frances left me several photos of Imogen. She had a tattoo in one of the photos, Ethan."

"What kind of tattoo?"

"I couldn't tell. It was too blurry. But it made me think..." Kate swallowed. "My sister obviously had a lot of secrets. Maybe she knew Heather Rigby. Maybe Kenzie did, too. There could be more photos of them with Imogen's belongings." Kenzie's car had slowed. It turned into a side road. Kate followed it. At the very end of the dead-end street, Kate glimpsed the sign for the self-storage building. "Maybe there are photos that would point to a different killer." *Like Kenzie.*

Kate knew that the police had hit a number of dead ends on the Heather Rigby case, the greatest roadblock being Frances' confession. Without any evidence to establish a different killer, they were stuck with it. "If we could find some evidence—"

"You can bet that Kenzie will go through everything right now, Ethan. We've just arrived at the storage locker. I'm going with her."

"Kate, hold her off until I get there. I don't need a search warrant under these circumstances. But it will take at least twenty minutes," he said, his voice a mixture of frustration and excitement. "We are at Frances' house."

"I'll do my best, Ethan. But if she goes in without me, what should I do?"

I can't let her get away with murder.

This wasn't about vengeance for her sister's destructive path. This was about justice for a girl who had never come home.

"Don't go in." But she heard what it cost him to say that. Evidence could be destroyed in minutes.

"I don't think Kenzie would ask me to come if she planned to hurt me. It doesn't make sense. She's smart enough to know that I would notify someone of my whereabouts. All fingers would point to her."

He exhaled. "Okay. Try to stall her. I'm on my way."

Kenzie parked in a dark corner of the parking lot. She hopped out of the car and gestured to Kate, pointing at her watch.

"I've got to go."

"Kate, be careful."

Kate deliberately parked under a streetlight, on the other side of the parking lot. Kenzie strode over to the security door. Kate hurried after her. Weeds sprouted between the cracks of asphalt, scrubby bushes flanking the pothole-ridden lot. The facility didn't inspire much confidence. It was rundown, with a hodgepodge of additions that created a rough L-shaped building. At the end of each wing, truck ramps led down to dented double-garage doors. A variety of loading bays dotted the building, the lower edges patchy with pieces of torn tire rubber. Punctures gashed the wood flanking the bays, no doubt the victim of careless drivers.

The entire place had a shoddy, derelict air. Kate was surprised that Frances would entrust any belongings to it. Kenzie stood on the narrow porch in front of the main entrance. She swiped the key and pushed the security door open. "Come on, Kate."

Kate stepped inside. It was totally black. No light whatsoever. Not very promising. "We need some lights, Kenzie."

"Just a sec." Kenzie groped around the entrance, flipping a bunch of switches. Fluorescent light flickered reluctantly along the narrow corridor, shedding barely enought light to see. Farther along the corridor, Kate could see a few dark stretches where the bulb had burned out and had not been replaced.

Kenzie stuffed a folded envelope between the door and the frame. "I don't trust this place. I'm going to leave the door open, just in case."

"I don't think it can lock us in, Kenzie."

"I'm not taking any chances. I don't want to miss my flight. And these lights look pretty crappy, too. If they go out, we'll be able to see the streetlight."

A sign with bright neon letters listed the storage units. Kenzie frowned. "I don't see 132 on this."

Kate shrugged. "Let's head in the direction of the one hundred series. It must be around here somewhere."

She realized what a foolish strategy that was about five minutes into their foray.

"This place is a friggin' maze," Kenzie muttered. "Whoever numbered it should have their head examined. We should have left a trail of bread crumbs."

It was the third time they had had to retrace their steps. There was a strange sense of camaraderie that made Kate uncomfortable. Kenzie seemed to feel it, too. The tattoo artist couldn't meet Kate's gaze as they turned another blind corner.

And the sight of the mousetraps edging the corridors did little to enhance the experience. *Well, at least it means that there are probably no rats in residence,* Kate thought.

"There it is," Kenzie announced, rounding a corner. She unlocked the door, slid it up and turned on the light.

The room was small, Kate noted with relief.

This shouldn't take long. Despite her bravado with Ethan, she was on edge about being in this place with Kenzie.

Two sets of metal shelving lined each wall. Document boxes had been neatly stacked on each shelf, marked in what Kate guessed was Frances' pre-ALS hand. *Closet. Bed linens. School projects. Garden. Old toys. Books. Misc.* And there, on the end: *Friends (Imogen?).* Kate's tension dropped a notch. So far, Kenzie had told the truth.

Various knickknacks and furnishings lined the shelf: a cube-shaped side table, a matching cube-shaped table lamp and a bookcase. Normally, Kate would have been incredulous that a mother would have stored a teenage girl's furnishings to keep for her estranged grown daughter, but these were unique pieces. Clearly chosen for style and design.

"Your mother was very organized," Kate said.

"I know. It was a pain when I was a teenager, but it has its uses." Kenzie hoisted the box marked *Friends (Imogen?)* off the shelf, and placed it in the far corner against the wall. "Here, have a look through that."

Kate glanced at the dim overhead light. The box was in the shadow, but the room was so narrow Kenzie would not be able to access the boxes on the shelf otherwise.

Kate crouched down in front of the box and flipped off the lid. Kenzie threw a quick glance at her, and then began to investigate the contents on the shelving unit, moving quickly between boxes.

Kate peered into the box. The hair on her arms shivered. This was a time capsule from a lifetime ago. There were things in the box that Kate had not realized were missing until she stared at them seventeen years later.

She pulled out Imogen's Language Arts binder, her sister's name written in a girlish, pretty script. It was purple. Her favorite color. A pencil case. Kate lifted it up, hoping to find some loose Polaroids hidden underneath, but something glinted. It was a chain. Her mother had given Imogen that chain for her thirteenth birthday. They had looked all over the house for it after she died.

A whoosh of a heavy object coming toward her head was her only warning.

She lurched sideways. But it was too late.

Her head exploded in searing pain.

She collapsed on top of Imogen's box.

50

Kenzie gazed down at Kate's head. Brown hair spilled over the edges of her sister's box. Blood glistened from the spot where the cube lamp had connected with Kate's scalp.

That was easy.

So was finding the gun.

Her mother had been very clever. When Kenzie saw the box marked *Garden,* she guessed that the gun was in there. Now the next, most crucial question: Would it work?

She retrieved it from the box and unlocked the catch, pushing the barrel down. The cylinder gleamed in the light. There was not too much rust. And there, in the final two chambers, sat the unused bullets.

The coke had carried Heather through the tattoo. It gleamed black and glistened red on the back of her neck.

"Do you like it?" John had asked Kenzie, ignoring Heather.

"I love it." Kenzie's mind raced, soared, flew. The cocaine had hit her system and her nerves sizzled on her skin. She couldn't believe John had set this all up. That's why he had been gone before their gig—he had

taken his tattoo kit and the booze out to the bunker and hidden it in the bushes.

He had done it for her. All for her.

John dug around in the backpack and pulled out the gun.

Heather had gasped. Kenzie snickered. The girl was such a drama queen. "Why do you have a gun?" Heather asked, her gaze darting from John to Kenzie, then to Lovett, whose eyes gleamed with excitement, and then back to John again.

John stroked Heather's cheek with the muzzle.

The sight of the hard metal pressing against her soft cheek was such a turn-on.

"It's for a game, darling."

Heather staggered to her feet, the combined effect of cocaine and vodka making her stumble as she grabbed her shirt from the ground. "I think it's time for me to go." Her voice trembled.

McNally grabbed her hand. "Not until you play."

She yanked her hand, but she couldn't break his grip. Of course she couldn't, Kenzie thought. John was invincible. So was she. They could do whatever they fucking wanted to.

"Let go! I want to go home."

John twisted Heather's arm behind her back. "You can't leave yet, Heather. We're not done."

The air within the small concrete walls was thick from Heather's fear, feeding Kenzie and John's excitement. Kenzie had never seen John so rough. Every nerve in her body snapped and crackled.

God, she loved him.

Heather shot a terrified look at Kenzie. "Tell him to let me go."

"*Don't be a baby,*" *Kenzie said.* "*It's just a game. We've all played it before. And no one got killed.*"

"*Really? You don't use real bullets?*"

Lovett pushed up behind Kenzie, while John took Heather's hands in his own. "*You have such pretty hands, Heather,*" *he said. He put the gun in her palms, and clasped both his hands around it, forcing the gun to point to the floor.*

"*Guests always go first, Heather.*"

She shook her head, tears springing to her eyes.

Kenzie swigged some vodka. "*Don't be a baby, Heather. You've got the best odds out of all of us.*"

Then Lovett grabbed Kenzie's arms from behind.

The vodka bottle crashed to the ground.

"*Look what you did, you idiot,*" *Kenzie cried.* "*Now it's all gone.*" *She tried to shake him off.* "*Let go of me, you jerk!*"

He glanced at John. Kenzie glared at him. "*Tell him to let go of me, John!*"

"*Here's the deal, ladies. It's winner take all.*"

The walls were spinning. Kenzie tried to focus. What was John talking about? "*I don't get it.*"

"*I'll get Heather to demonstrate.*" *He cocked the hammer.*

Kenzie waited for him to push the gun up to Heather's temple.

Instead, he aimed the gun at Kenzie's chest. He winked at Kenzie over Heather's head.

"*What the hell are you doing, John?*" *Kenzie yanked her arms, trying to break Lovett's grip, but Lovett held her fast.*

"*Don't miss, McNally.*" *Lovett's voice was tense.*

"*Winner takes all,*" *John said.* "*Pull the trigger, Heather.*"

"Will you let me go if I shoot?" the girl asked McNally. *Her makeup ran in two black streaks under her eyes.*

He grinned. "If you are the winner."

Heather closed her eyes. Her chin trembled.

The gun gleamed. Hard, cold, its edges smudged. Kenzie could not keep her eyes from it. John's gaze locked onto her face. You'll be fine, baby, his gaze said. Trust me.

His hand, covering Heather's, pulled the trigger.

Kenzie tensed, bracing herself.

The gun clicked.

Heather sagged.

The rush that went through Kenzie was like no other she had ever experienced. Her mind soared, spinning, flying, exulting.

This was the biggest high of them all.

She wanted John. Right now. Against the concrete wall.

"It's my turn," she said. Her voice was high, thin, not her voice at all.

John tossed the revolver to Kenzie.

Lovett ducked.

"You are fucking crazy, man!" Lovett cried. "It could go off." But he was grinning.

Lovett covered her hand with his own. It was a strange contrast of sensation: cold, hard metal on her palm; hot, sweaty flesh on the back of her hand.

"I can do it by myself," she said. Everything swayed. The gun's grip pulsed against her skin.

She aimed the gun at Heather.

The girl stared at her.

Don't. Please, *her eyes begged.*

"Pull the trigger, Kenz," John said. "She's all yours."

Kenzie barely noticed. The gun curved so naturally in her palm. It was meant for her hand, it was meant for her body, it was meant for her.

And no one else.

She pulled the trigger.

In that split second, she knew.

A bullet had been in the chamber.

A loud crack exploded in the small rear bunker. Then a gasp.

"Holy Mother of God!" Lovett cried.

Heather fell backward against McNally. Blood bubbled from her chest.

Kenzie yanked her hand from Lovett's.

"You did it, Kenz," John said. He grinned.

"Help me," Heather moaned.

Blood streamed from the wound in her chest.

John let her crumple to the ground.

She moaned again.

Kenzie's mind crashed to a halt.

She had played this game and had never been beaten by the bullet.

All the coke and vodka rushed up into her throat.

Oh, God.

What had she done?

The smell of blood filled the small concrete room.

John grinned at her.

What would happen when they left these walls? In a few hours, when dawn broke?

She had just shot a girl.

Her. No one else.

And John was going to strangle the girl.

She knew it. She remembered what he had drawn on that sketch.

She was going to puke.

She lunged out the door and broke into a sprint, still gripping the gun.

It was only later, while rinsing the gun in the sink, that she had discovered the other two bullets in the gun's chamber.

Jesus, she could have killed herself with that while she had been running.

Then another, more chilling thought hit her.

Had John meant it for her?

Would he really have killed his obsession?

She still didn't know. But she wasn't going to hang around and find out. She snapped the cylinder and locked the gun, weighing it in her hand.

She had told McNally to wait ten minutes, and then come find them.

She was ready.

She didn't think he was armed, but she didn't know for sure.

And she sure as hell wasn't taking any chances.

The guy was definitely psycho.

And he would never leave her in peace.

It was either her. Or him.

Then she would kill Kate. She had no choice. If Kate lived, she would talk. Kenzie would be convicted. If Kate died, it would be a tragic murder-suicide. Two bullets from the same gun that killed Heather Rigby. A rather neat solution, if she did say so herself.

She heard a rustle.

She flattened herself against the wall, cocked the gun and waited.

Blood hammered in her ears.

A low groan broke through the silence.

Kenzie darted a frantic glance at Kate's crumpled

body. She moved, trying to get her hands under her body to push herself up.

Did she have time to knock her out again?

Footsteps. Getting louder. Faster.

Shit, shit, shit.

McNally was just around the corner.

Kate pushed herself into a sitting position. She leaned against her sister's box and put her hand to her head. Her face was white.

Then her eyes focused on Kenzie. With the gun.

She staggered to her feet. Blood trickled onto her forehead. She gripped the edge of the shelving, and swayed. But her eyes were hard with fury. "You tricked me."

McNally was at the door.

Kenzie's blood pounded in her ears.

Kate lunged toward her.

Her finger tightened on the trigger.

This is your chance, Kenzie.

Do it!

McNally burst into the room. He was a blur of speed, backed up by mass. Kenzie pressed herself to one side.

Kate crashed straight into him.

He threw her against the shelving.

Kenzie pressed the gun against the side of his head.

"You bitch!" he screamed, raising his hand.

It was then that Kenzie saw he gripped a pistol.

Where the hell did he get that?

Do it.

Now.

The thoughts moved in tandem with the pistol McNally aimed at her head.

Now!

Kate sprang forward, kicking the pistol from

McNally's hand. It flew into the air and spiraled down into the box holding Imogen's belongings.

Before McNally could move, Kenzie pressed the muzzle hard into his temple.

She braced for the kickback. *Die, you bastard!* She pulled the trigger.

The trigger did not budge.

She strained, pulling with all her strength.

The mechanism was frozen.

Oh, God.

McNally smashed the revolver from Kenzie's hand and twisted her arm around her back. "You had this planned the whole time, didn't you?" Pain and anger flashed through his eyes. He shoved her arm high up her back.

Kenzie yelped. Something in her arm snapped.

"Don't move!" Kate yelled. She held McNally's pistol. She had retrieved it from Imogen's box. Her voice echoed in the storage room.

Sweat ran down McNally's temple. In the small space he seemed bigger than ever, everything pumped and straining to explode. Kenzie half-collapsed against him, her body caved where he twisted her arm.

"Kill him, Kate," Kenzie panted. "Or he'll kill us."

McNally snorted. "You're one to talk. You killed Heather."

Kate's gaze darted from Kenzie to McNally.

Do something, Kate. Before McNally does. If she didn't do something now, he would overpower her.

God knew what else McNally would do. She remembered the blood lust in his eyes on Mardi Gras night.

"He wanted *you,* Kate," Kenzie said, her voice desperate. "He told me to call you. He was going to do to you what he did to Heather Rigby."

The only sign that Kate heard was a flaring of her nostrils. "Kick your gun over here, Kenzie."

Kenzie kicked the old service revolver toward Kate, squashing her fear as her only protection slid away from her.

McNally sensed her panic.

"It's a worthless piece of shit, anyway," he said, tightening his grip on her arm. It was a message: *you tried to kill me, bitch. And now you have to pay.* "You didn't seriously think it would fire after all this time, did you?"

Kill him, Kate. Kill him. "He wanted to kill your sister, Kate," Kenzie cried. She felt McNally's entire body tense. "He tattooed her with his mark."

Kate threw a wild glance at McNally. "You wanted to kill Imogen?"

Kenzie flashed a triumphant glance at him. *You bastard. You are not taking me down.* "Imogen was supposed to be his first victim."

51

Kate's head swam, but Kenzie's voice sliced through the wooziness. "What do you mean, his mark?"

"It was a raven," McNally said. "Ravens mate for life."

"She was only fifteen," Kate said. Her blood whooshed through her head, as if her arteries were a roller-coaster track. Up, down and all around.

"It was Kenzie who wanted to put the bullet in her head," McNally snarled, jerking Kenzie's arm back.

Kenzie moaned.

It was true.

She could see it in Kenzie's eyes.

Kenzie had planned to kill her sister.

"Kate, don't listen to him. He has this sick, perverted fantasy. He wants to rape you and strangle you to death. He planned to do it to Immy."

Kate's muscles trembled, caught in a tug of war between fatigue and adrenaline.

"Kill him, Kate. You have to do it. He'll never let you be in peace again. He'll haunt you, he'll send you messages, he'll hurt everyone you ever loved. He will make your life a living hell!" Kenzie's voice shook.

"He is evil incarnate. And he will not stop until he gets what he wants!"

McNally's eyelid flickered.

It was the only warning Kate got.

He shoved Kenzie into a shelving unit and lunged toward her, fist raised, mouth snarled in a battle cry.

"Pull the trigger, Kate!" Kenzie screamed.

Kate jerked her finger on the trigger.

McNally's body jolted. Blood spurted from a tiny hole in his chest. Kate could barely see it.

Then he kept coming at her.

Shoot him again.

He threw himself on her, ripping the gun from her hand.

Oh, God. He's got the gun.

Blood began to stream from his chest.

He pointed the muzzle at Kate.

She shrank back into the corner. "Kenzie. Help me!"

Kenzie stood behind McNally. Her gaze locked onto Kate's.

Those eyes. Merciless.

They had always been merciless.

They were still merciless.

She's going to let him kill me.

McNally made a gasping, choking sound. Blood bubbled from his mouth.

He staggered. Kate lunged forward and grabbed the hand holding the gun. She twisted it, smashing it against the metal shelving. McNally's mouth opened. He gasped but no air could pass through his blood-filled airway.

Kate smashed his hand again. The pistol flew past Kenzie. It hit the concrete floor in the corridor and skidded to a stop.

McNally crumpled at her feet.

She stumbled over him, staggering against the shelving unit.

Kenzie stepped in front of her. Kate looked up.

Kenzie raised the old service revolver with her good arm. "Thanks, Kate."

Are you friggin' kidding me? Would this never end? She was pissed off. She just wanted to get out of this hellhole. "Kenzie, put the gun down. It doesn't even work."

Kenzie's jaw clenched. "I'm not going to jail."

"Kenzie, you're not making any sense. Even if you kill me, you'll still go to jail. There's no way you can cover this up."

"I'll take my chances," she said. She aimed the revolver straight at Kate's forehead. Her finger was on the trigger.

Her eyes shone with death.

What if the latch became unfrozen?

"Put the gun down, Kenzie!"

"I can't." Kenzie shook her head. "Sorry." Her gaze mocked Kate's.

I was always smarter than you, Kate.

"Did you really intend to kill my sister? Was that why you tattooed her?"

Kenzie studied Kate. Finally, she said, "McNally tattooed her. She was in love with him."

Imogen. So trusting. So desperate to be loved.

Her little sister.

She had been a baby.

"How can you live with yourself?"

"How can you live with yourself, Kate? She only turned to me because you were so controlling. She didn't need another mother. She needed a sister, a friend."

Kate's body began to tremble. "Some friend you were. Why would you do that to someone?"

Kenzie's eyes hardened. "It was McNally's idea. Besides, it was fun." She raised the gun and aimed it at Kate.

Kate jumped onto the edge of the bottom shelf, and using it as leverage, threw herself straight at Kenzie.

Kenzie squeezed the trigger—

Kate's body plowed into Kenzie's.

They went flying through the doorway.

Kate heard Kenzie's head hit the concrete. Hard.

She had landed on top of Kenzie. For a moment, their hearts raging against one another, two heartbeats that would never be in unison.

Kate pushed herself up with her arms and staggered to her feet.

Which way should she run? She swiveled to the right.

Something black gleamed on the ground.

Right by Kenzie's feet.

It was McNally's pistol.

Shit.

Kenzie saw it at the same time.

Kate dove for it.

Kenzie kicked her in the face, scrabbling for the gun.

Kate's cheek exploded in pain.

Black spots. Swirling, dancing, dying...

She shook her head, dislodging the spots from her vision.

Kenzie had the pistol.

Kate pushed herself up—grateful for the muscle memory from all those push-ups—and kicked Kenzie's injured arm.

"Jesus!" Kenzie screamed and curled her body in pain, clutching her shoulder.

Kate snatched the pistol. Her blood raced with adrenaline, whirling crazily with the black spots in her head. Her ears rang.

And her heart raged.

Kenzie was not going to get away with this.

She had tried to kill her. Even when Kate saved her from McNally, she had tried to kill her.

And Kenzie had wanted to kill her little sister. She and McNally had planned to shoot her and strangle her, just as they eventually did to poor Heather Rigby.

She had deliberately lured Kate to the storage locker.

Knowing that McNally would join her.

And that he had planned to murder her.

Kate was not going to be a victim.

Ever again.

The gun was hard in her hand.

It felt damn good.

Smooth. Powerful. Sleek and deadly.

She gazed down its sights. Straight into Kenzie's eyes.

They mocked her.

They mocked her sister.

That apology had been crap.

Her blood surged.

All she had to do was pull that slim metal band. It was easy.

Pull the trigger.

She could do it right now. Make Kenzie pay. Make McNally pay.

Make the whole fucking world pay.

Her finger was slippery with sweat.

"Do it, Kate. Do it," Kenzie said in a whisper. "Put a bullet in my head. It feels good, doesn't it?"

A chill ran along Kate's scalp.

Kenzie's gaze locked onto hers. *Do it. I want you to do it.*

"You can do it, Kate. You think you are so high-and-mighty, a frigging hero to the masses, but underneath that pure white skin, you are just like me." She raised a brow. "It takes guts to do this, Kate. Not anyone can be a killer."

Kate's finger shook so violently, she couldn't control it.

"Do it, Kate."

"Goddamn you!" Kate yelled. She lowered the gun. Her body trembled. She staggered, lurching forward. Then she began to run.

"You can't run from yourself, Kate!" Kenzie cried.

Kate heard her stumble to her feet.

But Kenzie could not hurt her.

Not anymore.

Kate half ran, half staggered outside.

She collapsed into her car, locking the doors and lowering her head on the steering wheel.

Spots danced and whirled.

Not everyone can be a killer. But you can. I see it in your eyes. You are just like me.

"Goddamn her!" Kate pounded her hand on the steering wheel. It was only then that she felt the blood, sticky and wet against her hand.

She fumbled in her purse for her cell phone and dialed Ethan's number.

"Kate! Where are you? I'm five mintes away."

"It's Kenzie. She almost killed me. At Bluenose Self-Storage."

And I almost killed her.

I was so close.

Too close.

His voice was urgent. "Are you still in there?"

"No. I'm in my car."

"And is Kenzie?"

"I think so."

"Lock your car doors and stay low in your seat, Kate. We're almost there."

Kate said quickly, "She's got a gun."

"Can you drive?"

Her vision kept darkening, then clearing. Dark. Light. Dark. Light. Was there nothing in between? "I can try."

"Go now. As far away as you can."

Kate started the engine.

The door to the self-storage opened. Kate watched as Kenzie lunged through and fell to her knees. She staggered to her feet.

Would she be able to drive with one arm?

Didn't matter. Ethan would find her soon enough.

Kate backed up, the car lurching as she fumbled with the gearshift. She drove slowly out of the parking lot.

She forced herself to stare straight ahead.

Not at Kenzie.

Not at the gun that lay on the passenger seat, gleaming under the streetlights.

52

A little later—Kate had lost all sense of time when she heard a knock on the front door of the Richardsons' house. She had been resting there, despite patrol's request to take her to the hospital. "I'm fine," she told them.

Kate had made one phone call when she arrived at Muriel's. To Finn. When he heard what had happened, he rushed over, his face white, his eyes stunned.

But he didn't ask Kate any questions. He could see she was in no shape for them. Instead, he took Muriel into the kitchen and kept her busy preparing soup for the patient.

There was another knock, louder this time. Finn and Muriel must not have been able to hear it. Kate slowly got to her feet and walked to the door, steadying herself on furniture. She opened the door.

"Kate!" Ethan rushed toward her and pulled her into his arms. "Why did you refuse to go to the hospital?"

"Too tired," Kate said. Despite Ethan's arms around her, everything kept lurching. "I need to lie down." He led her back to the sofa.

She sank back and lowered her head on the cushion.

Ethan leaned over her. He brushed a wisp of hair that was encrusted with blood. "You need to get this stitched. You are still bleeding."

"It's superficial, Ethan." Her eyelids kept drifting closed.

"Kate, look at me."

She opened her eyes.

"I'm taking you to the hospital."

"Tomorrow," she murmured.

"No. Tonight."

He slipped a hand behind her back and eased her up. "I need to ask you some questions, but they can wait."

He led her to the front hall, leaning down to help her with her shoes. "For heaven's sake," Kate muttered. But she couldn't bend over. The pain in her head was crushing.

Two hours later, the emergency room physician had stapled her scalp wound together— "fairly superficial, although you may have a small scar at your hairline" — and confirmed that she had a concussion. "Ever had one before?" she asked Kate.

"No."

"Ever been hit in the head before?"

Kate closed her eyes. The lights were so bright in here. Pain crashed back and forth through her head. "No."

Ethan glanced at the doctor. "She was hit on the head a year ago. Knocked unconscious."

The doctor looked at Kate. "Do you want to tell me about that?"

"Oh, yeah. I forgot." God. The concussion must be bad to make her forget about that attack. "I was hit on the head and passed out."

"Did you have any of the same symptoms as you are experiencing tonight?"

"Just a headache. And blurry vision. But it went away."

"Ms. Lange, you will require rest, a darkened room and no stimuli for the next few days. If the symptoms persist, we will need to reassess you. If you had a previous concussion, it can take longer for this one to heal. We want to keep an eye on brain swelling."

Ethan helped Kate off the examining table.

"Whoa." Kate swayed.

Ethan put a steadying arm around her waist. "Can you walk?"

"Yes." There was no way she was spending the night in hospital. She'd done that last year. She wasn't going to make it an annual event.

The drive home was dark, silent. Kate closed her eyes and rested her head against the seat.

"Ethan," she murmured.

"Yes?"

"I almost killed Kenzie."

He put his hand on her knee. "It was self-defense, Kate."

Darkness billowed through her head. Clouds and clouds of darkness, cloaking her anger and her fear in the soothing comfort of night.

She was half aware of Ethan walking her upstairs. He laid her on the bed, drew the covers over her and closed the door behind him.

When she next awoke, it was two in the afternoon.

"I've got some tea all ready for you," Nat said, smiling.

Kate pushed herself up on her pillows. "Have I got a scoop for you."

53

Finn knocked on Kenzie's hotel room door.

She'd had her shoulder set at the hospital last night, and had been released on bail after lunch. She called him as soon as they gave her back her phone. But she hadn't been sure he would come.

She opened the door.

He stood in the hallway.

His gaze took in her sling, the bruises on her face.

But his eyes sliced right through her.

She forced a smile. "Come on in."

"No, thanks."

"I just wanted to explain—"

"I already know."

His eyes said, *You are dead to me now.*

"It was a mistake, Finn. I was young. McNally was controlling, abusive—"

"What about your mother?" His voice shot through her denials.

The police had "leaked" the fact to the press that she had been seen leaving her mother's bedside just before Frances died.

Kenzie stared at him. Her eyes swam with tears.

Her mother had been sleeping when Kenzie slipped in

through the back door. The room had been still. Peaceful, except for the sound of her respiration machine.

She brushed her lips against her mother's cheek, still smooth, still warm.

"I love you, Mom."

She gently lifted her mother's head and removed the pillow.

Her mother's eyes opened.

"Thank you," she whispered.

"Sweet dreams." Kenzie placed the pillow gently over her mother's face.

And held it there.

After a while, she lifted her mother's head and slipped the pillow back. She smoothed a wisp of hair off her face.

"Be at peace."

She brushed her thumb—the one with "tranquility" tattooed in Kanji—over her mother's cheek.

And then she called Kate Lange.

A tear threatened to tremble.

"Enough." Finn shoved his hands into his pockets. "I shouldn't have come."

"I know I don't have the right to ask this of you…"

He stiffened.

"I know I'll go to jail on that assault charge—" she couldn't bring herself to speak of Kate in front of him "—but I wanted to ask you to look after Foo." Her lip trembled.

His face softened. The tiniest fraction. "Okay."

"Thank you."

"I'm not doing it for you, Kenzie. I'm doing it for an innocent animal. He deserves a good home."

"It's not forever."

His smile was grim. "Nothing is forever, Kenzie."

He turned and walked away.

54

The team assembled in the war room. Ferguson elbowed open the door, carrying two trays of Tim Hortons coffee with a box of doughnuts hanging on for dear life on top of one of the trays.

They passed around the coffee, squabbling good-naturedly over the lone Boston Cream doughnut that was nestled amongst the others. Ethan drained his cup, soaking up the caffeine in his sleep starved body. The sugar doughnut helped, but he really needed another coffee to feel remotely human.

"Okay, let's get this party started," Ferguson said, her eyes bright. "Ethan, what's the status?"

"We've got Kenzie Sloane under arrest for the murder of Heather Rigby, although she still proclaims her innocence. Kate Lange stated that John McNally told her Kenzie shot Heather Rigby."

"Do we have any evidence to back this up?"

He shook his head. "McNally is dead. All we have is what Kate says she heard him say. And that was after she'd been unconscious."

The team exchanged looks. Not a great start to building the case.

"What about the gun?" Ferguson asked.

Ethan grimaced. "I don't think they are going to find anything. Any original prints are now gone. In terms of the chain of evidence, Frances clearly had possession of the key to the storage room before giving it to Kate Lange. Kate gave the key to Kenzie and accompanied her into the storage locker, so unless she was carrying it on her person, the gun was stored by Frances in the locker. And…Heather's cause of death was inconclusive. It wasn't clear if she died from the gun wound or the asphyxiation, so even if we could prove Kenzie fired the gun, I doubt we'd get a conviction."

"Were Kenzie and McNally the only ones at the scene when Heather was killed?" Ethan asked.

Lamond shrugged. "The only one who is talking to us is Kate. Does she know if there were any other players?"

Ethan shook his head. "She told me that McNally and Kenzie only identified each other as being present during Heather's murder."

The mood in the room had sobered. "And what about McNally? Who shot him?"

"Kate. Self-defense." Ethan's voice was curt. Ferguson raised her brows at Lamond. Lamond shrugged.

"Did Kenzie shoot anyone?" Ferguson asked.

"No. All we've got on her is assault."

"So do you think Frances Sloane's confession still stands?"

Ethan shook his head. He wished he could make it stick, but he was sure that her son would fight it tooth and nail. Lack of capacity was sure to be bandied about by his legal team. And they could be right. "No. I think Kenzie did it. With McNally. But we have absolutely no proof Kenzie did it. We did find a tattoo kit and a rope in a bag hidden by the bunkers. We believe it belonged to McNally. We are hoping we can match the rope with the one used on Heather, but it's a long shot."

The way things were looking, the case could go from "missing girl" to "unsolved murder."

It made him sick to think Kenzie was getting away with murder.

He wished Kate had shot her.

An eye for an eye.

But he knew Kate would never have gotten over it.

"Lamond, what did you find out about Frances Sloane's death?" Ferguson asked, chewing thoughtfully on a honey cruller.

Lamond flipped open his notepad. "Her caregiver told me that she thought she saw Kenzie leaving through the back door that night."

Ethan straightened. "You mean, she killed her mother?"

"Hard to say. But the caregiver did see her. And I checked the list of phone numbers on the call screen, and she had made a phone call to Kenzie about an hour before she died."

"What did the autopsy results show?" Ferguson asked.

Lamond grimaced. "Basically, Mrs. Sloane stopped breathing. With her condition, that was entirely to be expected. Whether it happened as a result of the disease or from a pillow pressed over her airway, it's hard to say. It would not have taken much pressure to kill her." So there would be little or no evidence of trauma on her body.

The team digested that.

"So…Kenzie kills her mother to ensure the confession stands. But McNally keeps harassing them. And she decides to take both Kate and McNally down. But Kate takes McNally down." Ethan rubbed his jaw. "What do you think?"

"Makes sense to me," Ferguson said. "She wanted to get rid of all the loose ends. But why would she want to kill Kate?"

"I don't know if she did," Ethan said. "I think her hand was forced by McNally. He sent her a text that night. He was clearly escalating his behavior. Kate says that Frances had asked her over a week ago to give Kenzie a key to a storage room after she died. If Kenzie knew that the gun was hidden in the storage room, she would have to get it before she left town. Otherwise her brother would have found it and turned it in."

"So, why did she have to drag Kate into it?"

"Because she told Kate that her sister was originally supposed to be McNally's first victim…. She even got the same tattoo as Heather Rigby. She thought that Kate would recognize it and make the connection."

Ethan exhaled. "McNally was a sick stalker. He had this thing about 'marking' his victims with tattoos."

"I had read once that tattooing used to be a stigma and criminals were marked with it," Lamond said.

"Could be that's where he got the idea. Anyway, the raven was symbolic for McNally. It mated for life."

"But why would he mark girls he was killing?"

"He wanted to be in control. They were 'his' and he had the power to kill them. Kenzie Sloane had one, too, according to Kate, but I think she was the queen bee. I think he wanted her to be the Bonnie to his Clyde. But she dumped him and became a celebrity tattoo artist, instead."

"Good career move," Lamond said.

"So, right now all we have is an assault charge on

Kenzie. The gun she pointed at Kate was broken. They both knew it," Ferguson said. "Damn."

"Just what every celebrity tattoo artist needs to add a little street cred to their rep," Ethan said, his eyes grim.

Unless they had a major break somewhere, Kenzie Sloane had gotten away with murder.

At least once.

55

The doorbell rang.

It reverberated through Kate's head. She hoped to God it wasn't the media again. She shuffled to the window and peered through the drawn curtain of the Richardsons' home. She longed to be in her own bed, but her window still needed repairing and her house needed cleaning from the fingerprint powder. Although people had been hired, the work was still not completed.

Fortunately, Corazon came every day to help, which was a huge boon because the hospital had decided to discharge Enid a few hours ago. Finn had brought her home, settled her upstairs and then left.

Kate had watched him go, her heart heavy.

Easygoing, laid-back Finn had new lines in his face, new hardness in his eyes.

Kenzie had done a job on him.

The doorbell rang again. Corazon must be upstairs with the Richardson sisters.

Kate hurried to the door, as much as her bruised body and aching head would allow, and opened it, squinting at the bright light.

Ethan held out a bouquet of orange tulips and some kind of purply-blue flower.

"Hi." She put a hand to her hair. She hadn't been able to wash it because of the staples in her scalp, and it fell in lank waves around her face. "Come in."

An awkward silence fell between them.

"Let me make you tea," Ethan said.

"No, I'm fine. I'm all tea-ed out." She tightened her robe. "Do you mind if I lie down? It's easier to talk."

He hovered behind her as she wobbled to the living room, and he sat down on the chair facing her.

"Ethan, I know you are busy wrapping stuff up," Kate said. "Everyone is taking good care of me."

"Trust me, I wouldn't be here if I didn't want to be here." He hesitated, then sprang to his feet and moved to the edge of the sofa, his eyes gazing down into hers. He took her hand. "Kate, do you remember when we met for coffee a few nights ago?"

"Yes."

Her intuition told her where this conversation was going—and she wasn't sure she was ready for it.

"I told you that I wanted to try again. Because life was too short. And we didn't know when something could happen—"

She managed a wry smile. "Famous last words."

He stroked her cheek. "I almost lost you. Before we even had a chance to start over."

Start over.

Was that what she wanted?

Ethan had been here for her. The whole time.

But did she love him?

She didn't know.

She thought she had loved Randall.

But she didn't know that anymore, either.

Her head felt woozy. "Ethan, I can't make that commitment right now." She swallowed. "I don't know if I can ever make it."

Hurt darkened his eyes. "I can wait."

That's what she had told herself when Randall left. But it was harder than it sounded.

"I don't want to do that to you," she whispered. "Life is too short."

Ethan's eyes searched hers. "He doesn't deserve you," he said, his voice fierce. "You know that."

"I'm not saying this because of Randall. I'm saying it because I don't want anyone to wait for me. That's not fair." There was too much hurt in his eyes already. What would happen three months from now? "Timing is everything, Ethan. And our timing has never been good."

He stood. "I really believe we had a chance. Everything was just like before."

"That was the problem. We were living in our past. We're not the same people anymore."

"I still believe in you, Kate. I still believe in us."

You are breaking my heart. "I know. But I don't want you to wait for me anymore."

He stiffened, shoving his hands into his pockets. God. She couldn't bear the hurt in his eyes. Was he right?

He bent and brushed his lips across her forehead. *"Au revoir."*

She gave a small smile, acknowledging his choice of words.

"Au revoir."

A small spark of hope lit his eyes. *Au revoir* was not goodbye. And they both knew it.

"Get some rest," he said. "I'll see myself out."

"Before you go, I just want to say thank you."

His eyes searched hers. "Anytime."

She heard him close the door just as she drifted off to sleep.

* * *

"Kate…" Enid's voice was hesitant. "Would you like some tea?"

Enid came into the room slowly, her step uncertain. They both had come so close to death. "You should be resting, Enid."

"My doctor told me I needed to get some exercise." She patted Kate's hand. "So I walked from the kitchen to the living room. Muriel and Corazon have made us tea and cookies." Corazon lowered a tray of tea onto the table, adding milk to the china mugs. "And now I shall sit here and you can tell me everything that has happened."

Muriel strode into the room, flourishing a plate of homemade shortbread, which she put on the tray. She sat down next to her sister on the love seat, her large frame leaning gently into her sister's diminished one. Brulée leapt onto her lap. Rather than feeling overhwhelmed by the trio facing her, Kate felt comforted.

"Eddie Bent told me most of what happened," Enid said. "But how did you end up with the stitches?"

Kate gave a brief—and heavily edited—rundown of her encounter in the storage locker. But when she told Enid how Kenzie had tried to kill her, her throat tightened.

"I've never shot a gun before." Tears pricked the back of her eyelids. "I wanted to kill her, Enid."

Gazing at these elderly ladies, with their china mugs of tea, Kate wondered if they could possibly understand. Would they think less of her?

But Enid's gaze was compassionate. Nonjudgmental. "I'm sorry, Kate."

"I almost killed her, Enid. It was so close."

"Kate," Enid said, her voice firm, "you were provoked."

"I wanted her to pay." A tear ran down her cheek. Her head pounded. *Vengeance is mine.* "She told me I suffocated Imogen." The tears came in earnest. Her gaze moved between the two sisters. "What if I had been less controlling? Maybe Imogen would never have hung out with her."

"Kate." Enid's eyes were fierce. Fierce with love. Fierce with the desire to protect her. "Kenzie was trying to manipulate you. She wanted to make you responsible. But don't you see? If you hadn't taken your sister from that party, if you hadn't crashed that car, if your sister hadn't died in that car wreck—then she would have been McNally and Kenzie's first victim. You *saved* her, Kate. You saved your sister from a terrible death."

The room was silent.

Kate hadn't seen it that way.

Until now.

"I wanted to *kill* Kenzie. I had the gun. It felt so good in my hand, Enid."

"Don't punish yourself over this, Kate. You are not a machine."

Muriel added a sugar cube to Kate's mug of tea. Then another.

Kate's eyes searched Enid's. "What am I, then?"

A killer?

Enid gave a small smile. "You are a survivor." She glanced at Muriel. "We are all survivors."

Muriel handed Kate the mug of tea. By now it held at least three sugar cubes.

Kate took it, her hands clasped around its warmth.

A survivor.

I can live with that.

* * * * *

Acknowledgments

This book has been a personal and professional odyssey. Life, as it has a tendency to do from time to time, imploded on me while I was in the midst of writing this book. I am deeply grateful to the support of my friends, family and colleagues who helped me on so many levels.

I am indebted to the experts who generously shared their time and expertise—and gave me a glimpse of their fascinating work. In particular, I would like to thank:

Detective Sergeant Mark MacDonald, of the Halifax Regional Police Department. Simply the best!

Dr. Marnie Wood, M.D., FRCPC, Medical Examiner, who helped me theorize about Canada's first bog body. So much fun!

Michelle Patriquin, M.Sc., who gave me great insight into forensic anthropology methodology and techniques. I will never look at a person's face the same way.

Susan MacKay, LLB, who helped with some of my legal scenarios and made me so grateful that I have such enduring friends.

Amber Thorpe, tattoo artist and owner of Adept Tattoos Studio, who showed me how the professionals do it.

Any and all mistakes are mine alone, and I apologize in advance to those who shared their expertise with me.

I would like to thank my team at MIRA Books for their support, and for pulling out all the stops to get *Tattooed* on the shelves. You are the best!

In particular, I would like to thank my editor, Valerie Gray, for her tireless support, for helping me make my books the best they can be, and for her compassion during a difficult time.

I also would like to thank my agent Al Zuckerman. His insight, experience and kindness guided me through a challenging year. He helped me see the forest through the trees, time and time again.

And thank you to my friends and family who were always there for me:

My husband, Dan, whose support has been unfailing and truly selfless.

My daughters, who are my biggest cheerleaders and my proudest achievements.

My brother, my sister and my dad.

My best friend and fellow traveler, Linda Brooks.

My critique partner, Kelly Boyce, who guided me with deep breathing during several points of this book's creation.

My writing peeps, Cathryn Verge and Julianne MacLean.

My writing chapter, RWAC, which has the most inspiring authors I know.

And last, but never least, my pug, Peaches. She makes me laugh every day.

NEW YORK TIMES BESTSELLING AUTHOR
KAT MARTIN

Millions of lives are on the line. But for him, only one matters.

It's not in bodyguard Jake Cantrell's job description to share his suspicions with his assignments. Beautiful executive Sage Dumont may be in charge, but Jake's not on her payroll. As a former special forces marine, Jake trusts his gut, and it's telling him there's something off about a shipment arriving at Marine Drilling International.

A savvy businesswoman, Sage knows better than to take some hired gun's "hunch." And yet she is learning not to underestimate Jake. Determined to prove him wrong, Sage does some digging of her own and turns up deadly details she was never meant to see.

Drawn into a terrifying web of lies and deceit—and into feelings they can't afford to explore—Jake and Sage uncover something that may be frighteningly worse than they ever imagined.

AGAINST THE SUN

**AVAILABLE NOW
WHEREVER BOOKS ARE SOLD.**

 MIRA |  HARLEQUIN®
www.Harlequin.com

MKM1350R2